Praise for *Leaving:*

'A unique collection of stories, wildly geographical with strong narratives and memorable characters. Each story illuminates a facet in the world, creating an exceptional anthology filled to the brim with absolute gems.'

Lynette Cresswell, Bestselling Author

'This diverse mix of stories introduces a variety of timely themes that readily engage the reader's interest and invite further reflection beyond the stories' endings.'

Jennie Liebenberg, Editor

'A collection of contemporary tales, many covering subjects that have been debated across Europe in 2019. They grab you right from the start, so go ahead, read and enjoy.'

Jackie Collins, Author

'This superb anthology gathers some of the best in modern writing from around the world.'

Hugh Riches, Journalist and Broadcaster

OTHER PUBLICATIONS:

Conflict
Award Winning Short Stories

Eternal
Award Winning Short Stories

Eternal
Award Winning Poetry

Tales From The Walled Garden

Precious
Award Winning Short Stories

Precious
Award Winning Poetry

Shakespeare In Debt
by Ted Stanley

Who's Afraid Of The Dark – Not Me!
by Sarah Smith

Cows In Trees
by Julian Earl

The Dog With The Head Transplant
by Julian Earl

25 Years On: Grimsby Writers
Short Stories and Poems

Leaving
Award Winning Poetry

LEAVING

AWARD WINNING SHORT STORIES
Edited by Ted Stanley

HAMMOND HOUSE PUBLISHING

LEAVING
AWARD WINNING SHORT STORIES

1st Edition published in the UK in 2020 by
Hammond House Publishing Ltd

ISBN: 978-1-91-609805-3

The right of the individual writers to be identified as the author of this work has been asserted in accordance with sections 77 and 78 of the Copyright Designs and Patents act 1988.

All rights reserved. No part of this publication may be reproduced, stored in a retrieval system, or transmitted in any form or by any means, electronic, mechanical, photocopying, recording or otherwise, without the permission of the Publisher in writing.

Page Design by Alex Thompson
Proofreading by Jennie Liebenberg
Cover Design by Ted Stanley

Cover Image *LEAVING* by Deborah Geddes, first exhibited in 2018. Produced by permission of the artist.
All rights reserved.

The opinions expressed in this book are entirely those of the individual authors and are not endorsed or supported by the publishers or their sponsor, University Centre Grimsby.

Contains language that may be considered unsuitable for a younger audience.

Hammond House Publishing Ltd
13 Dudley Street, Lincolnshire
DN31 2AE, United Kingdom

www.hammondhousepublishing.com

LEAVING
AWARD WINNING SHORT STORIES

Enjoy this eclectic collection of short stories that brings together award winning writers from around the world.

LEAVING is the fourth in a series of short story anthologies, each featuring a different theme and including the winning and shortlisted stories from the annual *Hammond House International Literary Prize*.

University Centre Grimsby

Includes the winner of the
2019 International Literary Prize

The opinions expressed in this book are entirely those of the individual authors and are not endorsed or supported by the University Centre Grimsby.

Contents

Introduction | *Ted Stanley*	x
The Moving People | *Guy Baillie-Grohman*	1
The Sound of Silence | *Rhys Barratt*	15
Dark Waters | *L.E Beacock*	28
Staying to Leave | *Mags Brown*	35
A Far Cry from the Poppy Fields | *Gillian Brown*	41
Rifle | *Joshua Bruyning*	49
Olivia's Plan | *Richard Burtle*	60
Like Paradise | *Oliver Bussell*	76
Six Letters, Two Months, One Year | *Verity Capstick*	84
A Woman Who Knows | *Kate Carne*	91
Slipping Away | *Peter Clegg*	101
Patchwork | *Clementine Collett*	109
Curiosity | *Jackie Collins*	118
Glimpse Into The Future | *Lynette Creswell*	121
Notice of Eviction | *Kevin Davis*	140
High Radon Gas Expectancy | *Sarit Elkon*	147
All That Cannot Be Helped | *Joe Eurell*	160
The Easy Now | *Blythe Eveleigh-Evans*	173

Contents

The Red Hand Of Rosie | *Joe Fuller*	180
Mirror, Mirror | *Lucy Grace*	188
Locked In | *Peter Hankins*	196
Leaving | *Clara Harland*	207
Émigré | *Sarah Hunter-Carson*	214
Murder Anonymous | *Steve Jackson*	216
Snow and Feathers | *Michelle Jager*	229
My Name Was Joy | *Alan Kennedy*	245
Gladstone's Sorrow | *Laura Ann Kenny*	253
The New Sieve | *Colin Kerr*	263
Cartolandia | *Enzo Kohara Franca*	277
The Cruellest Leash | *T. H. Kunze*	284
Rootless | *Hanne Larsson*	296
The Accident | *C.S Lawrence*	304
Left | *Jennifer Liebenberg*	314
The Milky Way | *Chrissie Maroulli*	323
You know there was a time I felt whole | *Tiyani Mhlarhi*	335
Bitten | *Adrian Mills*	344
Stale Peaches | *David O'Dwyer*	347

Contents

No Answer | *Eamon O'Leary*	355
Sarah | *Christopher Owen*	363
Running Up That Hill | *Jonathan Page*	372
Chrysalis | *Dylan K Page*	383
Cowboy Boots are Waterproof | *Andrew Peters*	387
More Ways To Leave Your Lover | *Don Rhodes*	404
Freeing Yasmin | *Wendy Riley*	423
The Levensons | *Tara Roeder*	438
No Two Ways | *L.F. Roth*	451
How To Become Crimson | *Richard Salsbury*	461
Tall Tails | *Peter True*	476
Bloodletting | *Kyle Waters*	480
Max Mustermann | *Lara Weddige*	495
Blessed Trinity | *Gordon Wilson*	510
Tenacity Penguin | *Matt Wixey*	516

Acknowledgments

Thank you to the University Centre Grimsby for supporting the 2019 International Literary Prize. Deborah Geddes, Alex Thompson, Leanne Doyle, Jonathan and Katherine Williams-Stanley and Richard Hall. Competition judges, Peter True, Anjali Wierny, Sarah Hunter-Carson, Adrian Mills, Steve Jackson and Hugh Riches. Jennie Liebenberg for her invaluable proofreading, and Lynette Creswell and Jackie Collins for additional judging. Finally, all the writers who submitted such an amazing collection of stories for this anthology. We are sorry we were unable to include more.

Introduction

Leaving has been a constant literary theme, from Romeo's sweet sorrow at parting, to George Elliot finding the depths of love in its agony. Hemmingway employed it as a recurring theme in *Farewell To Arms* and, in popular culture, Willie Nelson declared he had been a long time leaving, but was going to be a long time gone.

As a theme for our 2019 International Literary Prize, it provided the inspiration for a new generation of writers to explore the human condition as its most vulnerable, with imaginative and unusual stories, poetry and screenplays. They did not disappoint.

Many highly personal stories were woven into the wider issues of climate change, mental illness, the refugee crisis and – in the case of the winning short story, *Tenacity Penguin* – the possibility of nuclear annihilation.

A record number of entries, spanning five continents, tested the judges' resolve to compile a shortlist of just thirty stories, before long and challenging deliberations settled a winner and runners up. Some of the panel's favourite choices that didn't make the shortlist have been included as *Judge's Choices*.

I have also chosen a selection of stories from non-English

speaking countries, allowing readers to enjoy the full diversity of cultures and settings represented by the competition. Our fourth annual anthology is completed by three winning stories from students at the *University Centre Grimsby*.

Thank you to all the writers who submitted their stories to the competition, allowing us to publish this outstanding body of work, and to you, the readers, for supporting new writing talent. I hope you enjoy these wonderful stories.

Ted Stanley

'We leave something of ourselves behind when we leave a place, we stay there, even though we go away. And there are things in us that we can find again only by going back there.'

Pascal Mercier

The Moving People
Guy Baillie-Grohman
United Kingdom

Shortlisted for the 2019 International Writing Competition

'Good afternoon, Turtle and Dove.'

A soft hiss sang down the line, the pause was always longer than expected.

'This is the moving people isn't it?'

The 'atmosphere adaptation relocation' biz was booming. Exploding in fact. Uncle Al had seen it coming, his head always several catastrophes ahead of the game. The calls had started slowly, a few billionaires at first, then those who actually paid attention to the news inferno. Now just anyone with a roof over their head were scrambling for the T&D hotline.

'Yes, that's us, the lifestyle transfer agency. My name's Joe and I'll be – '

'Turtle and Dove?'

'That's right, named after East Anglia's ecologically unique migratory dove species.'

LEAVING

Sticking to the standard call script was easy, though it seemed callers' interest in endangered bird species was rather limited.

'Dove what?'

'It's a species of dove that was once quite widespread in –'

'Look, we just need to move, okay?'

'Of course sir, what are your criteria?'

The criteria had been a stroke of genius, at least initially, but things were changing fast. The slabs of cut-price Scottish scrubland Al had snapped up for the 'build your own' option were long gone, now just the flat-pack options remained. They seemed popular though – solid, safe and Swedish.

'*Criteria*? A house that isn't underwater.'

'We have the Serenity Green package, or the Forest Breeze option. For you sir, I'd recommend Serenity Green.'

'Where is it?'

'That depends, normally Scotland, but we do have the Northumberland option, it is a bit more expensive though.'

'What's the difference?'

This was where he earned the money. There was no difference, only comforting nonsense. Lives were becoming drenched, charred and tangled at an increasingly absurd rate. People wanted a sense of control. Control only Turtle and Dove's impeccably produced brochure could offer.

'Well, Serenity Green includes a detailed community research brief, so you can consider whether or not your current lifestyle –'

A heavy sigh rustled down the line.

'My current lifestyle involves wading through my sitting room fishing out books from a syringe strewn sludge.'

Some lime green digits on his screen blinked at him impatiently;

twenty seconds in and he'd yet to get his details.

'Some of them were first editions, worth hundreds you know.'

Books! This was the key. He'd build the relationship from here. They had all received a week's coaching on how to forge connections with callers based on subtle conversational giveaways.

'Are you a professor sir? Plenty of our resettlements have a rich intellectual community.'

The line hissed a little louder, he'd fallen quiet, something had alarmed him.

'*Resettlements?*'

'Relocation communities, yes'

The dread was setting in again. Eight months since starting and he still couldn't quite bring himself to quit. He'd almost managed to say something, but something in his uncle's eye had stopped him. He was stuck, unable to make a decision either way, a small part of him putrefying a little more every day. How was this legal? Would anyone stop them? What *was* this?

'I'm a neurosurgeon.'

'And where are you based?'

'Look, just, just tell me what to *do*.'

The guy was desperate, his taut voice holding back a tide of swirling insecurity. The dread was starting to fade, replaced by a fuzz of smug cosiness that rose up through his body whenever he was on the phone to an unravelling life. He had tried to force it back down, but it was unstoppable, he just had to make peace with the guilt. Joe Francis Hartley was winning the dizzying game of climate change roulette because his uncle knew how to make serious money from serious problems.

'Sir, please, where exactly do you live?'

'London, what's left of it anyway, look I just need – '

LEAVING

'London, thank you sir.'

This guy though, yes, he could still help, still do his thing. Sure, he wasn't the neediest of prospective clients, but something about his fragile voice touched him, its anxious creaks echoing his own crumbling certainties.

'Look, I just need to move as soon as possible.'

His voice was starting to crack – he could hear the fear. The green clock started flashing a little quicker.

'We've got a week before the sheriff declares a zone zero on our street and my wife is seven months pregnant.'

Pregnant! Yes, this would be it. Mr Neurosurgeon and his family would be it: his project number one. Screw Serenity Green, they deserved Holy White. There was a tragic energy to this guy's manner; as if the faster he spoke the faster he would escape the lapping sludge. Something about his fervid panic reminded him of his mum. She'd died years ago but her voice had never left him, the way it had gently tightened whenever something had worried her. Mr Neurosurgeon was channelling his mum's endearingly fretful grip on life, *and* his wife was pregnant. Something deep inside him had connected, this was fate: they *had* to be moved.

'What's your name and contact number, sir?'

Fzzzzz. The line went dead. No doubt another electricity raid by some off-grid bandit brigade.

◆

Slipping off his headset he peered through the tinted windows. Two seagulls picked at some chips, a man cycled past on an expensive looking bike, it all looked very normal. Even the weather seemed normal, a few smudges of faded sunshine forcing themselves through a bank of altostratus. His cloud knowhow had been increasing ever since 'the pamphlet' had arrived, a fifty page booklet sent to every household in the country containing practical and psychological guidance on how to live with 'atmosphere adaptation'.

The office had crowded by the coffee machine, the usual routine when the lines went down.

'We need to get their numbers *first* okay? The package options can come later.'

Uncle Al's voice filled the office. His unflappable self-confidence was impressive; despite almost daily power cuts there was no let-up in his enthusiastic demand for 'clients, clients, clients'. In fact he seemed positively buoyed by the challenge. He had made a fortune in the bowels of the zinc sourcing trade. There was no way a few off-gridders with shotguns were going to derail his latest enterprise.

'We might be able to retrace the calls. If the switchboard is rewired, I might be able to sort it.'

A jolly exclamation rose from the crowd; it was Computer Tim, Al's technical wonderkid. Computer Tim could sort everything; he'd magic Mr Neurosurgeon's number out of the ether and send it his way. Operation save the neurosurgeon would be back on! He'd call him, arrange a location visit and secure him the best site he could. The Joe Hartley Holy White package. Al's voice rumbled across the office.

'Joe, stop skulking, come and have some coffee.'

He was shattered, the last thing he wanted was a dose of his uncle's indomitable bonhomie. He did want some coffee though, their supplies were running low, and god knew when the next batch might arrive. Rising from his desk, the unblinking eyes of Dr Alice swivelled towards him. Without her the whole operation would collapse, it was all too much to handle without a serious amount of weekly counselling.

LEAVING

She watched closely as he made his way across the very loud wooden floorboards, her unwavering gaze taking in every inner synaptic crackle. She blinked, slowly. That was it! She knew. She knew about Mr Neurosurgeon. She'd call him in for a special session and he'd be forced to read the manual aloud: *Every client should be treated equally, no preferential treatment should be offered to anyone regardless of personal circumstances.* He felt sick, the coffee tasted apocalyptic. His uncle continued to rally the troops.

'As we all know, these unfortunate interruptions are becoming ever more common, so I've asked the governor to provide some kind of back up generator, but until then we'll just have to take things as they come.'

Al was sleeping with the governor's wife so they'd get a generator soon enough, but his bland practicality in the face of thermodynamic collapse never failed to amuse him. Everything about the whole operation was desolately comic – the 'land guardians' deal with every farmer north of Manchester, the vintage cars used for location visits, the Turtle and Dove branded water pistols given to the kids. It was all too much, a rainbow coloured waterslide to oblivion, but they were all getting very rich very quickly so quitting wasn't really an option. Anyway, half their clients were theirs through a government contract, so it was democratically legitimate. It was ethically fine. Ish.

'So let's enjoy the coffee while we can!'

♦

Dr Alice nodded slowly. Too slowly. This was her thing, slow down time a notch to perplex you, get you stuck in a temporal swamp before swooping in to pick at your freshly exposed thoughts.

'So Joe, this neurosurgeon and his family deserve a relocation more than our hundreds of other clients? What makes them so special? You know the criteria.'

Her voice was thin and cold. Quite why Al had employed her to soothe the company's battered psyches was a mystery. Or maybe that was the reason; she'd cool everyone down enough to stem an office wide meltdown. There was always some sort of logic.

'Yes, I know, but…'

'*But*?'

The session was off to a bad start. The cognitive evisceration had begun. Joe shrank back into the sofa. It was surprisingly comfortable, definitely new. How Al was managing to source premium leather sofas when cows were disappearing as fast as beaches was anyone's guess, but it felt good – firm and friendly.

'Joe, an answer please.'

He edged further back into the leather. Her lips twitched as she leant forward.

'Okay, it's because he sounded like he just really needed helping. Just something about him. I know everyone needs it, but why can't we just *help*?'

His voice was cracking, he'd exposed himself. A smile broke across her heavily made up face.

'But Joe, you know the rules. This neurosurgeon doesn't fall into the premium bracket.'

The premium bracket had allowed Al to skim off an extra twenty percent from a desperate stratum of bankers and tech execs. But they paid a *lot*; there was no way Mr Neurosurgeon could compete.

'And he can't be included in our government intake, neurosurgeons aren't exactly the neediest in our society, are they Joe? We can't take everyone. We are a business after all.'

A speck of spit landed on his lower lip as her tongue snapped back behind her lips. He winced.

'But –'

Her tongue leered out again.

'A *family* business in fact.'

He wanted to vanish. There was no way Al could be aware of this, or maybe he was? Maybe this actually *was* the core of the business, the secret power source of his retro-feudalist empire.

'So Joe, what shall we do now?'

Shuffling further into the depths of the sofa he looked around for some sort of escape, a tastefully framed photo of some frost covered leaves stared blankly back at him. He was stuck; the more he struggled the further he sunk into the swamp. *Breathe Joe, breathe.* The fates of two innocent people and an unborn child hung in the balance.

'Please can I have some water?'

She paused. He'd caught her off guard, he had time to collect his thoughts.

'Still or sparkling?'

'Sparkling please.'

The bubbles felt good, cleansing; fizzing the grime from his synapses so he could push back nicely refreshed.

'So Joe, what are we going to do now?'

She was reaching towards a bookshelf. She was going for the manual. Al had once joked about the manual during a meeting, 'the rules of engagement' as he'd put it. They had all laughed, he was quite a funny guy. But as his eyes had drifted from his uncle to Dr Alice a twinge of panic had consumed him, she had smirked knowingly, the manual evidently *did* exist. For the first time since he'd started he had felt dangerously out of depth. A soft thud snapped him back to reality as she placed a hefty black book onto the table.

'Joe, are you listening? What are you going to do?'

'Read the manual I guess.'

Her lips curled into a sickly smile.

'No need to be facetious now.'

A few bubbles popped their way back up his throat, he tried to swallow but nothing happened. The room was getting too hot. He needed to cool down. Just think of Mr Neurosurgeon and his wife desperately dredging up their favourite belongings from a noxious brown soup. That was why he was here, for them, to help. Everything else was peripheral. A drop of sweat edged down his brow.

'Sorry, yes, I'm just a bit tired. I'm sorry for getting confused about the criteria, we've just been so busy'.

He'd play dumb, hope she'd get bored and let him leave. It would give him time to think of a plan. There was now zero chance he could relocate them by the book; he'd have to go rogue, persuade Computer Tim to mix up the records or something.

'You probably haven't read appendix twelve of the manual, have you Joe? Don't worry, no one does, it's quite verbose.'

More bubbles fizzed up his throat. It was all wrong. She'd clocked his just a bit tired shtick a mile off. He'd blown it. She was going to unleash something savage. He tried forcing himself further back into the leather, but there was no more give. The sofa had abandoned him, he was completely alone.

'Some more water Joe? You look peaky.'

His hands tingled with anxiety.

'Thanks, yeah, it's just quite warm in here.'

She blinked slowly, time was starting to slip off-piste again. He was being drawn back into the swamp.

'Joe, so what we're going to do is this. You're going to drink your water and then consider appendix twelve. Okay?'

His eyes spun around the room, the frosted leaves remained as serene as ever, they had abandoned him too. He raised his water glass to his lips and took a long slow sip. Dr Alice's eyes zeroed in on his throat, each fretful swallow monitored for any tell-tale signal that he might do something rash. The water tasted metallic, the bubbles were dying. His thoughts too. They were dissolving into a grey slush of nothing. The heat was atrophying everything.

'Here you go, now turn to page 220.'

The book looked ominous. No slick fonts of the company's client facing literature here. Instead a simple embossed gold title reading 'Turtle and Dove Employee Practises and Procedures'. It looked bible-like, final.

'Just page 220?'

'Yes.'

She looked excited, as if he were about to open what she knew to be the perfect present. He turned to the page. A spike of terror shot down his spine. It was blank. His eyes rose to meet hers.

'It's blank.'

She nodded slowly.

'Precisely.'

'But –'

'But what Joe? Were you expecting some neat instructions telling you how do to rectify the situation?'

He glanced again at the page; apart from the small page number it was completely blank. The white expanse terrified him.

'What do you want me to do?'

His voice jittered with exhaustion.

'Now Joe, the executive board took the decision to revise some policies last week.'

He swallowed in acknowledgment.

'We thought it better company practise to allow employees to come to their own conclusions with regards to matters of problem clients.'

'Problem clients?'

'Yes, those that fall between the premium and the government brackets. The normals if you like.'

'The *normals*?'

'Yes, like your happy family of neurosurgeons.'

A rip of white light coursed through his retina. An adrenal gland must have woken up somewhere. Mr Neurosurgeon! Yes! He was still his; he wasn't out of the game yet.

'So the whole thing's up to me now?'

'Well yes, though obviously you'll have to be prepared to deal with the consequences of whatever decision you come to.'

'Consequences?'

'The board will judge each individual case on its own merits, but essentially it's your call. We're keen to inspire a bit more agency in the workplace.'

The adrenalin tempered out, he was hers for the taking. She'd almost drowned him in the swamp, and was now dragging him to the bank to resuscitate him with crap about agency in the workplace.

'So it's completely my call?'

She nodded slowly.

'Yes Joe, like I said we're keen to give everyone a bit more control over their client portfolio.'

His mind attempted to spin, but it was stuck. A smouldering mess of burnt out synapses filled his head with an impenetrable fog.

'Right.'

LEAVING

She smiled an almost genuine smile, her tongue remaining firmly behind her lips. She was starting to seem vaguely human again. It was over. What had happened? Was everything actually just fine?

'So if you're happy with the potential ramifications I think we'll call it a day.'

Ramifications. Another hot flash tore through his head, the emergency hormones had returned. What were the ramifications? Had she said, had he missed them, did they even matter? He tried to think, nothing happened. All his body could do was to continue pouring sweat into the sofa. Splintered images of cloud formations floated through his vision.

'Joe, *Joe?*'

◆

'I Love The Smell of Warming in the Morning'. His favourite mug throbbed gently at him across the desk. He wasn't quite sure what had happened, but he had woken to Computer Tim dabbing his forehead with a cold flannel. Apparently he had fainted and Al had sent him home to rest. A vague recollection of a terrifying encounter with Dr Alice hung in his thoughts, but the details were blurry. Only a week before his holiday though, it would be fine, just grind on through.

The office seemed relatively quiet, a soft gurgle of phone calls and chitchat drifted towards him, a standard day on the apocalypse frontline. A dull ache beat through his forehead, everything seemed a little unsteady, but coffee and painkillers were levelling things out. It would all be okay, just take it call by call, Al had halved his targets for the week.

'Joe, feeling better?'

Computer Tim jerked enthusiastically towards him, a lifelong limp lent him a stop-gap animation quality. It suited him though; he was undeniably the company's friendly cartoon character, his sunny disposition a near miracle given the news cycle.

'Okay, yeah.'

'Good good, so I've managed to find the number, the neurosurgeon guy.'

Yes, Mr Neurosurgeon, flooded with his pregnant wife. A wave of hazy recollections washed into his consciousness, something horrifying had happened, maybe. He turned to Tim, his quizzical eyes searching for clarity.

'You spoke to him yesterday Joe, before the lines went down.'

'Right.'

'I think you went to speak to Alice about it, not sure though.'

'Okay.'

'Anyway, here's the number.'

Tim passed him a scrap of paper with a barely legible number scrawled across it.

'That's 4429 right?'

'No, 9929.'

Yes, that was it, they'd been granted carte blanche to take on whatever clients they wanted, the brackets were gone, *agency in the workplace*. Yes, call him back up and explain the phone line outage, then crack on with getting them moved. The premium package was probably a step too far, but he could get them to Scotland, out of London at least.

'Thanks Tim, appreciate it.'

He watched him jerk his way back across the office. His head felt lighter, he was feeling good. Everything was fine. He reached for his coffee. It tasted good – delicate and fragrant. Everything was very good. He'd call and get everything back on track. He could help, move them, do his thing!

LEAVING

Uncrumpling Tim's scrap of paper he tapped the number into the phone. A drawn out series of bleeps hummed down the line. Spinning around on his chair he scanned the office, Jess making tea, Marty on the phone, Dr Alice stepping into her room. *Dr Alice.* Something inside him glitched.

'Happy with the potential ramifications.'

A buried knot of anxiety unspooled through his stomach. It was all crashing back; the frosted leaves, the sofa, the manual. The bleeps howled through his head. He was back on the sofa. What had she said? *Problem clients, normals, consequences.* It wasn't good. It was appalling. What were they going to do, what was he going to do? Bleep, bleep, bleep. His nerves were fried, he could almost smell the burning. He clenched Tim's scrap of paper, the only thing that felt safe.

'Hello?'

It was him. He'd actually picked up.

'*Hello?*'

What to do, what to do. Do his thing? *Consequences.* Every synapse was screaming.

'Is anyone there?'

He span his chair towards the window and looked out. A few clouds drifted overhead, some seagulls were picking at some chips, it all looked very normal.

The Sound of Silence
Rhys Barratt
United Kingdom

THE HARSH RINGING OF GUNSHOT reverberated throughout the room. Art imitates life as the remnants of the President's grey matter wetly splatter against the militaristic painting behind his desk. There's a cacophony of heavy footfall and the panicked barking of orders approaching from outside the room, then quiet. Simon's last conscious thoughts are that this is real and the idealistic hope that Cherubim play half as passionately as Viola did…

First Movement

I'm awoken by the sonorous ringing of the alarm, its listless tone the perfect accompaniment to my day. It isn't even concrete yet; my schedule, but I already know to expect monotony. It's a credit to the army's sheer lack of creative thought that I'm assigned to the armoury. They either couldn't muster the reasoning to find me something better suited to my talents, or they simply couldn't care. I'm not quite sure which is more depressing if I'm being honest. Yes, there isn't a pressing need for a man of my particular skillset in this soulless regime, but relegating me to cleaning the barrels of rifles and shoe-shining is a little reductive to say the very least.

    Structured, that's what the President said in his inauguration speech. He would usher in a new era of peace and prosperity, all the standard spin for a budding politician. Ex-military definitely gave him an edge in his campaign however, really helped play on the populaces' sympathies. The conflict with the violent 'savages' to the east had left the country in disarray, true. We consequently needed a brawn-over-brains warrior to stamp out culture with an iron first, false. But he riled up those patriotic, post-war emotions and whipped them into a frenzy, driving even the pacifistic toward his totalitarian viewpoint. Reminded me of a talented fiddler I once tutored, made it seem like the instrument was an unwitting partner in a dance he directed. Every speech the President gave was designed to invoke a certain emotion in a certain sect of people at the height of the subject matters' importance. It sounds like pretty obvious stuff, but he struck the chords just so.

    Not much point dwelling on the past though, but I sure wish they wouldn't plaster President Bradley's smug mug on every bus that happens to drive past. Right about now I would be indulging in the ethereal melodies of Beethoven or the scaling arpeggios of any number of talented guitarists. Instead I listen to the click-clack of heels on pavement and a steady thrum of multiple conversations leaking through government-mandated mobiles and interactive billboards. No fun allowed, no artistic expression, no disagreement. Sure, there's less violence, but it's manufactured, a non-verbal treaty signed by fearful citizens under the looming threat of a firing squad. Looks like they've plastered some propaganda on the vacant stretches of wall just before Main Street, mainly anti-Soldan; what a surprise. Must have being put up over Sunday when I wasn't working. You wouldn't think they had an assigned nomenclature that they utilised from the sheer breadth of slurs used as substitute.

Turning onto Main Street and I'm greeted with the monolithic Central HQ, a grey monument to all of our sins. There's a heavily armed guard stationed outside the strikingly grey lobby, standing ever vigilant against the perilous threat of stray pigeons and other such enemies of the state. It's a rotation of four soldiers, changing at noon and midnight, on the dot. I've seen some of the same faces interspersed throughout the week, but I couldn't put a name to a single soul. It isn't a plebeian's place to know such things of course, but it's probably a good thing in hindsight, wouldn't want to start associating names to faces, faces to people and people to personalities, that might make me feel some base level of empathy with the bastards.

Even as I'm striding up the unnecessarily wide, grey steps I notice the withering glares levelled at me, a silent reminder that they don't carry those guns for show and they certainly aren't afraid of throwing their weight around. I've witnessed it, the sad resemblance between the grey, brutalist structure behind them and the brutality they enact on anyone getting rowdy. A grotesque cascade of red runs down those steps and into the boulevard, a body sent tumbling down the sanguine falls to a depressing lack of fanfare. The sound is sickening, the cracking of bones and a general squelch of skin not quite fitting a frame so tightly anymore, followed by a thuggish jeer from the four jumped-up men gleefully hopping down after their prey.

I'm past their glares now, it's too much effort to crane your neck when you have another equally detestable artsy type coming right up behind evidently. The inside of the lobby is mostly, you guessed it, grey. There are some paintings left hanging, but they're purely for effect. Renditions of battles with the Soldan, of which we're always decisively crushing. They're amateurish at best, outright offensive at worst, a product of government dogs without an iota of emotional connection to their work other than an order to do so and the chance to express some not-so-subtle racism in oil form. Garry's sat at the receptionist desk, looking morose as he applies his critical eye to the piece sitting across from him. It's sad that he tries, beyond all reasonable measures to find something of true merit in the work he stares at for twelve hours a day, six days a week. I suppose there's little else to do when you aren't being harassed by military desk jockeys and surly soldiery.

'Hi Garfunkel, how's it hanging?' I ask in hushed tones.

He doesn't look particularly amused that I chose today to play our game. 'Hi to you Simon. Miserably, as you well know.'

He begins stamping my documentation the moment a rather unflattering woman turns her head our way. She crooks her lips in a particularly sinister manner and goes back to her conversation with the mountain of a man casting a shadow over our own chat.

'Get to your embroidery, or shoe polishing, or whatever it is you do nowadays.' He sounds sour but I can't blame the man.

'It could be good ol' paperwork today Garry, don't get my hopes up to high.' I get the genial smirk I once had the pleasure of waking up to in reply.

Now that my small stack of personal information has being stamped with Bradley's fist, which is of course grey, I can get on with this laborious day. A rather harsh pull on my available wrist brings me face-to-face with an altogether more serious Garry.

'I wasn't going to say anything, I don't think you deserve it, but ask Viola about the sensitive documents she found.' It sounds rather insulting, but intriguing nonetheless.

'Okay Garry, I will. Speak to you tomorrow.'

Second Movement

The gang's all here as expected. It isn't like they have a choice in the matter, but pretending that they do and still choose each other's company makes the day a little bit easier. I can hear Mark rummaging through the supply closet for all of the crap he'll need for his time down in the armoury, he doesn't sound too pleased all things considered. Viola looks awfully stern for someone so beautiful, it's rather vain and awfully soppy that I wish I could change that. I remember listening to her performances at the amphitheatre, a veritable masterclass on all things string. She captured the minds of many a musician, the hearts of anyone that enjoys music and turned the heads of anyone interested in women. That's the real shame with this anti-art establishment, the palpable sadness that accompanies it. Life seems rather empty without the aural pleasure of music, the immersion in pointless prose and musing over pretentious paintings with boisterous friends. I want to blame the Soldan for breeding a man like Bradley, but I would be bending to the whims of the propaganda machine. Without the ancient Soldan people, music might never have come to be, or maybe it would be purely functional like it is now, military marches and little else.

Mark grunts a customary pre-labour greeting before demonstrating his displeasure with a harsh slam of the door. The rattle sends a loose stack of documentation sprawling to the floor and Eddy lets out an audible gasp before immediately glancing to Viola in a rather amusing look of shock. What isn't amusing being the sheer expression of hate marring her features, not directed at the paper carpeting the carpet, nor the doorway through which Mark stormed. She's looking dead ahead, trying to compete with the sun in who can cast a stronger glare on the solitary

LEAVING

office window.

Laura breaks the silence with her trademark dulcet tones, 'Morning Simon, as you can see tensions are a little… high right now.'

'That's the understatement of the century don't you think, babe? Viola looks like she's about to put her foot through my ass any second.' Eddy's antics always brighten the mood, but I can't possibly care for his comedy act when Viola's breaking down in front of my very eyes.

Her change in moods is, as always, infectious. Everyone looks about as sullen as I suddenly feel and Laura has moved to Viola's side to comfort her. I don't know what to say. We've had some rough days before – that much is true – but Viola was always the face of stoicism. Stepping towards her I'm given an uncharacteristically stern shake of the head from Eddy and it's accompanied by a suitably vague remark,

'Learn to fight your battles kid, this ain't one of them and shit's about to go down.'

I don't appreciate the kid remark, even if the man's junior by twenty years. 'I don't appreciate the kid remark Eddy, even if you are getting on a little, but just clue me in would you. Garry was being awfully clandestine this morning, even compared to our usual verbal sparring.'

Eddy sighs seeming somewhat exasperated. 'Look at the papers, really look at them. Viola doesn't think you should get involved, I don't either, but you aren't going to take no for an answer.'

Bending down to look at the papers isn't particularly enlightening and I'm frankly already tired of this miasma of misery hidden behind riddles that I'm evidently not qualified to answer. There's something about a couple of the papers that does catch my eye, they look pretty faded, two-tone, in the light. Flipping one over is enough to make me feel nauseous, nostalgic and utterly defeated in one fell swoop. It would appear that someone has gone to great lengths to attach some rather ratty note sheets to the back of the standard supply reports Viola deals with. It has been a long while since I've seen musical intonation, even longer that it has meant so much to me. Someone had clearly found something hidden away and taken the liberty to show it around. Obviously it has to be someone forced to work in this soul-sucking place or else they wouldn't take the risk, wouldn't be so brash as to practically staple signs of their dissention on official documentation.

Viola's hand thrust towards me is pretty startling, in her death grip is a small letter of some kind. It requires gently uncurling her fingers to get at it and my straightening of the note is accompanied by a small hiccough from her. My momentary lapse into self-loathing is justified that I find it endearing and marginally attractive. Laura looks positively demonic as I skim the contents of the secretive correspondence,

'You don't know me, perhaps in a more professional fashion years ago, but we aren't friends. The time for lamenting that fact has passed, and we feel that the time for President Bradley and the anti-art movement is also at its end. Central HQ is a time-bomb of unrest, as it was always destined to be, for in all of his infinite wisdom that intolerant, insufferable prick decided to confine everyone he reviles inside his most strategically important infrastructure. There aren't many of us in the resistance, hence the purpose of this letter. It is our hope that you will see an end to your suffering, this country's suffering, by any means of which you are capable. You will find some note sheets attached to reverse side of the usual documentation. It is our hope that you have enough spirit left that you remember what we've suffered through, the sins our military committed that we repent for even now. Bradley's security will be found awfully lacking today, it only takes one of you to do the right thing.'

It started in a relatively innocuous fashion, the anti-art movement that is. Bradley made some rather overt remarks regarding the Soldan

LEAVING

people and their love of the arts, how it made them weak and unclean. This would have normally upset a lot of people, it certainly pissed me and Garry off at the time, but the thinly veiled homophobia and bashing of femininity was more or less glossed over. Because who gives a shit if it's directed at another group of people we dislike, especially when they aren't so close to home. There were some protests shortly after the fact, I even went to one despite pretty much all of the gang warning me not to. I should have listened, because that balmy night I witnessed the truly vile side of war. It wasn't the bloody battles, the slaughtering of townsfolk in counterattacks or the unending fear that you were going to be uprooted from your beds by the savages from the north. That stuff was awful sure, sickening even, but it was expected. We had faced conflict before on a greater scale, hell, one could argue that we even lost one along the way, but the atrocities I saw happened after the war, when things were meant to be peaceful and the country healing...

 I love music, it's in my very nature to do so I think. The ability to say so much without any need for words or expressions, no room for misunderstanding. You can't talk to a mirror without looking at least a little strange, but you can compose any number of pieces and be adored for doing so. It's a deeply personal, individual aspect of humanity that personifies everything good with the notion. You wouldn't think that man, or woman for that matter was capable of ruining that, not an individual like Bradley, nor a small mob of angry bigots, you would be right. It was the idea, the notion of hate for hates sake that prevailed over common sense during that night ten years ago. The protest was relatively dull as they often are, the standard sights of drum circles and picketing, obnoxiously blunt t-shirts worn by equally obnoxious protesters. But it was real, it was that liberty afforded to us by our freedom. The war was over, now was the time to complain about the smaller worries, hope the everyman's voice was heard.

Eventually it seemed someone had listened, or at least grown tired of the chanting outside of Central HQ, for a small army of stern looking uniforms began corralling people closer to the boulevard. I found it somewhat amusing from my distance at the time, I was there to be a statistic in the paper more than anything, make the numbers look good. Things started getting a little heated and the volume steadily rose. It wasn't pleasant by this point, there wasn't that general hum of sociable conversation amongst the repetitive backdrop of piss-poor drumming anymore. I could vaguely make out some slurs amongst the general shouting of the crowd, the military firmly in Bradley's camp when it came to the artsy pansies. Then a gunshot sounded, solitary and deafening, more significant than its foolish catalyst could even comprehend. A chorus of its brethren followed, accompanied by the backing of pained screaming.

Things escalated quickly and violently from that point on. Media spin made Bradley look like God of course, the blame being firmly placed on the violent protestors. It wasn't a lie, hell, it was an incredibly easy pill to swallow for anyone pushing the Bradley agenda, and it helped topple a lot of people still on the fence. A flood of speeches and laws followed, each more ludicrous than the last. Protestors would be arrested on the spot. Musicians, writers and artists were to have government mandated inspections to ensure they weren't Soldan sympathisers. Soldan refuges were shot on sight attempting to enter the country, or taken to government black-sites if the rumour mill was to be trusted. Only marches were to be played in public, only political propaganda was to be published, only art depicting the glorious campaign against Soldan. It went on and on until anyone that made a career from the arts, or openly practiced any as a hobby were sentenced to their new position at Central HQ. It wasn't said, but the threat of death hangs like a spectre even now.

Viola's shouting, I think. It's much like a fade-in for the next song, increasing in volume and clarity until it suddenly registers…

Third Movement

'You aren't getting involved in this, none of you are!'

'But Viola,' Eddy starts, 'they say that Bradley's going down, the bastard deserves it after what he turned this country into.'

I silently agree, but evidently Viola isn't swayed by the notion of Bradley's death.

'We don't know who *they* are, for all we know this could be a trick to weed out anyone still stupid enough to resist.' There's barely a breath, 'And what would any of us do anyway? March into Bradley's office guns blazing? I think that it will be our office getting redecorated.'

Eddy is barely deterred in the face of thorough upbraiding, hell the guy used to be a stand-up and not a particularly good one, he's had his fair share of heckling.

There's an edge to his tone now. 'Listen Viola, I'm fucking sick of this deafening silence hanging over our heads. At this point I live purely to keep Laura going,'

She doesn't seem shocked by that frankly depressing revelation.

'There isn't any joy in life anymore. I thought maybe I could get used to a diet of work or die, with the caveat of having a Sunday to do nothing that brings me joy, but turns out it's pretty bland. Bradley needs to die, his laws need to be repealed and people need to see that what we're doing isn't living, it's existing.'

Laura looks like she's about to speak some hard-hitting truths, and I'm more than tempted to get my two cents in but Viola isn't having it.

'Listen, Eddy. If you think that Bradley's death is going to make a lick of difference your understanding of politics is as poor as your comedy act.'

Ad hominem isn't very becoming and everyone in the room knows it. Eddy doesn't even take the time to look offended and Laura's hand isn't resting on Viola's shoulder anymore.

Laura starts, commanding the room, 'Baby, Viola, let's just take a moment and think this through. Airing the first thing that comes to mind is likely just going to make things more volatile. Also, keep your damn voices down or we won't have a say either way.'

There's that sound again, the sound of silence. It truly is deafening like Eddy says, I always thought the phrase rather stupid. But it's all intellectual, the sound is all of the unspoken words in a conversation, the tension slowly building until something has to break it. That's something I miss just as much to music, those moments of quiet without expectation, without pretence. I've been robbed. At some point after that damn protest some malicious deity robbed me of my reason for being. It isn't just me though, just standing here is enough proof that everyone's in the same boat. Except we aren't sinking, there isn't a calamity waiting to happen, we're just sitting in the still water.

'Maybe we should try and get in touch with some of the other offices? See if anyone else has had a visit from the civil uprising fairy. It's like he, she, they, whatever said, it only takes one person to put a bullet between Bradley's eyes. Why does it have to be any of us?'

'Laura, you're the smartest person I've had the pleasure of knowing, but the letter only says that so that someone suicidal will feel that they have a purpose. It's working evidently, just look at your husband.'

Eddy looks pissed at that; clearly Viola hasn't noticed that he never volunteered himself, only agreed with the general sentiment. Eddy has

Laura and the reverse is also true, they're both too selfless to leave the other one alone, because that would turn them into the person Viola's accusing Eddy of being. Viola isn't a coward, but she still values her life for what it is, real. You can't really undo that whole dying thing unfortunately, or perhaps fortunately. I suspect that most people that have that same letter, if they exist, would find the excuse to keep on going. The ones that don't could probably convinced by everyone else. I'm in agreement with Viola's main worry, no one's going to commit, and any mistakes gets everyone killed. Guess I should interject my opinion, for what it's worth.

'Listen guys, I think we can all agree that this argument is circular. I don't think it's a good idea, but it's something that could change this game we've being forced to play for years. We've being given a time limit by this resistance, and clearly none of them are willing to get their hands dirty beyond whatever opportunity they're affording us.'

That's all I want to say, it isn't enough to make them worry. If they worry they will presume, and that leads to more talking about things that may or may not happen. They're friends, but friendship is something forged through shared experiences and finding joy in mutual interests. We don't really have experiences anymore; it's just one amalgamation of time passing whilst recalling ever fading memories. That isn't enough, Eddy's right about that. I don't have a Laura to keep me here, so I might as well do something real, something that might afford me my own crescendo before that fabled tranquillity I've missed.

'Simon, what's your point?' Viola retorts.

'Wasn't one really Vi, just thought I would demonstrate how it's circular you know? I've always had a flair for being dramatic.'

'You have, that's why I'm going to ask you not to do anything you can't take back. I care about you. All of you, even the flaws,' she says, shooting a look at Eddy full of something I can't quite place.

Eddy returns it.

Maybe in another life Viola would have had the chance to love me, let me love her. Not now though, it can't happen in this grey world.

'I'm off to the armoury; maybe I can find some slightly less miserable sorts down there. I'm going to run this note sheet business by Garfunkel, see what he makes of it.'

Picking up one of the forms turned plotting device I turn to leave. Shutting the door behind me is the hardest part, because now it's real and it's suddenly overwhelming. Briskly is my preferred pace towards the armoury, past the lobby were Garry has gone from grimacing at the painting to pitying it. All manner of nosy grunts could be stopping me, but that's the thing with complacency, why would they? I'm not really sure what the next step is, but Tom is in charge of the gun cabinet so I flash him the note sheet as discretely as possible. Within seconds I'm pocketing a revolver and I've never felt so alive…

Dark Waters
L.E Beacock
United Kingdom

Winner of the 2019
Student Category

SHE'D ALMOST GROWN ACCUSTOMED to the metal binding tightly against her wrists. Almost. But how was one supposed to willingly adjust to a life of enslavement? Struggling to come to terms with her oppression, Ebele's mind fell into an endless cycle of torment and fear. To think of her future was inconceivable, so she chose to focus on the now, whatever that entailed.

The rotting smell of malnourished bodies clung to her senses. Black skeletal bodies huddled and clung desperately against one another in the dark, their feeble limbs unified by rusted shackles and chains. The moans of the ill and starving echoed the hull, chilling Ebele's bare skin endlessly with their awful lowly hums. To distinguish between the living and the dead seemed impossible.

How long had they travelled across the ocean like this? Bound to the aching arms of strangers by heavy chains and rocking their bodies back and forth to the ruthless rhythm of the Atlantic waves. How long had she endured the stench of decay, imminent disease and faecal matter? No human should have to bear such pain she thought, but thoughts were futile. The end was nigh and all that was left to do was to wait patiently for its arrival.

Hoping to console her crippled spirit with sleep, far too weak and constrained for anything more, Ebele found herself stirring uneasily against the wood instead. Distorted voices from the white men above grew loud and energetic, more so than usual, and the frightened slaves below shuffled closer to one another in anticipation for what was to follow. Had the time come? To finally meet their end? To be torn limb from limb and feasted upon by the red-faced cannibals dancing and roaring on the slaver's deck?

As their heavy-footed tramples became erratic, Ebele searched her surroundings for a sign of assurance or guidance from the others, yet the widened eyes of her fellow slaves only presented her with looks of concern and fear in return.

'*In ugo?*' She heard spoken amongst the huddled people, and the occupants of the hull shuffled anxiously at the ever-growing commotion taking place above their heads. There hadn't been so much movement amongst the slaves in many months. Yes, they had *all* heard, and although none could quickly identify the cause, they would shortly find out.

With a piercing squeak and a hefty pull, the hatch door of the slave deck swung open wide and the blinding brightness of the blue skies shone down ferociously into the darkness. Promptly obscuring the rays of light with his tall figure, the apprehension of the slaves heightened at the man's ominous visage, and in their desperate union, they all attempted to hustle further back in their shackles as far as their frail bodies could permit. Although she couldn't see above the heads of the many, Ebele

LEAVING

hadn't needed to see the cause of further distress.

'Since we don't have enough arms, I'll be taking six of you to fight with me!' His voice boomed and echoed the wooden planks of the lower ship in a language strange to the slaves, and yet a tone now all too familiar.

The man known only to the people of Igbo as Mr Markham was a merciless creature. More so than any of the other seamen aboard. Elijah Markham was the boatswain of the slaving ship, a sadistic man who was most uncaring for the lives of the ship's cargo. Unforgiving in his torture of Africans, he flogged and threw Ebele's brethren overboard should they have foolishly disobeyed his words.

His shiny black shoes of leather trod distinctly against the wooden steps with his descent, a walk mannered with subdued haste. He could not quite hide his stress. Though his voice and demeanour had been unmistakably fearsome as always, Ebele could sense urgency in his stature. His beady blue eyes, sharp and seeking, caused her to observe his movements with care. Something was happening. Or rather something was *about* to happen. Something far worse than what they had already endured.

Quickly tilting her head to one side, just to peer past Mr Markham's shoulder as he became level with the floor of the deck, Ebele glanced up and out through the open latch door. She saw sailors running erratically amongst and into one another, their pale faces etched with absolute terror. This chilled the young girl to her adolescent core. What exactly could be far more frightening than they? Had there been other kinds of monsters that ventured the sea in white-winged dungeons on their own?

'You.'

Reluctant to look up at the tall fiend standing before her, Mr Markham's broad figure cast a perilous shadow over her small seated frame. The menacing silhouette seemed frightening enough to consume her entirely, and the thought of being one of the unlucky chosen to be eaten stabbed at her mind once more. At one point or another throughout her journey, the thought of death had provided comfort. An end to her misery, however attained, calmed her thoughts. This would not last an eternity. And yet now, for her moment of death to arrive so forthrightly, Ebele denied all of her previous desires.

If she was to die it would *not* be by this man.

Smiling toothily, a yellow-tainted grin with plaque and holes, Mr Markham sank his hand deep into the pocket of his smoky grey breeches; and promptly revealed a rusted iron key. To most, a key would signify release or freedom, but it was most feared by the Igbo captives.

After all, a slave was only to be removed of their manacles should they have fallen to illness and risked a spread of disease. Or to be flogged as a way of punishment and likely thrown to the ever-impatient sharks that followed below the ships that generously fed them.

Yielding to the boatswain's looming impression, Ebele slowly met with his blue eyes and froze at the sight of the sickly smile stretching against his sun-peeled face. Mr Markham was a hard man to study. Although rather unsightly with his long greasy ponytail, his crooked sneer and oversized ears, his sailing attire was impeccable in contrast.

The strange clothing that he wore, that signature white cuffed shirt and sagging slops, always looked unsoiled from any of the natural elements of sea travel. Maybe this was due to his obvious disdain for rigorous duties aboard. The only physical task that the boatswain enjoyed was the whipping of slaves and ill-behaved underlings.

'Let's start with you. Looks like there's a bit of fight left in there. Even for a woman, you might come in use.' He reached down and took hold of her constraints, forceful and rough with his calloused fingers. She twisted and turned her scabbing wrists beneath the shackles, hoping that another of her fellow slaves would come to her aid and push Markham from her grasp, but alas, her yearning was in vain. He lifted her with little to no effort, almost tearing at her scarce rags during the struggle. Maybe there had been a bit too much life in this one.

'Stop it, girl! Unless you want to die under my hands instead of that of a pirate, you'll do as I say!'

Dismissing the threats of his foreign tongue, Ebele continued to resist under his hold, pulling away at iron and scratching at his hands whenever he came too close. Cursing her disobedience, he tightened his fingers around her wrist and quickly unlocked her shackles, maintaining and furthering his strength against her arm. Any harder and he would've surely broken bone.

'I'm not the one you should be fighting, you filthy little Negro! Do as I say!'

'*I don't want to die. I don't want to die today!*' Her newfound declaration roared from within, and just as she was able to accumulate enough energy to strike out a smack, the entirety of the ship thundered with a mighty quake. The occupants of the lower deck fell to one side, altogether tumbling over their kin. Screams of pain and terror consumed the hull and Ebele found herself crawling out from beneath the heavy body of a lifeless man.

Mr Markham lay lifeless at her side, the left portion of his face completely blown away into gruesome obscurity, the flesh and bone of his jaw exposed and pouring with blood, caused by the roundshot that had so mercilessly pierced through the side of the ship. Coughing and wiping at the dust obscuring her eyes, Ebele scanned amongst the wooden debris, broken barrels and loose rope in search of the livelihood of the other slaves. And as if by the grace of a higher being, they all seemed to be alive and moving, save for some bleeding wounds and dirtied rags and faces.

Without hesitation, she turned her attention to the open latch. Thunderous explosions rumbled on relentlessly, as did the harrowing cries of men at battle and the scraping of connecting metals.

After she had told herself she would not so willingly die that day, Ebele remained exactly where she had fallen, her eyes fixating back and forth to the latch and the corpse of the boatswain bleeding at her feet. Whatever or whoever else was to step down those stairs next she would face head on. Whatever else blew through and into the side of the hull next she would face head on. And in seeing the resolution in the young girl's eyes, the slaves grew closer to her side. They held tightly onto one another, steadfast and prepared for the fate of their future.

'*Gidi gidi bụ ugwu eze.*' Sweet and heartening, Ebele's words uplifted the souls of the slaves, their hands tightened securely into one another's despite their constraints. *Unity is strength.* Reminiscent words of the village elders resonated within her thoughts. Maybe she had been reluctant to die, but it wouldn't have been all that bad to die alongside the unity of her people.

A step. One heavy step followed slowly by another. The screaming, shooting and fighting began to still from somewhere above and the deep treads of another stole the slaves away from their solidarity.

Now this individual was different from any of the other seamen that boarded the slaver. *Distinctively.* Their walk was leisured and playful with a sway of their arms, behaviour unfamiliar to Ebele and her knowledge of nasty and violent sailors. Long black boots, surely weighing more than those of Mr Markham, implied mass and power, as did the curving blood-smeared cutlass swinging merrily in their right hand.

A number of the slaves fell back at the sight of the newcomer, their chains chinking against the wood and catching the attention of the stranger. They tilted one of the three corners of their tricorn hat and peered over the crowd of Africans, finally revealing their face in its entirety.

A woman. With skin as dark as their own and a variation of deep scars that decorated her right clouded eye and lower lip. Unmistakably beautiful, the young woman surprisingly carried an aura of time and experience, her stance casual and composed as she took in the faces of the lost and stolen souls. Her thin fingers and wrists were accented with bands of jewels, revealing with a childish smile that even various teeth had been replaced with gold. How had a woman of their colour, no doubt of their land, come to dress and be like those of a distant one?

Ebele caught the attention of the woman with her uncomfortable fidgeting, and the mysterious individual knelt down to her level. The ends of her extravagant frock coat slithered over the ignored corpse of Mr Markham, as if to so coldly indicate that nobody else in the World mattered at all. Death had been no stranger.

Pulling out a small handkerchief from the sleeve of her coat, the woman softened her smile and reached out to wipe the dust from Ebele's cheeks,

'I see the fire in your eyes, my little sister. Shall I grant you your freedom or will you join me in the fight?'

Though the eighteenth century would be cruel to those of her kin and colour, Ebele would waste no time dwelling on her decision. She would rebel for them at the side of her new Captain. And as she had come to realise, Ebele was reluctant to die, and it wouldn't have been all that bad to die alongside the unity of her people.

Staying To Leave

Mags Brown
United Kingdom

Shortlisted for the 2019 International Writing Competition

HER HEART POUNDED and her hands were wet with sweat. Anxiety was both her familiar friend and ruthless enemy, whilst her medication was neither.

Her soup bowl was in front of her, a spoon relaxing on a napkin by its side.

Her stomach growled as her hands trembled. The aroma was intense and inviting and, for the first time in a while, her taste buds were alive. But the spoon was lying on its back, on the napkin, whilst her hands were firmly in her pockets and neither could reach the other.

She was oblivious to the others around her, to the chit chat and companionship of like-minded folks in, what was for them, a familiar situation; likewise to the quiet ones who stayed separate, isolated by their own demons.

Her only crime was the desire to leave – to leave her home, her parents, her family, her tormentors, herself. Why had she been stopped?

LEAVING

Been silenced? Been seduced into thinking that perhaps life wasn't so bad after all?

Because it was bad. Very bad. Her opinion and her experience. All subjective and personal and real to only the one person – the central character in the story of life. And that, for the moment, was her.

She took a deep breath and tried again to reach the spoon, to assuage the hunger pangs and prolong her unwanted existence, but it was too much. Far too much. She shuddered, shook and ran, through the swinging doors and along the long, dim corridor to reach the relative safety and privacy of her room, under the bed and amongst the cobwebs missed by the cleaning team.

Life hadn't always been like this – she had been a happy young child with an infectious laugh and a face which, not always helpfully, spoke before her words came out. She made light of her bullying brothers and escaped into books, her mobile library being one of her best friends and she devoured 'What Katy Did', 'Ann of Green Gables' and 'Black Beauty'. And childhood dreams and hopes and wishes flew like dandelion seeds in her head as she ran with her friends on warm summer days.

Chores were always there and were a way of life, something to be accomplished to the best of her ability (and then some!) as a six, seven, eight year old. She learned not to complain as her brothers went out to play; life was very different for the two sexes and she had drawn the short straw by being a girl. Oh well! She made the most of it, took pride in doing her best, then escaped back to books, writing and time with her best friends. She took pleasure in pleasing people, in singing on the bus en route to see relatives every weekend, in dressing in her best dress and party shoes so she could please an elderly aunt even although she would rather have been at home reading or playing. Bringing pleasure to others became her strength and, ultimately, one of her greatest weaknesses, which would bring about her downfall.

Because some people can never be pleased.

Some people can never be happy or content.

Damaged themselves, nothing will ever help some people, ever. But that is an observation and discovery for later life.

From under her bed she could hear her name being called. She wanted to reply. Wanted to respond, hoping that she was missed, wanted, cared for. But experience told her the opposite and that she would be in trouble, again.

She had tricked herself into that hope just too often. For a young person she had experienced more than her tender years could understand and it would be a long time before she realised the truth and complications of relationships, responsibilities, recourse.

So, it was all up to her. To answer? She would soon be found anyway so probably no sense in delaying the inevitable. She crawled out of her temporary safety, ready to face the next few moments. Brushing herself off she stretched her cramped limbs, lifted her tired head and raised her fragile hopes.

What came first, the chicken or the egg? Which has most impact, nature or nurture? When is the most impressionable age for a child? What effect does a parent's personal problems have on their children? These were questions I would have asked, had I had the vocabulary at the time. Instead, I spoke with my actions. Angry and frightened, lonely and afraid, I screamed, kicked out and generally caused trouble at school, which was why I ended up where I was, unable to eat my soup, hiding under the bed and wondering if the nurse calling my name would be sympathetic or frustrated or borderline cruel because of her own personal inadequacies. Sometimes I was accused of 'playing dead', but I wasn't playing. Sometimes my whole being was overcome with emotion

LEAVING

and just shut down, often to be reawakened by a sharp slap on my face. But that, of course, was the least I deserved.

For hurting others.

For making them uncomfortable.

For making them aware of their own demons.

For not being able to understand.

For not being able to communicate from the depths of my being.

A kindly nurse spoke to me, explained I would be moved to somewhere where I could be looked after and helped to find my way through the plateful of thick sludge that was puberty (and the beginnings of a life-long mental health issue) with a side order of dysfunctional family and extra chips. Not that those were her words, nor mine. Words come later, I've learned.

A cottage in the woods! A small garden! Two locked outside doors and sixteen peers (eight boys separated from eight girls by two locked internal doors and several intimidating looking nurses). A small kitchen, a formal lounge resembling an old people's home with chairs arranged in a circle, a dormitory with eight metal beds along one wall and an armchair, small table and anglepoise lamp placed by the door where the night nurse would spend her night reading and clicking her knitting needles. The desire to leave was overwhelming (a distinct theme in my life) but my quick sprint came to a sudden halt as I barrelled into a large male nurse. Size, age and experience triumphed over slightness, youth and sheer panic.

'Draw me a picture'. So I set to with dark paints, large jagged lines and felt so much better until a fellow inmate told me 'they' didn't like that sort of thing. If I ever wanted to get out I had to draw rainbows and fluffy clouds. So I painted over my emotions and re-covered them with something more acceptable. To get anywhere in life, I was continually discovering, you have to do what you have to do.

I volunteered and helped out cleaning and made sure there was never any dust or cobwebs under the beds. I spoke quietly with some of the other more intimidated girls. I sang and had all eight of us relatively tuneful and word perfect in 'I'm Nobody's Child'! And I ate! Oh how I ate! Cereal, toast and cooked breakfast, cooked lunch, cooked dinner with sponge and custard, bread and butter with everything too. It all arrived in a large stainless steel box and I had no preparation to do at all, no washing up either. I could just sit back and enjoy it, which is exactly what I did. There were no mirrors in our little cottage so I didn't see my elf like face get rounder and it was easy to just leave the top button off my trousers. This would be a problem for another time, another life-stage, another therapist.

But I was restless and uncomfortable and needed to leave, despite the amazing food, the two (out of six) kind nurses, the rather odd but highly entertaining teacher who made no effort to keep us up to date with the educational curriculum and, despite not really wanting to go home, I really had to leave. If ever I was to reclaim myself it could never be done in the isolated, secure and sterile environment of those trying to help. They didn't know what I needed and I didn't know how to ask. Words, again, come later.

So I learned that in order to 'leave' I had to learn to 'stay'. I became the model patient and used the desired colour of paint and pencil no matter how I felt; I learned to plump the cushions and replace them 'square' and not 'pointy' and learned to sleep on my back, legs straight and arms by my side. It was actually quite a nice game to think myself into and I appreciated some security whilst burying myself deeper. It was in a good cause – it would get me out. I could perform the actions needed. Words, real words, would be articulated eventually.

LEAVING

And I left. Or rather, I was escorted out. The staff patted themselves on their backs and celebrated another success (the paperwork was all very positive), another life put back together (they didn't know the building blocks were still faulty) and another family reunited (and they had no idea that they were actually happier when I wasn't there). Back home, where things would be awkward but where nothing would change. Back to school to face awkward questions, wary teachers and friends who had missed me.

Slowly I reintegrated myself into a different version of my old life, which wasn't really different at all – home, school, chores, study, medication, repeat. But some things were different although I didn't recognise it at the time. Recognition, like words, has its own dynamics.

'Leaving' would become a good friend to me in time, time which would have its own pace and plan. 'Leaving' would introduce me to 'Going' and between them I would find 'Being' and the whole richness and quality of the physical, the emotional, the spiritual parts of which we are all made. And words. Finally, the right words.

A Far Cry from the Poppy Fields
GILLIAN BROWN
France

EDITOR'S CHOICE

MY REFLECTION STARES BACK FROM THE MIRROR. With my black hair cut short and brushed high on top, I look like a typical fifteen-year-old boy. And yet, something is missing. But some things never change. A smile parts my lips as I remember my brother calling me "broccoli ears". I cover them with my fists, let out a deep sigh and slump onto the bed. My mother's dark, sad eyes appear from nowhere, drowning me in another wave of guilt.

A knock at the door makes me jump. That'll be my therapist. Martin understands Farsi but we speak English as I need to practise. He lowers himself onto the only chair. Despite being a small man, something about him demands my attention. His gaze seems to burrow under my skin. I turn away and pick at a broken nail.

'How's things today, Gorbhan?'

His cockney accent can be hard to follow but I'm getting used to it. I shrug and drop my head, staring at the frayed laces in my second-hand trainers. 'Okay.'

He laughs, throwing his head back in that way of his. 'It doesn't sound like it.'

'I've been in London six months now. Sometimes I feel I left Afghanistan for nothing. All they do is shunt me from hostel to hostel. I want to go to school. I want British citizenship. I want a proper life.' My sigh fills the room like a dark cloud. 'All I do is watch telly or listen to music all day. I haven't enough money to go out.'

I've told Martin this a thousand times. My mood dives further as the cold and damp English summer presses up against my tiny windowpane. I think of the heat and dust and beauty of my homeland. My chest tightens.

Martin clears his throat. 'Is there something else?'

I squirm under his stare until my thoughts burst out. 'Nightmares. Last night I dreamt about the boy who fell overboard in the storm that night on our way to Greece. He screamed in the dark, choking for his life. We didn't stop or go back for him. His cries grew fainter and fainter until the boat's engine drowned them out. His scream stayed in my head. Some nights it gets so loud it wakes me up. Then I just lie there – scared – till morning.'

'Are you taking your medication?'

'No.'

Martin's thick eyebrows meet. 'It will help you sleep.'

'I don't want pills. I want to go to school. I want to learn. To work. To do something with my life.' I punch my mattress in frustration. 'Please, Martin. Can't you make something happen?'

I watch Martin's chest rise and fall, straining the buttons on his clean white shirt. As he turns from my gaze, his Adam's apple bobs up and down. He mutters something under his breath, then clears his throat.

'Progress is being made.' I gape in disbelief. He sounds like a robot. 'Your case is complicated.' Just as I'm thinking he doesn't care, an exasperated grunt escapes him. I've heard him swear when he thinks I'm not listening but all he says is, 'It's not my decision.'

I clench and unclench my fists, biting my lip to stop myself exploding. The air grows heavy. The walls close in.

Martin folds his arms and stares at his knees. I'm used to his silences. It's his way of calming me down or letting me gather my thoughts. Perhaps his too. But this time I'm not calm. My heart is hammering against my ribs. Blood drums in my ears.

A burst of anger burns up my throat and jumps out. Soon I'm screaming at the top of my voice. 'I'll start a riot. I'll do anything to catch attention. I don't care if they throw me out on the street. This immigration system is rubbish. No-one listens. All I want is a better life.' I pause to steady my voice. 'I wish I'd been blown up with the same bomb that killed my father.'

Martin's head jerks up. 'What did you say?'

'You heard me.'

His eyes blaze. 'Have you forgotten the 12,000 kilometres of hell you went through to get here?' he shouts. 'Hidden in lorries with hardly enough room to breathe. Jammed into overcrowded boats with nothing to eat for days. The fear. The loneliness. All that hardship and misery and you can talk like that?'

'Yes.'

'No, Gorbhan! This is about you. It's your future. It's what you dreamed of.'

I throw my hands in the air. 'My case worker never listens. She makes me want to give up. She doesn't care.'

'What makes you think that?'

'She peers over her glasses at me like she wishes I'd disappear. She never smiles or offers any hope, however much I beg for help.'

Martin presses his lips together. He stands up and starts to pace. Three steps one way. Three the other. There's no more space. He scratches his head so hard I'm afraid it might bleed. 'I'll have a word with that b—.' He bites his lip. 'I'll see what I can do.'

He sits back down and draws his chair closer, taking a deep breath. 'And your family? Do you ever think of them?'

Memories swarm in. Mama is crouched down, a knitted shawl around her shoulders as she milks the goats. Together, we empty the pails of milk into steel containers. Next day, I'll take them to market. My brothers are working in the poppy fields for a pitiful few afghanis a day. I think of the kite fighting and the chess I played with Papa before he was killed – before the Taliban banned both kites and chess as useless pastimes. I remember the hatred in the eyes of my stepfather, who fought with Mama every time she wanted to see me. Once Papa was gone, her brothers forced her to remarry and I was banned from their house.

Martin interrupts my thoughts. 'Your family is part of your identity, Gorbhan. Your own flesh and blood. Have you been in touch since you left?'

My mouth turns dry. 'No.'

'Why not?'

A knife tears at my insides, as it does every time I think about it. 'I left without telling my mother. Now I'm too ashamed to speak to her.' My heart cramps up. 'But I had no choice. She'd only have stopped me.'

'A difficult decision. I understand that, but you could contact her now.'

Once Martin has gone, I turn the idea over in my head a thousand times, until I can't stand it any longer. I log onto Snapchat and search desperately for any "friends" I have in Afghanistan. My real friends and family have no Internet. One boy comes from the next village to mine. I click on his profile. I've never met him. I ask him if he can post some photos of my village. They're blurry, taken on a cheap phone – flat roofed houses, distant mountains, fields of purple. They tug at my memory. My heart skips a beat. I give him my mother's name, to see if he can find her. Days later, he messages me her new phone number.

I memorise it but don't call her. What can I say? I need to prove myself first to justify my leaving. But Martin is right. My past is as much a part of me as my future. This truth comforts me, and the storm in my head quietens a little.

A week later, a miracle happens. I'm given a place at the local secondary school. I dance around the room, beaming from ear to ear. I want to call Mama. But I don't.

When I tell Martin my news he shakes my hand with the force of an ox. 'Brilliant, Gorbhan! At last we're getting somewhere.' Then a concerned look clouds his face. 'You'll be bullied at school, you know. There'll be racist comments.'

'I don't care if they beat me up or spit on me. I'm going to school! I'm going to school!' I repeat the words over and over until I run out of breath.

'I admire your courage, and speaking good English will help. Just be warned.'

Martin is right. Insults are hurled at me as fast and sharp as hunting knives. One cuts too deep. 'Son of an Afghan whore!' I reach out with my fist but the guy is too big and too quick. He knocks me down and pins me to the floor. 'Fuck off back to where you belong,' he says, before kicking me, laughing with his mates and running off in triumph.

Bruised inside and out, I struggle to my feet.

LEAVING

Just when I'm thinking things can't get any worse, a vision pops into my head. Fields of mauve and pink poppies sway before me. Their stems are bent double with the force of the 100-day wind, which sweeps across the poppy fields every year before harvest time. It tears at their petals and they shiver and shake, but against all odds they cling on. Their strength brings a flutter of hope to my stomach.

I cut out my routine of press-ups and weight-lifting, and study all my free time. I remind myself I'm doing this for Mama as much as for myself. Martin too. I don't want to let him down.

Things get better for a while. My classmates find someone else to pick on. Ben becomes my best mate. Or so I thought, until the day he announces to the whole class, 'Gorbhan may think I'm his friend.' My jaw drops. He hesitates, then swallows hard. 'But I'm not. I never want to speak to him again.'

Ben avoids eye contact but I notice dark bruises around his face and on his arms. These bullies could seriously harm him, or worse. I must let him go. A void opens up inside me. I've never felt more alone. I force back the wetness behind my eyes and run from the room, slamming the door behind me.

That same night, I gather the savings I've made from odd jobs around the place, and go out and buy a six-pack of extra strong lager from a man who asks no questions. I've never touched alcohol before. If it kills me, who cares?

The more I drink, the more vivid the images in my head become. I'm playing Pajpar, or Five Suits, with Mama. Her work-worn fingers grip the cards. Her brow creases in concentration. A surge of love for her overwhelms me and I let her win the hand. She laughs with such joy, I join in and give her a hug. She strokes my hair, like I'm a child again.

I crack open another can. And another. My mind tips. Mama starts shouting at me. 'Why did you leave without telling me? Why are you drinking alcohol?' Next, she is hitting me. Slapping my face. I take another swig. Her features becomes a blur. Her words muffled.

With the last can, I sink into a pit too deep to crawl out of. I'll never see my mother again. She'll never forgive me for what I've done. My heart breaks into a million pieces, which scatter like shards of glass across the floor. I take a last gulp of lager, stagger to the basin and grab my razor. The world narrows down to a sharp blade and the pulsing vein on my wrist.

I don't remember any pain, just a sudden spurt of blood.

'Luckily, you screamed,' Martin tells me later. 'The neighbours heard you, and saved your life.'

Luckily? I'm not sure.

With Martin's help, I get back into the routine. Days seem like weeks, months like years, but I never touch alcohol again and bury myself in my studies. Finally, I'm rewarded with top grades in my A levels. A ton of weight slips from my shoulders. I stick out my chest and punch the air in the Anglo-Saxon way. 'Yes!'

My dream is getting closer. Soon I'll have my British passport. I'll belong. A surge of relief sweeps through me.

I can't put off calling Mama any longer. My hand shakes so much I can hardly hold the phone. It seems to ring forever, like an echo from the far side of the world. Then there's a click and a suspicious 'hello'. The sound of her voice in my ear is as sweet as the sheer pira dessert she is famous for. My favourite.

My heart is still pumping the next day when Martin comes in. 'Have you won the lottery?' He throws his head back, laughing.

'I passed my A levels.'

He grins from ear to ear. 'Congratulations, Gorbhan!'

LEAVING

The words gush out. 'And I spoke to my mother.'
Martin's eyes light up. He lays a hand on my arm. 'And…?'

'I told her everything. About my journey with the smugglers. How I speak good English now. How I passed my exams and want to be a teacher. How I'll soon be a British citizen. How, as soon as I get a job and can afford it, I'll fly out to Afghanistan to visit her and my brothers and bring them lots of presents. And money.' I pause to catch my breath, looking hard at Martin. 'The money should stop my younger brothers from joining the Taliban.'

I drop my head in my hands and burst into tears.

'Gorbhan? Are you all right?' Martin squeezes my elbow. 'Has she forgiven you? What did she say?'

I sniff and look up. My voice quakes. 'She said she was proud of me.'

Rifle
Joshua Bruyning
United States

Shortlisted for the 2019 International Writing Competition

Between the wooden coffee table and the dusty television stand, John pressed his palms into the oak floor as if to move it. He counted to himself every time his arms straightened, 'One, two, three…' Easy. The rhythm remained, gradually slowing to a contemplative chant, his voice retreating into his head with every push.

At sixty-one years of age, the muscles required more attention; and with sixty-one years, forty of which were spent laboring in the United States Army, John's mind adjusted to deal with the unthinkable, that which was too difficult – some would say impossible – for a man of his age to endure. 'Eighty-three, eighty-four, eighty-five…' The blood gathered into his chest, his arms swelled, and in his mind, he sang a song.

He never looked down, always straight ahead where he could see his old rifle mounted on the wall. In truth, it was not his rifle. It had once belonged to a Vietcong during the senseless Vietnam war. After two days of sitting in the wet trenches, huddled with the living and the dead, his

LEAVING

platoon had gained enough confidence to proceed to the enemy's camp. When they arrived at the village, they were able to see the fruit of their labor with their naked eyes. John must have stood there for a half an hour taking it all in when something had possessed him to pluck the rifle out of the bloody hand of a fallen Vietcong. He retrieved it as if he owned it.

And why shouldn't John have taken it? The weapon which he held in his hands with such reverence was responsible for the death of the men he was supposed to protect. John knew that rifle well, not personally, but conceptually; and John knew the bullets that had exited it and had entered (and in some cases exited) the bodies of his brothers. He had been plucking bullet fragments out of living flesh for the past two days and nights. Why should he not claim this rifle?

There was a single splotch of blood on the front of the dead man's shirt, middle of the chest, dead center. John wondered if it was his bullet that had made the wound. Could have been Jefferson's, or Jameson's, or Frederickson's. It was just as right for John to believe that it was his own bullet, no need to verify the claim by reaching a finger into the wound – just as right as it was for him to think that the weapon which he now held close to himself was responsible for the death of all his comrades, including Jefferson, Jameson, and Frederickson.

Where blood had not ruined the shirt, John tore off a piece with which to cover the rifle. After wrapping it tightly, he noticed the smallest drop of blood. He contemplated: was it worth it to unwrap and then wrap this damn thing all over again because of a tiny spot of blood? What difference would a drop make? He carried it back to camp, clutching it firmly, discarding his own rifle in the tall grass, and no one asked him about it. The army had rules about bringing such things back to the States. The helicopter landed, gathered all the men, and flew back to base camp. Even upon entering his own country, John remained silent as he clung to his mummified weapon of war. When asked what it was that he carried, knowing full well that he was breaking some law, he spoke only in nods and shakes of the head. They let him through customs. The war must have been written on his face – 'please don't fuck with me' – silent words undoubtedly read from a distance.

'One hundred and five, one hundred and six, one hundred and...'

There comes a time when the breaking of concentration is very much like the breaking of solid bone. A sound he thought he'd never have to hear again startled him out of his morning routine. He moved to the city to avoid the senseless noises of country living; still, there are a great many other sounds which are almost as devastating, such as jackhammers in the morning when there's construction on the main road. But a jackhammer was a jackhammer, and with a few breaths and a couple hundred pushups, his brain and body would also come to realize this fact. But the sound which had broken his rhythm was the unmistakable firing of a .22.

POP! POP POP, POP POP!

When the shots had all been fired, he was still on one hundred. No one likes to be awakened from a deep sleep, no one wants their earphones yanked out of their ears during their favorite song, but at least most people have the luxury of entering a world of normalcy after the initial shock is over. For John, there was no natural world to come back to. He froze, feeling his hands, callused and thick, sink into the hardwood floor. The silence after the shots was torturous because, in the quiet, he could still hear gunshots in his head. Five shots. Five shots. For fucksake in the goddamn city, where he thought he would find relief from the constant firing of hunting rifles. At least in the countryside, it was known that the shots ended in the death of a deer or pheasant, and he could deal

LEAVING

with those deaths by way of mental and physical exercise. But in the city, a gunshot means murder. Those bullets had names written on them.

Genich was not a corrupt city. Some might hardly call it a city at all. John had only to contend with the distrust of his neighbors, the beautiful people of 1511 Rose Avenue who had imagined many charges against him. He often kept to himself, responding to all inquiries with a nod and a shake of the head. The neighbors thought that he was rude, and when the rumors were in full swing, it was unanimous that he was a racist and a bigot.

There were twelve apartments in the building. John occupied the largest on the top floor, number twelve. It was the only apartment with gas heating, and on the south wall, there was a tall, broad window with a full view of the neighborhood.

He got up, dusted off his hands and knees, and walked to the window. Drawing the blind, he looked out to see if someone was lying in the street. He could see only a sliver of the main road. The shots could have come from anywhere. Apartment buildings had distorted sound as well as sight, and John was left with his imagination.

◆

Mrs. Mavis, a round black woman, wore a shiny weave that had been given a bowl cut. Everyone knew that Mrs. Mavis wanted John's apartment since last May. She even put in a request with the front office for them to keep it for her when, if ever, the former residents vacated. When they did leave, Mrs. Mavis was surprised to witness a tall, old, grumpy-looking white man hauling a small sofa, a tube television, something wrapped in a blanket (or something like that), a few boxes, and many books into what was supposed to be her new apartment. She phoned the front office – using all of the expletives in her vocabulary – to tell them how they wronged her.

For the entire afternoon, John sat in his leather armchair and tried to fill his mind with the sort of things that usually got the song in his head to die down. After the war was over (and while he still lived in the country), to drown out the song, John would read Austen, his favorite novelist. Faulkner was a close second. He liked these books because the lives of their inhabitants were so full, and yet so empty. Sure, they talked about the war, but it was the kind of war that could be fought by gentlemen at sea in the Caribbean Islands, probably complete with suntan lotion and beach chairs. Austen never wrote of the kind of war where men dug trenches to shelter themselves from an endless barrage of gunfire, where bullets fell like rain and, in the trenches, turned into rivers of blood. In Austen's books, the war was pleasant. Everything was nice. His city had been excellent, until… *POP! POP POP, POP POP!*

He began to meditate, actively trying to silence the song in his head until he heard voices, like marbles in a bag, coming from the hall just beyond his door. He stood still, wearing only his white boxers with blue stripes, careful not to make sounds on the floor. He tip-toed to the door for a better listen.

He could make out one or two of the voices. One for sure was Mrs. Mavis. He confirmed this by peeping through the little glass hole in the door. He had never used the damned thing and was slightly put off by the way the people looked: elongated and broad; distant and close. He looked only for a moment and then counted them. There was Mrs. Mavis, Brandon, and two other black boys he did not recognize. Four in total.

Whoever had lived in the apartment before must have broken the lock somehow, causing it to rattle when the door is pushed ever so gently.

LEAVING

John pressed an ear to the door, being careful not to press too hard.

'There were cops and firetrucks and everything,' said Brandon. 'They even had police on horses out there.'

'That's too much,' said Mrs. Mavis, hands on her waist, shaking her head. 'Where did the horses come from? Do they have a stable around the corner that I didn't know about?'

'I don't know,' sighed Brandon. 'They must have been somewhere.'

One of the other boys laughed. 'I seen them galloping down the road, dodging cars, jumping over stuff like you see rich people do on TV.'

'It's not funny,' said the other boy.

Brandon and Mrs. Mavis agreed. Silently, John agreed with them.

'What a stupid way to die,' Mrs. Mavis said. 'He probably deserved it. It's a war out there, them people coming from Chicago. They fucked up their own neighborhood, and they gonna fuck up this one too.'

'It's not like that,' Brandon said.

'How you figure?'

'Because I knew this dude. He lives on the block with the laundromat. He had a job, he was about to get married –'

'To a white girl,' one of the boys interrupted.

Brandon continued, rolling his eyes. 'And they just had a kid. This dude was not a gangster.'

Finding his way into the conversation, one of the boys plucked his arm from his hoodie pockets, spread his feet wide apart, and said, 'What had happened was, the dude who got kilt was trying to protect his little brother. The brother had beef with this other dude. They were gambling, and he lost. And this other dude, who had won, told him to pay up. He didn't have the cash, so the dude just left. They saw him at the laundromat this morning and roughed him up. Told him to get the money. The dude went home fuuuuuucked up and told his brother, the dead dude, what had happened. Dude hopped in his car and drove to the spot where they beat up his brother. The dudes were still there. Dude got out of his car, and they got into an altercation. When the dude took out a gun, dude ran back into his car. You see how the fence by the cemetery is all fucked up? Well, that's where they killed him. They jumped into a car and chased him from the laundromat to the cemetery. He was so fucking scared that he drove his car into the fence. One dude jumped out of the car, walked up to him, and *POP! POP POP, POP POP!* Blew his head off.' The boy said this... laughing.

John was so engrossed in the story and so disgusted by the boy's laughter that he had forgotten he was eavesdropping, and, pressing his ear too forcefully onto the door, he accidentally rattled it. The laughter stopped. They all stared at the door as if they could see beyond it.

After about thirty seconds, Mrs. Mavis was the first to speak. 'Mr. John, if that is you, you might as well come out here.'

John froze. He peeped through the little hole in the door and waited, half expecting them to go away. But he also wanted to know if they caught the 'dude' who shot the other 'dude.' He did not understand why he wanted to know, he just wanted to know. The song in his head continued, and like any song, if he were to hear the end of it, maybe it would stop. Perhaps if he found out who killed the 'dude,' it would stop.

When it was clear that they knew he was there and that they were not going to leave, John slid the chain, turned the deadbolt, and turned the knob. He had forgotten that he was still wearing his white boxers with blue stripes. They did not seem to care. He stared at them, and they stared at him.

Mrs. Mavis spoke again. 'How much of that did you hear?'

John stared at her. It was not that he was trying to be rude, his mind just went blank.

LEAVING

She asked again, remembering from previous brief encounters that 'yes' or 'no' questions worked better. 'Did you hear all of that?'

He nodded.

'Did any of that make you upset?'

He nodded.

'The part about the boy being shot?'

He nodded.

'Must be happy that there's one less nigger to worry about,' said one of the boys.

He shook his head.

Mrs. Mavis was not entirely convinced John wasn't a racist, but at least she now knew that he didn't want black folks dead. 'You gonna just stand there?'

He nodded.

'Well then, I guess we'll go.'

He finally spoke – because there was an obvious question in his head and the response would settle his mind, ending the god-awful song ringing in his head. 'Do you know who killed him?'

Mrs. Mavis, annoyed, but startled by the coolness of John's voice, turned back towards him and said, 'I don't know who did it.'

'Nobody knows who did it,' said Brandon.

'I mean,' said the boy who had been telling the story, 'we know who did it, but not who did it. We know it was a dude, but not which dude.'

John nodded and slowly retreated into his apartment. He slid the chain and turned the deadbolt.

◆

Four days later, the song was still playing in his head. *POP! POP POP, POP POP!* Who done it? *LA LA LA LA, DI DA.* He needed potato chips and thought of driving to the store, but decided that a walk would do him some good. The fall colors were out, and with a good windbreaker, he felt the wind without feeling the cold. Whenever he walked, he walked on the sidewalk east of the lake. But whenever he drove, he drove by the front west bank of a small lake that no one bothered to name.

Just as the store was in view on the street opposite the lake, he saw about twenty helium-filled balloons tied to a lamp post. The balloons struck his eyes first because they were reflective red, reflective green, reflective silver, and the midday sun shone brightly upon them. He walked a little farther and saw that in addition to the balloons, there were teddy bears, candles, toys, letters pinned to the lamp post, and words written on everything. He crossed the street to get a closer look.

He stood and read and reread everything. He wished that the army would have done something like this for his friends. He did do something like that – he believed – by mounting the Vietcong's rifle on his wall. Justice. There would be no justice this time. He had been reading the papers and knew that the cops were not going to find the killer. They never do. The police will find someone who fits the description: black, dreads, tattoos. They find twenty 'dudes' and simply choose one to blame. All the way to the store, he thought about the words at the vigil. The song still blared in his head; there was an accompaniment.

Potato chips in hand, he walked out of the store. He crossed the street, deliberating that on the way home he didn't want to walk too close to the vigil. He felt that it would, in some way, be disrespectful. He saw the bright balloons in the distance, and as he walked a little closer, straining his eyes, he saw a dark figure by the lamp post. It was moving erratically, yet as if dancing to the tune in his head.

As his walking closed the distance between himself and the figure, he saw that it was wailing. It wailed and shouted at the lamp post. It

LEAVING

flung its arms and threw punches in the air, but never touched any of the objects: it was holy ground. The figure cussed and flared and cussed. It hated what was before it, but also worshipped it. John strained his better eye, placing a hand over the other one, and saw (as if through the little hole in his door) that the dark figure had a face, a black face framed with a black hood. John stood and watched. The words were indistinguishable through the wailing; and yet, John understood. The orchestra was in full swing. The song was a symphony in his head.

◆

In his apartment, hanging on the wall, wrapped in deadman's clothing, was the rifle. It was the conductor and the baton that would silence the song. He opened the blinds as far as they could be drawn. Pressing his head against the glass, he looked at the window as far left as he could. Barely visible, distinguishable only by shimmering, the balloons danced. He once again closed the blinds. He turned all the lights off, unplugged the fridge, and turned off the gas heater. He walked over to the wall where the rifle was hung and plucked it from its place. Carefully, he unwrapped it for the very first time. He mused to himself, this, this will be my salvation.

He got into his car, settled the rifle upright in the passenger's seat, and drove to the police station.

When he walked into the station, he could see on the cops' faces that they didn't know whether to arrest him or let him walk right up the counter with that thing in his hand; but I guarantee you that – if he were not white – he would've been laid out, sprawled out, shot up, and shut up for good. He continued all the way to where two earnest rookies were sitting, and with reverence placed the rifle longways on the counter.

The song would never have been complete without knowing who

killed the young man; and knowing that the answer would never be satisfied – the song, too, would never be satisfied – and knowing that even if the authorities were to catch the killer (they would not); and needing desperately for the song to be over, for justice, for the wailing brother to find peace, carrying in his heart the certainty with which he had first asked the question – John confessed: 'I killed him.'

Olivia's Plan

Richard Burtle
United Kingdom

Judge's Choice

'Excuse me. It's Olivia, isn't it? Olivia Harkness?' There was a shrill, piping quality to Desmond's voice. He shifted a hot plastic coffee cup from hand to hand as he spoke, finally settling it precariously between thumb and middle finger.

She turned the screen of her phone downwards and looked up from her easy chair. 'Yes, that's me. Now then, where have we met before?'

'School, Saint Pete's,' – she showed not the slightest flicker of recognition – 'we left in 2001. We were both in W, right through to GCSE.'

She frowned and pursed her lips, so as to give the impression that she was at least trying to remember him. Sounding nervously apologetic, he pressed on. 'We didn't have much reason to meet after that, we did different A Levels.'

'That's probably why I can't place you.' Again she frowned. 'Well then. Who are you?'

'I work in IT now – at Global Reach. I've been there five years.'

'I see.' She looked up at him quizzically. 'So could you possibly tell me your name?'

'Desmond... Desmond Casey. I usually sat at the back on the left. You were front right. You had shorter hair then and I still had all of mine. Do you mind if I sit down here?' He hovered over the vacant seat next to hers.

'No, of course not, Desmond. Sorry I can't remember you. In W it was always girls at the front, boys at the back, wasn't it?'

Desmond sat down, shakily placing his cup on the low table in front of the chairs and slopping some coffee on to one of its stock of tatty magazines. 'Have you been waiting long?' As he spoke, he barely turned his head towards her.

'About twenty minutes,' she replied glumly. 'The clinic's running late today, as usual.' She turned over her phone and resumed the game she was playing.

Desmond looked around the waiting area and counted eight other patients. How many times had he been here before? And he still couldn't tell how the queue worked; the lack of information irritated him. He could have asked one of the nurses but they were always busy – he didn't want to trouble them. Was it old-timers first or was there priority for the more serious cases? He ruled out alphabetical order. Perhaps they somehow randomised it? Hopefully it wasn't down to the whim of the consultants.

For a couple of minutes Olivia continued to play her game. Desmond picked up a gardening magazine, thumbed his way through it in search of any article that might be even slightly interesting: failing to find one, he shut his eyes and tried to compose himself.

'So, Desmond: how far have you got with this palaver?' She touched him gently on the elbow as she spoke and he opened his eyes.

LEAVING

'Nine months.' He pulled himself up in his chair and stared hard at the reception desk. 'I'm here once a month now – the Tuesday clinic. No more chemo though, thank God.'

'I'm usually Thursdays. That's probably why we haven't met. I've just completed eighteen months. I've had two rounds. Hopefully that's it.' She made it sound like a military tour of duty.

'Eighteen months, eh? That's pretty good going. I mean…' He realised too late what he was saying, his voice inevitably tailing off.

'Don't worry,' she said brightly, 'I know all the odds.'

He remembered her far better than she him: in the top two in every subject, always first in maths, frequently given individually-tailored extra homework, in a notation incomprehensible to the rest of them. Of course she would know the odds.

'For me it's one-in-five up to a year,' she said, 'shortening to one-in-three at two years, and fifty-fifty after five. By ten,' – she shrugged her shoulders – 'zilch. Just a few lucky sods left really.' She could have been talking about the National Lottery.

'But, at our age, the prognosis can often be a bit better – if you're otherwise healthy, that is.'

'No bucket list then?'

'Just a tattoo – I've always wanted one. I'm having it done next week.'

A smiling nurse pushed through the swing doors at the end of the room; the waiting patients all looked up hopefully.

'Olivia?' There was no need for a surname. She rose and walked rather stiffly toward the doors. The nurse held them open, letting her patient go through first, just as the tall figure of a man came the other way. Olivia paused in the doorway and stretched out her arms to him; they embraced. Desmond watched as the man's grave expression broke into a broad smile, which he recognized as belonging to the other star of W. It was Alex Bancroft.

Desmond didn't expect Alex to recognize him or even acknowledge his presence, even though it was quite normal for fellow patients to at least smile at each other as they came and went, particularly the familiar faces of those who had waited together before. But that would never have been Alex's way. He sat down on a straight-backed chair and waited for a few minutes before standing up suddenly and striding purposefully along the corridor toward the hospital's main entrance.

As he sat and waited, thoughts of school days flooded into Desmond's head and especially memories of his personal hero, Alex. He remembered him being led into a maths lesson by the deputy head, introduced to the class and given some books before getting straight down to work. At break-time a few of them had shown him round. Up to that point privately-educated, he'd arrived at their comprehensive near the end of year nine. 'Dad's gone bankrupt, can't afford the fees. It happens.' He'd given a shrug, screwing up his face. 'They say this is a decent school. We'll see.'

After the summer holidays, he'd quickly settled into 10W and established himself as equal top of the class, alongside Olivia. Not that they'd ever been obvious rivals: they always knew they were both headed for A* across the board; it was left to their classmates to speculate as to which of them was the more brilliant. Desmond had made a spreadsheet for himself, giving every member of W marks out of 10 for each of ten categories: intelligence, hard-work, imagination, wit, good-looks, sex appeal, sporting prowess, creativity, social skills and cooperation (this last one chosen because it had frequently appeared on his own school reports, thus giving himself at least one high score on the matrix).

Returning from the hospital to the parental home, where he was

LEAVING

still living, Desmond took a print-out from a battered manila file. Olivia had scored 93, Alex 91 – the difference largely because he'd given the former a 10 for sex appeal while the latter had only merited an 8: he should have asked a girl to rate him but, in those days, Desmond hardly ever dared talk to girls; he now realised for certain that Alex should have been given a 10; he was tall, he was dark, he was handsome and – as Desmond had observed in the showers after PE – also very well-endowed. He had to admit that there'd been more than a touch of jealousy involved in docking him those two marks.

◆

A month later their appointments once again coincided. Desmond arrived just in time to get a glimpse of Alex's back as he went through from the waiting-room; Olivia was sitting in exactly the same seat as before.

'Do you mind if I wait with you again?'

'Of course not, Desmond – it is *Desmond*, not *Des* or *Desi*, isn't it? Why didn't you introduce yourself to Alex last time? He remembers you from the cricket team, says you were a very dependable middle-order batsman.'

'Oh… really? I did enjoy playing but I wasn't much good.' He'd played four times in all for the first eleven, averaging eight from three innings, top score twelve. Alex had been captain (obviously), opening bat and leg-spin bowler (frequently match-winning).

He waited for her to reconfirm Alex's opinion of his prowess but she said nothing. She looked straight ahead, apparently deep in thought, no mobile phone on her lap today. The other half dozen patients were silent too. After a few minutes, Desmond felt impelled to break the silence.

'Are you and Alex together… not just here today I mean… that is, are you an item?'

She turned her head upward and to one side, focussing on the strip light above the corner of the room. 'Are, we, an, item? Do you know, I suppose we are.' And Desmond was suddenly back twenty years, to Room 15A, English, Mrs Potter, and those long rambling conversations between teacher and pupil in which Olivia had often appeared to be in charge of the argument, while the rest of the class sat and listened – some more attentively than others. *Is Shakespeare anti-Semitic? Do you know, I suppose he is.*

'Not married then?'

'No, not married,' she replied sharply. 'Living in sin. What about you? Any significant other?'

'Not at the moment. I was married for a while but it didn't work out.' He tried to sound nonchalant, narrowly failing.

They discussed their lives in the seventeen years since leaving school (without, on this occasion, ever touching upon the nasty twist of fate that had conspired to visit the same affliction upon three former members of 11W).

As was only to be expected, both Alex and Olivia had pursued very successful careers – she as barrister, he as pharmaceutical chemist.

'You were always argumentative – gave a lot of the teachers a hard time.' He smiled nervously, half afraid she would take this as a criticism. He himself had always been a bit of a goody-goody – though of course she wouldn't remember that: she'd hardly remember him at all.

She smiled back. 'I always tried to stay one step ahead of them. I realised early on that the trick was to do your homework *before* the lesson, not after. That works in the law too: you have to master your brief or you're up shit creek. But if you know more than your opponent, it can be very satisfying. Sometimes, as a bonus, you may even know more than the judge – not that it happens very often.' There was delight in her eyes as she spoke: she clearly loved her job.

'So you and Alex went different ways – academically I mean.'

'It was a conscious decision. We didn't want to be rivals. So I went for Law and found I enjoyed it: he started in Medicine. Classic cliché subjects for high achievers.'

'I thought you said he was a chemist?'

'He switched after a year: he loved the science but hated the whole illness thing – not the sight of blood, more the prospect of having to deal with people's physical frailty. He hates imperfection.'

'He was a charming guy though – must still be, I'm sure. He would have had a good bedside manner.'

'You think so? Well, maybe. You know, an awful lot of innocent creatures died so that he could get his PhD.' She reached into her handbag, pulled out her phone and switched on the screen to find the time. 'I hope he won't be too long today.'

Again they fell silent. Like Alex – now in the day ward and, cannula in place, just about to receive the last one of his regular therapeutic doses – they were soon absorbed in their own thoughts.

◆

'Until now I've not wanted kids, I've left that to my sister Sally. It's not that I don't like children, babies included. Sally's are great – all three of them lovely in their own distinctive ways. No, up until recently, it's been more a question of losing control of your life as soon as you become pregnant, and thereafter for the next twenty years. Of course there's the whole career thing too – though that probably wouldn't be a major problem, now that I might not be around for much longer. But being in control is so important to me – always has been, sex included. I allow Alex to make love to me and he gives me pleasure, but it's always on my terms.

We do love each other, I think. Not enough to want children together though. The idea of a child, my child, being half Alex and only half me – well that's giving ground to your rival, isn't it? I know we've always said that we don't compete with each other but, as time's gone on, I've come to realise that we'll never really be a team. That's rather sad, I suppose. It might sound crazy, but I believe that having a child with Alex would be allowing myself to be infiltrated by the enemy.'

♦

'I don't think I'm cut out to be a dad. My own father was usually a bit distant – often away somewhere, supposedly on business. Mother was always there for me, despite the wrench of being sent off as a boarder, though I soon adapted, like most of the others, and enjoyed it really – until dad's outfit went belly-up and I had to come home and go to St Peter's. Dad came through the whole bankruptcy crisis pretty well, all things considered: more modest house, smaller car, salaried job – he worked hard and survived. But it was the loss of status that killed him. Not literally of course – that came ten years later. To be honest, I think I was part of the whole status thing too: not so much a son, more of a 'my son the doctor'. When I was awarded my PhD, it was: *Well you took a different route but you've got there in the end.* If I had a son or daughter, I've a horrible feeling I might think like that too.'

♦

'It's not ideal, living at mum and dad's house, but at least I get my washing done and the meals are good; I can come and go as I please. I pay a nominal rent and it's a lot cheaper than renting from a proper landlord. The guys at work take the piss but, financially, they're not as well off as me.

LEAVING

'Who am I kidding? I hate it really. But beggars can't be choosers.

'It was all Daisy's fault. *Daisy & Desmond, Desmond & Daisy*: the ampersand gives it away. We were an item – from age seventeen onwards. All that 'love's young dream' crap – in the sixth form and right through university, even though we were two hundred miles apart. I guess we were in love but I'm not sure I really loved her.

'It took literally years to get her to sleep with me. She was a Baptist, just like mum (that's the main reason they always got on so well). I don't think Daisy actually said that we had to be engaged before we could get into bed with each other but she made it clear in general terms: being a theology student, it was easy for her to bring it up in a theoretical sort of way; so we avoided any awkward misunderstanding – and I was always the perfect gentleman. (Jesus! The number of times she patronised me for being so bloody patient – not that I thought of it like that at the time: I pictured myself as halfway to being some sort of virtuous, chaste monk – rather noble, really. Who am I trying to fool? – as usual, I just wasn't assertive enough).

'I visited her every other weekend in her hall of residence. It took me six months to finally get from the mattress on the floor and into her bed. So that was it: we slept together, we got engaged (rather than the other way round. Did that mean that she tricked me into it? It didn't feel like that at the time).

'We moved back home after graduation, bought a little flat and, a couple of months later, got married.

'Then it went pear-shaped – it's easy to see why. It was a classic student romance: neither of us had ever had another sexual partner or seen much of the world; we were just too bound up with each other, I guess. She became a teacher and, to cut a long story short, had an affair with a colleague, John; she got pregnant, decided to keep the baby and we divorced after three years. She kept the flat – it was all very grown-up and civilised, so that I didn't suffer financially – and I moved back into the family home. End of story. We meet occasionally, just by chance, and it's all very friendly: *John & Daisy, Daisy & John* – and daughter Dottie. She's ten years old now, a lovely little girl, very out-going and frighteningly clever. I often wonder whether, if I'd been the father, Daisy would have given birth to an equally delightful child. I suspect not – which would be a depressing thought if I were to dwell on it. Of course, these days I have other things – well, *the* thing – to worry about.'

◆

'Alex is off to Antwerp for a conference. Why don't you come round for dinner? I've a proposition to put to you.'

The invitation came out of the blue. Desmond had only been to their house a couple of times in the six months since first meeting them again at the hospital – and then only for a quick cup of tea and a chat. He wondered whether someone else had been invited and cried off at the last minute, so that he'd been drafted in as a late replacement. And what was Olivia's mysterious proposition?

He half expected there to be other guests but, as he entered the house, he saw that there were just two places set at the dining-table; Olivia's first words were to inform him that she'd just received a text from Alex to say that his plane had landed safely.

She gave him a glass of champagne. 'We might as well enjoy a decent drink, while we still can.' He nodded but said nothing except a polite thank you: he was generally fatalistic about his medical condition but still felt awkward when referring to it, even when talking to a fellow patient.

As expected, the meal was delicious. He was used to his mother's plain home cooking – or his own, which was equally straightforward. Olivia gave him fillet of beef: his mum would have done a roast with Yorkshire puddings.

'This sauce tastes really good. Did you make it yourself?' It was a silly question, immediately regretted.

'It's a Hollandaise with horseradish and tarragon. If you like, I can give you the recipe.' She reached across the table and, without asking if he wanted it, poured him a second glass of red wine – Bordeaux, he'd noticed, guessing that it was probably about five times the price of his usual supermarket plonk.

'Shall we wait a few moments before we have our pudding?' She pushed back her chair, turned it forty-five degrees to the table and stretched out her long legs. 'Can we talk about this proposition I've got for you?' (Later, when he thought about it, he realised how matter-of-fact she had sounded as she'd laid out her proposal and they'd discussed it. But that was Olivia, just as she'd been at school – often argumentative but ever the analytical, systematic student).

'Right, Desmond. First things first: how long do they say you've got?'

'Six to eighteen months.' Had it not been for the wine, he might not have answered her question, might have pleaded ignorance. But the alcohol was by now doing its job.

She smiled and said sympathetically, 'They don't like referring to it as one year, do they. For me the latest estimate is twelve to twenty-four months. Does it sound more hopeful? – putting it in months rather than years I mean. I'm not sure.' She turned her head to one side and added, rather wistfully, 'Of course, near the end, when you're down to less than six, they can be almost certain.'

She took a sip of wine. 'So, this proposition of mine: it's about children. Have you ever wanted children, Desmond?'

Where the hell is this leading? He too took another sip.

'The way I see it,' she continued, 'there are two reasons to want kids. Number one is that you like the idea of having them around. My sister has three: they're seven, five and four. Watching them grow and change – well, they surprise and delight you every time you see them. Being an aunt is just great. Do you have any nephews or nieces, Desmond?'

'Afraid not: I'm an only child.'

'Oh really? Just like Alex.'

'My parents used to spoil me rotten – mum especially.'

'Yes: ideally there should be more than one.' She puffed out her cheeks, before letting the air escape through puckered lips. 'Anyway, reason number two is that one might want to leave behind something of oneself. Actually I don't think most couples think of it like that but it's certainly part of the equation – not that it's always a deliberate decision: these things aren't ever completely objective.'

At this point Desmond wondered whether she was in the process of asking his advice: was she perhaps using him as a sort of therapist, to help her come to terms with her childlessness? But, if so, why him? Why not Alex? He bowed his head over his wine-glass and rotated the stem nervously between thumb and first finger.

For the first time in the conversation, Olivia looked not at Desmond but towards the French windows, through which late evening sunshine was streaming. 'I want a child, Desmond. Before I go, I want a child. And I want you to be the father.'

◆

And so it came to pass.

The act of conception was remarkably easy. Desmond had drunk just enough wine; Olivia made the whole process run smoothly; it was over in fifteen minutes.

Afterwards, as he lay next to her on the dining-room floor, he felt a strange mixture of post-coital *tristesse* and something more profound: a sense of lost integrity. What on earth had they just done? Why, in God's name, had she chosen him? She'd used him, hadn't she? In any case, there was every chance that she would not fall pregnant. And then there were the medical complications…

Of course she'd thought it all through. She'd discussed it with her sister months ago: 'You'd look after him (I think of it as a *him* – I don't know why) and you'd bring him up as another son, wouldn't you? That's after I've scooted off to heaven – unless I don't. But that's unlikely. You'll love it, Sal – admit it.'

Sally presumed that Alex would be the father; Olivia said nothing to suggest otherwise but neither did she confirm her sister's inference – and, when the announcement came that she was indeed expecting a happy event, the rest of the family followed suit.

'The medics tell me I should be able to carry it to full term, other things being equal.' They all knew what she meant but none of them was going to question the wisdom of continuing with her plan (though, at first, apart from Sally and Desmond, none of them was aware that there'd been a plan, Alex included).

Desmond and Olivia met from time to time during the nine months but never discussed the matter except in general terms: he offered the usual solicitous enquiries as to her health and the health of the unborn child. It was all very dispassionate, even clinical. And – since they always met in public spaces such as the hospital – even if he'd wanted to say more, that was virtually impossible.

Naturally he continued to wonder what she was playing at – although 'playing' was the wrong word: Olivia never *played* at anything. But it was not in his nature to rock the boat; as the months passed, he just accepted that she'd been in charge of her own destiny, that she was perfectly entitled to go ahead with the pregnancy, and that he had no right to interfere. The whole affair became a sort of unreal romance, in which he possibly had a stake but which he found himself observing from an ever-increasing distance. From the outset, he'd wondered whether Alex was infertile or indeed impotent: it didn't seem likely. So it could be Alex's baby, couldn't it? Perhaps his and Olivia's mildly drunken liaison had been a mistake, which she'd immediately rectified by making proper, passionate love to a *real* man, the *real* love of her life. Or maybe the whole bloody thing had been a twisted dream.

And then, seven months in, he had something much more pressing to occupy his thoughts.

◆

She never told Alex that the baby would not be his and – as she had calculated from the start – circumstances weren't going to let him find out.

'You're not going to go through with it, are you?' It was more of a statement than a question: in his mind it was, 'You're going to get rid of it, of course. It's not what you and I have ever wanted – before, when we discussed it, you were as adamant as I was.'

'No, I am going to have it,' she said firmly and went on to explain the agreement she'd made with her sister.

'You're mad,' he said. 'Have you talked about it with Dr Bedi? And what about the financial side? Have you and Sally given that any thought?'

It took him a week to come round; he apologised for questioning her mental state and began to see it from her point of view: in the best-case scenario she would probably have months, or even years, to spend with her child. The likelihood was that he himself might not have such a chance – but then he'd never thought of himself as a potential parent. However, the more he considered the prospect of fatherhood, the more he began to see it as a definite boost to his self-esteem: he'd have the satisfaction of having produced a son (like Olivia, he pictured the child as a boy), without needing to commit to the practical and emotional responsibility of bringing him up.

◆

They were about to take Alex to see his new-born son when his condition worsened and it was deemed too risky. He insisted but they demurred; by that time the pain relief was reaching its maximum and he was drifting in and out of consciousness. It was decided that Olivia was sufficiently recovered to allow her to bring the baby across to the hospice: in the event, they were too late.

She sat outside Alex's room, rocking the baby to sleep. Should she say something to him about his supposed father, lying on the other side of the lime green door? His eyes closed, re-opened and closed again; she leant forward and whispered, 'I'm going to name you Josh, not Simon.'

Yes, I know Alex and I have always called you Simon, from the day we found out that you were on the way, but – I don't know why – Josh seems to be the sort of name Desmond would have liked. Desmond, your real father – you were with me at his funeral, tucked away inside me, safe from the wind and rain. It was a rotten day, just a rotten day.

And now your pretend father will also need to be packed off – next week probably. You won't be there: Mrs Harris next door has already said she'll look after you – such a kind woman. You'll be fine with her: she's a motherly type, like your Aunt Sally – and unlike me.

They say that a mother's love trumps every other consideration but the problem is that you can't tell whether that's going to be the case until you're some way into the nine months. (Has it really been nine months? Did it seem that long to you?) So it has to be a leap in the dark (or, in your case, a summer's evening jump on the dining-room floor – Gosh! I don't think I should be telling you that. Not appropriate, not at all appropriate).

Being the sort of marvellous person I am (I can say that because, dear Josh, you're not going to be able to think otherwise), I've always wanted to leave behind something of myself but I've worried that I might not be cut out for motherhood. So, when I was told that I only had X months left, getting pregnant gave me just the opportunity I needed to… to… to what? Fulfil my destiny, I guess, while at the same time avoiding the possibility of being a rubbish parent. (I'm sorry, my darling, but sooner or later you'll find out that I've left you. But I'm not abandoning you: I'm leaving you in the care of a wonderful aunt and adoptive mother).

Why Desmond and why not Alex?

Behind the crematorium there's a rose garden, where the family can meet the congregation after the service to receive their condolences; it's beautifully tended, not a weed in sight, everything just perfect. Beyond the rear hedge there are some allotments and they're far from perfect but they display a sort of cheerful practicality.

I prefer the allotments.

♦

Ten months later, Olivia scooted off to heaven.

Josh would grow into a happy, uncomplicated, easy-going young man. Sally would love him dearly, never pausing to wonder whether the joy he brought to their family was down to his parents' genes or to the home into which he'd been welcomed as if he were their real son and brother.

Like Paradise
OLIVER BUSSELL
United Kingdom

SHORTLISTED FOR THE 2019
INTERNATIONAL WRITING COMPETITION

THIS IS NOT HOW SHE IMAGINED IT AT ALL.
Lying on the rocks, hair flicks tediously into squinting eyes. She loops it behind her ear where it wriggles free, heading seaward, flicking back, slapping at her lids like a persistent fly, sticking to drying lips.

For God's sake. She pulls her hairband out and tries to wrestle it into a knot, but it snaps and pirouettes away, landing between two rocks. She stands to retrieve it, freeing her sarong which flutters towards the water where it settles, momentarily dry before elephants are swallowed and patterns darken and sink. She abandons the hair tie, leaping forward to retrieve the drowning fabric, dense with seawater, spattering rocks in darkness. She has cut her ankle, sliced it on something in the commotion. Blood disperses above rock-pool commuters.

Inhaling deeply she snatches up her book and heads towards dry land.

It is three months since Laura quit her job, said the words to her boss that made him turn pink and then cry, beg for her return. Only a fantasy. He had shrugged, shaken her hand, and she was showing her replacement how to change the beer kegs before the week was out. No big farewell, no drama at all, although she had refused to return her uniform.

Three months since she had stopped paying rent on her flat – that tiny basement box with weeping walls and sighing windows. The scuttling of rats and the smell of their dead, squeaks of their living. One month's rent was all she needed to break the contract. A tanned man in a white polo had bought the flat from her landlord in cash on the second day of viewings. An Exciting Development Opportunity.

Three months since she had told her friends: jealous of course, so happy for her, we'll miss you hun; gone now. Words of encouragement, Facebook likes, Instagram hearts, you look so good, girl. Kisses and hugs. Then fewer. Fewer hearts, fewer likes, fewer kisses. Did you even see that last photo? Yes, it looked great. But not good enough to 'like'?

Jealousy then.

It is three months since her father died and left her his fortune.

A new beginning: just what she had always wanted, what they had all dreamed of. Is that not what they'd been striving for all of these years? To leave? Why they filled out their lottery tickets each week, went to bars that rich men like, called elderly relatives with a clockwork regularity that signposted chilling intent. Nothing. That is what they all desire. Enough of something to let them do nothing. Enough of nothing to do something – take up painting, write that novel, work on that tan, become a star, read the classics, watch the classics, learn a language, teach, do something great, truly great. And that is what she has at last: nothing.

Greatness awaits.

But for now: nothing.

LEAVING

She shakes the soaking rag and wrings it between her hands. It will dry quickly in the sun. Limping between rocks, feet tender on jagged lava forms, she straddles the tired rope that demarcates a footpath. Where to now? Nowhere to go, no one to see, no one to please. How freeing, she thinks and feels a brief flutter somewhere in the middle of her chest. She tilts her head to the sky and lets the bubbles rise, filling her cheeks so they part, freeing teeth from ear to ear and as if on cue, the sun peeks out from behind a cloud to drench her in warmth. She is so alive! Why did she not do this before? Why did they all not do this before?

A small chuckle escapes her throat, her diaphragm spasming to a full-bellied laugh. She opens her hands out wide, runs her fingers through delicate sunbeams, spins slightly, lets the wind caress her thighs, her face. She takes a deep, shuddering breath and gulps down lungfuls of pure joy. But then it begins to fade – an inevitable drainage problem that sucks it all back inside of her from the top of her head, down past her torso and out through her toes into the earth beneath her feet. It slithers free and she is cold – a half-thawed chicken breast, poisonous ice crystals at her core. She tries to chase the feeling, tries to get a finger on it but cannot. She can flare it momentarily if she concentrates but it is an exhausted breath on dormant coals.

Stupid body. It doesn't know how happy it is.

She longs for the feeling to return.

So what now? she thinks. A photo she'd seen that morning on Instagram: a bare-backed woman, arms spread wide, clifftop, forest below, Freedom written in delicately curled letters across the sky. Free of judgement then. She unloads her bathing suit from her shoulders and frees her pasty-white breasts. The breeze excites her nipples, and the sun's rays breathe warmth into her skin. Memories of her youth: topless bathing on dark Portuguese sands, warm wine, laughing girlfriends. But not in years now, and never so publicly as this; on a footpath where anyone could see!

She feels that warmth rise again, that happiness. She smiles, excites it, makes it welcome, wishes she knew how to make it stay. One day she will know; she is sure.

As she makes her way along the coast, her limp begins to lessen, her sarong drying on bare shoulders, and she casts her eyes over a violent ocean that plunges into rocks and reaches for her with salty spray. She puffs out her chest and walks tall, turns like a sunflower, evening out the warmth across her face. There is no one else around. She has seen hardly anyone since she arrived, few people her age anyway: old couples, expats with tanned leather hides and patriotic beach towels.

She is on an island, Spanish speaking, sun and sea. A small apartment to herself, bought outright, hilariously cheap when she thinks of her years of renting; views of dark walls, carparks, the doughy buttocks of dressing neighbours. And here: a glimpse of sea, a taste between houses, east-facing, and with enough money left-over to live carefree for another year or two at least. More than enough time to find herself. Space to think, away from the bustle of the city and the flowering wombs of contemporaries. Free from constant reminders of everything she lacks.

Except they are there – all of them.

Captured in moments of joy, happy despite her, happy in spite of her. Babies, new homes, every minute of what she is missing so that she is not missing it at all; as if she were still in that dingy apartment, hours after her neighbour's final light had been shut off, peering at those other lives infinitely better than her own.

But now hers is better, surely – this new life.

Surely.

This morning she had posted a photo from two days before with the caption Another Day in Paradise: her pedicured feet crossed at the bot-

LEAVING

tom of the frame, the view of the sun rising from her bedroom window. Really, it had been cloudy this morning, night then day, shades of grey with no intervals of drama. The apartment had felt small and dark; the single coffee cup and plate, tragic. She must buy more crockery. She must buy more things. There was an unexpected heatwave back home, a day for winter barbecues, friends gathered, cold beers, smoked meats and rouged cheeks. So Thursday's sunrise it was. No time for reality; never in times of war.

She wraps the sarong, now dry, around her hips and presses her fingers into her breast bone where the skin whitens and springs to pink. She should have brought sunscreen. She dreads the agony of hot nights with burnt skin, the orgasmic relief of a cold shower, sick satisfaction in peeling away dead layers. A memory: sunstroke, delirious in her father's arms, through an abandoned building or carpark maybe, floppy hat, cold bath and stroking hair, pure delirium but his face a constant. The warmth of the memory is cancer at her core. Maybe this is how it starts, she thinks, perhaps this is how it had started for him. A lump in the throat, a heaviness in the stomach – a turgid python – then dizziness, tiredness, thirst, headaches, sleeplessness, diagnosis, regret, death. But she is getting carried away, enough of that. The moment. Living in the moment. Is that not what her audiobooks advise? What is happening in front of you right now?

There are birds: small grey doves that flap their wings and glide on the wind like kites, settling on street lamps and fence posts. There are dark footprints of clouds that slide down mountaintops like passing blight. A blanket of spattered blue holds a single plane, an unbroken contrail that slices the Heavens in two. She wonders where it might be going, what its passengers are escaping. There are wild dogs on the beach, fighting over shade, panting, digging, chasing one another, snouts a natural smile. And then the shout of a small boy up to his elbows in rock-pool, his father bent over him, he looks up as she passes, eyes meeting and then dipping slightly, he taps the boy, and they both stare at her.

Exposed, she grasps her hands over her breasts without thinking, turning away from them. Silly, silly, what does she even care if they see? But it is too late, they can see her shame. The spell is broken. Her cheeks redden, but she hides behind the sun's blush. She waits until they are out of sight and then feeds her arms back through her bathing suit and wraps the sarong tightly around her shoulders. Ashamed. She pictures her father unconscious in the street, his exposed white buttocks a beacon for mothers delivering children to school. Covered eyes. She pulls up his ripped trousers, gagging at the smell, drags him inside with her sister's help. This is the last time, the final straw. He needs help! Shouting over his lifeless body. He knows well enough what he's bloody doing.

She reaches the end of the footpath and so what now? Glancing at her watch, she sees that it isn't even ten o'clock. She finds herself wishing it were later. Late enough to justify a long lunch that could kill at least an hour or so. She had started a painting yesterday – a smudge of blue acrylic on a blank canvas. Self-portrait perhaps. Her dad had always wanted to be a painter, but she had never liked it – the doing or the observing – and so she wonders what made her think that now would be any different. She could read some more perhaps, but her book is boring her. Who decides a classic anyway? Maybe she should pick another – her suitcase is almost full of them – piles of books that she's amassed over the years and has never read because she hasn't had the time. Excuses no longer hold water.

She finds herself staring at her phone, seeking out the shade of a palm so she can see the screen. She wants to speak to someone. Her thumb moves quickly through Jenny, Rachel, Will even. What would she say to them? Yes, it's perfect here; no I'm not trying to make you jealous; well if I had to find fault, I'd say the food is getting a bit tiring, lots of fried things. How's work? Same as always? Well, what could they bitch about now? She finds herself sidestepping her own life to dive into theirs, longing to hear their complaints and moans and secretly wishing that she could chip in with more of her own. Sure, she has her problems, and she could describe to them the overwhelming sadness that solidifies inside of her each morning, mere seconds after she opens her eyes, the grief she can only keep at bay with moments of mindfulness that her phone has to remind her to take; but no, that is not the type of thing they would want to hear. That is not the truth she wants them to know because she has escaped and she is free and they are not. And so she asks them about their days and feeds off their misery and hides behind her own. She calls Jenny but it goes to voicemail. The time difference, of course. She is far away from everything she knows.

She thinks of her final words to her father, her dismissal, her loathing, slammed doors, crying, a decade ago now. She thinks of his shrivelled corpse in the casket, half the man he was, thick makeup clown-like on an almost-bare skull, only human after all. Pathetic. All along perhaps. Does the money atone for his sins? Does it atone for hers? She wishes she had called him in those final years. Maybe it was her own hatred that had metastasised, edgeless after so long but an object of battery nonetheless; an eyeless worm, eating him from the inside out. He had died alone, they had said. It was the smell that caused the neighbours to call the police, they had said. If only she could have felt his suffering somehow, just to have known, she wishes he could have at least given her that.

She decides to walk down to the port. One of three pueblos on the island with identical white-rendered houses, green shutters, a handful of rarely-open restaurants, an old wooden pier that carves the blood-soaked beach in two where the fishermen haul in their catch. The town from up here is a flock of scared sheep, huddled at the union of two dark mountains, beautiful in its lack of order. Care-free somehow.

The fishermen are hauling the last of their wares up onto the sand as she steps into town. Locals inspect them – yay or nay – haul off great cartons of sea life. She knows most of them by sight already: dark-skinned, big-bellied, none by name. She still doesn't speak the language – yet another of the things she will achieve when she has no distractions but has somehow not found the time or energy to do so yet. For now she likes to hear the meaningless sounds of their voices: guttural rolling R's and lackadaisical L's, dramatic hand gestures, thick-eyebrowed frowns and smiles from the eyes.

Hola, she says raising a hand as her eyes meet with a captain of indecipherable age: that rotund, European purgatory between youth and death. *Hola señora*. They haul the last of the buckets onto the sand, throw seawater over the entrails and let the creeping tide deal with the rest. Some of the younger fishermen drag the boats with gnarled rope to moor them to the pier. Then they are off to the bar where they will drink a frosted pint as the sun gears itself up for a midday roasting; they will talk, smoke, laugh. She is free to join them of course, because there is nothing else she has to do. She watches them drag seats from inside to snag the gaps between lengthening shadows. Another day perhaps. She unlocks her phone and flicks through old photos.

Be in the moment, a voice from somewhere says. Be here now.

Here now then: cold tears stutter down sunburnt cheeks.

Six Letters, Two Months, One Year

Verity Capstick
United Kingdom

Shortlisted for the 2019 International Writing Competition

I AM RUNNING OUT OF TIME. I can see the hammocks swinging from side to side. I have a cigarette; it burns out too quickly, the ash falling amongst this crumpled paper. How much time do I have left? What do I know? I can't fashion it into words anymore. This is what I see:

Strange stillness.

Flat pictures.

Warm sweat trickling under my armpits.

It's yellow heat – and thick – and I can see it. I can see it weaving its way across the bent-back tree branches, between the ancient logs of the makeshift mud-huts and through the bony legs of the starving white-skinned cows. It brings beads of sweat to the foreheads of the rice-planters, as bent- back as the tree boughs, brown faces shaded under triangular hats amongst the rich green rice fields. The swaying palm trees are paralysed into memory-form.

I can see hazy clouds set against the shadow of green mountains on the distant horizon. Or are they purple mountains? I don't know – memories are strange beings; they are insubstantial creatures: sights, sounds, smells, touches. They shift every time I look at them and never stay the same. What is it that I see?

I see a sky as blue as washing-up liquid.

I see a girl – no, I was the girl: in socks and sandals, clutching a backpack twice my size and ripping at the seams with scuffed trainers dangling precariously off the strap, clinging on by the thread of a double knot of string. They swing from side to side. I hover on the threshold of the gate as the rattling tuk-tuk rattles away. Then I step over it.

The slim tanned hands of someone in charge takes my backpack, the seams of it splitting and then sewn up again only a few weeks ago with unstable fingers. Sometimes the needle slipped and there was blood. Only a little bit, but enough – enough to know that it hurt. And then my socks and sandals follow a long dark ponytail (too long for a man) across a yellow dust-path across a makeshift school shaded under the swaying palm trees, with children of smiling faces and bright brown eyes who are just waiting to grow up. They are waiting for me to teach them something, but what do I know? I don't know yet.

Then there are words from the mouth of the man with the long dark ponytail which tell me where I'm staying and where I'm teaching and what time breakfast is at and I can see the whiteboards and marker pens and old rattling desks and the hammocks with the other volunteers, with faces like mine – but not quite like mine – with blue eyes and brown eyes and green eyes, swinging lazily from side to side in the stifling sun. There are polite smiles and nice to meet yous and where have you come from? and why did you decide to volunteer here? and what do you know? I don't know yet. There's a disturbing hiss from the old black rice pan in the kitchen and the sharp sweet smell of green chilli.

LEAVING

I follow the trainers swinging even more precariously than the hammocks against the side of my patched-up backpack to a dorm room and a metal bunk which breaks my back at night and bruises my left hip first a dark blue, then a lilac-purple and finally a sickly yellow-green until the mark fades away into nothing. Then tanned arms shift my backpack to the floor and I see his face: dark eyes – too dark for a man – cheekbones too sharp, and a ponytail longer than mine. He is twenty-six. I am nineteen. I ask him for a cigarette; it burns out too quickly.

The days are a blur and the nights are even blurrier. Cigarettes are only forty-two pence. Time happens; a swinging pendulum like the way the hammocks swing from side to side under the swaying palm trees and I am scared that I am running out of time. I swing from side to side in the hammocks.

Little children's fingers grasp my hair and I press a kiss softly onto their brown cheeks, and their brown eyes watch me stutter in front of the whiteboard wondering what it is that I can teach them, what it is that I am supposed to know. I watch the other volunteers and see their blue eyes and brown eyes and green eyes crease up at the corners into smiles and their lips twist into strange sounds of laughter and I wonder what it would be like to be able to smile like them, to laugh like them – to not be afraid of them. And all the time I see him with the long dark ponytail and I wonder if he ever really sees me. I am running out of time. I watch the hammocks swing.

I watch the hammocks swing and I get better: better at standing in front of a whiteboard and not shaking when I lift the pen to the board. I get better at smiling at the blue eyes and brown eyes and green eyes and asking questions like how was your day? and how were your classes? and are you going out for a beer this evening? I go out for beers in the evenings at a dimly lit café under the twilight shade of the swaying palm trees and I get better at not sitting on my own and drinking them. Cigarette smoke curls into twisted clouds. I learn how to play cards and to laugh at jokes and to forget what people think of me. But I still steal a moment to watch the stars on my own sometimes – even though I know I'm not supposed to. Someone once told me, as a child of golden curls in the concrete playground, amongst the ball games and the skipping ropes that it was sad for me to sit on my own. I told them that I was listening for fairies to flutter their wings. They told me that fairies didn't exist. How did they know that? What did they know? What do I know? What do I see?

 I see the wheels of a bicycle deep in Cambodian rice fields and I see the same girl: the one that I was, the one that I no longer am, balancing precariously on the bicycle like the trainers on the back of the stitched-up backpack which is slowly unravelling. Sand-coloured blonde hair blows out behind her in the hot wind. I see myself, distorted through the picture-frame of memory, smiling at the sunburnt grass, the falling down mud-huts, the curved roofs of golden temples, at the smiles of the faces of the motorbike riders, whipping up a curling cloud of thick yellow dust with two wheels and shiny helmets as they pass. I see her speaking to the man with the long dark ponytail and dark eyes, late at night with a half-smile and a tilted head wondering what it is about her that he knows. He cooks her rice in a porcelain bowl with bittersweet green chilli. She likes the way he laughs, with his tongue at the back of his teeth. At first taste the chilli is sweet. Then it burns.

 I see her again in the sticky heat of the whitewashed walls of the classroom with a pocket full of pens and an exercise book clutched in hand and there are brown faces at the desks who now know her and listen to her and learn something from her, whatever it is that she knows. She perches on the side of a desk with her socks and sandals swinging

LEAVING

from side to side giving out ticks and crosses and well-dones and smiley faces. They give her something back in the form of scraps of crumpled paper with wobbly hearts in smudged pencil. There is a mark on the wall of the whitewashed classroom where he has inked his name with a fading marker pen which runs out too quickly: four letters, two months, one year. When is she going to write hers? She doesn't have much time.

She's there – tangled blonde hair and running barefoot on the hard dirt track and yellow dust of the schoolyard, colourless eyes laughing at the brighter eyes of the children she teaches surrounding her. And I think that out of the corner of his eye he is watching her too – but what would I know? I see her laugh; I watch her smiling. She smokes too much.

And then I can see a night; a starless night – a night fashioned of a borrowed checked shirt and a conversation at a bar and tequila shots: 1, 2, 3, 4… how many…I don't know. There is a crowded bus back, which empties into that starless night, and then there is a question from the girl in the borrowed checked shirt to the man with the long dark ponytail. Can I have a cigarette? There is another question. This time I say yes. On a crumpled duvet, on the hard floor, amongst broken beer bottles and torn-up papers and half-read books and empty packets of cigarettes: 1, 2, 3, 4… how many times… I don't know. I can feel the heat weaving through the window with the makeshift curtains and amongst the clothes strewn across the floor. It's yellow heat – and thick – and I can see it. I can see it as it leaves a glistening sheen of sweat across the outline of our collarbones, shoulder blades and down the bones of our spines. Hands touch, fingertips travel across and up and down the outline of our collarbones, shoulder blades and down the bones of our spines. He smiles at me. He tells me lies. There's a bruise that hurts from where his lips press against my neck and that bruise will be dark blue tomorrow, then lilac-purple and finally a sickly yellow-green until the mark fades away into nothing. I tell him the truth. Afterwards we have a cigarette; it burns out too quickly, the ash falling amongst the crumpled sheets. Now I know what I know.

The next day I bleed. Only a little bit, but enough. Enough to know. Enough to know that it happened – enough to know that it hurt. But what do I know?

I know that there was a boat trip and an island and twenty other people with us who don't know – can't know what we know. I can feel salt in my tangled blonde hair and the burning sun on my sunburnt face and sunburnt arms and sunburnt legs. I see an ocean as sharp as glass and undercut by dark rocks which are even sharper. We cling onto stolen time: the touch of a hand, two glistening bodies tangled together at night in the darkness and sharpness of the ocean amongst the glowing-plankton glimmering like fairy dust; little flickers slipping between our fingertips. They told me that fairies didn't exist.

Mosquito bites sting for a moment and then they start to itch: they are an aching and throbbing kind of pain that nothing can numb. How much time do we have left? The stitches on my backpack are unravelling.

Now his eyes are glassy as the sea; they cut straight through me. There are strained smiles. He tells me things that he doesn't mean when he's sober and things that he does mean when he's drunk. He drinks too much; too many people see. I watch him drown in his own dark ocean and stab me in the back with the shards of glass. I try to stitch my backpack back together but the fabric begins to disintegrate and fray. What do I know? I know that we've wasted too much time.

I know that a boat will cut too quickly back across the glassy sea and a crowded bus will brush up yellow dust into curling clouds through the green Cambodian rice fields. I know that I will ink my name onto the

LEAVING

wall of the whitewashed classroom with a fading marker pen which runs out too quickly: then there will be nothing left of me except six letters, two months, one year and a pair of white lace knickers left amongst the crumpled sheets. I know that I will pack up my clothes into my breaking backpack and tie the trainers to the strap with the thread of a double knot of string so that they will swing precariously off the back: side to side as the now empty hammocks under the swaying palm trees. Now I'm running out of time.

And now I will step over the threshold of the school gate into a rattling tuk-tuk which will take me into streets of blaring horns and bright poster signs and the smell of noodle soup and bittersweet green chilli. I know that now my socks and sandals will take me with a stream of people who don't know what I know across ticket barriers and through passport control and into a metal machine which can defy gravity and cut through the washing-up liquid sky as swiftly as the wings of fairies which don't even exist. I know that they will take me away: from the smiling brown faces and purple painted mountains and the bent-backed trees in the rich green rice fields. They will take me away from a man with too dark eyes and a too long ponytail who will forget too quickly what he knows and I will never see him again. The stitches on my backpack disintegrate and fray and it finally falls apart. I have a cigarette; it burns out too quickly. Now I've run out of time.

A Woman Who Knows
Kate Carne
United Kingdom

Shortlisted for the 2019
International Writing Competition

WHEN WE SEE CARLO, a kid from the village, running up the rutted track, we know it must be urgent.

'It's Dona Catarina,' the scrawny boy says, bending to catch his breath. 'She says you must come quick with your truck. She has paid for some bales and needs to get them up to her place before the rains come. She says she needs you straight away.'

Paulo thanks the boy and watches him run back down the hill. Leaning against the wooden post of the veranda, he surveys the storm clouds gathering to the west and rubs his arm. 'She's expecting too much this time, *claro*.' He tries straightening the right arm, but it's swollen to twice its normal size from an impetigo infection. He grimaces and brings the arm back to right angles. 'No way I can drive… pity. We could do with the cash.'

I am also on the veranda, sitting in a plastic chair that had probably once been white. I glance at Paulo's arm, but it makes me queasy, so I look into the distance instead. It's such a magnificent scene, the hills forested with monkey puzzle trees and the mountains beyond. This shack lies at the end of a dirt road, pushed up against the wilderness. Living here was meant to be temporary, just till we got work and money coming in. We've been here nearly a year. Of course, if I'd had any idea of the isolation, the poverty, of the awkward, fumbling way it feels to be always a foreigner, I'd never have left London. But the thing is, you never do know, do you?

'I'll do it,' I say. My stomach tightens, waiting for Paulo to react. Usually whenever I speak, we end up arguing.

'Fine,' is all he says. He hands me the keys.

◆

The truck is an old four wheel drive pick-up that has twice gone round the clock. It's a waste of time carrying things for people—it barely pays the repair bills, but not that many locals have cars, and something that can get up dirt roads in the rain is rare. It is not exactly a public service, hauling things for the people here, but it is a way of fitting in, of hearing the gossip, of getting a few eggs or a sack of flour. It's also a way of getting out, which, at the moment, is all I want to do.

I climb into the cab, pull out the choke, coax the old diesel engine into its uneven grumble.

Dark clouds sag down onto the village. Dona Catarina is standing in a queue, waiting for the only public phone in the whole of the valley.

'Ay, Dona Lucy, thank you for coming. Women should always help each other, no?' She cancels her phone call. 'My horses are needing the hay, and I got a good price.'

Dona Catarina climbs into the truck and directs me to a broad valley where a large lorry sits at the side of the road. 'Says he can't risk his big truck on these country roads…just pull up alongside.'

The lorry driver tosses the bales of hay onto the pick-up, while Dona Caterina and I shove them into place.

'This won't all fit,' I say, but Dona Catarina is determined to get it all home before the storm. Dona Catarina is not the kind of person you want to contradict. Although she's barely five foot tall in her cowboy boots, and round as a pumpkin with a long dark plait snaking down her back, she has a reputation for being tougher than any man. There was the time (so the story goes) when one of her horses threw a tourist, who landed impaled on an old metal fence. Single-handedly, Dona Catarina (who has the arms of a wrestler) lifted him off the metal spikes, stemmed the flow of blood with her bare hands, ripped off her shirt to make a bandage, and (bare-breasted) flagged down a car to take him to the nearest hospital, two hours away. Everyone says she saved his life. But there were other stories too. Dona Catarina, according to the rumours, is a *bruxa*, a witch. She is a woman of potions and spells. This means everyone is afraid of her. Another time, people say, she caught a man beating a horse with a plank of wood full of nails. She shouted so loud, like the voice of God himself, that the man had a heart attack and died right there on the road. Other versions of this story involve a knife. Anyway, Dona Catarina led the bleeding pony home and nursed it back to health. The police never came to question her, even though there were witnesses. In fact when people around here tell you this tale, every one of them will tell you they saw it with their own eyes.

'Dona Catarina, please, the suspension can't take anymore. We'll come back for the rest. Here's a tarp we can use, just leave the hay by the road. No one will take it if they know it's yours.'

Dona Catarina pauses, both to think and to receive the compliment. '*Vamos*, Dona Lucy, let's get this load home before dark.'

We cover the bales we are leaving behind and climb into the cab.

LEAVING

'*Amiga*, you don't look too good,' Dona Catarina observes.

I sit up straighter and take a deep breath. 'Just tired. It's hard work, living out here.'

'*Claro*,' Dona Catarina agrees, and we drive.

◆

The track to Dona Catarina's place is cut into the side of a steep hill. Normally it's just Dona Catarina walking up and down with her horses. I get out and shift the truck into four wheel drive. As I hoist myself back into the driving seat, the first fat drops hit the windscreen. '*Vamos*,' she says to the truck, feeling its wheels grip onto the rough dirt and ease us forwards. There's a mile or more to Dona Catarina's, and we need to do it before the road becomes a mudslide.

When rain comes to the tropics, it comes wholeheartedly. I switch the wipers on, and the headlights. Even in second the truck complains. People live in the craziest places out here, half way up mountains, carrying all their stuff home on their backs. At least Dona Catarina has her horses. In mountain reckoning, this makes her a wealthy woman.

The rain pounds on the steel roof of the cab, but the road is holding up. 'I think we're gonna make it,' I say.

Suddenly the front nearside wheel collapses. I shift into first, then reverse, but this only makes both front wheels sink lower, as if they have landed on marshmallows. Dona Catarina shakes her head, gets out of the truck and walks ahead to survey the situation.

'It's the grave,' she says solemnly as she climbs back into the cab.

I look at her. At first I think I must have misunderstood what Dona Caterina is saying. My Portuguese is rudimentary, and out here people have accents like their mouths are full of molasses.

'Josefina's grave. I buried her here, maybe three weeks ago.'

I frown. 'Who?'

'Pretty Josefina, one of my ponies. She died on the way home. So I buried her. It was hard work.'

'You buried a horse in the middle of the road?'

'On the side, actually. I couldn't pick her up and move her, although I tried. She was such a good pony, the one who got beaten with nails. Ever since she bites any man who comes near. She was my favourite you know, even though she was old. I didn't want the vultures getting her.'

'Our wheels are sunk into a horse's grave?'

'*Sim, claro.*'

I get out. The truck is sunk in the mud up to its headlights. I look around in the increasing gloom for some planks of wood when the smell of Josefina hits me. I bend forward and vomit, and vomit again, leaning against the side of the truck to stay upright.

'How deep did you bury it?' I shout through the downpour.

'Oh, not so deep…probably the front wheels are greeting Josefina right now.'

◆

In the dark, in the rain, in the mud, we walk the rest of the way to Dona Catarina's house. The old woman seems to have owl's eyes, she can see exactly where she is going, but I am finding it hard to keep up. I stumble, landing on all fours in the mud. After that Dona Caterina holds my hand. It takes us nearly an hour to get to the old shack. Wooden walls, corrugated roof, a single room. I'm grateful to be out of the rain. I take my boots off, feel the cold concrete against my feet. This is the moment the shivering begins. First my neck and head, and then my whole body begin to tremble uncontrollably. I am sweating, hot fine sweat. I know if I don't sit down, I will faint. I don't want Dona Catarina to see what's going on, partly because I am embarrassed, and partly because, to be completely honest, she frightens me. 'I need the toilet,' I say, stumbling my way outside.

I guess she must find me out there somewhere, in the darkness, in the mud. I guess she hauls me back inside. I can feel my clothes being taken away, my skin being rubbed with a cool damp cloth. The next time I have any clear notion of what is going on, I am lying on her bed. All I want to do is get up and walk out of there, but I am naked, and the muscles in my legs have disappeared.

I watch. Dona Catarina lights candles and builds a fire. The stove is the sort that all the locals have – built of bricks, a long space open at one end for the wood to slide in, and a rectangular metal plate on top that holds the pans. The light of the fire makes the room flicker and dance.

Dona Catarina begins pulling dried herbs from bunches that hang overhead. She boils water. She sings softly as she does this, strange words, as if she truly is a sorcerer, as if she is casting a spell. Back in civilisation, such things do not exist. Life down there is rational, with right angles and electric lights. Up here in the mountains, the wilderness has a different way. A different power. The night is filled with unseen jaguars and poisonous toads. People say that night is the time when a *bruxa* can cast her strongest, most dangerous spell.

'I need to get back,' I say weakly. 'Could I borrow a horse?'

'No one takes one of my ponies out in a storm like this – you would both break your necks. And also,' Dona Catarina pauses, 'in case you have not noticed, you are standing at the abyss. If I am not able to release you, by morning you will be gone.'

Just as she says this, I come back into my body. It is burning, so hot that I cannot bear for my arms to touch the sides of my body. Every bone begins to ache. My mind darts through the heat and pain like a caged rat.

Dona Catarina brings a bowl of thick brown paste. She fingers up some of this muck and wipes it over my forehead, on my neck, into my armpits, into my groin. It is cool, gritty, and smells of the earth.

'Malaria?' I whisper.

Dona Catarina shakes her head. 'Nothing so simple,' she says. 'You know, if you have a plant, growing in the rich dark earth, and you pull it up and ask it to grow in the desert, the hot, dry desert, do you know what occurs?'

'It dies.'

'Exactly. In a human, it is the same. Only in us the *alma* goes. Disappears. Searching for its home.'

I want to ask questions, but somehow the words will not take shape. This is when Dona Catarina begins her song.

It is a song that seems to go on for hours. At times she is sprinkling water onto my skin. At times she is covering me with a sheet. At times my mind leaves the body and hovers, watching her as she sits there next to me, as if it is a strange, art-house film. The shadowy room, lit by candles and the fire, the rain pounding down on the roof like a dozen tribal drums. Sometimes I am aware of her face, and sometimes there is no awareness at all. At some point I fall down a deep, black hole and die. I remember thinking: *Well, at least this is the end.* But it is not the end. At the other end of the hole I find myself climbing out of a limestone cave, standing on a pebbly beach where a whale is stranded above the tides. I watch, and see that this huge creature is still breathing. I know I need to push her, to roll her down to the surf and release her back into the sea, but I am not at all sure that I have the strength to do so. I push first with my shoulder, then lean into the smooth, hairless flesh with the whole of my back, hoping that the whale will understand that I mean no harm. My feet slip and slide among the pebbles, but finally I feel the whale shift her great weight down the slope of the beach. Somehow she seems to grow even larger. Air snorts from her blowhole. The colour of my skin becomes her colour, a bluey grey, and my outbreaths fall into a rhythm with hers. Somehow we are communicating, both dreaming of the buoyancy and ease that is so close by, and just out of reach. I keep pushing and pushing, as if my life depends on it. Meanwhile the sweats go on and on until there is no moisture left within me, until even the blood has gone solid in my veins.

I am Catarina, a woman who sees things

I am Catarina, a woman who knows

The rest of her endless song continues in a language I cannot understand. Somewhere within that song, everything is erased and I float on comforting waves.

◆

Light cracks in beneath the ragged door. Dona Catarina's round body lies next to me, softly snoring. She smells of leather and horsehair. I am cold. The sweat has dried, stiffening my skin. The inside of my mouth longs for water, but even if I can move, which I am not sure about, I do not want to wake her.

I lie, staring up at the corrugated roof. Something is different. I feel more whole, and yet no longer entirely here. I have entered a different space, a strange realm, a place I do not quite believe in.

◆

Dona Catarina wakes, heats the kettle, pours water into a large metal bucket with fresh herbs. She orders me to stand in it and wash myself. It surprises me that I have the strength to do this.

She gives me clothes – a man's shirt, some old jeans. I have many questions, but she shakes her head. 'It is not permitted to speak of the *otros mundos*,' is all she will say.

♦

Dona Catarina saddles up two ponies and we ride off to find Paulo. With Dona Catarina there, explaining about the truck, he does not dare expose his rage. She waits while he goes to get a shovel. As they head off together on the ponies, I feel the huge relief of being alone.

♦

The next day Dona Catarina comes to see how I'm doing. How I'm *going*, as they say here. I want to ask her so many things – what song she sang, what herbs she used, what exactly happened up there in her cabin, and most importantly of all, what I must do now not to break the spell. She smiles, she shrugs, she shakes her head.

But she does tell me about Paulo and her pony.

'In daylight,' she says, 'the smell was even worse. I told him that I had paid for the delivery, and I expected it to be done. He had to unload every bale of hay, and then prise the wheel out of mud with planks of wood. And once he got the front wheels out and started to drive, next the back wheels got caught in the grave. I have to tell you,' she shakes her head, 'that it was hard work for me, not to laugh. And then he had to reload all the hay, and drive it up to my place. After all that he was afraid of driving the truck back down and getting stuck again. And he stank so bad of rotting horse-flesh that he stripped off *everything* and went to wash himself in the river. He had to walk home wrapped only in a blanket. This morning people told me they were laughing behind their hands as he hurried by.'

Dona Catarina will make certain that everyone hears this story.

LEAVING

'Oh,' she says, slapping her short tough thighs, 'My little Josefina, even in death, she is still taking her revenge on any *bastardo* who comes near.'

◆

As she swings up into the saddle, it comes to me that Dona Catarina is completely part of this land – the mountains, the herbs, the horses – all these live within her, giving her strength. I could almost envy her. Belonging is a subtle business. Roots are fussy things.

As if she can hear these thoughts she says, 'You know, do you not, that you must leave?'

I smooth the flank of her horse.

'And then you must tell people how it really is to live in a place like this.'

'Yes,' I say, 'I promise that I will.'

Slipping Away
Peter Clegg
Italy

Editor's Choice

I AM HOLDING A SMALL TREE, an Acer, with golden leaves, small enough to grow in a pot. Around me the street market grows ever louder and more crowded. I am feeling a little confused and disoriented. My wife has gone ahead to make the lunch. There is a fourteen-year old girl with me who says she is my niece, but I do not recognise her. I have two nieces, but they are much younger. Lovely girls, but I haven't seen them for a very long time. My wife said things would be easier if we lived closer to her sister so the family could help look after me and now I'm always followed by this girl who is set to spy on me. We moved here from… but the name slips away in mid-sentence like an oyster from its shell. This happens more and more these days. It's easier just to keep quiet.

'Uncle John,' says the niece who is not a niece, 'could you wait here a second please? I just want to get something from that stall over there.' And she slips into the crowd. I wait. I wait for quite a while.

LEAVING

'This is silly,' I tell myself, 'I'm perfectly capable of finding my own way home. I have no need of a minder, I just walk along the high street and take the second left.'

Off I go with a spring in my step, away from the noise and bustle and prying eyes, proudly holding my Acer. My minder told me I shouldn't have bought it, that they didn't need an Acer in the garden, but I like Acers. We had several Acers in the garden at... where we were before, and I'm not going to be bossed around by some snotty nosed kid. Fifteen minutes later I see the street where I now live on the left. I cross, ignoring a tooting horn, and set off down the hill.

There is something strange about long rows of Victorian terraced housing. Only the paintwork and the state of the front yard, distinguishes each from its neighbour. Time and again I think I've found the house only to realise as I get closer that it's not quite the same. Numbers don't help, few houses have them and anyway, I can't remember ours.

And where is the railway bridge? There should be a railway bridge at the far end of the road. I know because I worried about it when we first arrived, afraid that it would keep me awake. But it's far enough away that I only hear a low rumbling when a train goes past, quite a comforting sound really. I like to lie there in the dark, thinking of all those people, all those journeys, remembering all those train journeys I used to make. Commuting to work, forward and backward, backward and forward, like those on the trains on the bridge. I feel a sort of connectedness with them, links to a world that is slowly, gently leaving me. Sometimes at night, when I can't sleep I like to look out of the window at the trains, scurrying across the bridge, little caterpillars of light against the dark night sky. It reassures me that all is normal and I go back to bed and sleep.

I used to enjoy commuting. I know that sounds strange, but I did.

The noise and the bustle made me feel alive, a part of something I cannot put into words. I loved the structure it brought to my life, the patterns it gave to my day. Patterns: the walk to the station in the morning; the muttered greetings to the other regulars; the scramble for seats which I always lost, too timid to push my way through; the rhythm of the wheels; the ritual dance as I raced across the concourse avoiding those racing just as fast in the opposite direction. It was patterns that gave structure and purpose to my life, now beginning to tangle and smudge.

Earlier journeys too, I remember. As children our holidays always started with a train journey on a real train, a steam train, to some unknown destination. Each year our father took us to a completely different part of the country, the South Coast, the West Country, Yorkshire, the Lakes and one magical year the West Highland railway to Fort William. I still remember the smell of smoke, the leather strap holding the window shut, which you could lower and lean out to see the engine as it rounded a curve, having a compartment to ourselves, the net luggage racks, the adverts for so many holiday destinations.

We were obsessed with trains in the 1950s. Not only Richard and me, but most of our friends could be found on even the wettest of Saturdays standing on a platform, trainspotters guide in hand, collecting numbers as the trains roared past. Even more exciting were our visits to a nearby marshalling yard. A footbridge ran across the yard and we would stand so the trains passed underneath us enveloping us in clouds of acrid smoke. One lazy summer Sunday, with only a single shunting engine leisurely at work, Ricky found a hole in the fence and through he went, me following reluctantly behind and in no time he persuaded the driver to let us spend the afternoon with him on the footplate. Utter bliss!

Richard my brother, small and wiry, always cheerful, so full of energy he could never keep still, his carrot coloured hair in odd spikes, uncontrollable no matter how much brylcreem he used, a bit like Richard himself. Richard the adventurous one, always getting us both into trouble and out again with his cheeky grin. Rickety Rick they called him at school. Even the headmaster had a soft spot for him. Ricky could always get away with some outrageous prank if his excuse made the headmaster laugh. School certainly taught him to be quick-witted if nothing else.

I worshipped my elder brother. Still do. They tell me he is dead, and I know that he is dead, but somehow he still comes to see me every few weeks, sitting on the edge of the bed, leaning right back with his hands behind his head, roaring with laughter over some half-forgotten escapade. Our hitch-hiking holiday to Spain is a favourite.

I gather holidays in Spain these days are commonplace, but for us, at that time, hitch-hiking was high adventure. Mainly, I think it was the people we met. First in France, the old man who had seen a dead Russian in Sputnik and who insisted in taking us to every bar in the area, introducing us to one and all as 'mes amis anglais'. We arrived too late for a bed at the hostel and too drunk to care, ending the evening sleeping under the stars.

Then Spain, Franco's Spain, heading for Barcelona. A lorry driver tossed me a coin with Franco's head on one side and a pig on the other. 'Which,' he said, 'is the bigger pig?' That evening another night under the stars sleeping on a deserted beach, until we were kicked awake by police screaming and shouting and waving machine-guns who had taken us for gunrunners.

The following night we hid under an upturned boat in a small fishing village and slept quietly until the fishermen found us in the morning. Roaring with laughter, they handed us ropes to help haul in their deeply laden boats, then slapped a fresh fish each into our hands and pointed us to a small café by the harbour wall to have our breakfast cooked.

Then on to Barcelona where the buildings still wore with pride bullet-holes, like medals earned in the civil war; where a rum and coke, a Cuba libre, was known as a Fidel Castro; where one of our lifts was cheered for going the wrong way in a one-way street. Three things I particularly remember.

Firstly, Gaudi's mad, yet magnificent church with stonework dripping as though covered in white chocolate sauce and spires like a kraken's tentacles. Adding to our feeling of unreality was the fact (if it was a fact) so we were told, that although still under construction, more was falling down than was being built!

The contrast with Barcelona's cathedral could not have been greater. Whilst Gaudi's masterpiece is an invitation to reach for the heavens, to dream, the cathedral was more a monument to Mammon than to God. The entrance was filled with stalls selling tourist tat or those little plastic limbs and foetuses that the faithful hang in front of their favourite saint to ease their arthritis or ensure an easy birth.

We attached ourselves surreptitiously to a group of American tourists being taken around by a priest who made no secret of the fact that he was utterly bored both with the tour and the cathedral itself. As we began to go down the stairs to the crypt I noticed an elderly peasant woman in black, one of those ageless women who could have been 50 or 80. She was tentatively following us down into the crypt, clearly uncertain if she was allowed, taking one hesitant step, then another. Looking almost with fear toward the priest, waiting to be reprimanded for her temerity, but drawn inexorably onward to gain a glimpse of St Eulalia's tomb, the saint who guarded her city, her people, her family and herself. A day that would stay with her forever. Meanwhile the priest droned on, the archetypical guide. We began to wonder if he expected a tip at the end of the tour and what he would do with it if he got one. The contrast between

LEAVING

her evident faith and the priest's total lack of it was enough for us and we left. I have distrusted organised religion ever since.

And the third thing? One of Ricky's practical jokes of course. We went into a nearby bar for a Fidel Castro, unaware that it was a gay bar. Indeed, I don't think that as teenagers we even knew such places existed (though Ricky probably did). As soon as he approached the bar, he began to be accosted. With a gentle smile he said, 'I'm sorry, gentlemen, I'm not interested.' Then his grin broadened as he waved his hand in my direction, 'But my brother!'

I am sitting on a bench in a small park, with a children's playground nearby. I have been here for some time, I think. I am not sure where I am or how I got here. I must have been lost in thought and not paid attention to where I was going. My wife complains that I do this all the time. Still, the sun is warm, the park is peaceful and the bench comfortable, so I feel no great compulsion to leave. Besides, I enjoy watching the children playing on the climbing frame, the swings, the roundabout and the rest. It reminds me of my own childhood. I liked the roundabout best.

After a while I notice that some of the mothers are giving me odd glances and whispering to each-other. A little girl walks past. I smile and say hello, but she just looks at me and scurries off to her mother. The suspicious looks increase. Time I think to move on. I pick up my Acer and set of along the path, then decide to take a smaller path in a different direction. I don't really know why; it just feels right. As I turn onto the new path I see in the distance my minder, the niece who is not a niece. I hide behind an old sycamore. It's the wrong time of year for the helicopter seeds, another childhood memory, like conkers. Did you know that the sycamore is an Acer?

I watch my minder stop and talk to the mothers and see them point to the path on which I'd left. Time, I think, to hurry away.

After a while, I realise that I am in another of these anonymous terraced streets and slow down to look around. I can hardly believe it but there in the distance is my new home. I hurry towards it and run down the side passage into the garden to see where I can plant my Acer. But something is wrong. This doesn't look as I remember it. A lady comes out of the back door and starts to shout at me. I've never seen her before and don't understand what she is doing in my house.

She says something about trespassing and calling the police. I get frightened and, dropping my Acer, run back into the street. My bid for freedom is not working out as I had intended. I just keep walking, not knowing what else to do. A police car drives past, then stops and reverses. Two officers get out and ask me to get into the car. Did the woman in my house report me? Are they going to arrest me? I am extremely nervous. However, they seem friendly enough, so I climb in and go with them to the police station. This proves to be a typical 1960s institutional building. Facing the entrance is a long counter with glass partitions to keep the public at arms length. The walls are exposed red brick. A row of lockers stands against the right hand wall. The left is dominated by a long wooden bench. A notice board with a jumble of papers pinned to it next to the lockers completes the picture.

'Please sit there sir,' says the older of the two, pointing to the bench before disappearing through a side door. For a moment I catch a glimpse of an open office with several officers. I think I hear a snigger as the door swings shut. I sit and study the floor. It has a random pattern of swirls and blotches. As I continue to look I begin to see distorted faces and animals in the pattern, reminding me of summer days, lying on the grass in the park with Ricky looking for pictures in the clouds.

A lady in uniform comes through the side door carrying a mug of tea She gives me a friendly smile. 'I thought you might be thirsty,' she

LEAVING

says, 'so I brought you this. We've been in touch with your family who were very worried of course, but everything is fine now. Your niece is coming to take you home so sit and wait,' she says, 'just sit and wait.'

So I sit, and I wait, as the last vestiges of freedom slip away.

Patchwork
CLEMENTINE COLLETT
United Kingdom

SHORTLISTED FOR THE 2019
INTERNATIONAL WRITING COMPETITION

I STOOD AT THE PLATFORM in South Kensington tube station wearing a light brown trench coat. My umbrella was propped up against me, trickling rainwater into a small puddle. The damp had made my hair more frizzy than usual, so I started to tie it into a tight bun on the top of my head.

'Scarlett?' I heard a deep Californian voice behind me, just as I was twisting the last bit of my hair-tie around, securing the bun.

I turned to see him.

'Oh my god! Eric!' By some kind of bygone instinct, I pulled his shoulders towards me and hugged him tightly, tilting onto my tippy toes and knocking my umbrella over in the process. I wrapped my hands around his shoulder blades. They felt broad and muscular even through his suit. His cologne lingered. A sharp, bitter, amber smell.

'Jeez. I haven't seen you in, god, I dunno. Ten years? Since graduation maybe, I dunno?' he said, squeezing me affectionately.

LEAVING

He pulled away and looked at me incredulously. 'Are you still with...?' he said. I leant down awkwardly to pick up my soaking umbrella, propping it up against a pillar.

'Dom? Yeah! We're...we're married actually,' I said, speaking quickly, flinging my hands up as if to say it was nothing.

'No way!' he laughed, 'Sorry, I just, I didn't realise. Well hey look, congrats! And you're...living in London?' he said, sneaking a glance at my ring finger.

'We're,' I cleared my throat, 'still in Oxford actually. I'm lecturing at the university now. I came down to see my brother, you remember Ollie, right? Well he's just had a baby with his wife, Angie. Anyway, I'm heading back to Paddington to get the train,' I said. I couldn't stop grinning.

I folded my arms uncomfortably and tipped my head sideways, attempting nonchalance. 'I thought you had gone back to America?' I said.

'I was. I mean, I was in the States. Came back a coupla years ago to head up the UK office. So... yeah. Living in Chiswick with my wife Jemima. Been married about a year now,' he said.

We examined each other's faces in silent disbelief.

A train pulled up on the other side of the platform.

'That's my train, but hey, give me a buzz this afternoon? You guys gotta come for dinner at ours, okay?' He pulled out a card from his inside jacket pocket and handed it to me. He got onto the tube on the other side of the platform, holding his dark brown briefcase so tightly his knuckles were like swollen mistletoe buds, all plump and white. I looked down at his card. A tingle in my stomach.

'Hey Scarl,' he said, just before the doors shut. I looked up at him. 'How crazy is this?'

◆

Eric and Jemima's house was set behind an industrious white gate with a buzzer.

Jemima greeted us at the door. She had wide, sapphire coloured eyes and golden hair which reached down to her waist like strands of silk. As she led us down the hallways, her figure sashayed through the air like a ribbon in the wind, her arms unfolding this way and that as she gave us a tour of their place. The house was lined with dark oak and black marble surfaces, embellished with mustard and purple velvets, and thick Persian rugs ran through the hallways. The whole place smelt like warm spice and wood smoke.

Eric was stood in the kitchen, squinting at the label of a bottle of Armand de Brignac. He looked soft and defined at the same time, as if someone had drawn him in pencil and then gone over it in one sharp line of pen. His hair was ruffled and moist, like he'd just got out the shower, and his face looked fresh, rosy-cheeked.

'Alright! You're here!' he beamed, striding over to us, slapping Dom's hand and shaking it violently, then kissing me on both cheeks. I could feel the aura of Dom's body clenching and clamming up beside me.

We ate delicate bits of food and drank lots of wine. Small talk gradually turned to reminiscing, reminiscing turned to politics, occasionally exploding into heated debates between Dom and Eric, and eventually petering out into non-sensical drunken discussions.

Just as we finished the shop-bought lemon tart pudding, Jemima jolted out her freckled arm to fill up Dom's glass, missing, and spilling wine all over the table. It stained the silky table cloth, spreading like a burst blood vessel. Jemima leant back on her chair howling with laughter, entertained by her own inaccuracy. Swinging to light a cigarette on one of the tall candles in the centre of the table, she puffed the smoke in a thin cylinder shape straight up into the air.

LEAVING

'Do you still keep up with anyone else much from Oxford then, you two?' said Eric.

'Not much, Eric, to be honest,' said Dom, pausing to drunkenly stumble over his words. 'Most of my time is made up of commuting to London nowadays. Don't have much time to socialise anymore.' He paused. 'No time for sex either,' he mumbled, turning to me.

I felt the room freeze. I looked at Dom, my mouth open. His lips were stained with red wine and his eyelids fluttered, twitching his hazel eyes in and out of view.

To try and defuse the tension I laughed nervously. I took a sip from my glass and swallowed back the lump in my throat, trying to get rid of the ball of heat which had formed in my chest.

Jemima's glowing skin illuminated the darkness like a pearl. She sucked on her cigarette, blowing the smoke out through her nostrils.

'I mean even living in London, Eric always seems to be commuting or working,' Jemima said, putting her bare feet on the table and crossing them, wiggling around her candyfloss coloured toenails. 'It's not as if we have much sex anymore either,' rolling her eyes and taking one last drag before she put out her cigarette.

'Jemima,' he said. Eric's eyes looked like a murky pond covered with a layer of ice, his pupils and iris homogenising and leaking into each other.

'I'm just saying, Eric. I'd like a passionate fuck every now and again,' she said, shrugging in Dom's direction. 'But you're too tired, busy or whatever.' She was tipping her hair backwards off the back of her chair. It was so shiny it looked sharp and metallic. 'Who knew it could all go downhill so quickly? We've only been married a year or something,' she laughed.

My cheeks throbbed from blushing. They were starting to pulse.

'We should go,' I said, turning to Dom. I took out my car keys and put them on the table.

'And who exactly will be driving?' he said, turning his head towards me but not his eyes. 'We've drunk too much,' he said.

'Oh, stay! You can't drive now,' Jemima announced, stroking her tanned, freckly chest with the tips of her long, elegant fingers.

My head was still turned directly towards my husband. There was no sound.

'We've got plenty of rooms here. If you do need to stay,' said Eric.

Jemima's arm leant over the table, making the silky table cloth slip like a piece of lingerie. She picked up my car keys and swung them on her index finger, looking at Eric, at Dom, not at me.

'We could...?' said Jemima.

'What do you mean?' I said, bluntly.

She cupped her hands around her face and shook her head. 'Oh no, never mind, I don't know what I'm saying. I just thought it sounded like we all need to spice things up a bit,' she said, biting her bottom lip.

Eric rubbed his closed eyes with his thumb and forefinger.

Dom swivelled to look at me. 'No?' he said, curving his mouth into a downwards arch and sticking out his bottom lip. I saw Eric and Jemima exchange a look. It made me sad, that look.

◆

About half an hour later I found myself in the upstairs bathroom. I had told Eric I would just be a moment, that I wanted to freshen up. Instead, I sat on the side of their clawfoot bath, staring at the tiled wall on the other side of the room.

I could hear Jemima and Dom. Jemima's moans, Dom's familiar grunting, the creaks of springs, the rhythm of the bed against the wall.

LEAVING

I felt hollow, unemotional.

I stood up and went over to stare in the mirror. My vision was blurry, like a camera trying to come into focus. Looking at my own face felt comforting and sickening all at once. Normally my skin was an olive colour, luminous, but in this light, I seemed almost bronze, dirty and tired. My mascara was all smudged under my eyes and my skin looked oily.

When I opened the door to Eric's room, he was sitting on the edge of the bed, checking his phone. The top of his shirt was unbuttoned. He looked up at me and smiled, putting down his phone.

'Hey,' he said. 'You look great.'

I shut the door behind me and stood there for a second. My throat cramped. I wiped a tear from my eye and then swallowed the rest back. Eric came over to me and held me in his arms. He didn't say anything. I could hear his heart beating, his slow breathing. He took my face in his hands and smiled.

'Can you believe any of this is happening? I mean. I just couldn't believe that we bumped into each other the other week,' he said, dropping his hands and walking over to the bed. He lay down and perched his hands behind his head.

'I've thought about what it would be like to see you again for so many years,' I said, going over to curl up on the end of the bed.

He smiled at me so warmly it made my stomach melt.

One night in our final year of uni, after our exams finished, we'd gone to a house party just off the Cowley Road. I'd ended up in the garden with Eric, sitting on a set of old white metal chairs. Eric had told me he was in love with me, that he thought Dom wasn't right for me. He'd tried to kiss me. I'd pulled away. I'd told him that I was happy with Dom. He'd apologised, asked me not to mention it ever again, to forget he ever said anything.

'Well,' he said, undoing his buttons on the cuffs of his shirt, 'I'd be pretty mind-blown if I'd been able to see what was happening right now...'

Neither of us seemed drunk anymore. We didn't kiss, we didn't even touch. But I felt closer to him than I'd felt to anyone in a long time.

I fell asleep fully clothed on Eric's bed, curled up like a foetus in a womb of fluffy Egyptian cotton. In the morning, I found Dom downstairs. He was reading a book on Indian artwork in one of the sitting rooms. I found the car keys, still on the wine-stained dinner table. We sat in silence the whole drive home.

◆

That night felt surreal and real to me all at once, like a dream that I could remember perfectly.

Dom and I had been trying to patch things up, but they'd been falling apart for so long, it seemed pointless. We'd tried ignoring it, we'd tried fighting about it. He was doing me a favour, he said; he knew how I'd felt about Eric ever since Oxford. He was leaving me, he said.

A month after that night I was travelling to Paris for a conference. It was a fresh winter morning. A blue sky and a layer of mist hung above the ground. In St Pancras, the light was streaming in through the tall walls of shimmering glass, refracting the light like a crystal and dappling diamonds and circles of light onto the floor. Commuters in suits and heels bustled past me, moving so fast they looked like streaks of paint on a canvas.

I bought a raisin Danish pastry and a black coffee and sat in a café reading the newspaper. I bit through the crusty icing and let the flaky pastry and the soft raisins roll around on my tongue.

'Scarlett?' I looked up, squinting through the brightness. It was Eric.

LEAVING

'Oh my god,' I said, folding my newspaper up hurriedly and standing to hug him, 'What are you doing here?'

'I'm just on my way to the office. Are you off somewhere?'

'Just a conference – a conference in Paris. I'm off – just for a couple of days.' I was flustered, flinging my arms around to create twitchy gestures, stumbling over my words nervously.

'I've got a meeting in 10 minutes, but could I join you for a sec?'

'Of course! I mean – I'd love that! I've been meaning to contact you.'

'You have?' he said, pulling out the chair and sitting down heavily. His tie was hanging loosely around his neck. He started to tie it up, winding one strand around the other. 'I've actually wanted to contact you too, but I wanted to give you some space,' he said, shuffling the knot up to tighten it around his throat.

I swallowed, but my mouth felt dry.

'I mean, space to sort out you and Dom. To sort out what you want. I didn't want to intrude,' he said.

I smiled. 'You're not intruding. Or if you are I want you to,' I said. His eyes were fixed on me.

'You do?' he said, flicking his gaze from one of my eyes to the other quickly.

I nodded. He let out a big sigh. 'I wish I could stay here with you, but I better get to this meeting,' he said, 'How about dinner as soon as you're back?'

I laughed, 'The four of us?' I said, 'Not sure that's the best idea,' I smirked. I meant for my voice to sound light and sarcastic, but it came out wobbly.

He stood up, laughing out of his nose, 'No, just us. If you'd like to?'

'I really would,' I said, getting up.

We looked at each other for a second. Then he leant in and I felt the breath from his nose on my lip. He kissed me, moving his hand up to my neck and behind my ear, pressing his thumb in and stroking my jaw. His hands felt dry and warm on my skin. He paused for a second to look at me. We smiled. We kissed again. He drew his body in close to me. Everything around me seemed to sink away.

'I've been wanting to do that for a while,' he said, stroking my cheek. My body felt full, relieved and complete.

On the train to Paris, I looked out the window. Through the glass, I saw gold and emerald fields, like patchwork, the train weaving through the seams as the growing plants lilted in the rising sun.

Curiosity
JACKIE COLLINS
United Kingdom

Karen's Diary, 18th July 2014
'It' arrived on the doormat at 10 am this morning. I stood for half an hour staring at it. I reached out and immediately pulled my hand back, as if it had been scolded. This was the final result of my stupidity. The same question I have asked myself a billion times in the last 2 years, went through my mind: 'Why did I do it?' Curiosity? 'Curiosity killed the cat', my mother used to tell me. I was always curious, even as a kid. Curiosity didn't take into consideration my faithful, loving, husband and my two adorable children China, 13 and Leo, 10. I said some bloody stupid things: 'It just happened.' 'It meant nothing.' 'I'm sorry.' 'Forgive me.' 'I love you.' 'I was curious.' There it is again, that selfish bitch curiosity.

Rob's Diary, 1st June 2012
Went to Helen-from-work's 40th last night. It was at 'The Paradise', big crowd of us from work there. Helen's family and friends. All us young guys in the office took a dare to see which of us could 'get off with' a 40-year-old woman. I set out to win the prize money. I made sure I looked good, haircut, clean-shaven, expensive cologne, clothes classy but

fashionable. Made a lot of effort to look effortless. Danny and me started chatting up Helen and her best mate Karen. Karen was a looker and she had a good figure for her age. My modus operandi is tried and tested. I'm a natural flirt; it amuses me to flirt with a woman, any woman. I've got a smooth tongue, I'm funny, intelligent (believe it or not) and persuasive, I lead them on, I play with them, flatter them. By that time, I know if she's green or red. Last night I got a green. So, I went, all the way, to her bed. Smiling at the guys like 'the cat who got the cream' as we left the party. 2 am in comes hubby, he didn't hit me or her, that makes a change, he just said 'get out now', so I did.

Paddy's Diary, 18th July 2014
Karen is the love of my life, and will be till I die. The skinny red-haired girl with the plaits who liked to climb trees. The daredevil teenager with porcelain skin, flowing red curls, and a smile to melt your heart, not to mention her kiss, oh that kiss. The young woman with the determination to get her degree in law and help the needy. The beautiful bride, supportive wife, great mum. She is a wonderful woman and I will always love her.

For me and for Karen, good relationships are built on trust. I trusted her totally, we had known each other all our lives; we had been married 15 years. I believe her, I know she is loyal and faithful, I know she loves me.

As I walked into the bedroom that night he was getting out of the bed. They were both naked. I was unexpected.

I told him to 'get out'. He grabbed his clothes and ran. I glared angrily at Karen, the words; I trusted you repeated themselves over and over in my head.

She garbled her story out, insisted she had done no more than kiss

LEAVING

him.

The memory of that night haunts me; if I had stayed over after the meeting instead of driving home I may never have known. I callously rejected Karen, left that same night and resolved to get a divorce. The woman in the bed was alien to me. Without her I am incomplete and unhappy. Karen and others have tried to reason that a kiss is not adultery, is it? A kiss this time, what next time she gets curious? I'm a crushed man with a broken marriage and two screwed up kids, there are no winners here.

I know every word she told me that night was true. She had been to Helens 40th, been chatted up by this young guy, had too much to drink, let him kiss her, got carried away, flattered, curious of what it would be like to have sex with him. We had only ever known each other. They came back, undressed, got into our bed. Suddenly, she thought: 'What the hell am I doing?' She asked the guy to go, then I walked in on them.

She stared at me wide-eyed, innocent, naïve. She was sorry, please believe her. I did, I do.

But I can no longer trust her. I can never trust her again and I cannot live like that.

This morning in the post I received the absolute.

Glimpse Into The Future
Lynette Creswell
United Kingdom

THE KNIFE WAS CLUTCHED IN HIS HAND. Rosa shot up in bed gasping for air. Sweat soaked her flimsy night gown.

'Hey, babe, are you okay?' Aiden switched on the bedroom light, reached across and pulled her into his arms. 'Same nightmare?'

Rosa nodded and clung to her husband. 'But the visions… the visions were more intense.'

'In what way?'

Rosa's voice wobbled. 'When he strikes, I sense her terror. Like I'm with her in the shadows.'

Aiden's grip tightened. 'Have you any idea who this woman is?'

Rosa shook her head. 'No. She's facing away when he attacks.'

'And the killer?'

'Six foot, male. Athletic build.'

'Did you recognise him?'

'He's wearing a balaclava.'

Aiden stroked her hair. 'You know… I thought your gift would make us rich, not give us sleepless nights.'

Rosa stared deep into his eyes. 'I wish I'd never been born a Romany.'

Aiden kissed her forehead. 'Yeah. Me too. Try and get some sleep. We've got an early start tomorrow.' He turned over and switched off the light. 'Jake's picking us up at…'

'But I said I'd meet Freya.'

'Eh?' Aiden rolled back. 'But…'

'Don't you remember? I promised to help her load the flowers and take them to market.'

'So you did.' Aiden snuggled beneath the duvet. 'We'll catch up at supper. I'll make Tacos.'

Rosa huddled closer inhaling his manly scent and drifted off to sleep.

◆

A car horn beeped. Rosa dashed out of the flat to the street where her sister's blue Mazda waited.

Opening the car door she slid inside, snapping on the seatbelt. 'Morning, Freya.' Rosa pecked her sister on the cheek.

Freya shoved a Styrofoam cup into her hand. 'Americano. No sugar.'

'Thanks. You're a lifesaver.'

Freya pushed the gearstick into first and set off down the road. 'How's things? Are you still having trouble sleeping?'

Rosa sighed. 'Yeah.' She sipped the coffee. 'And the visions are getting worse.'

'Same woman?'

'Uh-huh.'

The traffic lights changed from amber to red. Freya hit the brakes. 'I think you should talk to someone.'

'Like who?'

AWARD WINNING STORIES

'The Police.'

Rosa choked on her drink. 'Don't be daft? They'll lock me up.'

The traffic light flicked to green and Freya indicated left. 'But you have to do something. You can't allow this woman to be murdered.'

'But how can I help her if I don't know who she is?'

'You must have some clues?'

'Only a flash of the coat she's wearing and the back of her head.'

'Well, that's something. Anything else?'

Rosa chewed her lip. 'It's twilight. There's a crescent moon…'

'No, I mean about the victim.'

'Oh.' Rosa fiddled with the zip on her jacket. 'She's got long, dark hair.'

Freya pulled up outside a group of portacabins. Switching off the engine she turned to Rosa. 'So all you have to go on is a glimpse of a coat and the victim's dark hair. You'll have to hope something significant comes to you before it's too late.'

Rosa got out of the car and spotting a litter bin, she threw the empty coffee cup inside. A man in black uniform, carrying a clipboard ambled towards them.

Freya smiled at the foreman. 'Hey, Mitch, are the flowers ready?'

'Yup. Around the back.' He scribbled on a sheet of paper and then passed it to Freya to sign.

She scrawled her name at the bottom of the form and turned to Rosa. 'Let's get the trailer hitched and flowers loaded.'

Mitch took a step back. 'Just so you know… Big Dan was here earlier. I don't want trouble.'

'Relax. Gavin's got it in hand.' Freya hurried off to collect her order.

Noticing her sister's smile had vanished, Rosa chased after her. 'What's going on with Gavin and Big Dan?' She tugged at Freya's sleeve.

-123-

LEAVING

'Hey, I'm talking to you.'

Freya spun around. 'Look. Don't sweat. It's like I said. Everything's under control.' She pointed to a large piece of tarpaulin. 'Grab that will you. We'll use it to protect the cargo.'

◆

Freya glanced into the rear-view mirror, reversing the trailer into the allocated parking slot.

'Now that we've stopped,' Rosa said. 'Are you going to tell me what's going on with this Big Dan business? Do you owe him a lot of money?'

Freya yanked on the handbrake. 'Let's just say enough to have him breathing down our necks.' She got out of the car and hurried towards the trailer to untie the rope on the tarpaulin. 'Thank goodness the flowers are already in buckets. All we have to do is get water.'

'But what about Big Dan…?'

Freya groaned. 'Leave it, Rosa. Whatever happens, it's down to me and Gav to figure out.' Her eyes shifted towards their pitch. 'It's not quite what I had in mind, but it'll have to do.'

Rosa followed her gaze. Flimsy pieces of timber held the stall together. The canvas roof was ripped and green with mildew. 'Hmm. Classy. Still, at least we're close to the main shops and Starbucks.'

'Huh.' Freya rolled her eyes. 'I don't know. You and your copious amounts of coffee.'

Rosa grabbed two buckets of pink chrysanthemums and carried them over to a tap jutting out of the nearby stone wall. Filling the tubs a third full she placed the flowers in a spot where shoppers couldn't fail to miss them. After a lot of to-ing and fro-ing she was happy with the finished display. She admired her handiwork. Dark purple tulips, white vibrant lilies and blood red roses transformed the rotting planks into a summer garden, drawing shoppers from every direction.

'I'll have a mixed bouquet and a couple of those lilies,' said a customer, heaving a multitude of shopping bags.

'And I'll have a dozen red roses,' said a man whose cheeks glowed the colour of the pink chrysanthemums.

◆

Freya rubbed her stomach. 'I'm starving, are you?' She glanced at her watch. 'Two o'clock. The pitch is booked until three. I don't think I can wait that long for food though.'

'Why don't I get us a cuppa and a sandwich from the coffee shop? My treat. I could go now as we've almost sold out.'

'Good idea. I can't let you pay though.'

'Yes, you can. I insist. Now what would you like?'

'Okay, I'll have a latte and a tuna melt if you're sure? I'll pay you back once me and Gavin get back on our feet.'

'No need that's what sisters are for.' Rosa checked her purse was in her jacket pocket and headed off in the direction of Starbucks. She'd just reached the door when she heard someone shout, 'Hey, you. You've dropped these.'

Rosa spun around, surprised to find a young woman hovering behind her.

The woman took a deep breath. 'I thought I was never going to catch you.'

She was oddly familiar. And that coat… Rosa shook the misgivings from her mind. 'I'm sorry but I think you've got the wrong person.'

The stranger's green eyes rounded. 'I'm pretty sure these are yours.' She jangled a set of keys.

Rosa gasped. 'Goodness. You're right. Those are mine.'

LEAVING

The stranger laughed. 'They fell out of your coat pocket.'

'Thank you, erm…'

'Gina.'

'I'm Rosa.' Rosa took the keys, but the second she touched the metal an excruciating pain shot through her fingertips. 'Argh.' A flash of light… A gruesome image flickered behind her eyes. 'No. It can't be...' Rosa's legs buckled beneath her and she collapsed onto the pavement.

'Hey, are you all right?' Gina's face loomed before her.

'I saw you.' Rosa held her forehead. 'A vision… You… you were lying on the ground. Your coat… it's the same… covered in blood.' Rosa clutched her chest, unable to breathe.

Gina helped Rosa to her feet. 'I'm sorry but you're talking gibberish.'

Rosa clung onto Gina's arm. 'Listen, your life is in danger. I know it sounds crazy. But you… you mustn't go near the lake.'

The woman's eyes widened. 'Are you serious? Are you on something?'

'No… I…' Rosa caught Gina's worried expression. She shook her head. 'Sorry.' A slight smile lifted the corners of her lips.

'Look it's okay. You must have hit your head. Let's find you somewhere to sit down.' Gina guided Rosa to an empty table outside the coffee shop and passed her a bottle of water. 'Here. Drink this.'

Rosa sipped the cool liquid. 'Thank you.'

'Can I take you home or to A&E? My car's just…'

'No, thanks. I just need a minute.'

'Are you sure?'

'Positive.'

Gina sat beside her. 'Should I call someone?'

Rosa shook her head. 'No, honestly. I'm fine.'

Gina rummaged inside her coat pocket and pulled out a business card. 'Look, take this, it's my mobile number, just in case you come over all funny again and need assistance... My shop's just on the high street.'

Rosa pushed it away. 'Thanks for your concern, but I'll be fine. My sister's just over there.' She pointed towards the stall.

Gina placed the card onto the table. 'I'll leave it here anyway. When you're feeling better why not swing by the shop sometime? I'll give you discount.'

Rosa laughed. 'That's one way of getting customers through the door.'

'I never miss an opportunity to do business.'

Rosa sipped the water. 'Do you mind me asking, how long have you had that coat?'

'Oh, a couple of months. Daddy bought it for me in Vienna.'

'It looks unique.'

Gina grinned. 'It is.' She did a twirl. 'The only one of its kind. Now, if you're sure I can't help anymore I must be off. Hope to see you in the shop sometime.'

Rosa waved as Gina disappear into the crowd.

◆

'What do you mean it was *her*?' Freya's bottom lip quivered.

'The woman from my dream.'

'But how can you be sure?'

'The coat… the dark hair…'

'But that doesn't mean…'

'I had another vision. This time I saw her face. She was lying in the dirt. Her body covered in blood. He'd killed her.'

'Fuck.' Freya pushed her fingers through her curly hair. 'What are you going to do?'

LEAVING

'What can I do? It's not as though I can knock on her door and say, 'Hello. Did you know I've seen you die?"'

'A bit drastic but it might stop a murder.'

Rosa sighed. 'Be realistic.'

Freya stared down at the business card Gina left behind. She gave a loud whistle. 'Windsor Jewellery and Antiques. I bet she's worth a pretty penny.'

Rosa grabbed her sister's arm. 'Wait… Do you think that's why he kills her?'

Freya threw the card down onto the kitchen table. 'This is getting weirder by the second.'

'I have to do something.'

'Why don't you visit the shop?'

'What good would that do?'

Freya shrugged. 'Get to know her better. Find out if she really *is* the woman from your dreams.'

'I could invite her to lunch.'

'That's a good idea. Ring her.' Freya picked up the business card. 'You've got her number.' She headed to the fridge and pulled out a bottle of wine.

Rosa took two glasses from the cupboard. 'You're right. If I spend more time with her I can learn about the people in her life and maybe work out who the killer is.'

Freya poured the wine. 'Worth a try.'

◆

Rosa got out of the taxi and checked her watch. She'd arranged to meet Gina at one o'clock. The jewellery store was just across the road. A sign above the tall windows shimmered with shiver embossed letters. The traffic was horrendous. While she waited to cross, she noticed a familiar figure step out of the doorway. Rosa hid behind a parked car. Peeking out, she spotted Gina with Big Dan. They chatted for a minute or so and then Dan leaned over and kissed her.

A sharp pain shot through Rosa's head and blood images flashed before her eyes. Could Dan be the killer? At six foot, he was certainly tall enough.

Dan walked off and Gina went back inside. Rosa crossed the road and made her way into the shop. A bell tinkled overhead as she opened the door.

'Ah, right on time.' Gina grabbed her handbag and headed towards Rosa.

Rosa stared up at a crystal chandelier hanging from the ceiling. 'Wow. Look at this place...'

'It's my father's shop. I just work here.'

'A far cry from the markets I'm used to.'

'Yes, it is rather glamorous.' Gina flicked the sign to 'closed' and locked the door behind them. 'I've booked a table at *Clarence's*.'

'The posh wine bar?'

'You said choose somewhere nice? Plus it's just up the road so I won't be late back.'

'Smart thinking.'

'I won't hold you to buying me lunch though as it's quite pricey in there.'

'I want to. If I'd lost my keys...'

'Anyone would have done the same.' Gina's high heels click-clacked along the pavement.

'I'd like to think so but...'

'Look, the restaurant is about a hundred yards up ahead. I'm a reg-

LEAVING

ular there so we'll get a nice table. Hey, watch out.'

Rosa jumped out of the path of an oncoming pushchair. 'Phew, that was close.'

'Those things are lethal,' Gina said, 'we're nearly there now.' They carried on up the main street.

'Here we are.' Gina ushered Rosa through the shiny glass door.

Rosa felt a stab of unease. This wasn't the usual eating establishment she'd visit. Pizza Hut was more her style.

They were greeted by the Maître d'. 'Good afternoon Miss Van Cleef.' He showed them to their table. 'Madams.' Once seated, he passed them a menu each. 'The waiter will be over to take your order shortly.'

'This is nice.' Rosa admired the leather seats.

'It's one of my favourite places,' Gina confessed, 'the atmosphere's great and the food's even better.'

The waiter came over. 'Would you like something to drink?'

Gina studied the wine list. 'A glass of Sauvignon, please.'

'I'll have the same,' Rosa said.

'And have you decided on what you'd like to eat?'

Rosa glanced at the menu noticing the meals weren't priced. 'I think I'll try the Chickpea curry,' she said, hoping that it wasn't going to be too expensive.

'I'll have lobster.' Gina handed the menus to the waiter.

Rosa looked around the restaurant, trying to hide her concern about how much lobster would cost.

'Honestly Rosa, you don't have to treat me. I have expensive taste.'

'No, it's okay. I said I would.'

The waiter returned, placed the glasses onto the table and poured a drop of wine in Gina's glass for her to try. Gina sipped the Sauvignon. 'That's fine. Thank you.' Once the waiter had left, Gina said, 'So what were you doing the day you lost your keys?'

'Helping my sister sell flowers.'

Gina fiddled with the corner of a napkin. 'I thought traditional gypsies only go door to door?'

Rosa eyed Gina over her wine glass. 'Sorry?'

'My friend said you're a gypsy. Has he got that wrong?'

'Well, err no… Which friend is this and how do they know me?'

'Well, aren't you?'

'Yes. but…who told you?'

'My boyfriend, Dan. I mentioned you to him.'

'Oh, I see.'

'So, tell me more about yourself. Do you live in a caravan?'

'No.'

'Why not?'

'Because I chose not to. My husband, or *gorger* as he's known by my family has a flat close to the river. When we married I moved in.'

'Gorger? What kind of name is that?'

'What's with all the questions? What's this Dan been saying about me?'

'Oh, sorry I didn't mean to bombard you. I'm just interested. I've never met a real, live gypsy before.'

Rosa took another sip of drink. 'That's okay. It all felt a bit like third degree and with someone talking about me, it just threw me. I understand you're curious about the way I live. Going back to Gorger, well, it's the term used for non-traveller.'

Gina leant forward and whispered. 'Do you tell fortunes?'

Rosa shook her head. 'Not anymore.'

'Why? Did something happen?'

Rosa hesitated. 'Look… people like me… well we try to help others

LEAVING

but more often than not our warnings go unheeded.'

'You've seen something about me, haven't you?'

Rosa placed her wine glass down.

Gina reached out and touched her hand. 'The day we met you tried to warn me but I couldn't make out what you were saying.'

Rosa pulled her hand away. Glancing to her right she caught sight of the waiter. 'Here comes dinner.'

The server placed the food in front of them. 'Can I get you anything else?'

'No. thank you,' said Rosa.

'We're fine.' Gina slipped the napkin across her lap.

The waiter gave a slight bow. 'Enjoy your meal.' He turned and hurried away.

◆

Freya pulled up outside the shop and Rosa got into the car.

'So how did it go?'

'She knew I was a Romany.'

Freya frowned. 'How?'

'Big Dan.'

Freya gasped. 'She knows that buffoon?'

'Yeah, they've been dating for six months.'

Freya opened her mouth wide.

'I was shocked too.'

'Then he has to be the murderer.' Freya's foot pressed down on the accelerator.

'Hey, slow down.'

Freya eased her foot off the pedal and the car slowed.

'Are you okay?'

'No, not really. Big Dan is bad news. If he's seeing that girl then it can only mean one thing.'

'Money?'

'What else?' Freya slammed on the brakes.

'What the—'

'Sorry.'

'What's got you riled?'

Freya bit her bottom lip. 'Big Dan's threatened to break both Gavin's legs if he doesn't pay up by the end of the month.'

'Jeez. How much does he owe?'

Freya manoeuvred the car into an empty space outside Rosa's flat. Yanking on the handbrake she turned to face her sister. 'Fifteen K.'

Rosa gasped. 'How much?'

Freya gripped the steering wheel. 'Gavin borrowed five grand and it escalated from there.'

'But he's never going to be able to pay that back.'

Freya burst into tears. 'What are we going to do?'

Rosa hugged Freya. 'Hang in there, sis. We'll think of something.'

◆

Gina lifted the champagne flute. 'I'm so pleased you could make my twenty-first birthday bash.'

Rosa grinned. 'Try keeping me away.' She turned to Aiden who chinked his glass with hers. 'Here's to a pleasant evening.'

'Enjoy the party. I'd better go and mingle.' Gina hurried away to greet the arriving guests.

A dark curl fell loose of Rosa's chignon. Aiden slipped it behind her ear. 'Hey baby, how much do you think this boat is worth?'

Rosa laughed, tossing her head back. 'Oh, let's not go there.' She let

LEAVING

out a gentle sigh. 'We both know this little beaut is worth more than we'll ever make in a lifetime.' She fiddled with the silk scarf around her throat. 'Let's watch the sunset and then go to the bar.'

The sun slowly disappeared. Aiden put his arm around Rosa. 'Time to check out the cocktails.' He led her away.

While queuing for a drink, high-pitched laughter caused Rosa to turn around.

Gina was on the dancefloor. She tapped the side of her champagne flute. 'I'd like to thank you all for coming this evening and making my birthday special.' A round of applause followed, and Gina gave a giggling curtsy. 'The evening isn't over yet. Daddy has a surprise so if you'd like to follow me.'

An attendant brought Gina's coat. Her father helped slip it across her shoulders. The same coat which Rosa had seen in the dream. The pale cream stripes embossed with black made it memorable. A shiver of unease wormed its way down Rosa's back.

Gina took to the gangplank with caution in her six-inch heels.

Her father took her hand. 'We don't want you falling, Princess.' He led her off the boat and onto a tiny island situated in the centre of a lake. Sconces, offering light, stretched along a small area of shingle. Noisy guests trailed behind.

The shore reminded Rosa of a scene in the *King Kong* film where the beautiful handmaiden is taken away and tied to a pole. Only the jungle drums were missing.

'Everyone, gather round,' Gina's father said to the guests. Family and friends huddled together. Laughter tinkled through the air.

'Why are we out here when we could be having fun on the boat?' Rosa recognised Big Dan's voice. She hadn't seen him all evening, but now he was pressing butterfly kisses on his girlfriend's hand.

Gina giggled like a schoolgirl forcing Rosa to turn her head away.

'Look, Gina.' Her father pointed to the sky. 'Your surprise.' A firework exploded filling the darkness with a shimmer of gold and silver stars.

'Ooh.' The crowd stood transfixed as a rocket zoomed high into the atmosphere.

Gina and Dan slipped away. Rosa nudged Aiden. 'They're sneaking off. We need to follow them.'

'Don't be daft,' he said, 'they probably just want some time alone.'

'But what if…'

'What?'

'My premonition…?'

'But we can't follow them because of a dream.'

Rosa squeezed his hand. 'Have I ever been wrong? Gina's going to die tonight if we don't help her.'

Aiden hesitated. 'But Big Dan's a mean mother –'

'Are you turning yellow?'

Aiden puffed out his chest. 'No.'

'You sure?'

'Okay. Come on, but don't blame me if Big Dan punches me for being a pervert.'

'A pervert?'

'For spying on him and his girlfriend.'

'That'll be the least of your worries if I'm right.'

'And if you're wrong?'

'Then you'd better duck.'

Aiden rolled his eyes. 'Thanks, but if someone does try to hurt her, how are we going to stop it from happening? You said the killer has a knife. What am I supposed to do? Stop him with my bare hands?'

LEAVING

'I don't know. You'll think of something.'

Aiden wiped beads of sweat from his forehead. 'I must be crazy but if we're doing this, we need to do it now. Head through those bushes over there.'

They shuffled along a winding path leading to another part of the island.

'Keep out of sight,' Aiden said, pushing branches away from Rosa's face.

'Shh.' She placed a finger to his lips. 'Look.' She pointed to a silhouette standing close to the water's edge. 'It's Gina but where's Big Dan?'

Aiden guided her behind a flowering Rhododendron. From their hiding place Rosa noticed Gina dipping her toes in the water.

'Did you hear that rustle?' Aiden said. Something dark rushed passed them.

'That's him.' Rosa chased after the shadow and to her horror, the dream unfolded before her eyes. A man dressed in black stood behind Gina. A knife flashed in his hand. He raised the blade and took a step towards his victim.

'Gina.' Rosa dived towards the assailant, knocking the knife out of his hand and threw herself on top of him. He stumbled and fell forward. Aiden grabbed the man's ankles forcing him to the ground. The knife glinted. Someone screamed. Rosa closed her eyes and waited for the fatal blow. A man's voice called out her name… She glanced up. Aiden was holding the man's arms behind his back, pushing his face into the dirt. 'Rosa, for God sake pick up the knife.'

She snatched the blade lying just a few inches away from her and stashed it the back of her trousers.

'Good girl. Now give me your scarf.'

She untied the neckerchief and handed it to him.

Gina rushed over and wrapped her arms around Rosa's shoulders. 'Thank you. If it wasn't for you I'd be dead.'

'What the...' Big Dan came hurtling towards them, throwing kindling and bits of driftwood to the ground.

'Dan.' Gina rushed to his side. 'He... That man... tried to kill me.'

Rosa stared at Aiden. 'If that's not Big Dan you're holding down then who...?'

Dan bent over the body and removed the balaclava.

A gasp left Rosa's throat. 'Gavin? But why?'

Dan dragged the man to his feet. 'You piece of filth.' He punched Gavin in the stomach causing him to crumple to the ground in a heap. Dan turned to Gina. 'Are you okay, baby?'

'Yes, I think so...'

'I'll go and get backup.'

'Shall I come with you?' Gina clung to his arm.

'No, best stay here.' Dan pulled her hand away. 'I'll be back as soon as I can.' He ran off into the bushes.

Rosa stared down at the man at her feet. 'Why, Gav. Why would you do such a thing?'

He looked up. His voice hoarse. 'He said if I didn't do it, he'd kill Freya.'

Rosa gasped. 'Big Dan put you up to this?'

'You don't expect us to believe such bullshit,' Aiden said.

'It's the truth.' Gavin glared at Rosa. 'Dan's taken out a ten million pound insurance policy on her. Go on... ask her.'

'It's true.' Gina pressed her forehead. 'But he said it was just in case... with us starting a new business together.'

'Oh, Gina.' Rosa hugged her new friend.

Aiden pulled Gavin to his feet. 'We need to get back to shore and

LEAVING

alert the Police about Dan.'

'He won't get far,' Gina said, 'He'll have to get back on the yacht with the rest of us.'

An engine roared into life.

Aiden spun around. 'What's that?'

'A speedboat,' Gavin said, 'should have been my getaway.'

'Christ,' Rosa said. 'He's done a runner.'

'And left me to take the rap.'

'Well, you're hardly innocent.' Aiden pushed Gavin towards the bushes. 'We'd best get back.'

Rosa and Gina trailed behind.

'I can't believe Dan would do such a despicable thing.' Gina wailed. 'He said he loved me.'

'I'm sorry,' Rosa said. 'Isn't that your dad waiting?'

Gina ran to her father's side. 'Daddy.'

He held her close. 'Gina, you're trembling.'

'He... he...' she pointed towards Gavin. 'He was going to kill me.'

'You,' her father said, 'you'll pay for this.'

Gavin lowered his gaze.

'Please Mr Van Cleef,' Rosa said, 'don't be too hard on him. Dan forced him to do it.'

The old man laughed. 'You don't expect me to believe such rubbish?'

'It's true, Daddy,' Gina interrupted, 'he fled using a speedboat. Gavin told us how he'd threatened to kill Rosa's sister if he didn't go ahead with Dan's plan.'

'In that case, once we're on the boat I'll radio the Police.'

Gina sobbed in her father's arms. 'If it hadn't been for Aiden and Rosa...'

'Thank you,' her father said, 'I'm indebted to your both.'

'Daddy,' Gina moved from her father's arms. 'Rosa saw it happening in a dream. She's a Romany gypsy. She witnessed my fate.'

'Shh, darling, you're upset. You've suffered a nasty shock. Let's get you inside.'

Aiden turned to Gavin. 'I don't condone what you've done, but I'll do my best to get you a good lawyer.'

Three security guards hurried down the gangplank and headed straight for Gavin. He turned to Rosa. 'I'd do anything to keep Freya safe.'

Rosa winced as they cuffed and led him away.

Aiden put his arm around his wife. 'Are you all right?'

'No, not really.' Rosa fought back tears. 'I never thought these premonitions would cause someone close to me to end up in jail.'

'But you saved someone's life, darling.'

She tried to smile but a bright flash behind her eyes made her wince. A man standing on a chair, a hangman's noose tight around his neck... She let out a deep sigh. 'Oh, no. Not again...'

Notice of Eviction
Kevin Davis
United Kingdom

SHORTLISTED FOR THE 2019
INTERNATIONAL WRITING COMPETITION

IT WASN'T MUCH TO LOOK AT, but it was my home. I can imagine how it wouldn't suit everyone. There was, upon reflection, a few cons as well as pros. OK, let's be brutally honest, quite a few cons. It wouldn't be to everyone's taste. No, not everyone's 'cup of tea' at all. However, as I've already said, it was my home, and as the song says, 'Be it ever so humble, there's no place like home'.

I moved in a few months ago and I admit, the place took a little getting used to, but right from the first day, I felt a good vibe about the place; you know, like we belonged together. It's funny how sometimes a house can feel like a home right from the start. You go in through the entrance hall for the first time and it's almost like you've been there before. Not exactly déja-vu, more a keen sense of familiarity and belonging, as if it had been waiting for me to arrive with a keen sense of anticipation. Me and my room were made for one another, and in a very real sense, we completed each other. It was somewhere I felt happy and safe; you know, a place where you can grow and develop as a human being.

It was, after all, my first home. The world is a big scary place for a wet-behind-the-ears youngster, and this home was my sanctuary and my safe-room. Nothing harsh or horrible could reach me once I was inside my comforting space. Like I said before, it wasn't perfect. It was not what you would call spacious converted loft-space living. My room was tiny, or as estate agents like to call it, 'compact and bijou'. Space was definitely at a premium. It was only a bed-sit, or in modern parlance, a studio apartment, and there was no storage room at all. Yet there always seemed room for the important things; always room for everything I needed, when I needed it. Room for my personal growth, you might say. The space seemed to adapt to my changing needs, as if it knew me and wanted to accommodate me.

However, it wasn't perfect. Natural light was at a premium. No, that's not strictly true. I don't want to be guilty of more 'estate-agent speak'. Let's be honest here and now; it was dark all the time. Day or night, the passage of time on the clock seemed to make little difference. Gloomy during the day and pitch black at night. However, there are lots of people who live in dark and dingy basement bedsits, who have exactly the same problem, and I have to admit, it didn't bother me. Quite the opposite, I found it comforting, like being wrapped in a soft woollen blanket. I felt at one with the room. It was as if I was taking on the character and personality of the space I inhabited. I increasingly felt myself being subsumed by the very room in which I lived. Not in an unpleasant possessive way, but in a way that comforted and strengthened me. The room fed and nurtured me with a feeling of sweetness but not cloying, sugary but not sickly, made-to-measure but not restrictive. Like I said, room for personal growth. Time spent in my room felt nourishing, as if it was feeding me with everything I needed for growth and development. Oh yes, I was a

LEAVING

very satisfied tenant in my dark, cramped, but personal space.

Of course, there was the damp. Even with an excellent heating system, the bill for which, by the way, was included in the rent, it couldn't solve the perennial problem of dampness. The wallpaper was a very dark pattern with occasional slightly lighter patches affording a limited contrast for relief. I have no idea why the landlady would have chosen such a dark pattern, given that the room was very small anyway. She had obviously avoided watching any TV make-over programmes. Sometimes I would lie back on the bed, kick off the proverbial shoes and stare for what seemed like hours at the strangely shaped patches of damp on the far wall. Not the most stimulating of pastimes I grant you, but I discovered over time that it constantly changed, and it was a more effective way of falling asleep than counting sheep. Every day a different shape presented itself to me upon awakening from my slumber. It was a little like looking at clouds and trying to work out their shapes. Sometimes it looked like a diving duck or a serene swan. The restful images would swim through my mind and lull me into a peaceful sleep. Other times, it resembled a large scary clown with a twisted malevolent leer spreading over its face. It's wild eyes, getting larger and larger, staring straight at me. I would feel panic rising within me, and sleep would be the last thing on my mind. On the occasions when the latter occurred, I would curl up into a tight ball and turn my back to the wall until the image in my mind re-emerged in a friendlier form.

Anyway, as far as I was concerned, the positives far outweighed any negatives. I was offered a great deal on the place. It was one of the factors that swayed my decision to sign up and live there. Can you believe it, all bills and meals were included? I know! I couldn't believe my luck. Take the heating for example. The room was always just the right temperature. A lot of small flats are either way too hot or freezing cold; sometimes both in the same week if you're unlucky. I don't know anything about boilers and radiators. It's all a foreign language to me. So, I have no idea what sort of heating system the landlady had installed but it provided me with a temperature that was consistently perfect. Cold days, wet nights, summer sun and winter snow were all the same. It took all weathers in its stride to provide me with a perfect environment. I know it sounds weird but it's as if it intuitively gauged my body temperature and switched on or off according to my needs

And then there was the food. She was a gourmet chef! What can I say! Jamie Oliver had nothing on my landlady. In comparison, Nigella Lawson wasn't fit to flip burgers, and Mary Berry would have hung her head in shame if she had tasted my landlady's strawberry gateaux. I neither knew nor cared what the meals were called, only that they tasted out of this world. I'd only been resident a few months, but I was already feeling the extra pounds piling on. I didn't care. The meals were irresistible. I just lay back and waited for the next serving of delicious delicacies. I couldn't refuse any of it.

Now I know it sounds crazy, but right from the word go, the house spoke to me. A lot of house-hunters say this, but I don't just mean in an abstract empathic way. Not simply in that way which signifies that you can imagine living in the house. No, I mean in a real audible way. Sometimes it was just feelings, but more often than not, it was an actual voice; faint but audible. It was impossible to make out specific words, let alone constructed sentences, but the voice was definitely there. I needed to be very still and quiet to hear it, but all the same, it was there. Not all the time, but most days, especially in the evenings. And the voice was always the same. The same tone, quiet and deliberate, soft and reassuring. If it had been a difficult day, full of uncertainties and unknowns, I would hear its soothing and supportive tones and be comforted. Many

LEAVING

a time I would fall asleep, gently rocked towards a peaceful slumber by the rhythm of the words. It engendered such a sense of well-being inside me. As each day passed, the voice became more frequent and clearer. I felt warm, loved and comforted. I felt like I belonged. I was home and all was well with my world.

So, imagine how crushed I felt when I accidently overheard the conversation about eight months after I had taken up residence. Surely, I must have misheard. It couldn't be right, but it put me in a real spin. I never really believed people when they said they were frozen with fear, or rooted to the spot, or immobilised in horror. But I was a believer now. I could feel my heart trying to jump out of my chest; its thumping, swooshing lub-dub sound, usually so comforting in the still of the night, now took on a terrifying persona. The noise was deafening. Panic overtook me, which only made the noise assaulting my ears even louder. I could feel it, vibrating through my body like the discordant clashing music from an orchestra of demons. I just couldn't comprehend it. I must have misunderstood. It couldn't be true. But however long I lay there, languishing in denial, I could not deny what my own ears had heard. It was obviously a conversation I was not meant to hear. She was talking with her sister; the usual mundane stuff, you know. My landlady's sister had been visiting with increasing frequency over the last few months and I had overheard these conversations many times before. Over the usual cup of tea and custard creams, the sister was working through her usual litany of woes; namely her husband, her kids and her thoughtless neighbours, whilst my landlady responded with her ongoing health issues, weight gain, excessive sweating and back pains. It was all following the expected schedule of topics, when I heard it. I heard my landlady say that her problems were all down to me and things would be much easier when I'm gone in a few weeks' time. There it was. It was out. My landlady was giving me notice! She was evicting me. I was being thrown onto the street with no home, no hope, no future. Through the fog of panic, the inevitable questions hammered in my head. Why blame me? What had I done wrong? How was it all my fault? I thought back with as much objectivity as I could muster. No. It couldn't be all my fault. I wasn't a bad tenant. I was quiet in my room, and unfailingly polite and appreciative. No late-night parties that's for sure. I had never even had any visitors to my room. Not that I'm anti-social. I simply didn't need anyone else. I had my room and my landlady, or so I had thought. Now even that was being taken from me. Now my whole world was about to be ripped from me. I smiled grimly as I thought this must be how 48% of the UK voting population feels under Boris' premiership. But bugger Brexit! This was far more important. This was my room and my life.

  I thought the next few weeks would drag slowly, but they flashed by surprisingly quickly and before I knew it, the day of departure was upon me. Don't get me wrong. I want to be absolutely clear about this and leave no room for doubt. I didn't want to leave. In fact, I would have given anything to stay here where I felt safe, warm and loved like never before. In fact, it was impossible to remember what my life had been like before I had moved in. I wasn't just leaving my lodgings, I was leaving my refuge, my home. The place where I belonged and felt complete. In a very real way, I was leaving a very real part of me behind. I belonged in my room. The room with all my memories, the damp patches on the dark wallpaper, the cramped space, the amazing environmental system and the delicious food. However, and I'm being nakedly honest with you here, over the last three weeks I had also felt something else, the beginnings of a vestigial yearning deep inside me. A yearning for something different. Perhaps it was simply a reaction to my enforced exit, but an inexplicable desire for change, growth and challenge began to form within

LEAVING

me. I could not form this desire into words, let alone understand it, but as the days passed, it grew inside, becoming stronger and more urgent. It frightened me, as if something alien was taking over, consuming and transforming me into I didn't know what, but I was helpless in the face of it and couldn't fight the urge to change.

Inexorably as each day followed the last, so inevitably came my day of departure. I moved towards the door of my room. Part of me willing to cross the threshold into new experiences, part of me fighting the motion, wanting only to return to the familiar and comforting space behind me. The emotional dichotomy was overwhelming. It felt as if I was being torn in half. The discomfort was increasing and what started as an internal anguish, quickly became a physical pain. My quiet shadowy solitude was slowly being replaced with brighter tones of colour perceived through heightened senses. The soft still voice of my room was fading into the background, replaced by more urgent noises, strange, sharp and pressing sounds which crowded in on my peace and solitude. As the door opened onto my new life, I was assailed by a cacophony of bright lights and piercing noises which immediately overwhelmed my senses and thoughts, save one: in order to begin a new life, one must first leave the old one behind.

High Radon Gas Expectancy
Sarit Elkon
Israel

Shortlisted for the 2019 International Writing Competition

HE WAS STARTLED the first time he heard the laughter. A woman's laugh from beyond the wall. Jakob looked at the door briefly, then raised his eyes to the murky grate attached to the ceiling. He glanced from side to side, as if the laughing woman might break through the wall, or emerge from between the shelves, or jump out of one of the brown folders he, himself, had written the names on.

He pressed his ear against the wall. It was a laugh entirely imbued with pleasure. And here he was on his own, completely on his own one might say. The voices all came from the outside. Never from inside this room. This room had no one.

'Relax,' he told himself.

But seriously, relax. Every morning, relax – look how tranquil everything is in here. A room that can't be considered large, but if it was ordered a little bit, the room definitely had potential. Two levels below ground. Cool. You couldn't see the sea from the room, but early in the

LEAVING

morning, before he parted from the sun and went back down into the building, the breeze whispered at the back of his neck. Other than this lively laughter, always preceded by a door being slammed at eight in the morning, it was quiet. And even it, the laughter, slowly diminished into a low fire on which bubbled velvet conversations followed by silences made heavy with bodies and sighs.

The rest of the day was quiet. He couldn't say it wasn't. People – how could he put it? – did not exactly stand in line to see him. Even light, real daylight, was not to be found in there. That same small dusty window that hadn't been touched for years is sealed over. Other than the window, there was just your standard lighting; a fluorescent bulb emitting grayish light. And there was the ceiling-fan, quite pleasant, actually, which had been replaced by a primitive air conditioner. In the winters – a standard electric heater. Recently, a yellowish halogen light had replaced the lamp. That sort of thing would never have happened without the official's report.

In that regard, and with reference to the lighting, things were better now.

◆

Jakob gave the official directions on his landline. He explained that he didn't give his private cellphone number to anyone.

'Why private?' the official inquired. 'I thought the office gave each of its employees a cellphone.'

Here we go with the interrogations! Jakob thought, deciding to be careful with his replies. 'I've grown used to my own,' he replied. 'The grip, the keys, the ringtones. All those modern extras just aren't for me. No, thank you!' The directions were simple: 'Use entrance A. From ground level, you go down to minus two on the elevator. Turn left to the stairs.

Go down another half flight, then take a right.' A bunker? Why denigrate? His speech was slow and clear. He repeated the necessary turns twice – left and right.

Trying to buy himself some time, the official decided. He knew it often happened when he announced he would be arriving; straight lines became crooked, the simple became complex, and directions complicated.

The report that came later discussed the question of location, which answered to no known standard. Not health, sanitation or the environment. And it definitely wasn't a suitable place for storing all the files, (there were roughly two thousand of them) that huddled in inappropriate conditions on the metal shelves. And an outdated filing system. Row after row, alphabetized. Family name, comma, first name. Tattered files, one file being swallowed by another, names mingling together. And they, the names, had been written with markers – in all the colors of the rainbow.

'That's it?' Jakob asked.

'Not yet,' said the official, a grim-faced character who wore spectacles. Behind the lenses darted little eyes that hid a missionary's glint. As pompous as his job required him to be. Keeping a stately distance, choosing his words and using professional terms. He wrote notes in a small ledger. 'What about Radon gas?'

'Never here,' said Jakob.

'Have you measured?' (In the ledger the official wrote, *he's close to retirement?*) 'You can't tell if you don't measure. One can't see or smell it, after all.'

'What are you trying to say?' Jakob asked.

'It is one of *the* major health hazards. And this is an area with a high radon gas expectancy.'

'What does it do?'

'Cancer. Do you smoke?'

'No.'

'It's as if you have been smoking your whole life. That's no laughing matter, especially at your age.'

Grayish and emaciated, clothes hanging loosely from his limbs, his thinning hair glued to his skull. *I should have washed it,* thought Jakob. Washing his hair would have taken at least a decade off his age. *The least I can do is stand up straight!*

The official gave him, Jakob, a look of profound scrutiny. Age had bent Jakob's back, his lips were bluish in the grey light. Then there were the sunken eyes – and what about that emaciation! *Perhaps he's already suffering because of it,* the official thought. With atypical generosity, he took a small, thick volume from his black bag. 'Here,' he said, opening the book, 'Quote. The environmental health authority determines that the maximum concentration of radon gas in a residential apartment is 200 becquerels per cubic meter (for your information – this is the unit used to measure radioactivity) and this applies to normal living conditions. Normal, yes? When higher levels are measured, immediate action must be taken for the gas removal. Such actions may include, ventilation, painting the room walls with sealants and additional protective measures. Unquote.'

'What other measures?'

'Let's not get into that now.' The official smiled. He undid his topmost shirt button. 'What about ventilation?'

Jakob felt his throat constricting. *Here we go,* he thought. *Trouble comes in threes.* 'There's a window up there,' he said aloud. 'We can open it.'

'Why is it closed then?'

'Because of the noise. They're doing construction work up there on the main road.'

The official wiped his forehead over and over. He picked up his ledger again. 'All right, that's it.'

'Excuse me – could I talk to you about doing some overtime? After all, I'm...'

Here come the confessions! thought the official. He said: 'All finance discussions should be addressed directly to the administration department!' He hardened his voice and went on. 'But as a general rule, you should know that there are never any free gifts in the public service.'

'He that hates gifts shall live,' said Jakob. 'Of course! But still...'

'If you don't deserve a raise ... well, there's nothing to discuss, then. All right. Like I said, that's it.'

◆

After the inspection, a whole swarm of upper level types began to bother him. From the production department, the computer department (which brought a computer and placed it on the table), the human resources department, the maintenance department (which sent a bundle of thick, black markers), the research and development department, and so on. They all landed on him like false messiahs, blabbering about the prohibition of consuming dry bones. They would stand by the narrow door, poking a hesitant head in, wishing to resurrect dead files without coming all the way inside. And they were all claustrophobic.

Jakob knew, everything was temporary. They'd come and go. Go and forget. And, generally speaking, the building had always had an air of dementia to it. Every request he sent upstairs ended up being forgotten. They said that it – the building – had been erected on the site of a graveyard. A Muslim one probably. Perhaps that explained it. The claus-

LEAVING

trophobia and dementia. It was completely deserted in there after five in the evening.

In the mornings, his ears were peeled to hear what was taking place beyond the wall. It sometimes happened that two women would neigh in there like fillies, and sometimes a thick voice would rise, and Jakob would close his eyes and imagine how she hurled herself into hands, four or five or six hands, pirate hands, adorned with hooks rising to meet firm breasts, and mouths pecking her neck with flattery.

It was hot. He opened his shirt buttons, exposing a white chest studded with tufts of gray hair cascading from it down to that little potbelly he'd grown since he had stopped his morning exercise routine. The one he used to religiously perform with that jumping spring of his. The corner dedicated to that particular activity, a small space between the entrance door and the row of shelves, A-B kissing C-D, was now occupied by cardboard boxes stuffed with files. Since that whole computerization thing had begun, more and more of these file boxes had been brought down from the upper levels to find a place on his shelves. Like stalagmites in a cave of boxes, ever rising from the floor, striving to meet the ceiling.

Before the auditor had come, he roamed the Elysian fields of the Archive uninterrupted. Now all energies were diverted to getting each of the files into the software. He would have done it himself, damn it, if it wasn't for that software thing. A trivial matter on the face of it; he had to encrypt the password with no less than eight digits and characters and symbols, then repeat the action in the row below.

The instructions were written in a black folder, thanks to the Instructions Department. On the first page, highlighted with a black marker was the technical support phone number. He called, but the line was busy.

He received a reproachful email. He 'wasn't moving on with the spirit of the times, properly utilizing the technology' and so on. A concealed threat was hidden in the closing lines.

Jakob thought, *I have permanency, I know the rules and regulations, and they can all just go to hell.* Out of the corner of his eye, he watched the files piling into taller mountains. Each day they brought another box. It was Dima, from maintenance, who came each morning to hurl in another cardboard box which would land with a muffled thud.

'Listen, Jakob, go get some instruction. People are talking upstairs. They say they'll send someone down here to bring some order.'

He sat at his desk and gazed at the window that opened on the computer screen. *Password required.* He tried: *B-l-a-k-e-W-i-l-l-i-a-m1234, M-l-t-o-n-J-o-h-n1234!* Tried again. *R-o-z-e-b-l-a-t-J-a-k-o-b!!1234.*

Error. He called technical support. No progress. This meant, he knew, that they regarded him as being rebellious.

Some lowly type from human resources came. He waded his way between the cardboard boxes. Black t-shirt and black elbows. He walked in, passing the length and breadth of the shelves with a gait that spoke of unspoken revenge.

'It's like a cave here,' he said with a humorless smile. 'Don't you ever get lonely? Perhaps you need a woman to turn this place upside down.' It seemed that this was his idea of humor.

Just in case it wasn't, Jakob replied, 'Just me – the fewer people, the better.'

A week later, an employee from information was transferred to him. She was already sixty, but had refused to retire. Quite understandable really, she wanted the bonuses. Kindly spirits had arranged for her to be transferred from job to job, which was how she ended up in the Archive. They set up a separate desk for her, in the G-H section. She sat there, all presence, like a fifth wheel. She immediately started complaining about the stuffiness and the stench, the absence of light, 'These were catacombs!' She protested. Also, she was hot. Flailing her arms before her face, she undid a button, deepening her cleavage. Nothing sexually oriented, but Jakob stole a glance and was reminded that he still had needs. Good thing he could hardly stand the lady. No dirty looks. He moved his own desk to section A-B and sat with his back to her.

She blurted out, 'Interpersonal relations is not a talent everyone has, apparently!'

The following day, she started nesting, fixing her own corner. Little cacti flowerpots on the desk, a scented candle that whiffed of tropical blossoms, a decorative stationery stand. She nailed a cork board to the wall and pinned exotic sunset postcards on it, waterfalls and galloping horses. When the lady started rolling in a little iron grated table – a most unpleasant example of government-style interior design – 'We'll have ourselves a nice coffee corner,' she said, Jakob said, 'No more!'

Her face retained a sour expression that whole day. As if making a point, she placed a white plastic kettle on her desk. And a large mug next to it. And cookies. All through the working hours, a thick, hardcover notebook sat in front of her. At the end of the day she carefully placed it in her drawer. On his way to the restroom he peeked and saw writing in cropped lines. He thought, *Perhaps she, the lady, has some affinity to culture.* Was she a frustrated poet?

He was almost tempted to say, 'Eve, we've started out on the wrong foot. After all, I am known, in certain circles, as a man of letters.' But he didn't.

He washed his head and shaved and even put on some aftershave. He wore a clean shirt, even inside the collar. And despite his aversion to social chit-chat and technology, was able to carve some words from inside himself. 'This is a nice corner you've arranged for yourself here,' he said.

'It is what it is,' she said, and started fidgeting with the cookie box, tearing the packing, inserting sharp, pointed nails. Like a bird of prey, she clawed out a cookie, holding it between thumb and pointer finger, the pinky raised at a peculiar angle. Other than the nails, nothing with her was in the right place.

'I've heard you'll be getting your own computer soon,' he said.

'You don't say?' She replied, opening her mouth. The cookie was gone, swallowed into the depths of her gullet.

In other words, not interested, thought Jakob, and he returned to his own desk. Good thing he hadn't said anything he would not have been able to take back. *And that,* he thought, *will be the end of it.*

Suddenly she stopped her munching. 'What's that?' She pressed her ear against the wall. 'Hold on, what is that?'

A single high-pitched feminine voice came from beyond the wall, then was joined by another. Two women. 'Oh my!' She was suddenly crimson. She could hear everything! As if it was being said in this very room! 'How come,' she wondered, 'I didn't notice earlier?' She jumped as if bitten by a snake. She clenched her fist and pounded on the wall with it. 'Hello! Hello!' She shouted. 'Look at that!' she said to Jakob. 'You can hear it all in here! Did you know? We need to bring that Ukrainian guy in. We need him to put some sealants on the walls or something. What is this, a commune?'

'It's better if we don't,' Jakob muttered. 'It's crowded in here as it is, I'd say.' Instinctively, he stood before the wall.

'Is that what you call it? Crowded? I say we need to call a spade a spade – there's a whorehouse beyond this wall!'

Ostentatiously, she went to look for Dima, leaving the notebook on the table. Jakob could not resist the temptation. He rose, went to her desk, peeked and saw what he saw. A written record documenting his every action. When he took his breaks. When he went to the restroom. And when he lingered in the restrooms more than was reasonable. When he was sitting idle, when he rose and made odd, unpleasant movements with his arms and with the jumping spring, when he left work (*Note*, she had written, *he's stalling for more hours*). This wasn't poetry.

She was back, Dima with her. Dima stood by the wall and listened. 'I can't hear a thing,' he said.

'A bordello! Do you know what a bordello means? And you can hear it all in here.'

'Perhaps the lady is hearing voices in her head,' said Jakob.

'We need to soundproof,' said the lady. 'This is a government office!'

'We need authorization from upstairs for that. Perhaps we could just open a window?' Dima suggested.

'Open a window? Do you know how much noise we'd get here? What with all the digging.'

'Yes, noise. But you wouldn't hear those other things. And this is a cellar. I'm worried about radon more than noise. You can get cancer without enough air. Have you ever heard of radon?'

The lady gave her cacti flowerpots a crooked glance. 'Yes,' she said, 'I have. Perhaps that is why my cacti are wilting away. And I water them all right. Not too much, and still – they wither.'

'See for yourself.' Jakob pointed at the dry cacti corpses standing on her desk like monuments. 'They're all dead.'

'They're not dead yet,' she said, protesting.

'But they are dying,' Jakob said. 'Isn't it a shame?'

The lady gave the cacti another, more tender look. 'Are they really dying?'

'Without proper ventilation, it's just a matter of time.'

Opening the window wasn't easy. It creaked, it grated. When it finally yielded, a plume of white smoke billowed in, and with it the sound of honking, and a cloud of black soot.

◆

He put his ear against the wall, waiting for the laughter to come like some unfulfilled heart's desire. At his age, he knew some things were better left in the unaccomplished darkness. That was why he pressed his ear against the wall. He closed his eyes and imagined. How lips fluttered with a slight tremor over the laughing girl's, weaving webs of desire. Someone emitted a peal of hysterical laughter, too high-pitched and loud. A bus came to a screeching halt over his head, and the basement filled with smoke and soot and the stench of the street. Soot and more soot, and Jakob breathed deeply, as if approximating the full extent of the damage. He coughed, waited a moment, then rose and dragged his chair under the window. He climbed up and slammed it shut. 'There, we're done now!' he said.

A murky silence settled. He glanced at his watch. The lady wasn't there, nor had she been for the past day or two. Nor the week before. Jakob took a deep breath.

Ten days later Dima came back. He took the cacti off the table. He removed the stationery and the notes, and he dragged the table out. 'What about the kettle, you want it?' He asked. The corkboard was still on the wall with its horses, waterfalls and sunsets. Jakob went over to the board, took it off the wall and tossed it in the wastepaper basket. As for the cacti, he put them on his desk.

And the laughter – it dimmed. Jakob stood, his ears straining to hear the laughter from beyond the wall. Each morning, he pressed his head against the wall and held his breath. Waiting. He was familiar with all the variations of this laughter. Joyful at times, a purring of words dipped in a smile at others. All that was fine. It was the disturbed, prickly, grating, hair-raising laugh that bothered him. Erupting from the other side and smashing against the walls. A woman from beyond the wall broke into evil laughter and his heart sank. Even the door no longer rattled the wall.

Sometimes a silence settled there, filling him with unrest. Sometimes a kind of cough sounded. *Perhaps she's sick,* he thought. *Or maybe she's alone, losing herself in a dry cough. She's in a basement too, and the radon has seeped into her lungs, claimed its hold on them.*

He gave the dry cacti a look, rose and walked, dazed, between the shelves like a man walking in narrow alleys, looking at names he'd written and they, all of them, were strange, and strangers, to him. The names, the handwriting, the girl beyond the wall – strangers all, and silent. Still, this silence that used to fill him with comfort has now turned into a burdening absence of sound.

Dima came back with sealants. 'Listen, we got a letter from the Ministry of Environmental Protection,' he said. 'About the radon gas.'

'Is it really harmful?' Jakob asked, no longer thinking of himself.

'You bet!' Dima said. 'Maybe it was why your lady died.'

'What's that? She's dead, you say?' Jakob remembered her, the lady. Each time he thought of her, an unsavory taste filled his mouth, like a piece of dry bread forgotten in the breadbox and consumed in a fit of hunger.

'They say it was a stroke, but go figure,' Dima said.

Jakob rose and left his room. Left and right, he ascended half a flight. Then two more storeys up in the elevator. Outside, dazzling noontime light blinded his eyes, the sun blazed blades straight into his eyes. Momentarily blinded, pressed against the wall, he suddenly began to fill with doubt. Still, he knew he had to take action. *He who saves one life saves an entire world,* he thought. And it had nothing to do with age, the saving of people.

His back still pressed against the wall of the building, he took sideways crab steps, heading toward entrance B. A bulldozer piled torn bits of asphalt into a large mound and a frightful drill bored holes in the ground and rattled the sidewalk under his feet. He raised his eyes and understood. Through clouds of dust, he saw the roots of tall, glass skyscrapers. Then there was this grunt, a restlessness of the world that surrounded him, as black as locomotive soot. He tried to toughen up. Onward! This was a matter of life and death!

And he reached the door. It was locked. He tapped with an open hand, then banged with a fist. 'Open up!' he screamed. Coughing, dust infiltrating his nostrils, his teeth gnashing at grains of sand that had snuck into his mouth. A tiny plaster fragment infiltrated his right eye. He closed it as he went on pounding on the door. His banging faded, swallowed in the din of the bulldozer, the honking of nervous drivers whose paths it had blocked, and passersby hissing curses.

'Goddamn!' they mutter. 'This is a living hell!'

All That Cannot Be Helped
Joe Eurell
United Kingdom

Shortlisted for the 2019 International Writing Competition

WITH NO FOOD FOR THE JOURNEY father feeds me and my sister lies. She sits on my lap so as the train lurches I hold her with one arm and brace myself with the other. We're lucky to have a seat though. Most of the passengers stumble down the overcrowded aisle.

'Is everyone else on holiday too?' she says.

Father tells me off for asking too many questions but with Aimi he only nods and gives a half-hearted smile.

If they are on holiday, there's no dress code. One woman straightens her skirt, pulls at tights with a pencil line running down them that disappears into her high-heeled shoes. The old man next to her is in overalls rolled to the knees and wriggles his bare feet. He's wearing his winter coat too, the open window showing him no mercy as it circulates warm, sticky air round the carriage.

I know why he's wearing it. We're only allowed two bags. Ours bulge between my feet, the black plastic sticking to my legs. Father sold our suitcases, the ones his parents bought across the Pacific so they could start a new life in California. He sold lots of things before we left, to help mother keep the farm going. There's another question I'm not allowed to ask. What kind of holiday is this without mother?

As the white alders disappear and the pale green scrub recedes I know we've left our home in Camerillo far behind. The view from the window is now copper-coloured dirt, so cracked and dry it has me reaching for my flask. Aimi won't stop fussing until she has some water too. Buildings cast slender silhouettes against the horizon and a Buick parks at the station up ahead. I wonder if this is our destination, a big brash city like Oakland or Sacramento.

The conductor shoves his way down the aisle, banging shutters over windows. The carriage gets dimmer, the old man forced to eat his lunch in the dark. The conductor hovers over us but I won't close my shutter. I will share my seat and share my water but the view is mine. He stares, probably because I'm the only person on the train who shares his blue eyes. Aimi's are blue too but her face is buried in my chest, my sister shy around strangers.

'I can't,' I say. 'She's sleeping.' If father can lie, I can too, a small price to pay to keep the smell of stale bodies and udon broth at bay.

The conductor leans across me and slams the shutter. The gun-shaped bulge at his hip tells me he's not the conductor at all.

'Perhaps he's jealous we're going on holiday,' I say.

Father silently seethes in the dark.

Eventually the old man's hunger outgrows his fear and he opens the shutter to finish eating. Others follow suit and since we didn't stop at the station it occurs to me that they weren't closed to keep us cool but to keep us hidden. When I open mine, my view is the mountains. Snow topped peaks in the height of summer. They look imposing, impassa-

LEAVING

ble, but I'll never know as the real conductor applies the brakes, wheels screaming as the train comes to a stop.

Outside we're greeted by the wind whipping up the dirt. I rub my eyes and spit and father cuffs me round the ear. We join a queue but I can't see where it leads, only the back of the old man's head, grey hair balding at the crown and angry skin that he scratches from the back of his neck.

His shadow is my only shade so I follow close, craning my neck at stars and stripes flapping against a flagpole. Taller still are two towers, wooden crisscross structures with a view of the desert for the men inside them. Men who are holding guns.

Aimi waves at them. Father drops our bags and gently lowers her arm.

'Wait quietly now, Aimi. Like a good girl,' he says.

The queue leads to a hut. My palms are slick at the thought of more men with guns, rivers running through the lines in my hands, but inside the soldier behind the desk is armed only with a pen.

'Name?' he says. But there's no inflection. It's an order.

'Jiro Tanaka,' father says, 'and my children –'

'Issei?' the soldier says. This means first generation, which means father was born in Japan.

Father nods and his name is ticked off a list, the scratch of the pen the only sound in the room.

'I'm Kentaro and this is Aimi,' I say, breaking the silence.

The solider takes one look at us and ticks our names off a list that reads *Nisei*.

We're ushered to a line of barracks. They're poorly constructed, a patchwork of wood. Workmen with tool-belts slung low on their hips hammer away at one, missing a roof.

I'm good at maths but don't need to be to realise there aren't enough barracks for the families huddled around us. This dawns upon them too and there's shoving, fighting as they race to stake a claim. The old man sheds his coat in a doorway, marking his territory.

Father drops our bags by the barrack without the roof. He seems to have dropped the holiday pretence too; both of us knowing no bellboy will collect them.

'Hungry?' he says, and this time I tell the truth. He leads us away and over my shoulder I see that the soldiers have tool-belts too, truncheons they snap off them to beat against the unruly mass of limbs. The old man is pulled by the hood of his coat, still slung over one shoulder. He falls and his arms are up, but they can't soften the wet crack of the truncheon against his temple. Father squeezes my hand. 'Ken, in life you never look backwards.'

The Mess Hall is like my school canteen, only the adults eat here too. The bowl I'm handed is ringed like a tree, yesterday's soup still crusted inside. As the cook ladles beef stew over my thumb I know how the hall got its name. All of the food is messy – there will be no such thing as a solid meal in camp.

I have my fill of watery stew, tasting beef in its juices but not finding a scrap as my spoon scrapes the bottom of the bowl. It's still swishing through my stomach as I lie in bed, looking at the stars. I can't sleep with Aimi tossing. There are only enough bunks to share and she takes it out on me, kicking my shins with her little legs.

'Why don't you go away?' I whisper.

'They won't let me,' Aimi cries, pointing at the watchtower, and without a roof my anger evaporates up and into the night.

◆

LEAVING

I stretch my arm upwards, shoulder straining at the socket.

'Yes, Kentaro,' Miss Goto says, pointing at me with a nub of chalk.

'Abraham Lincoln freed the slaves.'

'Very good, Ken.'

'And he was the sixteenth President of the United States and he was a lawyer and when he was a boy he almost drowned in a creek.'

My voice breaks in the middle of *creek* and I wish one would swallow me up as everyone laughs. At my old school balls of paper – and worse – would be thrown at me, but here there's no paper to spare. I stare at my desk, so ancient it has an inkwell in the corner, and wait for my face to stop flushing.

Being an eighth grade honour student counts for nothing here so I need to show Miss Goto that I belong outside of camp's barbed-wire walls. Only the brightest are released for college, the rest left to gamble on whether war ends before they're old enough to be drafted into it.

We're dismissed and the boys rush to batting practice. I don't have to ask to know I'm not invited. Instead, I pick Aimi up from nursery. A dusty day, the clay darkens my shoes as I walk. It hides the bloodstains where they rub and pinch, my feet growing quicker than the rest of me.

Past women doing their afternoon calisthenics and those scattering seed for the chickens, workmen put the finishing touches to the Post Office. Camp changes like the wind, but unlike us, the wind isn't something camp can contain.

It teases the hem of Aimi's dress as she skips towards me. I'm surprised father let her wear it as her dress is for special occasions and there's nothing special about living in a tar-papered barrack. But today is Aimi's fourth birthday and when she holds my hand, it's sticky. Her teacher has given her jam and I wonder how many more birthday spoonfuls are ahead before she learns of a life where this isn't a luxury.

Father is tending to his vegetables so when Aimi greets him with a hug he raises his arms in surrender as not to dirty her dress. The patch is his new obsession, in the rain, in the dark, and I wish he'd spend half as much time nurturing me. He wipes his hands down his overalls and beaming like the sun above, pulls half a chocolate bar from his pocket.

'Happy birthday, chan,' he says, for once speaking Japanese without cursing – unlike when reading the newspaper, Mitsubishi fighters on the front page and headlines of *Yellow Peril*.

Aimi's eyes grow wide, the jam long forgotten. Black market goods have their price though and with fewer carrots in father's patch, the currency he deals in is clear.

'I wish Momma was here,' Aimi says, putting a pang in my chest. I was beginning to think that after a year here she had forgotten her.

'Your mother's sending lots of birthday love,' father says, pulling a letter from his pocket and a photo of mother next to a bumper crop of corn. While her green fingers were never in doubt I'm old enough to know it's the colour of the rest of her skin that meant she wasn't sent here too.

Father snaps when I try to read the letter, his temper these days shorter than his supply of vegetables.

'No baseball today?' he says, his tone softening. 'Go on, the amount you strike out, you need the practice.'

I'm not built for sport with my narrow shoulders and lithe arms that look like an extension of the bat when I hold it, but father understands how sport fills the hours. In camp, time is the real enemy, not Japan. But his words still sting like the blisters on my feet. He's always wanted a son who can swing a bat and not just quote batting statistics.

I run the whole way, eager not to miss another innings, and in trying not to trip over my laces I almost bump into someone, head first. I

LEAVING

freeze at the sight of his blue eyes and fair hair. The guard from the train. I must be staring at his hip as he says:

'Don't be afraid. They're for your protection.'

The shadow of the watchtower criss-crosses between us.

'Then why do the guns point inwards?'

I run off before he can answer and take a bat. With the teams uneven no one complains. The sun has bleached the pitch flaky white so I can only make out the painted lines from where my teammates stand, bases loaded. I grip the bat like Johnny Mize. Lining up the knuckles, keeping it out the palm. Johnny hit 43 homers for the Cardinals last season, 43 more than I ever have.

The boys whoop and bang the chain-link fence as the guard strides over to the mound. But he's not confiscating the ball. He wants to pitch. With his top-heavy frame it's no surprise when I hit the ground with bat and ball in a cloud of dust.

I know it's bad even before the guard walks away and pain blooms along my hip. In the days to come, the bruising swirls across my skin like marble and all the boys in class want to see. It becomes my badge of honour. Honour from the Japanese half of me, which unlike the bruise, will never fade.

◆

I wake up and pull back my blanket. Rough as hessian, it scratches against my straw mattress and between them both it's amazing I sleep at all. I sneak past Aimi, now in father's bunk, treading only on the floorboards that won't groan under my weight.

Dawn crowns on the horizon but the cold still bites to the bone, making the hairs that have sprouted on my legs stand on end as I pace to the latrines. They're separated by six inches of air; no partitions, no toilet seats and no privacy. My stomach squirms as three days of sticky rice and vegetables vie for their escape. I rule out the toilets with stained bowls, those splashed yellow. Toilet paper, like everything else, is rationed and I won't waste a square on other people's mess.

I choose the cleanest seat and exhale sharply. My bottom will never get used to the shock of cold porcelain. My breath uncurls in the air like steam and my mind drifts to being first in the shower block for warm water, when something fleshy probes my leg. A man knocks knees with me, grunting from the very next toilet, rolls of fat spilling from under his ribs. I pull my trousers up as quickly as I pull the rusty chain down and leave.

The shower wipes away my shame as I cry from the pain in my gut and water cold enough to slow the blood in my veins. I ignore the grey bar of soap on the side and pull one from my trouser pocket, squeezed together from old slivers. I traded this supply for the last of father's vegetables and there won't be any more now he's sick, in the infirmary. The patch has withered without him and I can't be next. The idea of Aimi all alone numbs me more than the shower. Father has always taught responsibility, with the farm and with my schooling, and now he's gone, forgetting we are his. I scrub myself raw, angry at him and his *kuso* vegetables, and when I'm done my skin is mottled like in summer when the mosquitoes have their fill.

Back at the barrack, everyone is up. Shuling bounces Aimi on a sturdy knee and feeds the stove with scraps of wood. I would tell her it's a waste, that the frost isn't even on the inside of the windows yet, but Shuling is an old Taiwanese lady with no better English than my Japanese.

Instead of feeding the fire I pack the floorboards. In summer this keeps the dust out, but the cold is worse, so I reposition the tin lids over the knots in the wood and fold up father's old copies of the camp

LEAVING

newspaper, *The Free Press Weekly*, to slot between the gaps. Miss Goto taught us about irony and it will take all my restraint not to use this in my homework.

I run out of newspaper so rummage through father's things to see if he's hoarded more copies. I find the letter from mother, and a gust flicks the photo of her towards Shuling.

'So pretty, your mother,' she says, but I'm not listening, scouring the letter, which says *assets frozen* and *foreclosure* and other things I don't fully understand. 'Pretty names for children too, Ken and Aimi. American names.'

She means that when you say them out loud and look into our blue eyes, you could never tell. Ken and Amy.

Shuling pats Aimi on the bottom to send her scampering. She picks up the photo and her knees creak, her huge breasts almost touching them. She takes another look at mother and sighs.

'Shikata ga nai,' she says to herself, the fist Japanese I've heard her utter. This means it cannot be helped, an expression in our culture I've never fully understood. She hands the photo back to me. 'Now school, both of you.'

It's as dark when we leave as when we return, and it must be playing tricks because it looks like there's a hole in our barrack. Two panels of wood stripped clean away.

Inside Shuling and her children wear coats, playing *Hanafuda*, the cards weighed down by stones. Not that it matters. The wind out there could toss rocks.

'What happened?' I say and Shuling talks in a rush of Thai, miming at the stove. I can't believe she'd be so stupid as to use wood from our walls but when I scratch the soot inside, it's cold. She doesn't mean our stove. Someone has stripped our barrack to keep their own warm.

For the first time in weeks I'm not cold. Rage flushes inside me like father's fever and I burst out the door. My feet carry me to the frayed edges of a flag that never stops flapping.

The guards are off duty. They have open collars and open bottles of whiskey and pass round a cigar that makes my chest feel tight.

'There's a hole in our wall. You rationed the firewood and now look!' But I'm not sure they hear me through their laughter or see me through the veil of smoke. The blue-eyed guard isn't laughing though as he stubs out the cigar on the heel of his boot.

He follows me to the barrack in silence, and inside, stares at the hole. I wonder if he came because he respects me now my voice is low like a man's or whether he still feels guilty about the baseball. I don't care as long as he fixes the wall.

The guard leaves, returning with a plastic sheet and duct tape, which he throws at my feet. My knuckles tense white but I'm too afraid to use them.

Before he walks out the door, the guard peers over Shuling's shoulder, her family still engrossed in their game.

'Match your Ume,' he says, taking a biscuit from her plate and snapping it in two. 'You've two special cards right there.'

It's strange how he knows the rules. Stranger than how he stares at me differently to the other internees. I follow him, chasing his shadow into the night.

'Nisei!' I shout. The guard marches over and grabs a fistful of my collar. With his smoky breath in my face I see the truth in the elegant features of his own. 'You're half and half like me.' I'm off the ground now, my tiptoes scraping the dirt, before he realises what he's done and drops me, his only reply footsteps quietening in the distance.

LEAVING

◆

The infirmary smells of bleach and lemons. Dead insects collect inside the plastic casing of fluorescent strip lights that are overly harsh, but at least paint father's skin with a healthy glow. The same can't be said for the rest of him. His pillow is sweat-stained and he's lost so much weight that his skin stretches over his skull like putty. This the man who worked eighteen-hour days on the farm, lifting hay bales like they were hollow.

I've imagined this day for so long. It's sustained me in ways the Mess Hall never could, but not once did our release involve father lying there and Aimi crying. I wonder if it's happening because of my run-in with the guard. Whether this ensures my silence.

'That fever hasn't broken yet,' the doctor says. 'He's simply not well enough to travel.'

Father holds a letter with mother's new address. Typhoid is highly contagious so the nurse copies it onto a piece of paper. He gives a few croaky words of goodbye, says he'll follow us when he's better and when the nurse looks away I squeeze his hand so tight, like he did mine on the day we arrived. Aimi waves goodbye and father waves back, a long tube jutting from his arm.

The conductor inspects me more than our tickets as people push past us on the platform, onto the train. Smoke pours from its stack, crowding a cloudless sky.

'She can't travel without an adult,' he says, staring at the wisp of hair that clings to my upper lip.

The guard comes towards us, checking each carriage door is locked. The first time I've seen him since that night outside our barrack.

He takes the conductor aside and faces press against windows, willing the train to leave, with or without us. The conductor shakes his head and blows his whistle but as he steps up into the carriage the guard picks Aimi up by the armpits and hands her to him. I follow and he slams the door on all three of us. The conductor only gawps, his whistle hanging from his lips.

'My wife, she always loved your father's vegetables,' he shouts as the train pulls away, and as he's lost to the smoke I finally know why those blue eyes were always watching, why he came here to watch us leave.

I stand mother's photo up against the window to keep us company. She lives in San Diego now and I daydream to tune out the baby wailing opposite and the sickly smell of cracked leather seats. I imagine waves unfurling on wet sand. Not a grain of it on my skin as I wake up fresh and clean each morning.

The train only goes so far, so we use some of the eight dollars per month father earns in camp for his unskilled labour and take a tram. When I glance at the conductor's hip there's only a change machine full of red pennies.

It drops us so close we walk the rest of the way with palm trees overhanging the sidewalk and the sun shimmering off the silver-blue ocean. Aimi doesn't even mind as my strides get longer and she laughs as I break into a jog and then we're running, both of us the whole way until we're under a street sign matching the nurse's note.

The address is a restaurant. Its neon sign razzes red in the middle of the day. *Jose's Mexicano*. A man in a string vest reads the menu, holding a Doberman on a short leash.

This can't be the right place.

The curtain above the restaurant twitches and mother rushes from the side-door, barefoot into the street. She looks just like the photo only her hair is grey, streaks of it at her temples, ageing her more than the three years we've been apart. Aimi tugs my shirt and hides behind me.

LEAVING

She's shy around strangers.

Mother holds us close, pulling me down by the neck as I'm half a foot taller than her now. Tears warm my cheek, impossible to tell who they belong to.

'My babies,' she says. 'Ken and Aimi,' and Shuling is right, to the man watching us from the window, bussing dishes, we look like any other American family.

Only this is not Camerillo. Trash overflows in the streets and can't hide the smell of piss coming from the alleyway where our front door is.

'Ken, I don't like it here,' Aimi says. 'Let's go home.'

But she's too young to remember the farm. Aimi is talking about camp.

I scoop her up and kiss her on the forehead, the three of us walking into the alley and up the stairs.

It cannot be helped, I say to myself.

The Easy Now
BLYTHE EVELEIGH-EVANS
United Kingdom

SHORTLISTED FOR THE 2019
INTERNATIONAL WRITING COMPETITION

THE JOURNEY OUT WEST WAS LONG, and even though both the man and the semi- truck were used to long journeys there was something about the swell of the sun and the mist that clouded out the windows of the front carriage that made this one particularly unbearable. It had been several kilometres since the last truck stop and all that remained of his oasis was a Styrofoam cup gestating a series of slowly melting ice cubes. The sun hung low and lazy in the sky and the man found himself drifting into an accidental lethargy, hypnotised by the zoetrope of wheat fields that swung by his window and the continual flicker of the newly ignited streetlamps, natural light mingling with artificial in a haze of colour and shadow. The road itself was like an artery, deeply entrenched in the landscape and busy all the time.

The man was large, partially balding both in the face and temples and containing within him a certain sadness that came from the open road and the changing landscapes and his own unease at what was essen-

LEAVING

tially a continual loneliness.

The man had never been good looking, and as he'd aged the fullness of youth had left him, and he had become increasingly deflated. Like the slow emptying of a bladder, until his skin hung loosely over a road of tendons and vessels. He looked frequently at his watch even though both the minute and second hand were broken and his t-shirt clung to him, white with salt and greying yellow with bacteria and foodstuffs. Not that he was dirty, just that the road demanded of its wanderers a certain sacrifice.

Sunset conceived along the horizon and the man felt himself become transient in the tangerine glow. He thought often about the other truckers, ones he saw occasionally out on the open road, exchanging a slight nod as they slid away from each other into darkness or obscurity. They all wore the same clothes, drank the same off-brand beer and squinted samely through the front carriage window. His tribe, though he has never met most of them and never would. He imagined them all together, hundreds of men making journeys from North to South and Wrexham to Peckham. Always leaving, never quite arriving. Stuck in a permanent state of motion, yet in the driver seat he sat perfectly still. The job itself was like hypnosis, like a cult or a religion; it dominated his thoughts and exhausted his focus until reality itself was a kind of dream. Not that the man didn't dream also, he often found his mind wandering to a woman with kind eyes and soft hands who would stroke the curve of his cheek and laugh in a way that muffled the empty time. They would sleep in the same bed and early morning when he left her she would cry. The children in his mind existed only in periphery, small dark forms: warm bodies and kinesthesis.

A truck stop crowned the mess of terrain in his front window. They all looked more-or-less the same, which he liked, and they all offered practically the same food, which he liked also. This one was especially small, turning on its edge and wrapped long ways around a bend in the road. He pulled into the car park and shed himself of his vehicle. The tidemarks of dirt and rust gave the walls a kind of written language. A monotonous sign spelled out *Tommys*, no apostrophe.

'What can I do you for?'

The woman was middle-aged and grey-rooted. Her eyes were rimmed in a layer of kohl and bloodshot, black and red rings around an iris that made her pupil look like it was the centre of a cartoon bull's-eye. He pretended that he knew her and checked his watch anxiously.

Later, once his food had arrived, the man watched the waitress leave out of the staff door to smoke a cigarette in the liminal space between the diner and car park. He imagined they were married; maybe they would get along, maybe their kisses would taste like nicotine. This was something that he did, not just to waitresses but also to the foreign woman at the table opposite and the women in cars who passed by him on the motorway. He owned them in his mind, where they lived together and were in love always. They ate and slept together, had children or didn't. Sometimes the women were opinionated, sometimes they were passive, their temperaments mattered less than the way they made him feel, and the fact they couldn't leave.

The eggs were vinegary, yet he cleared his plate and sat watching the ebb of evening diners as his tongue turned slowly numb. It was a kind of dance: the way they entered, the movement of their bodies against each other, waitresses swaying away from leering men and towards family travellers. The bell at the door forming a rhythm of arrival and departure. It was a kind of hyper reality, the white and black linoleum checked floor and the juke box ignored in the corner. An American-ism that was in itself a parody considering that he was in the heart of the West-Mid-lands. The walls were dotted with pictures of famous people, and old people, and vinyl records of songs that hadn't been popular in decades, though the man was old enough to remember them.

'Hey lady giv'us another cuppa.' The man interrupted himself, as he often did. The woman didn't notice him immediately, and in that short window he watched her unencumbered. Her uniform clung to her unflatteringly, her eyebrows were thin and over-plucked and on the inside of her right wrist was a tattoo, *Jacob*, underlined.

'And…a pie if you've got one.'

The woman nodded wordlessly and disappeared behind the busted whitewash door of the kitchen, reappearing moments later and spilling coffee over the tablecloth in her carelessness.

'Y'all right there missus?'

She looked at him properly for the first time that evening, and let out a short joyless laugh that impregnated the air between them with an inarticulate sadness.

'Getting on.'

'What time d'you get off?'

'I leave eleven thirty.'

The woman actually closed up around one most days, missing the last bus and having to make the journey home in a darkness punctuated with street lights and the far off blink of aeroplanes she liked to mistake for stars. It scared her to walk alone, but leaving was better than staying the night in the small cot in the back room where the hum of the boiler made sleep a flirtation she could never quite consummate.

The man asked her to sit for a while and so she did. They talked about nothing in particular and didn't ask each other's names. She learned about the open road, how he felt leaving city and county in perpetuity. How in a short time he would leave here too, head east and most likely forget about the truck stop all together. They blended in his mind, he said, formed a tableaux of coffees and pasties and shit-stained bathrooms. You remember the landscape even less, he said. The man spoke like he was rehearsing the lines in his head before giving form to them out loud, with his mouth lagging oddly behind his eyes. He checked his watch often and seemed far away from the diner they both sat in, but he was lonely and scared of the empty seat opposite him, so she stayed. Sometimes that's what people need, she thought, a moment of singular connection.

Right before the man left, some hours later, and after he had paid for her third cup of coffee, he tried to give her a phone number.

'It's mine.' He shoved a ripped-off piece of paper with a series of digits written in scratchy biro into her hand. She couldn't meet his eye.

'Thanks.'

The semi-truck pulled out of the car park slowly and with much reluctance. Its headlamps were misted and so the red and white lights were somewhat dampened into a soft orange and faded grey. The side of the carriage bore an advertisement that was impossible to make out in the night and as she watched the man was blotted out by the shadow of the driver's seat. The slip of paper sweated slightly in her hand, and as she fumbled in her pocket for a cigarette the woman let the number fall from between her fingers and away into the mess of rubbish that lined the edge of the street. It wasn't that she didn't like the man, hadn't constructed a version of herself that married and kept him. Wasn't capable of inventing a future between them that didn't end in total unhappiness. But her world was three streets and the idea of a fourth. Shadows reflected back at her through post cards and tourists and calls from her cousins in Scotland. She was Andromeda, chained the proverbial rock of a truck stop which smelled of burger meat and had only one working women's toilet.

LEAVING

This was it in the end, she supposed, reaching for something you were destined to fall short of. She had read it in a book once, about rich men in old America, and though her memory disappointed her on the details she remembered a fast car, and a woman and a green light. A traffic light she supposed, though she much doubted the type of light mattered one jot. Just as the last glut of engine noise died out amongst the harmony of the motorway the woman forgot about the man and his truck and his loneliness altogether. Likewise for the man leaving the truck stop, the impression of the meal and the woman refused, quite disagreeably, to sit properly in his mind. Soon all he was left with was a small stain of pie filling on the hem of his shirt and the image of a woman whose eyes, black and red like range targets, spun ceaselessly round in their sockets.

The road, which stretched endlessly out in front of him by day, was shortened to the immediate stretch of visible ground by night. A cage of light moving slowly through an invisible sea. Consciously, the man knew that the world around him still existed, that the trees and rape seed fields passed him unknowingly in the darkness, but still he liked to imagine that beyond the confines of the driver's carriage there was simply nothing.

Sometimes the man imagined he was a shark, moving constantly under threat of death or drowning. It made the journey easier if he believed there was no alternative, that he was built this way and that it would always be like this.

Sometimes the man imagined he was on a submarine, that the smaller cars that passed by him far below were fish. Sometimes he imagined he was in outer space, surrounded by a vacuum and tethered only to the *terra firma* by a long range radio: his truck radio. Ballads became articulations of his own loneliness; songs of the stars; weather reports became scientific predictions of impending meteor showers. Sometimes the man imagined that the voices on the other end were loved ones calling from far away,

'Oh yes,' he would say, 'tomorrow's a scorcher –'

'Highs of thirty-eight degrees...'

'But I'll be home soon, wake us up with a cuppa –'

'Drivers are advised to take care...'

'Yes,' he huffed softly, 'yes, I'll take care...'

The Red Hand of Rosie

Joe Fuller
United Kingdom

I T SEEMS AS IF I AM ENAMOURED WITH LEAVING.
Leaving something of myself at every turn, like a cat cheek brushed against brick.
To come back in a threadbare, blue ripped hoodie.
Reliving what I left.
Feels counter-intuitive to leaving.

◆

Picture the scene on a sun-shy July night with cloud obscuring but never hiding the scorch, the tarmac is bubbling hot and would easily cook walking shoes and bare ham feet. Rattlesnakes slither, things pop up and descend, speed up and slow down. A humid air crawl, the dash is slick with sweet sweat. My head is cracked spiderweb style with blood claiming orifices like travellers on parched landscapes. Her scent, still unwashed from the contours of my neck giggles and plays with my inhibitions as my arm plays hand games with the handbrake. I might clock it up and clock off, rolling stone it until I hit a cliff in my dream daze, recourse and steer the ship because nothing would be nothing when you're dead. I make myself look half presentable in a wing mirror dash: scooping and sculpting greasy long hair, checking my turkey basted skin that's gone cough drop coloured in the confused cold hot mix. I finger dance with a box of matches, strike up the band and huff that cancer-stick till I'm semi high, before my foot inches down on the tiger pedal and the roar of it startles.

◆

I'm after clapping my hands to the bar in shadows and silhouettes.
 She's hot and got text thumb.
 Inside, she slathers my steak in Peruvian sauce.
 'Your fly's undone. Your shoes are undone. This steak. Is well done.'
 Known only in these parts and mean parts as 'Rodeo Rosie', her pink hair has been curtain dangling from my bed for seven years. Ask my little rodeo if we're in love. I'd like to think she'd stitch you up porcupine style with the shutterbox of toothpicks she always fingers.
 'I'll lace them when we split.'
 I mean it, I have no intention of getting head wrapped by those cali legs. I fumble with my fly to compromise and gaze up at her minty eyes as she brings two utensils down on a poor crustacean, who I swear simpers on a death blink.
 'Hmm,' Rosie muses, cross slicing my eye peppers with red shrapnel. The table clotted with red bombshell. 'Hmm?'
 She tugs damn hard on the hem of a shirt of a wandering waiter. 'You're paying right? You don't mind?'
 My eyes milk over, a courtesy wave stops hand cramp. I watch her spidermonkey the teen with delicious long nails that snap on his collar like cashew nuts, whispering feverently, slapping a collar kiss, she lets the poor guy retreat to the kitchen to breathe his orgasm out.
 'What was that?'

'I was just ordering a bottle of cham…'
'No.' I say delicately, smoothing a napkin 'That was you being –'
'Friendly.'
'Extremely, and that's putting it nice.'

Rosie changes her story to something about discounted drink babble and I make sure to cuff my ears at every angry interval.

'You wish you had friends who touched you like that –'
'It's twenty two fifty, with a bit of feeling –'
'I'm taking Poco home with me tonight –'

It's not even the mention of Poco – our residential shared brown bred tabby – but I'm already lighting sparks with cutlery friction when she utters the atom bomb.

'It's not gonna work out.'

I stop before I hit ignition, the choir of diners around us seem to sing 'good call'. Putting the wine boys and girls on the back foot, I swipe a glance at a gaggle huddling in the doorjamb, texting bored, cautious. Nervously stoned.

'What do you mean it's not gonna work out?'

My teeth grind pepper grounds.

'I don't like you dictating how friendly I can be. The kid didn't mind.'

Waiter boy is back with a breeze in his step, a clink of glasses between thumb and index. He does not introduce the drink but it's a vampire pulpy concoction. Bloody red sting.

'I'm not paying for that.'
'You are paying for that or I walk.'
'Then fuckin walk. It's over anyways, right?'

The bottle lands on a dime spin, I pour myself a quick thimble, the tipple tumbles.

'On the other hand, if you wanna stay, just swig that bottle and we'll forget this whole thing.'

She slips on a pair of white gloves and strangles the bottle shaft, it gives me the gigs, Rosie gets comfortable and swills the drink raw. Comfortable fingers, wet, soggy, snapping, she flicks red marinade over the carcasses of swan napkins and spatters me with the violent juice. I wrestle it back, fill up a chalice and grin, hiccuping ecstasy. Reminiscing, painting a grape canvas on skin, a torrid affair in my blood. A passed out tongue that slithers and slimes as we hiss about all we hate through the night.

♦

Fast forward an hour and we're advised on the pudding options. Rosie has my plastic card and barely stutters, but I'm too far gone to care. She swipes on the bounce growing glee, saucer eyes, money hungry. Putting the kids out of step, pace and time. They're siren-called by her possession and attracted to my money as she ruffles a few shirts on the passing, which causes me to bite my lip bloody. By the time the creamed, whipped brownie hits the deck, my oxygen suckers are too sore to lick.

'Looks nice.' I drunkenly gesture to her puddling, a curt curd and a wafer boat.

'It's average. Little dry. Too crispy on the edges,' she grunts, spitting pastry shards into the lemon sea. I glare a retort and twist my neck into a left, right headrush, giving the final few working stiffs a white chinned, chocolate dribble scare. There's shadows by the bar, couples talking suppertime talk, Glass talk, sex talk and brittle bone talk. Slurring mullets, scarves, mustachios. My little Rodeo is glowing euphoric, pink, and I feel the glee of a teenager, despite her general asshollery, in knowing how the outside wind will buffer and batter her skirt.

She snaffles the curd.

LEAVING

I suck down the brownie.

'I just need the –'

'Toilet?' she slurs. 'Same.'

Coming close in a hold-me-up drunken waddle, she snatches her cold hand flesh in my warm bruised gripper and slides me to the toilets by the bar. Semi derelict in a different world, back to back slabs of oak blacked and stained with the smell of old brew.

'I was thinking, we could have a good time?' And as my shadow crosses her, she barks like a choking dog: 'Not that! Not yet!'

Rosie feeds me a sticky bag of blow. Safe in the dim dark we split her sole note in half and rip apart whichever president is in charge. I'm all questions with electric prickled fingers but she plays her nose xylophone style and winks like a shuttering blind. Questions procure answers. Proceed, baby. Proceed into a deep, dank tomb.

The toilet has all the noise of a shower because the sky outside has cracked into triangles. It pelts rain like a freshly crying baby and encourages lightning strokes, which charm up the mirrors with flash and dazzle. The bulbs are popped glass dripping scolding fluid, and the sole window, partially split, enters me into a flooding zone.

'Anyone in here?' I goad the waiter and he stalls: 'I'm locking up!'

Drip. Drop.

I jangle a pair of pocket keys to illustrate my point, ripping the rust peel away like a banana to reveal shiny slivers of metal skin.

The scabs drift away around my piss soaked boots and I trawl to the line-up of mirrors, satisfied, I pinkie pinch the note, smoothing the hell and transgressions out of a green face. I give the middle mirror a good hammering knock.

One…

Two, three….

AWARD WINNING STORIES

And wait for the retort..

I'm increasingly puzzled as a minute stretches into two because this is our blow bar; when we go to our respective piss rooms we always signal our misdeeds with a heady three point knock, we have for months, and she hasn't knocked back so I'm feeling antsy.

'Rosie?'

I ditch the sticky bag for a second and pound on the mirror as panicked as a drowning crewman, dislodging some tile shards in the process, racing squelched footprints to the other oak door I creak it open a bit...

'Rose?' I croak into the void.

The void gives me nothing but that cold drip feed of finality. From what I can make out, it's an edge less soaking and sodden but a drop more dead. Desolate, even. I go to call again when a hand seizes me from the shadows.

'Hey man, it's okay.'

He's a mothball man in a tartan coat, old, kindly type whose bones would break as easy as his walking stick. 'If you're looking for a little pink haired lady, she went to catch some air some minutes ago.'

I breathe my thanks and give the guy a wide berth as he clears my vision to take off for a bowel movement. Passing the bar, slanderous murmurs, drunk chick talk while fingers flop into the nut bowl.

Out in the chill, I clear the awning without much trouble and squint to the far end of the car park in which running feet have been ran bloody. Footprints dissolve and are reborn by the torrential overhead. There's three rust buckets parked up, not chundling but capable. There's blood in the water and a pink high heel doing a dolphin dive.

'Rosie?' I question, making for the sinking shoe. Metal taste, eel slipper touch. Smell wrapped in a perfume, concrete, grass and sand charmer touch. Past the pub wall curve, I'm hit by a double-whammy.

LEAVING

Ugly cologne and the batting side of a steel pipe.

'You done fell for it! You done fell for it!' chortles a southern hillbilly with scuffed up boots and torn jeans, his voice, just a nipple twist away from female. I see nothing but blue and I'm knocked blind onto my knees. Hanging position assumed, he takes swings into my guts. Swears open a gouge on my neck, causes a shiner and dots my scalp with spit salivated, tossed carelessly. On the floor my head rings tolling bells of fire and pain, leaning down he blows a cloud of menthol gum my way 'You need to take off those rose tinted glasses son, she don't give a damn about you –'

A siren cuts the sting of gum short, painful. Chunky blues and thick warning reds glaze the ground, the vehicle whoops, the window slides down and the hillbilly slides to his feet. A slit in my eyelids gives me fair show of a tired, rounded head behind the motor. Black? White? It's possible.

'What's going on here?'

My throat fails me, my chest feels crushed as if by a heavyweight demon from the heavens, I'm certain a rib or two is in peril. The hillbilly assailant changes tact, he walks big-balled to the vehicle until ordered to grind the brakes.

'Let's hold it there. Why is that civilian on the floor?'

'He's a hophead, sir... a druggie.... he attacked me.'

'You always go carrying around a big ole' pipe just in case?'

'Needs must, I'm pretty banged up.'

'Nevertheless. I'm going to have to ask you to set the weapon down and get in the backseat. I'll have to dial the other guys for the sad sack, assuming he still has breath in his body.'

Neither of the two share anything apart from a yawn, as if my beating was a common street occurrence. A beat or two passes before…

'Backseat, fella. And this time, I'm not asking.'

'I'm beyond cold and wet, officer,' the hillbilly groans, lowering his voice to a shrunken shrimp mewl.

'Then the backseat is the best place for you, I got the heating on all roasty toasty.'

'I have cash…' and the order of the day changes magnificently, the officer drops his radio, snags a wad of big bribe money and snarls: 'Get out of my sight.'

♦

I'm fed into the car park gutter where the rain collates, semi stripped, jacked of a fair wallet of backup change and curled up like a newborn baby left to catch pneumonia.

'If you got any sense, you'll stay dead.' He toussels my hair and hops into a four door. My four door. There's a girl with him, naked foot pressed against the done up glass.

♦

I give them a two day start, rolling in a hotwired six wheeled nightmare, rolling in stolen clothes and wearing stolen pomade. There's chewing tobacco and partly chewed cigarettes from glovebox to behind to beerbox to cooler. The tiger pedal jammed down in a mad rush, the sun shy July giving no mercy tonight because I'm round the bend from my abode baby, and you'd be dumb to be here. I pull up and scoop up Poco on his nightly rounds.

The neighbours will later report a curse of gunfire.

It seems as if I am enamoured with leaving.

Mirror, Mirror
Lucy Grace
United Kingdom

Shortlisted for the 2019 International Writing Competition

THE HOUSE IS QUIET NOW, it settles and breathes out beneath me. I can relax whilst they're not here. I'm sure they'll be back. I am not leaving. People think that because I'm old, I don't understand what's going on, but they have no idea. I see everything.

The crying is a mewling, a raw scraping like when the cat got caught in the gardener's mole snare. It's coming from the lady's bedroom. From my place at the top of the stairs I can see the corner of the landing where the man of the house is pacing outside the door. They won't let him in. Water is pooling on the steps, sloshed from a basin lip by the harried housemaid. Silence thickens like sauce on the hob. The doctor isn't here, nobody called for him. There is movement at the bedroom door and the man is stepping back. The housemaid rushes from the stifling copper taint of the overheated room and past me, quickly returning with the cook. What on earth they need cook in there for I have no idea. It's a roomful of women now, the only men in the house are outside the closed door and outside the kitchen window, where cook's eldest brother waits. He covers and uncovers greased black hair with his cap, eyes dark with not knowing. Both men are walking and waiting, one upstairs and one downstairs.

The bedroom door is opening and the man of the house swims in as cook swims out holding a bundle tightly against her bosomed apron. She is shaking her head to the man and from inside the room there is crying again, only this time it is not a rasping newborn but the lady of the house, diminished.

Cook pauses at the top of the stairs to gather her skirts with one hand. I see the swaddled baby open its eyes and they are as black as coal, the hair dark and silky thick, and the baby looks directly into me, into its own reflection. I know this is the beginning of the secret. Cook is running down the stairs on surprisingly deft feet, and out through the kitchen door where she hands the bundle to her pacing brother and he is crying and looking and they all hold together briefly, three dark heads in a blackberry clump. The brother sets off around the back of the house down the lane where he still lives with his mother and younger siblings, some still at school, but most in service in other, bigger houses.

♦

Everyone has been wearing black all week. The house is held darkened under cloth like a silenced parrot. The lady is up and out of bed, on occasion taking walks down to the bottom of the orchard. There is a patch of newly turned earth there. Sometimes the man accompanies her, but she returns alone, skirts dirtied in the mud.

No-one can find the lady. Tea was due to be served half an hour ago, but she isn't sewing in the sitting room. She is vanished. I know where she is, but no-one ever asks me. No-one has thought to look outside.

LEAVING

Cook is startled by a single knock at the window; leaving the jam boiling she follows her solemn brother down to the dirt patch where the lady is scrabbling on the ground. Tears fall on a clump of violets she is trying to plant in stony mud. Cook's brother and Cook help her up and back to the house, until the housemaid comes out to take his place. The brother melts away as the jam burns.

◆

Another baby comes. She carries this one over the winter and it is birthed in the bedroom. This one has pale skin and pale hair and the man is proud. I hear cook tell him it looks just like the one that was lost. Only a few of us know that is a lie. The man is pleased he has mended the broken past. When he looked into me at the top of the stairs, I told him he was a fool, but he didn't listen. Some people only see what they want to see. He will learn.

◆

It has started to snow. The house is so cold that someone even painted the inside of the windows last night. Jack Frost is the one who does that. I don't remember letting him in, but sometimes people slide underneath the doors. I've seen them.

◆

She is talking to herself again, a half-whispered singsong of nonsense. As she passes me on the landing I look hard at her, showing my displeasure at the choice she made. Every baby deserves a life no matter how black its eyes, and it is wrong of her to deceive the man like this. Each time she looks at me I show her her wickedness and she loses a little more of her mind.

Soon she will forget that her dark-eyed child is growing in the cottage in the village and will believe she actually lies under the dirt. She deserves to feel this.

◆

The man has gone from the house. He left in a uniform when others came to collect him. The postman brings letters from France, but the lady puts them on the mantlepiece, unread. I am worried they might fall into the fire, but she has little concern. She moves as if underwater, slowed. Her pale daughter, Viola, is beginning to adopt these mannerisms too, drifting through rooms without leaving an impression, taking on quiet hobbies such as reading and sewing. She rejects musical tuition, alarmed to leave a noise. Her mother loses sight of her and both begin to fold inward, but separately.

◆

Cook's brother is here again. He ran up to the house when he heard the news, but it was no use. The telegram said, 'Lost At Sea', but the man was lost to his lady wife a long time ago. She is still underwater. She no longer paddles and instead floats through dark reedy days, barely surfacing. Cook's brother cannot reach her.

When they were together before, there were sparks of love, secret moth murmurs and fingertip brushes. Only once was there the hurried connection on the floor in the sitting room, urgency and longing spilling out under skirts and buttons. She briefly stroked his skin, so different to her husband's, and after he had gone she cried and knew that she could never live properly now. Once was enough.

She looked at herself as she passed me on the stairs and I told her how it could be, but she wasn't brave enough. Some of them aren't.

LEAVING

There is a knock at the door and an air of excitement amongst the staff. The pale daughter has a pale suitor, and today he is taking her on a boating lake. She is unable to swim and a little afraid but knows he is her chance to leave. I look at her for the last time as she steps down the stairs, and I feel it is a shame that it will inevitably end here.

♦

Today is another black day. The lady does not cry. I hear the staff talking about her after the service, how she stood at the empty graves side by side, father and daughter, looking without seeing, imagining their bodies in the watery depth. Cook finds it difficult to console her. The patch of bare soil under the tree at the bottom of the orchard has been reclaimed by weeds long ago and no-one goes there now. Few know it too is vacant – they choose not to be reminded it is there at all.

♦

The house is filled with emptiness. Sometimes I forget that the lady is still here. She makes no noise as she slowly passes, her reflection is fading. I was disturbed this morning by a scratching at the window, but it is only the blackberry brambles enquiring against the glass. She does not see them. She is barely alive.

♦

She has been dead and alone for several weeks. I keep an eye on her body as it passes through the indignity of rank smells and wet decomposition before it begins to desiccate. There was not much of her to begin with – she began to dry out when the staff left. Cook was the last to go. She too was elderly, and the money had ended years before. All that remained was the house – men in brown overalls came to collect the clocks and the dining table and the chandeliers. They tried to take me, but I clung to the wall with my fingers of brass screws. I am this house. I'll deal with the next ones when they get here.

There are many more.

◆

There is another sign on a stick in the garden. I watch the man from the van trying to put it up, but the brambles do their job and keep him on the other side of the wall. In the end he nailed it clumsily to the gate post, but I was pleased when the vines told me of the smears on his trousers, how the blackberry juice mixed with his blood from pricked fingertips and stained the painted white wood of the sign. That'll show them.

◆

It is autumn. There is a plump, shiny man with a clipboard in the hallway. He has glanced up here but not been to see me. I'll give him the benefit of the doubt – he has not yet realised it is my house.

I hear a car stop and a door slam, and the man moves towards the door. It opens onto a woman with eyes as black as coal and a dark, silky rope of hair. She seems familiar, back from the dead. She has not been in this house before. I watch as she steps gently over the threshold. The shiny man does not speak. He moves aside as she walks along cold tiles, busies himself with his phone as she explores the downstairs rooms. I steel myself to show her reflection as she passes, and she smiles at me. It is the second time I have seen eyes as dark as hers.

All will be well.

There are others here. She has come here to live, and she has brought others. I hear them downstairs. The woman has a man with her, a man with beautiful skin and fierce hair. He walked past me on the landing and

LEAVING

I reflected him directly, true and strong and proud of his family. I will allow him to stay.

The girl children have surprised me. Here they come – the first one up the stairs is a replicant of her mother, smiling and shining and glowing with youth. She rakes her fingers through a dark fringe as she passes me, acknowledging yet not lingering, recognising my purpose and position in this house. She is quickly opening doors into rooms, putting her head in and out like a jack in the box, sure of herself and trusting her quick decisions. I like her.

She enters the end bedroom, the one with two windows, and I hear her feet on the boards as she walks to the window. There is a scrape of stiffened sash as she raises it four inches and puts her mouth to the gap.

'Lily!'

Our silence is broken as she calls out to the garden. I am startled by the youthful sound – it is not unpleasant, but unknown. It will take some getting used to.

Back in the hallway there is a softer tread. The first girl runs down to the half landing, greeting her sister. Side by side, the twins walk up the stairs. As they approach, I look again, unable to make sense of what I see. Both are the same height, weight, build, and have the same features – undeniably sisters.

Yet whilst Poppy's eyes reflect the deep black centres of her flowery namesake, Lily's eyes are as pale as her skin. Her hair is blond and disappearing at the edges, her freckled skin reflected in my speckled glass. None of them know why she is the only white duckling in this family, but none of them ask, either.

◆

It is Christmas, and the house is full of warm smells and light. There is a party, and during the evening I finally see her, the baby who was not underground. She is an aged woman now, almost a century old. Her once black hair is silvered and iron grey, her skin polished chestnut.

She rises carefully up the stairs towards me, trembling hand on the rail, and I know in an instant that I will show her mother just once. After all, it was me who punished those who made the wrong choice years ago, I have a role here. I wait until I am sure it is her, until I hear someone calling, 'Tea, Violet!' from below the stairs and then I know. I will give her the answers, she will want them. But people don't seem to matter about such things now. It's all strange to me.

She's nearly on the top step, it has taken her a while to walk up the stairs on her aged legs. As she approaches and glances at her reflection, I show her. She stops and looks at the image of her unknown mother in the mirror. She touches the blond hair wonderingly, the translucent skin, she holds her hand to the blue veins on her neck. I see her notice the shape of her body fill the pale reflection perfectly; she turns, holding out her arms and lifting her chin to look directly into blue eyes. Raising fingertips to the mirror, she reaches out to touch herself, to connect with her mother and her secret past, just once. As she touches the glass I let go of the lady's image and return the reflection of Violet's centenarian self, and she looks.

◆

I don't interfere with this family much now. They seem to get on well without me. Sometimes, secretly, I show the girls who they are, but never when they are looking. I wait until they are walking away from me, high ponytails swinging, and I lay their retreating reflections one on top of the other, dark over blonde over dark over blonde, until I can see no difference. I'll get used to them.

Some of them get used to me.

Locked In
Peter Hankins
United Kingdom

3rd place in the 2019 International
Writing Competition

'It's painless, effective and quick,' Norma said, squeezing my hand, 'You'll be dead in no time, darling, without any discomfort. I just need to *source* a couple of things, and we need to make sure we get half an hour alone. But don't worry. I'm on the case – it won't be long.'

No! I was thinking. *Stop! I've changed my mind! I don't want to die!* But she couldn't hear my thoughts. There was nothing at all I could do. I was paralysed, unable to move. They didn't really believe I was still there; but I was. 'Locked-in Syndrome', that's what they call it.

She smiled and pushed her glasses back up with one finger. I'd noticed in the past that when she was excited she did that frequently. Why? Did a burst of enthusiasm somehow make her glasses slide down quicker? Did it cause an excess of nose-sweat or something? I noticed that I was becoming needlessly irritable; that wouldn't help. I'd learned to stay calm now. She glanced around the sunlit room, gave me a quick kiss, a plucky smile, and left.

I could not complain about God's injustice. In fact, making due allowance for His mordant sense of humour, I had to admit that he had given me pretty much what I deserved, right on the button. I was hoist by my own petard, if 'hoist' means 'condemned to death' and 'petard' means 'endless talk about the right to die'. Whatever was wrong with me, it hadn't affected my memory, which in quiet moments – I had a lot of those now – replayed to me with pin-sharp fidelity my many lectures to Norma on the desirability of voluntary euthanasia.

There we were after Norma's excellent cassoulet, for example, me clearing up what was left of the second bottle of unoaked Rioja at the grand old dining table her uncle had left us.

'Was that OK?' she asked.

'What? Oh, yuh,' I said. Actually it had been superb, and the product of many hours of 'sourcing' and cooking, but at the time that hadn't seemed important. 'You see,' I said, 'we still behave as if suicide was a religious issue, but *rationally* it's simply about quality of life.'

'Yes,' she said, 'of course.'

'I mean,' I said, 'if I couldn't live a full life, I'd want to end it.'

'Would you?'

'Of course. I mean, if I was like, paralysed; what's the point of living? If you can't do anything? But it's actually illegal to kill yourself! Can you believe that?'

'No.'

'You know what Damon Runyon said? "In this town, suicide is strictly illegal, though I am never able to find out what it is they are able to do to a man who has killed himself"! I mean, whose life is it anyway? You know? Like that play? Oh forget it, you never know about stuff, do you? But you get my point?'

'Of course.'

'I want you to promise me,' I said, like a drunken idiot, 'if I'm ever, you know, mentally gone, or lost my marbles, or crippled, I want you to take me to that place in Switzerland. The one where they help you bump yourself off.'

'Are you sure, darling?'

'One thousand per cent!'

Although I remembered that conversation, and others like it, with painful clarity, I could not remember how I came to be paralysed. I could remember a normal August day, and then waking up in September in this pleasant hospice room, totally unable to move or speak. It *was* an agreeable room, with good quality wooden furniture and cheerful daffodil paint on the walls. Opposite me by the door hung a big, swirly, abstract painting which I expect was meant to promote calm spiritual reflection, though to me it looked like a hurricane in a paint factory.

To my surprise I was indeed getting some calm spiritual reflection done. I was forced now to lie still, keep calm, and pay attention to the quiet moving chain of the minutes; the gradual passage of sunlight across the room and the slow changes in the weather outside the window. I had to give my full attention to the music they occasionally played for me, from my own collection, and I passed many hours reviewing my memories. For the first time in my life, I stopped spending most of my mental energy on preparing what I was going to say next. I was, to put it frankly, forced to shut up for once. It soon became clear to me, as it never had before, that I loved life; that a quiet hour in a sunlit room is a gift beyond price. How had I not known that? I thought of a friend who had had a fatal heart attack. He never saw this day, I thought, but I see it, and I am glad.

I got to know myself a little better, too, and it wasn't all good news.

Playing back my memories in the quiet hours I came to realise that I was not quite as clever or interesting as I had thought – but my God I liked the sound of my own voice! Poor Norma had always got the brunt of my lectures and I never realised before quite how much patience and attention she gave me, and how little she got back. This was a painful thing to discover, because although I was evidently a boring, conceited git, I really loved her and wanted her to be happy. Nothing in my ruminating self-explorations ever cast the slightest doubt on that. Now it seemed that God had neatly arranged for her to bump me off, awarding her the richly-deserved revenge that somehow, she didn't even want. Anyone else would have killed me six times over by now.

She was back next day, pushing up her glasses. She sat down, looking excited. She liked to have a mission, especially one that involved procuring unusual items. She hated Amazon for taking most of the challenge out of that process, but she loved finding stuff in the internet.

'I know you said you wanted to go to that place in Switzerland,' she said, 'but this is so much easier and simpler. Let me explain...' she stopped and looked at me, 'you never liked me explaining things, did you darling? You would have told me to keep it brief or shut up! But you don't mind now, do you, because you're not really there, are you?' She looked at me fondly and then sort of cancelled the smile, as if she thought it was improper, in the circumstances. 'All right. You see, people often talk about putting a plastic bag over your head and suffocating. But if you do that, your system detects the build-up of carbon dioxide, and it makes you gasp and choke. It's not nice at all, and you can't help struggling.'

'But your body doesn't detect a simple lack of oxygen! So if you could pump nitrogen into the bag and keep expelling the CO_2 as well as the oxygen, you'd suffocate quite happily, without ever feeling short of breath. Simple! Now nitrogen is not that easy to get. But cylinders of helium are for sale everywhere, to fill party balloons, and it works equally well. People have used helium to suffocate themselves very successfully.'

'Anyway, at first I thought we should actually use a plastic bag. How silly of me! Of course, we don't need to. You're already breathing through a mask! All I need to do is buy a cylinder of helium and connect it up instead of your normal one! It's as easy as that.'

No! I thought. *I don't want to suffocate! Don't kill me, Norma! I was an idiot when I said those things! I'm alive, and I want to stay alive!*

She leaned forward and gently brushed my hair back from my forehead.

'Are you still in there, darling?' she asked, not as if she expected an answer.

Yes! For God's sake, yes! Help me, Norma!

'They say you're not. I wish you were, though. I could discuss this with you. But it's a comfort that you talked about it a lot before your accident, so I can be sure what you would have wanted. You were so clear! I remember you telling me once how no-one could really be afraid of death, because being dead is being nothing, so to be afraid of death is to be afraid of nothing – which is impossible! I thought that was so well put!'

Christ, what an ass I am. Would you tell a man who's starving that he's only afraid of having nothing to eat – so he's really afraid of nothing? Please, Norma; don't kill me because of my own dodgy arguments, however much I deserve it!

'I wonder whether the connectors on gas cylinders are standardised?' she said, peering at my oxygen mask, 'I expect there's a European Directive or something. I'd better check...'

Please God, don't let gas cylinder connections be standardised!

I couldn't help noticing I was thinking about God rather a lot, given that I was a lifelong materialist. No atheists in foxholes, they say, and I suppose there aren't many in hospices.

When she'd gone I spent a few hours remembering the occasion she had mentioned, when I set out my debating point about fearing nothing. I had had a small promotion at work, and to mark the occasion she had made a wonderful cake, like a fairy palace – and it tasted magic too.

'Do you like it?' she asked, as I hoovered up the last crumbs of a large slice.

'It's fine,' I said.

'The lattice-work was tricky,' she said.

'Mh. Can we stop talking abut the cake? I haven't got any clean shirts, by the way. Took me ages to find one this morning. Some idiot on the radio – *Thought for the Day* – was sermonising about the fear of death...'

I wondered now whether this would be the reality of Hell; having to recall again and again every terrible, self-centred thing I had ever said or done. Whatever afterlife there might be, there would, I realised, be a day here on earth when I was gone, yet the world would go on much the same. It was strange to think of all those days, weeks, and years that I would never see, like lost children.

A nurse looked in to check me over. The hospice staff were efficient and did everything to keep me comfortable, but there was no doubt in my mind that they were all with Team Death. It was pretty clear to me that my remaining alive so obstinately irritated them, as if I were an empty beer can somehow left over from a party that finished last week; something that really should have been tidied up by now. One day soon, I thought, they would make their move, if Norma didn't forestall them.

She was back next day with a bigger bag than usual. When she put

LEAVING

it down there was a metallic clank that clearly announced a cylinder of deadly helium.

Norma, if there is any reality to telepathy, please hear me now. I don't want to die. Please don't suffocate me. I know I said I would want to die, but trust me, it's different when you're actually lying here.

'I researched the connector issue,' she said seriously, 'It was hard to work out what was what, but then I found this very useful site called *Max Bar: the board for pressured gas enthusiasts*. I posted a question there and this gentleman called Gaskin posted this...' she rummaged in the bag and found a sheet of A4. Why did she always have to print everything? I detected rising irritability again and checked it. 'I gave him a "best answer" rating. This is what he says: "Assuming you're in the US, the standard for helium would be a CGA 170 9/16" with internal thread. Oxygen's a 540, 0.903". Long story short, you're not getting those to couple. It could be that you could do it by chaining adaptors, but instead of going down that rabbit hole, I reckon the easiest way is to remove one of the connectors from the pipe to the mask and replace it on your own pipe so you can use the hospital's own connectors on both sides. Or you could remove both connectors and use a two-way on the bare pipe ends. Worst case, I reckon raw pipe ends and duck tape might get you through good enough in these circumstances. One thing about taking off the original connection is, you put it back afterwards and not only is everything back to the way it was, you've got yourself an alibi too, because hey, your tank doesn't even hook up with the mask!"' Norma looked at me fondly.

Curse Gaskin and all his seed unto the seventh generation! May they all suffocate or be throttled with duck tape!

'I've got spanners and tape in my bag, dear,' she said, 'it'll only take a few minutes. You'll be on your way at last.'

Don't do this, Norma!

'It seems so strange for me to be rattling on and on like this, while you lie there quiet,' she said, looking at me wistfully, 'you were always the one who did the talking, weren't you? Shall I tell you a little secret? I suppose it can't do any harm now. *I didn't really listen to you*, most of the time! Not to what you were saying. I listened to your voice – you always had a lovely, resonant voice. That was one of the things that first attracted me to you. I enjoyed the sound of you talking, and watching your dear face, so lively and excited. I'm sorry I didn't pay attention, but we both enjoyed ourselves in our own ways, didn't we, those evenings after dinner? Those were good times.' She squeezed my hand.

Oh, Norma!

All at once, she looked concerned, and leaned in close.

'Is that – it's a tear, trickling down your cheek! Can you hear what I'm saying, darling? Are you still in there after all?'

Yes, yes! I'm here, I'm here!

She got up clumsily and went into the corridor; a moment later she was back with Dr Jens, the regular fellow, sandy-haired and freckled with a permanent look of faint surprise.

'You see, doctor? On his cheek? It's a tear! He's crying!'

'Oh no,' said Jens, calmly, 'I don't think so.' He took a little cotton wool wipe and swabbed the tear neatly away. 'You know we have to put drops in his eyes because he's not blinking adequately. Most likely it's that. Or it could be that the drops have opened up a couple of plugged Meibomian glands, and we're seeing some excess run-off.'

'It's not... a tear of emotion?'

'No, I'm sorry but I'm pretty sure it's not. You know we've done all the tests. There's only chaotic and background activity in your husband's brain.'

You know nothing about the activity in my brain!

LEAVING

'Perhaps this is a good moment to talk?' said Jens, and they both sat down beside my bed. 'I've been wanting a chat. You know we're pretty satisfied that your husband is in what we call a persistent vegetative state. That means that although his body continues to function, his mind is completely gone, and will not come back. It's been over a year now.'

What? It can't have been!

'Now there's no hurry, but it's maybe time to think about whether we should help him on his way.'

'I thought euthanasia was illegal?'

'Oh, we're not talking about euthanasia. We don't kill anyone. But when a patient is clearly on a terminal path we might adjust our approach to pain relief, and we might *withdraw support*. Things like intravenous nutrition, or even liquids, if relatives judge that it's kinder not to prolong the process unnecessarily. If your husband's views are known, of course those should also be taken into account.'

'Oh, they're known all right,' said Norma.

'Well, I won't put pressure on you now,' said Jens, 'but have a think and we'll talk, eh?'

When he'd gone, Norma shook her head.

'Oh dear!' she said, 'there was me, smuggling in my ridiculous cylinder of helium and roll of duct tape, and there was no need! They'll finish you off after all. I think you got that bit wrong, didn't you darling?'

I did not 'get that bit wrong'! You just don't understand properly.

'I would tell him to get on with it straight away,' she said, 'but the sight of that tear on your face – I'm afraid it's upset me a bit. I know it doesn't mean anything.'

It does! It does mean something!

She kissed me and I tried to cry again, but I couldn't.

◆

I stayed awake all that night. I think I stay awake all night every night now, but it's a little hard to be sure somehow; deep thought and shallow sleep might merge now and then. I thought about why I liked to talk so much, and why I hadn't given Norma more attention.

We are all more or less solipsists (I know I am, anyway) – we believe sincerely in our own existence, but the reality of other people is, to us, just a working hypothesis, something we take on trust but don't feel the truth of so vividly. That's why I felt it was urgently necessary for me to explain things – I didn't really believe there was anyone else out there who understood them the way I did. That was why, terrible though it is to admit, I didn't think Norma's thoughts and feelings were quite as real or important as mine; I just politely and half-heartedly pretended they were. And that's why I was afraid to die. I thought that when I died, something uniquely important would be lost. I thought that if I ceased to exist, the Universe would lose its narrator.

I knew now that wasn't true. I had at least a faint sense that there really were other people with other minds like mine. Nothing much would be lost when I went. The sun was coming up now, beginning one more day. I wouldn't see all those future days I'd thought about, but they wouldn't be orphaned by my absence; they would be seen, just like all the other days. My arguments about euthanasia might have been debatable, but in a way I had been right all along; there was nothing – nothing much – to fear.

I closed my eyes and folded my arms on my chest – not really, of course, but in my imagination.

Come on then, God, if you're there. Any chance that there's room for one more egotistical scumbag in your forgiving embrace? Seriously, look

LEAVING

after Norma will you? Don't let her be captured by another selfish bastard.

There was no answer, of course, but deep inside I felt my spiritual connectors begin to disconnect.

Sorry you didn't get chance to do it yourself, Norma, but this one's for you.

There she was a few hours later, holding the cold hand of my corpse while I seemed to float above it.

'So in the end, you just went quietly in the night, all of your own accord?' she said, 'I'm sorry I wasn't quicker getting things organised, dear, but perhaps this was the best way.' Her eyes filled with tears. 'Wait for me if you can, darling,' she said, 'we still have things to tell each other.'

You have no idea.

And that is the end. Universe, you're going to have to manage as best you can by yourself from here on in.

Leaving
Clara Harland
United Kingdom

Shortlisted for the 2019
International Writing Competition

Late again, she trips over the cracks in the frosty pavement, skidding a little to remain upright. She glances about to check no one saw her falling over her own feet and then assumes an air of nonchalance before resuming her scuttling pace to the station. Not that there is a need to glance about at this time in the morning. It is barely light and she is more likely to see a fox foraging in the bins than hear the tentative frozen notes of birdsong.

She arrives at the station, making her train seconds before the doors slide closed, and autopilots to her usual seat in her usual carriage. A puff of slightly sweaty warmth exhales upwards from her body and escapes between the collar of her shirt and her damp neck as she plumps down, cursing her many layers and her inability to leave the house on time.

Looking about her, she recognises the faces of her fellow commuters, all either asleep or absorbed in screens. No one looks up. She sighs and tries to forestall the daily existential crisis that's taken to swamping her as soon as she has time to think. Far too early in the morning for that and, besides, her days of commuting are due to end in a week or so anyway. She imagines herself at the airport, already taking off, leaving this all behind, albeit temporarily; a three month sabbatical to go out and see the world. In moments of defiance, she thinks she might never come back.

The train slows into a station and a gasp of cold air breezes in with a man in a duffle coat, scarf wrapped up to his ears. He sits in the one remaining seat and slips his phone out of his pocket, no doubt checking emails, work dripping over the sides of normal working hours, seeping into the whole day. She's seen him before, of course, every morning in fact, and has dreamt up at least ten scenarios where they speak, they go for dinner and they fall in love, the clichés tumbling one after another. She doesn't really believe in this fakery though, left it behind in her twenties, but it passes the time while she waits for the monotony of the journey to end.

Collectively, they rise from their seats an hour later. There is a sense of resignation, a re-setting into game faces for the office; shoulders straightening as they step out onto the platform and stride with purpose away. She peeps one last look over her shoulder at the man in the duffle coat and watches as he bends to pick up a scarf that's fallen to the ground. He calls after a woman, proffers it to her, and their faces break into friendly smiles. Irrationally, she feels annoyed, imagining herself in the woman's place as if this is some kind of missed opportunity. She blinks away that piece of silliness, wiping it from her mind.

At the office, the sunlight shimmers off the glass panels, separating her from her colleagues, each in their own battery hen cubicle. The walls are tastefully decorated with super-size posters of the ad campaigns they've worked on and the atmosphere buzzes with importance.

Once, this had impressed her; she'd felt part of the buzz, had enjoyed the shmoozy lifestyle, but eight years on and the glitz isn't enough anymore. She isn't sure when the sheen wore off and sometimes she isn't entirely sure that it has completely gone; they'd land a new client, she'd produce a pitch and follow it through with a successful campaign, soaking up the murmurs of admiration. Then she'd forget the downsides, the feeling of being worn and jaded, and the effort of competing with the energy of the newbies that bounced through the door like a mocking parody of her younger self.

She sighs and swings her chair round so that she's pondering the city skyline, grasping her coffee cup, mentally exiting the building, drifting back to the platform that morning where she drops her scarf. He picks it up, hands it to her, amusement beaconing from his eyes. A chirrupy digital ring bursts from the phone on her desk and she realises she's been smiling inanely out of the window for at least five minutes. Swivelling back, she returns her brain to the office and takes the call.

Saturday night and she's sitting in a restaurant, making forced conversation across a candlelit table. Bob, or whatever his name is, doesn't look anything like his picture but then when do they ever? This wouldn't be a problem, except Bob isn't anywhere near as interesting as his profile suggested either. He's also not good at asking her any questions and, to judge by the way his gaze keeps slipping to her chest, he's clearly hoping to skip to the bit of the evening when he can find out if the probability of getting into her pants is a good one.

Letting herself into her flat at the end of the evening, minus Bob, she stands in the hallway and listens to the silence. She removes her coat, the chill of outside damp in the dew that rests on its sleeves, and reflects on another night designed to punctuate the loneliness of a stuttering love life but which has left her feeling lonelier than ever. She'd been pushed into online dating by her friends a year or so after the end of a relationship that had taken her through her twenties. Now, she's lost count of the number of candlelit dinners, the acres of time lost to small talk, the air aching with the lack of sparks, thin with the superficiality of choosing someone from a pick and mix of pixels.

At the beginning of the working week, she sits on the train, wearing her professional person outfit, her happy person mask firmly in place. The man in the duffle coat steps on and she fails to catch his eye. Maybe he's no more interesting than Bob, but she'd much rather find out in person, face to face and straightaway, without being duped into a date by an online presence obscuring reality. An idea forms and she smiles at its naivety. Deciding to humour herself, she unravels her scarf, clutching it in her hand as she steps onto the platform before gently letting it slip to the ground. Fighting the urge to look back, she begins to walk away, already feeling ridiculous.

A voice calls and her heart lifts, but it's too high, too young and when she turns, she sees a child of perhaps five years old, her scarf mostly bunched in his hands but still trailing an end in the dust. The boy looks up at his mother who smiles indulgently. She urges her son forwards, looking on as he returns the scarf, proud of his impeccable manners, gloopy with affection over his sweetness. A grateful smile and a thank you, a crest in the wave of an otherwise ordinary day, and they disappear, reabsorbed back into the crowd.

At work, it is jokily pointed out to her at least three times before her first meeting that she has just over a week left before she's off and gone. There is an edge to these comments; those who started with her at the company and who have since got married and had kids tell her she's lucky to have the freedom to do what she wants, a wistful envy lacing their tone. Not that they would trade, of course, as they tell her, but it must be nice to be able to drop everything and go. Her grin doesn't reach her eyes as she listens to this and it strikes her that the grass is always greener, whatever the choices we make. The child from that morning floats across her mind's eye, fuzzy at the edges, fluffy like her scarf, and she feels a pang in her heart, her grin faltering before regaining its rigidity. The next morning, she drops her glove on the train and looks back in time to see it being kicked, unnoticed, beneath the seats.

She picks her way over the toys strewn across the floor at a friend's house on Friday, taking in the homely chaos and scents of food from the oven. The husband is handing out drinks to guests, his wife apologising for the mess; the kids have only just settled upstairs, tucked up in their beds. A weary happiness is written across their faces while they take long, relieved gulps of wine from their glasses. She sits, preparing to regale her friends with funny stories from work, skewing the story of her latest date into something witty, bubbling with excitement about her upcoming trip, a thin film of paper covering the gaping cavern where her loneliness and insecurities bounce around in echoes. She watches as her friends' expressions turn to pity; she's the only one left at this coupled up table, and they've known her too long, can see through the cracks, know that she's trying too hard.

A screaming child bellows down the stairs partway through dessert and the rest of the evening is backed by a near constant wail, punctuated by parental distraction and strained by any attempt to continue adult conversation. It is with relief that she stands in the hallway of her flat that night, listening to the silence, wondering why on earth she'd want to get into all of that anyway. The thought strikes that perhaps she should be pitying her friends, not the other way around. Maybe that set up will be for her one day, but not right now. Unfortunately, that mantra has failed to convince those around her the closer she's edged towards forty.

LEAVING

She flings her bag down on a chair, huffing out her irritation at having to justify herself under the burden of societal pressure and against the backdrop of nature's insistent tick-ticking.

It would be nice to have someone in her life though, she thinks, as she watches the man in the duffle coat get on the train on Monday. She wonders whether she'd be craving the need to escape her life so fervently if she had the steadiness of a relationship to anchor her down. Dropping her other glove as the doors slide back, she convinces herself it was accidental, that she's not behaving like a romantic lunatic and as she's berating herself, a voice calls after her. She turns and he's there, the grey duffle coat accentuating blue eyes. They smile at one another and, as she takes her glove from his hand, a frisson of energy dances between their fingertips. How strange it is, they say, that people can sit together on trains every day and never speak. They laugh; numbers are exchanged and the day takes on a new brightness.

The following evening, she sits across from him at a candlelit table. He is the antithesis of Bob. More laughter, unforced, rallies from one to the other and back again, an easy flirtation growing into the expanding pleasure of shared humour and interests. She thinks: this could go somewhere. They kiss on the pavement after dinner, soft drizzle floating, unnoticed, and she pushes from her mind that she is leaving in two days.

Her final day of commuting and she has someone to sit next to at last. Absorbed by shared smiles and murmured phrases, their shoulders rest gently together, the carriage fading to greyness around them. She heads into the office, her mind full of him. Her colleagues take her elation to be excitement at leaving and she thinks of her travels and is torn.

The airport moves around her, a bustle of people, suitcases, trolleys and flashing departures boards. She wavers, the announcement for her flight a distant flutter of dislocated syllables scattering and reforming until she registers what has been said. Turning towards her gate, she clings to the words uttered from her bed that morning:

'I'll be here when you get back.'

Émigré
Sarah Hunter-Carson
United Kingdom

I ONCE DESCRIBED HIS EYES IN A POEM AS 'SEA-COLD', and really that description was perfect for them; I shrank from their gaze when he was angry, or even just stern. The 'kh's of his speech will mark him out for the rest of his life as Russian; I think that's probably why he prefers speaking French to English, he doesn't have to worry about the h sound in French. He used to tell me proudly that in Paris they couldn't believe he wasn't a native speaker. Sometimes, though, he flounders for a word in French, and in an emergency, or even if things are just going wrong, he'll always revert to Russian. If he thinks he's lost some money in a cafe he'll reach, panic-stricken, for his wallet and begin counting. *Dvesti, trista, chetirista…*

I don't know if I still love him; I cling to him because I needed to believe that my love for him, for which I sacrificed so much and for which I committed sins which still cling to me like smoke, wasn't all a colossal mistake. In Turkish, if you want to express an immense contempt for someone, you say 'I wouldn't even give him my sins.' I'd give anyone my sins, but you can't do that.

Sometimes I think he's getting sicker. Always pale, the dark rings under his eyes are almost black, but he keeps up his habits. He wanders around, utterly lost, really, but every morning is a victory of a kind. He used to be a diplomat, once; it's hard to believe. He seems sometimes to be searching for his former responsibilities as one might look for a mislaid letter, or an umbrella. Perhaps we all live several lives in one. He takes pills; to sleep (most of all to sleep) to settle his nerves, to settle his stomach. The greatest fear – the day the pills stop working.

I wonder what it's like to have been born in a country that no longer exists.

His hands are still beautiful, though they tremble sometimes when he signs his name, writing in another script for some reason daunts him; he is frightened of getting it wrong, making a mess. He likes autumn, especially late autumn, when it feels as though nature is trembling and the air is fresh; that's when he's most energetic, that's when he starts hesitatingly to talk about the future, about the things he needs to do 'next year'. He gives lessons, though few students seem to stay with him for any length of time.

I am ashamed of my need for him, which is now not really a need, but a habit. I used to feel greedy to know all about him, but it comes in glimpses, frustratingly incomplete, like something from a dream, insubstantial and unreliable. I think he hardly knows which are his own memories now.

Our luck is running out. Perhaps I have clutched at him too tightly. I feel the emptiness of everything, the impossibility of really understanding someone else. What is it to love someone so unknowable?

Why are we here? Mayakovsky said, *Listen, if stars are lit, it means that somebody needs them.*

Murder Anonymous
Steve Jackson
United Kingdom

Cheryl left me ten days ago. Said she couldn't stand how I'd changed, couldn't understand what had scared me. I wouldn't go out no more. Stayed in the penthouse apartment, looking through curtains like a nosy neighbour, afraid to move, answer the intercom or the door. She'd never seen me afraid before.

I'm on borrowed time. It could be anyone. In the car parked out front. The guy waiting in the shade of the palm tree on the corner. A marksman on the neighbouring rooftop. My life, my plans, all in ruins. All because I wouldn't trust, wanted to close the last loose end. He would never have betrayed me. He had no ambition to take over. He was happy where he was.

◆

It all changed starting with that news headline. I can even remember the date. The 22nd of November 1995 it was. I've still got the cutting somewhere.

Mass Murder Site Discovered!
Contractors widening the A6068 road near Keighley have un-

covered a number of buried human remains. Investigations by forensic experts seem to suggest that they have been buried here individually over a period of several years. Two of the deceased appear to be fairly recent burials, probably within the last year. These two have already been successfully identified from dental records and missing person reports. Their respective families have been contacted for formal identification. Careful excavation is ongoing, but so far, another five bodies have been discovered. Evidence currently suggests the work of a dangerous serial killer. What connection the victims might have had with each other is unknown: so far, no evidence has come to light linking the deaths with any known criminal. Investigations are proceeding.

When I first read the report I'd always been expecting, I went really anxious for a while. Had I been careful enough? Had I closed all loose ends? I trusted Jack with my life, but were any of his team in a position to betray me? As time passed, and the police inquiries faltered, I began to feel easier. No further bodies beyond the seven were discovered. My other burial site nearby, with another four bodies already in it, remained undiscovered. However, sooner than I expected, the find had had another consequence: I found myself without a living!

◆

For the past eleven years, I'd had a good thing going, taking care of other people's unfinished business. I'd worked with Jack Vance from early days, when he was just a local bully boy working his way up through local protection racketeering, with a bit of drug dealing and prostitution thrown in. We'd been mates from school. He'd always taken the lead, and

LEAVING

I'd always backed him up. That was the way it was. Jack did his own strong-arm stuff then as well as me, enjoyed it in fact. But then, so did I. I liked the power I had over people, liked seeing the fear in their eyes when they knew they were going to get done over. I guess you might say we'd found our vocations.

We were a convincing act. I'd always been big and muscular. Back then Jack was thinner and lighter, but had a dark look in his eye that always had people on edge. We took over Leeds like the Krays took over the East End. Everyone was afraid of us and our reputation for toughness.

♦

Then, one day, suddenly, it had gone wrong. All over a stupid takeaway owner who wouldn't pay his due. Akhbar, I think they called him. We only meant to damage him, but Jack'd been far too keen that day. Anyway, when he ended up accidentally dead on his own shop floor, I was there too, a material witness, you might say. It was Jack's doing though. So Jack kind of owed me.

We never mentioned it again, and Jack rose through the ranks to become Leeds' top racketeer. His best move was to take over a dead and alive joint, centre of town, called the Blue Moon. The owner was glad to offload it. In exchange, he got his gambling debts to Jack cancelled, and got to keep all his fingers and toes. Jack's 'friends' in the council fixed the planning applications, his business pals put up the cash, and the Regalia Club was born. In no time at all, the Regalia was posh, glitzy, the place to be seen. That was front of house. Behind the regal façade, all our old operations carried on like before. Jack led the empire from his posh office overlooking the club casino. But there wasn't anything he wasn't into by then.

I stayed with him, his first officer, you might say, just like before. I didn't really have the polished manners required for front of house. Anyway, I couldn't stand sucking up to the ponces who thought they was someone because they knew Mr. Big. So Jack and some oily Italian slime-ball he'd hired, Mario, looked after the Regalia Club proper. I took care of the other jobs, kept the ball rolling, the 'fixer.'

With a complex outfit like the Regalia, you need to remember that its posh, up-market customers weren't all squeaky clean. Behind the scenes were the usual drug and prostitution operations, our bread and butter through the years. I'd become good at operating all these with a firm hand. As well as that, some of its posher clients had, you know, 'special needs'. A business rival needing to be strongly advised against a certain course of action, say, or a local official needed reminding how vulnerable they really were. So I still kept my hand in with the tools of the trade: threats, blackmail, physical stuff where necessary.

When one particularly difficult client finally needed removing, the progression to killing felt quite natural. And once I'd done it the first time to protect Jack's and my business interests, it was soon clear that there were always other people who wanted it doing. A business rival, someone interfering with the wife/girlfriend/boyfriend, upstart rivals to our drug or prostitution business, that sort of thing. We did the business the same way we'd done other stuff for years. Jack took care of all the arrangements in the front office, and I became, as Jack put it, 'the executive branch.' For the run of the mill bully boy stuff, I had a good team round me. But the killings: I did them by myself. Completely by myself. Only me and Jack knew about them. Not just the killing: removal of evidence became my speciality. Although burials seemed clumsy and old fashioned, you didn't need to involve anyone else. You could do it alone. So it was much easier that way. No involvement of other people, so no loose

LEAVING

tongues. Easier, that is, till now.

◆

Once they'd identified all the bodies, even the plods could figure out some connections between them. One of the obvious ones was, of course, the Regalia. That number of bodies, and the nationals were on the scent like Sherlock bloody Holmes. So it was no surprise when they turned up. One day, I'm downstairs in the back office like usual when the phone rang. It was Cheryl, Jack's 'secretary.'

'Dave, can you come up here now. There's policemen here, asking some questions. Jack wants you with him.'

'On my way, love,' I answered, thinking.

This must be somebody new. Jack'd got all the local constabulary under his thumb. If it was just the local police, we'd have been able to wrap things up fairly easily. They wouldn't come asking questions without warning. Anyway, we'd already got our act together, Jack and me, with what to say, just in case, like. Even so …

When I entered Jack's office, he'd already got things organised. The two policemen, keen-looking bastards in wrinkled suits and – would you believe – trench-coats, were sat opposite Jack's desk, nursing cups of coffee. Cheryl was fussing round them, topping their cups up, giving them plenty of distracting views of leg and cleavage. Jack was sat back, cool as a cucumber.

'Dave, come in,' Jack began. 'These two gentlemen are London CID. Inspector Holmes (really?) and Sergeant Simms. They're making enquiries about ...'

'Thank you, Mister Paulden,' inspector Holmes interrupted, turning in his chair to look me over. '*I'll* explain the nature of our enquiries if I may.'

This was not so much a request as a command, from a voice well used to giving orders. I looked him in the eye. Medium height, thinning, greying hair, mid forties probably. Wrinkles around the eyes, greying complexion of a heavy smoker, typical cop, but ... his eyes were glinting, penetrating. This was a man to be reckoned with, I knew. Still ... despite our past, neither Jack or me had any form. We had nothing to fear – other than that we'd done it! Still, innocent until *proven* guilty...

'We're conducting enquiries following the discovery of seven bodies near Halifax about two weeks ago,' he said calmly, watching my eyes all the time. 'Possibly you've seen something of this in the news?'

Breaking his gaze for a moment, I moved to sit in the only other available chair, near Jack's side of the desk. Once there, I met his steely gaze once more before replying.

'Yeah, I saw it in the news. Looks a bad business,' I said off-handedly. 'How can we help you?'

Holmes set his coffee cup down on the desk. The sergeant, Simms, almost a clone of his inspector but without the steely eyes, pulled a notebook from his trench-coat pocket, and a pen from his jacket, and sat, looking expectant. I almost burst out laughing. Was he ready to take down our confessions? 'It's a fair cop – we did it!'

'It seems that all the victims had some connection with the Regalia Club. Mr Paulden's shown us your membership records. We're enquiring if there was any common ground between them – debts, for example.'

At this, Jack leaned forward on the desk.

'Inspector, we don't make detailed enquiries into our members' financial status,' he said calmly. 'They pay their membership fees, they pay their dues, if any, in the casino, and that's all we know. We value the privacy of our members very highly.'

Inspector Holmes turned to his sergeant with a gesture. Simms closed the notebook and returned it to his pocket. The inspector turned once again to face Jack and me.

'Let's not misunderstand each other here,' he began. 'I've talked to your local plods – the ones you've got under your thumb. We know what goes on under the umbrella of your 'respectable' club. Up to now, we've not been concerned too much. You're just big fish in a little pond. But this business has gone too far. You've gone too far. We're going to get to the bottom of this, understand?'

Jack leaned back in his chair, spread his hands wide. He wasn't fazed in the slightest.

'Wilbrow the Tailor,' he said with a smug smile.

'What... what's Wilbrow the Tailor got to do with this?' said Holmes, angrily.

'I'd be willing to bet,' replied Jack, 'that all your victims bought their suits from Wilbrow's. My members like to be smartly turned out. Maybe you should be making your enquiries there?'

The verbal fencing went on in this way for quite a while, but two things were clear. One, they didn't have anything on us. Two, they knew it was us, they just couldn't prove it. I knew about DNA stuff, of course. It was the coming thing. But proper use of DNA evidence was still some years away, then. We were clear, but...marked men. Looked like this part of our operations had just come to an end. In the event, the plods had nothing to go on, other than basic suspicion. With no leads, the enquiry eventually got dropped. Our usual financial arrangements in place with the local plods made sure that the remaining evidence from the site soon got 'lost' in the system.

◆

But, not so long after that, Jack died. Really. A list of enemies as long as your arm, and he just died. Heart attack. In the office. Cheryl said she found him dead. He'd had a thing going with her from day one. A sideline, because he was married with kids and all. I had a soft spot for her, and he always treated her like shit, but if she had anything to do with it, she was saying nothing, to me or anyone else.

However, what was sure was that, with his death, our business and me and Cheryl's jobs died as well. We'd been able to buy off the local police when necessary, but not the Inland Revenue. Her Majesty's leeches slithered in and went through the books. By the time they'd finished, there was little enough money for his wife and kids. He'd always kept them out of the real business, and so me and Cheryl were out on the street. C.V.? Ability to hurt, extort, murder, didn't seem a career future. I mean, you couldn't advertise it. The plods in London still had their suspicions. I was sure they'd watch me forever now, for any sign of 'business as usual.' My living was gone. Looked like I might even have had to get a *real* job, for fuck's sake! However, at least it meant that me and Cheryl got together. Also, I had a plan. Had it for some time, in fact.

◆

The year before, I'd had to visit a bloke on what me and Jack politely called our 'Debtors List.' The usual thing, about money, gambling debt, reluctance to pay. However, he wasn't the usual type. Brian, a little, scruffy guy in a little, scruffy council flat. I didn't even take any of the team. I knew he'd give me no trouble. Once I got there, it was obvious he had no cash, nor ever would have. Nothing in his flat except some serious computer kit. However, once I started talking to him, I realised he *did* have something I might be able to use. The Internet was a new thing then, but he knew a lot about it, and I thought his knowledge might be useful one

LEAVING

day. Just a hunch. So I'd told him I might be back some day, for a favour. Then I'd let him off with a warning never to return to the club. There didn't seem much point in breaking anything, him or the computer gear. He didn't have any friends, so it wouldn't have been a warning to anyone. I had no particular idea what he could ever do for me, then. Now I did.

I had this idea, but no way to carry it out. The Internet thing had stuck in my mind, though. And here was a way. When I'd gone to collect from him, he was obviously broke. I'd kept him as my Chance Card, for the future. And the future was here. He could possibly use the Internet in a way I wanted.

◆

So the 'Murder Anonymous' website was born. That wasn't its real name. I'm not saying what that was. Its real name and how to find it on the Net kept it anonymous, and only available to those in the know. I still had lots of contacts in the criminal world which, as we all know, is very connected to the 'respectable' world. There were plenty of people who wanted other people removing. Plenty of demand for a service I could provide. Here's how it worked.

You wanted somebody killed, a business rival, say, keeping you from making a packet. *You* can't kill them. You'd be number one suspect. So, you contact Murder Anonymous. First thing, you'll pay. £10,000 up front. Then you'll be given a name from the system. Someone you don't know, have no connection with, but someone else wants dead. You don't know why, don't need to know. Better if you don't. You've got to kill them. When and how you do it is your choice. And your risk if nabbed. However, your safety is, you've got no possible connection to the person you are killing. Provided you don't have a police record, you should easily get away with it.

Yes, you've still got to kill someone to get *your* job done. That tests your level of commitment, ties you to the system and guarantees your future silence. If you won't go through with it, I've got your £10,000 anyway, and you're off the books. If you do kill as arranged, there's nothing to tie you to that murder. Unless you're stupid enough to get caught in the act, you're free and clear. Once you've killed your named person, you pay another £10,000. Then your own target goes on the list for someone else to dispose of. Job done.

This is an executive service, designed for rich and ruthless people with little conscience and great need for money. I know that a murder can be done much cheaper. However, if you don't take the risk of doing it yourself, the mug you employ is likely to be known to police (their MO, fingerprints, even DNA) so odds on long-term success are poor. Done my way, the killer is anonymous, motiveless, so baffling to solve. *You*, the obvious suspect, will always remain squeaky clean.

So there it was, up and running. Out there on the Dark Web (as my computer nerd Brian called it), it seemed to be working well. New clients applying all the time, from all parts of the globe. I was an export industry!

◆

I'd 'inherited' Cheryl from Jack, and she seemed as happy with the arrangement as me. As the money rolled in, we'd moved from dismal Leeds to Marbella on the Costa Del Crime, where I already knew lots of people. My sort of people.

They knew I was doing okay, but didn't know what my business was, didn't ask, didn't care. We lived a great life. Cheryl only had the faintest idea what kept me at the computer screen part of each day. She thought it was something to do with stocks and shares. Anyway, she'd kept shtum

LEAVING

about Jack's activities over the years, and was tight as a clam about mine. I'd paid Brian well for his efforts, and he was on a rolling commission which let him move to a nice flat in Headingley. He didn't want anything more. However, he was the only problem, the only niggling doubt in my mind. All the years with Jack, I'd never let anyone get a hold on me, get wise enough to take me down. After a while, I figured I'd learned enough to run the Internet system on my own. But Brian knew it all as well. He might get greedy, sell out to someone else, get an attack of conscience, fall ill… The overall risks were too great. I had to do one last killing myself, to put things beyond the possibility of failure.

◆

So I told Cheryl I had to go back to Leeds to sort out a small business deal. She was okay with that, and so one dark November night, I turned up at Brian's door. This was to be a simple in and out killing. All the outer clothes I had on were 'new' from Oxfam. I had a woolly hat on, but underneath was a plastic bag. I was taking as few chances as possible with leaving DNA, even though I wasn't on file as far as I knew. A quick suffocation, back to the cheap car I'd bought cash, out into a nearby lane to torch it, a walk back to somewhere I could pick up a taxi. Job done.

I put my gloves on before ringing the bell. I didn't think he'd notice. Brian, surprised, let me in.

'What are you doing back here, Dave? Is everything okay? With the system?' He was instantly on edge, but that was just Brian.

'No hassles at all, Brian,' I answered calmly, easing my way in so he would back down the hall and allow me to close the front door. 'I'm back in Leeds to do a bit of other business, but, while I'm here, I just thought I'd call on you. Something minor I wanted to ask you about the system.'

'Sure, Dave,' Brian replied, relief evident in his voice. 'Come through, and we'll look at it.'

He led the way through a junk-filled hallway. Brian could make a palace look like a tip inside three days.

'Want a drink?' he enquired, pausing in the doorway of his study room.

'No thanks,' I replied. Not only the chance of catching something nasty from his scruffy kitchen – DNA again.

Brian hunched down in front of his computer, quickly saving the crapulent video game he had on pause from when I rang his doorbell. As he typed in the logon and passwords to access our website, I watched his hands. No problem, he was using the same passwords he'd given me. He obviously didn't have any special access I didn't know.

'What was it you wanted to look at?' he asked. Something in the way I must have paused, or some sixth sense made him start to turn towards me. Too late. I had the plastic bag down over his head in no time.

'Wait, Dave wait, you need to listen to me...' His voice was muffled, distorted by the heavy bag. I wasn't going to wait. I twisted it closed round his neck, holding him down in his chair, his threshing and twisting too little too late. His heels drummed on the carpet as he struggled for the clear breath he would never again take. His hands tried unsuccessfully to tear the toughened bag from his face. He would never know that, to make me let go, he should be trying to poke at my eyes. It was soon over.

I left him in the chair, pausing only to clear his web browser's history, and close his computer down. I knew he never kept any of our data on his local system. Removing the bag from his head, I left him in the chair, quietly left the flat, and returned to the car without being seen. In the quiet lane I'd previously identified, I burnt the outer clothing carefully, then torched the car. Brian was a loner. It might be days before he was found, I reasoned, and it would take the autopsy results to reveal his death to be unnatural, to be murder. I'd be long gone by then. I was. I was back in Marbella, back in the sunshine of the rest of my life in less than twelve hours.

♦

It was about three weeks later. I'd just logged into the system to see how things were going, as there were several clients on the books at that time. Looking through the pages, and there was an assignment I didn't recognise. I put in the extra passcodes to access the general info about client and assignment and – my name's there as the assignment, for fuck's sake! I've been assigned!

It's Brian's doing. It's got his hallmark on it. Then, when I try to cancel it, as he's shown me, the whole system evaporates, with just a laughing joker face on screen. It's gone completely, or so it seems. Then the message:

'Dave: if I haven't logged in via my own computer for seven days, then foul play must have taken place. You won't be able to see or use the website again. The full database is still there, however, safe in the cloud. Six months from now, that full database will be turned over to the Metropolitan Police. This may not affect you too badly, however. Your name and details will have already been assigned to five current clients as a change of target. Good luck – you'll need it.'

Snow and Feathers
Michelle Jager
Australia

Shortlisted for the 2019
International Writing Competition

Bird sits on a branch in the forest and watches two girls, mirror images of each other, baskets in hand, collecting wood. With bright red coats they are easy to see, easy to follow. Bird hops from branch to branch, flutters from tree to tree, shadows them as they move quietly through falling snow. Arm in arm, they go. They do not chatter or giggle as other girls do, other girls Bird has watched.

Bird cocks her head from side to side, hops closer, flaunts her feathers. She is small but beautiful. Look at me! Sapphire, indigo, emerald. Look at me!

One girl stops and points to the branch Bird is sitting on. Bird puffs her chest and warbles – an intricate, joyful combination of notes. One of Bird's finest. Both girls stare at her, eyes luminous in the anaemic landscape. But neither says a word. Bird is calling, but they do not answer.

◆

LEAVING

Bird remembers a time when she could not answer. When she couldn't speak or warble or sing or make sound of any kind. Or none that any would take notice of. None that could be heard by anyone who would help. This was before Bird was Bird.

Bird was like the girls. Walked instead of flew, pale instead of bright, trapped instead of free.

◆

The girls smile at Bird, and she sings for them. One holds out a hand and Bird, cautious at first, landing near, flitting over her head, finally sits on her palm. Bird feels her heart tripping in her chest, but there is something in the girl's eyes that calms her. Makes her stay and sing. The other girl rests her head on her sister's shoulder.

SISTER.

Big, bold, soothing. Sister. I had a sister.

The sisters listen to Bird's songs, shed tears silent as snowfall. Bird dances over their heads, makes her song happy – the sisters dance, clap hands, footprints decorate the snow.

'DAUGHTERS OF MINE!' Violent, a voice, shatters the air. MINE. Familiar. Possessive.

The sisters freeze, Bird flies. Sits atop the tallest tree; her breath comes heavy, comes fast. She watches the girls walk towards a woman, a house.

HOUSE. The word flashes in her mind. Big, bold, alarming. House. The word settles, becomes quieter. I lived in a house. Bird shudders. A house with four walls and a roof and locked windows.

◆

Bird goes to the house every day. A solitary building in the middle of the forest. Just the woman and the two girls live there.

Early each morning, before the sun is up, Bird perches on a branch and sings. Two faces appear at a window. Four hands press against glass. Two faces smile. Stay there until the woman cries out: 'DAUGHTERS OF MINE!' And they disappear.

◆

Every day, bar one, people line up at the door. People of different shapes and sizes. Bird watches them: tall and short, fat and thin, soft and hard, dark and fair, ugly and beautiful, young and old, but all grown. None are children.

They come and wait until the woman opens the door. She stands there with a bowl. One person at a time, coins chink as they drop them in, two gold coins each. The woman smiles. Her teeth are large and white, laughter tinkles, hands beckon, voice soft, dulcet. But Bird notices the tune is slightly off.

Bird studies the faces of the people going in. All have one thing in common – strain when they enter, relief when they leave. All day they come and go. Bird sits and watches and preens until the sun goes down.

And then she sleeps.

◆

Bird! Bird!
    Two voices calling.
Bird! Bird!
    Voices – hoarse and unfamiliar.
Bird! Bird!
    Urgent. Croaking.

LEAVING

    Bird! Bird!
    Frogs, thinks Bird, and wakes.

◆

Bird remembers someone else calling her name. Her name when her name wasn't Bird. Bird can't remember what her name was then, but she remembers the tone. The urgency. And snow falling. Snow is always falling when her name is called.
    Sister. Was it Sister calling?
    Only the voice remains. The sentiment. Calling Bird back – but back from where and why?
    SAD. The voice is sad. Bird wants to ask the voice, the memory – why are you sad? But she can't. She wants to ask – what can I do? Bird tries, she says the words, but the memory will not answer.

◆

Snow falls. Night is here. The morning was spent singing while the girls collected wood, but now Bird watches. Bird listens. She sits on the windowsill, looking in. There is the woman and the two girls. Candles light the room. The woman counts the coins and the girls are cleaning.
    Every other day, the woman is smiles and laughter when greeting. Now her eyes empty, her body shifts in on itself, her voice hollows. Bird is alarmed at the transformation.
    There's only the woman's voice –
    It's so hard, so difficult for her. Twin daughters, mutes, no man will stay.
    'You unsettle them, scare them. No one, not even your father would stay. He left because of you. And I – you are so lucky – because I kept you, I raised you, I made you my whole world. What would you be, where

would you be, without me? You don't understand how hard it is for me, what I've sacrificed because I love you. Because I am your mother.'

FATHER. Angry, the word stands. Booming. Bird flinches when she thinks of it. Father and Sister. Words, feelings, lost, returning. FATHER – this woman. MOTHER. Two different words, but Bird feels, when she looks at the girls, that these two – this woman, Bird's memory of Father – the same?

On and on the woman speaks, and the girls clean, and the candles burn, wax dripping, pooling.

And then, after an hour or so, the woman gets up, puts out all candles but one, walks the girls to their room, and goes into another.

Bird does not move. Shaken, fear and sorrow and Father cling together in her mind. Bird sits a long time. Snow gathers, wind howls, an owl cries out.

◆

Bird! Bird!

Croaking, the words come.

Bird! Bird!

Two faces follow. Moonlike, the girls come into focus.

Bird! Bird!

Bird is shocked to hear the words uttered from those lips. Voices that seem too old for little girls.

Help us, Bird! Help us, as you were helped. Help us be free. We're filled with words, so many words, all day long – but none are our own. They come and speak their pain, their wickedness, their secrets, and we can only listen. Only in dreams can we speak. Only in dreams do we meet and speak and share our own pain in words. Only in dreams do we dare think of freedom. We're scared, Bird. We're tired, Bird. We're sad,

LEAVING

Bird. Help us!

The words fade, little more than whispers; faint threads fluttering in the wind, breaking.

◆

Bird flies close when the people come. She flies down and sits on the windowsill. She watches the woman welcome the first visitor of the day into the kitchen. The two girls sit at the table waiting, their backs to Bird. The woman pulls out a third chair and beckons for the visitor to take a seat, all smiles she is, all white teeth, and sparkling eyes. Blue and golden, she is. Dark-haired, the little girls' heads do not move – still as statues.

'Thank you, Mary,' says the stranger. Stranger to Bird, but not, it seems to Mary.

'Alma, Dara,' the stranger nods at the girls, but does not look at them. The stranger looks beyond them, to the window, to Bird. Bird looks back, but the stranger doesn't seem to notice. Bird is just Bird, after all, and today she is drab. She doesn't want to be noticed. Doesn't want to be seen.

Alma. Dara. They have names.

Alma, Dara.

Mary.

'One hour,' says Mary.

'One hour,' says the visitor.

Mary leaves, shutting the door behind her.

The stranger begins to talk as soon as the door closes. He can't wait, can't hold it in a moment longer, the words burst out. Burst out low and soft, aware that still someone might hear, someone might be listening, eavesdropping – but still – the chance to speak!

'I cannot sleep. Can't sleep for thinking of her face, the sound of her voice....'

His daughter. For an hour he speaks of his daughter – lost beneath the ice, frozen below, out of reach, beyond his touch, his warmth, her mother's. An accident, a stupid unforgettable, unforgivable accident. He let her out of his sight. His lapse in concentration. His fault.

'I see her hair spread, her mouth wide, her fists....'

His eyes fill, Bird's eyes fill.

'So hard, so cold. And I look at my boy – I look at my boy and I think –'

Face twists, lip curls.

'I think –'

Don't say it. Don't say it, Bird thinks. I can't unhear it. They can't unhear it. Don't say it.

'Why not him.'

Now the stranger looks at the girls, at Alma and Dara. Long he looks, as if daring them in some way. Speak his eyes seem to say – speak. Condemn me. Then he grasps his head in his hands, pulls at his hair, sobs.

On it goes. On and on. Bird listens all day as the girls listen. Bird, Alma, Dara listen.

A mother doesn't love her baby; a husband beats his wife; a grandmother weeps because her daughter won't speak to her and she hasn't seen her grandchildren in over a year; a man trembles because he can't sleep for seeing the eyes of every man, woman and child he killed in battle; an old man smiles while recounting how he got away with strangling a peasant girl. And on it goes – a man, a woman, a man, a woman. Sad, lonely, angry, bitter, delusional, frightened. The sound of coins hitting the bowl, Mary's laughter, the chair scraping the floor. A man, a woman,

LEAVING

a man, a woman ....

♦

Bird is wretched by the end of the day. Bird is sick. Quiet she lies, exhausted. Pressure, like a thumb pushing on the back of her head, pushing her down. The weight of the words. Bird remembers – remembers her own sister. Lying together, side by side, in bed. Remembers the pressure, the tightening of chest, the nausea, neither sleeping, the swollen air, tight with his coming, treacle darkness, the creak of the bed, a moan...

♦

Weeping. Mary is weeping. The sound brings Bird back to the room behind the glass.

'Daughters of mine' – softly, the woman who is Mother, who is Mary, speaks – 'Daughters of mine.'

Mary's face is red, eyes ice-blue. Deflated, crying, she calls to them. Sitting in her chair, crumpled, she calls.

'Alma, Dara, my little ones,' she beckons.

Alma, Dara watch her, stand close, but out of reach, hesitant, trembling. Dark-eyes uncertain. On and on, she calls, beseeching, unrelenting, like the words of the others.

Dara steps forward, touches her mother's shoulder, Mary enfolds her in her arms and rocks with her, eyes shut, sobbing. Alma does not move. Alma only watches. Bird watches. Bird can see Alma waiting – waiting for what?

Rocking, rocking, Mary cries. Dara disappears in her grip. Rocking, rocking, faster, faster, faster – until she stops.

Bird's breath stops. Everyone is still. A wail – long and loud erupts. Mary begins to shake Dara – 'What did I do to deserve this? What did

I do?' Alma rushes forward, pulling at her mother's fingers, trying to break her sister free.

Mary pushes Alma to the floor. Rising up, holding tight to Dara, jabbing her finger at Alma – 'You,' she says, 'You who won't comfort your own poor mother. Ungrateful brat. After all I do for you –' and then she sinks back in the chair. Releases Dara, and weeps.

The girls back away, crying, facing their mother, moving towards their room. But Mary does not move, Mary doesn't notice even when they shut the door.

◆

Bird! Bird!

Alma, Dara calling.

Bird, remember – remember how you were saved. Remember for us.

Bird's dream shifts, it coils in on itself – a canary. Buttery-yellow, soft, sweet. It sings to Bird and her sister. A present from Father. The little bird in a cage, the little bird with a mighty song. She and her sister sit spellbound. Something so small that's so loud. Unbelievable! It sings as if it calls to all the other birds out there – Help me! – it seems to say – Rescue me from this cage!

When Father goes out, they set it free to fly around the house. They cannot bear for it to be trapped inside, they feel its distress, its pain.

Bird is Bird, but not Bird. Bird is Lola. Lot is her sister – Bird remembers. LOT. LOLA.

Dream-Lola and dream-Lot dance around after the canary, clapping their hands, whistling, laughing. Tears fall – happy, sad, tears of longing. The canary settles on Lot's shoulder, it looks at the girls, at their tears. Its little head beckons, Lola puts out her hand, the canary hops

LEAVING

onto her palm.

Fee. Fi. Fo. Fum.

They stop. They hear his terrible step, the sound of the key in the lock, his throat clearing.

Fee. Fi. Fo. Fum.

The canary nips Lola's finger – the lightest of pecks. Lola cries out, a tiny bead of blood swells.

Fee. Fi. Fo. Fum.

The hinges creak with his terrible weight.

Fee. Fi. Fo. Fum.

Onto Lot's hand it hops –

Fee. Fi. Fo. Fum.

Nip. Split. Bead of blood. The canary sings a song, full and strong, it flies –

Fee. Fi. Fo. Fum.

– up the chimney. They are alone with Father.

Father's eyes bulge, his mouth opens wide, spittle flies, and he says – Nothing.

Father can only watch as Lola sprouts feathers. Green and blue and purple they push through puckering skin. Lot, too. They start at the fingertip and spread. Orange and pink and yellow for Lot.

Bird watches, but Bird can remember, too. Can feel the bones contorting, shifting, shrinking, rearranging. Nose hardens, elongates and swallows mouth, separates – beak. Arms lengthen, dwindle, taper – wings flap.

Lola is Bird and Bird is flying. Round and round the room she flies, opens her beak and sings, round and round and up and down – the joy, the release, out of the reach of Father, up through the chimney, hurtling towards the bright light of day.

Bird is free! Over trees and houses, the sun on her feathers, houses far below. Houses with their four walls and roofs and locked doors and dark rooms. A river winds its way alongside them – a river she has never seen, only heard about. Bird follows it. Flits through reeds and chases dragonflies.

Catching her breath, she admires her reflection – spreads her wings to feel the space around her, the cool air, and she turns to share her delight, turns this way and that and –

And Lot is not there.

LOST LOT.

Bird lost Lot. Bird wakes and it floods back. Bird left Lot behind and Father trapped Lot in a cage. Bird tried to get back in, tried to make her way back down the chimney, but Father kept a fire burning. Always a fire burned, always smoke poured from the chimney, billowing clouds of grey. Seasons changed. Lot called. She called to Lola, to Bird, the sound throbbed in Bird's dreams. Bird tried to get in, tried to bear the smoke, crack a window with her tiny beak, slip in the door when Father left or returned. But to no avail. She watched from the window her sister in a cage, small, pitiful, unable to fly in such a small space, plucking at feathers till bald spots bloomed, pink and angry. Snow fell. Lot's song dwindled, the cries in Bird's dream became more frantic.

And then one day no smoke rose from the chimney, there were no dream-cries for help, and Bird knew that Lot was gone.

◆

Bird waits. Bird watches. Bird listens. The people come all day, every day, in and out: coins drop, tears fall, secrets spill. Mary becomes more errat-

LEAVING

ic. Manic smiles in the day, yelling or silences at night.

Bird shares the weight of the words with Alma and Dara, the weight of Mary until the Sunday. Mary's day of rest. Mary's day for sleeping and counting. In the morning, though, Alma and Dara collect wood. Bird will wait for that. For the girls to be outside.

The girls call to her in dreams and Bird tells them – I am coming, I am coming.

◆

Snow falls, sun breaks through trees. Bird waits for Alma and Dara to step out of the house, bundled up in their red coats, baskets in hand.

But the girls do not come.

Bird alights on the windowsill to see their bedroom empty. She checks another window to find it covered up – and another and another. Bird can't see inside. Bird can't hear a thing.

All day she waits, but no one stirs.

◆

Bird sleeps, but her dreams are quiet. Filled with falling snow and feathers and twin heartbeats.

◆

People come the next day, but Mary smiles and sends them away.

'My girls are not well. No one can come for a week at least, maybe more.'

Bird hears cries of protest, tears are wept, one or two ask if there is anything they can do.

'No, no. We'll be fine. I'll look after those daughters of mine.'

'Such a good mother,' the people say. 'For all she's been cursed with, look how she's carried on and made those girls her whole world with all the hardships that's entailed.'

◆

Windows stay boarded up, house is quiet except for the occasional curse or the low sound of crying. Bird can't tell who is crying, but she knows who yells. Smoke curls up from the chimney. Again, Bird is shut out.

But, Bird can't be quiet. Won't be quiet.

Night and day, Bird flits from window to window, tapping on the glass with her beak, brushing her wings against it, squawking. Mary swears and occasionally comes out to chase Bird. Throws a ladle, a book, rocks from the ground.

The beat of Bird's wings, the tone of her cries: I am watching you! I am watching you! Remember I'm here, watching you!

'Leave me be! Leave me be!' Mary sobs back. 'You don't understand.'

Gaunt, guarded, she slips back inside.

◆

Bird collapses into sleep now, night or day, exhausted. She dreams of snow and feathers and Mary's fractured gaze, brittle voice.

SAD. Thinks Bird.

Twin hearts beat faintly in the background.

SICK.

Bird changes tack. Sings soft songs, soothing songs, lullabies. Tired, so tired, is Bird. But on she goes, on. Throat raw, wings aching, fear rising.

Gentle, Bird thinks. I must be gentle. I must tread carefully.

A week crawls by.

LEAVING

◆

And then, in a dream –
    Bird. Bird.
    Softer than ash.
    Bird. Bird.
    Along with the heartbeats, brittle and breaking.
    Bird, she has killed us. Bird, we are not dead, but she has killed us. You sang your soft songs and she relented, but she can't undo what is done.
    Sobs muffle the words. Alma, Dara strain to be heard:
    She was scared, Bird. Scared that we would leave her. That we would find a way. She said she saw it in our eyes, felt it in her heart. We would leave her like Father. So, she shut us away and told us we were sick. Here, my girls, my little ones, she said, have your medicine to make you better. But it made us worse, Bird. Rotted our insides, made us weaker than babies. You tried, Bird. We know you tried. We heard you. But it is too late.

◆

A howl, forlorn, in the space between dream and waking.
    Bird shoots into the air with the sound.
    The door's wide open. Mary shuffling into the night.
    And then it's a blur – Bird moves but is barely aware of it. Bird is flight and fury and fear. Images separate but converge out of order – Alma and Dara on the bed – Mary weeps, wanders in the snow– Alma and Dara, damp, pale, sticky – Mary throws her hands up to the sky – Alma and Dara, vomit stains the sheets – Mary mutters to herself: sorry, sorry, sorry – Alma and Dara, Bird hears the faintest heartbeat and it all slows down.

Bird nips the girls' fingers, one after the other – nothing. Not a stir, not a flinch. It's not enough.

And so, Bird pecks at the chest of one girl, then the other, wasting no time, moving between them, pecking, worrying away, through flesh and muscle and bone. Metallic, warm, the blood covers her face, blinds her, but still she works until two weakly throbbing hearts reveal themselves. Bird pierces the thick protective sack of Alma's, pushes past the soft membrane into the centre, parts her beak, and sings. Blood gushes forth, fills her throat, Bird feels she will drown, but still she sings.

A jolt! A gasp!

'Bird,' a croak. 'Da - ra.'

Stunned, Bird watches Alma trying to sit up, tugging at her sister, words croaking, not in a dream but now. Feathers are pushing through her skin: orange, yellow, pink. Alma's shrinking, changing, words shifting into birdsong – a sad, desperate melody, pain-stricken at moments with the sound of bones cracking, realigning.

Bird, tired as she is, exhausted, heavy with blood and strain, hops onto Dara's chest, plunges into the cavity, sings. But though she sings and sings, Dara's heartbeat grows fainter. Tears pour into the song, mix with the blood – not again, thinks Bird, not again –

– and then, another song, stronger than Bird's, joins in. A warm body, small and feathered next to her own: Alma.

Song floods Dara's heart, forces it to swell and beat –

shudder, cough

Darkness swells, Bird blacks out.

◆

Bird is not alone. There is Alma. There is Dara. Identical. Feathers like the bloom of a new day.

LEAVING

Bird has sisters.

Dara and Alma clean Bird. Wash her, preen her feathers with their beaks, combing them gently, tenderly, till they lie flat and glossy.

Bird is weak at first. And then she's strong.

Bird, Alma, Dara they fly. One, two, three, they swoop and glide. They sing. They pause. They listen.

Speak, speak, we can speak! We can be heard.

Only in dreams do they hear her calling –

Daughters of mine

hear Mary, feel her sadness, her fear, taste her tears. They understand, but they cannot reach her, cannot be where she is, cannot help. Can only listen –

Daughters of mine –

distorted, barely there. As if her tongue's been plucked from her mouth, or her voice is muffled by snow and feathers.

My Name Was Joy
Alan Kennedy
Spain

Judge's Choice

'MY BIRTH NAME WAS JOY, though I experienced none till Krishna found me.' I memorised this speech for newcomers to the temple. My real name was Rhona, Rhona Binnie.

In the summer before starting medical school, my boyfriend, Drew, planned a three-month trip to India, the birthplace of Krishna. After two weeks of enduring cramped local buses, then four days squeezed into a greasy room watching Drew getting smashed on cheap dope, we arrived at a pink marble temple with peacocks strutting around the sweet-smelling garden. The mixture of women chanting coming from inside and the aroma of sandalwood trees made me dizzy.

Next to the latrines, twenty featherless peahens fretted in a row of cages with not enough room to turn around in. I gagged at the stench. Once a day, Govinda opened them to scrape out the droppings. Five men loaded a queue of gaudy lorries with wooden boxes stuffed with statues of Krishna.

LEAVING

We stayed in separate quarters, which was fine by me as I made a friend in the same bunk, but didn't suit Drew. 'I'm with these bald guys who drone on about the material world. Did they tell you we had to stay celibate? They frisked me for hash, flushed it down the toilet. Losers! I detest that bossy geek, Govinda.'

With no money to contribute to the ashram, they ordered Drew back to Scotland, to cut his long hair, find a well-paid job, send half his earnings to the centre.

'You can't stay here, Rhona. This place will rot your mind.'

'I have no intention of going anywhere. This chanting makes me – I don't know – happier than ever.'

'What about uni?'

'Krishna gives me all the knowledge I need.'

'What? Rhona, you've lost it. I'm not leaving without you.' He grabbed me, yelled, pleaded with me to return. The temple manager Govinda told Drew anger caused harmful vibrations before beating him up with the help of four other saffron robed priests, then expelling him. I sobbed for days.

◆

The following month, my sister, Kyla, arrived with no warning. Through tears she shouted at me. 'Rhona. What in God's name have you done to yourself? You're a skeleton. Why don't you write?'

'How did you find me? Did Drew…?'

'Drew? – Rhona, didn't you…? – They found him floating face down in the Yamuna River not two miles from here. Suicide. He sent a typewritten letter to his folks.'

'What? Drew couldn't type to save his life.' I laughed at my own unintended joke. Drew belonged to an incarnation of which nothing remained.

Kyla glared at me. 'Listen. It's mum. She's not too good. Please come home. She...'

Govinda, who reared the peacocks and led the chanting, butted in: 'Joy can visit in her mind. On this important transition between worlds, she will accompany your birthmother, surrounded by her siblings.'

Kyla looked the well-fed, well-spoken, orange robed Englishman up and down. 'I am her sister, curly! Her name's Rhona. Who the hell are you?'

Govinda held in his paunch and followed her gaze. 'I am the brahmachari, the leader of this centre. You have an hour to vacate the premises. If you'll excuse me, I must feed my girls... Joy! Back to work! Our statues won't paint themselves.' Four silent priests placed themselves behind Kyla and marched her out the front gate.

Mum died the following month. My sister never spoke to me again.

◆

After my mother's passing, Govinda told me of a special ritual to symbolise the union of Krishna with his handmaidens. I wanted to consult Kamalehka, my new friend, but he said it was a secret privilege. In his room, he instructed me to disrobe, to confirm that my birthmark was a sacred sign... my mouth dried up... I couldn't move. How did he know about my birthmark...? The showers...! I was bewildered. We were to stay chaste. He alleged Krishna manifested himself through the brahmacharis. I was a virgin. Men didn't interest me that way.

Govinda rammed me into the wall. The rusting drainpipe sent a wave of pain down my back. I yanked his top knot, the ponytail meant to pull him up to heaven. He squealed as my other fist swung up to smash into his windpipe. I ducked from his hand which slammed into the plaster. He grasped my shoulders. He soon discovered my temper, so did his bruised eye, not to mention his blackened, bleeding testicles. My knee rose and fell again and again, pumping into his groin. He buckled, swearing in a non-spiritual way. I stamped on his head and ran out.

I sought Kamalehka, who burst out crying. 'He tried it on with me last week. I didn't know who to tell. He threatened me.'

'Let's stuff the spyholes in the baths with clay; the creep won't be able to spy on us in the showers.'

We quizzed the other women, but half didn't talk, the others looked away. Coming out of the female quarters, I was seized, branded as an animal and locked in a cage they used for the peahens. I couldn't stand.

Govinda came to gloat when he left hospital three days later. He was limping, walked with a cane and a nappy bulged out of his robes.

'Let me out, you worthless piece of –'

'Now, now, Joy. We don't want to upset the birds, do we? We need their eggs.'

'My name's not Joy, you mental case. Open this door. A joke's a joke, but…'

'Krishna's brought out the spirit in you, that's good. Better leave you in here a while till you find your inner peace.'

'I'll shove my inner peace where the sun doesn't shine, you –'

'Here, in Krishna's gaze, the sun shines everywhere. Now, I've come to see my handmaidens. Hello, my lovelies, did you miss your beloved Govinda?' He turned to the other cages to talk to the silent, staring fowl.

Every two days, the same four thugs that arrested me opened the cage, picked the scabs off the scratched outline of the brand and retraced it with a compass. I passed out the first time.

◆

The following month, Kamalekha got dysentery, the only one in the temple. No doctors came. They chanted instead, but she died three days later.

When they let me out to attend the funeral prayer session, I saw my chance to escape. They tracked me to the station, carrying me back to the ashram, hiding my sandals. Four of them started to thrash me with branches of sandalwood. They blindfolded me but I recognised Govinda's panting. I pleaded with him to stop. He spoke to me as if I were excrement. 'Krishna doesn't allow you to desert.'

The cage creaked open.

My birth name was Joy, but I never experienced any.

Period.

◆

The Guardian of India – September 5th
As part of an ongoing anti-drugs campaign, local security forces in Vrindadrin stormed the English-run Holy Krishna temple yesterday at dawn.

Tipped off by the families of four missing adults, the officers found five pounds of white powder inserted into statues, ready to be exported to Great Britain. Several kidnap victims, showing signs of torture, were released from cages. One young Scottish woman, back bent and scarred, stated she was there for two winters. Doctors doubt she will ever be able to straighten up again.

The leader of the ashram remains at large. As they burned the records in the assault, his alias, Govinda, is the only clue the police have. The investigations continue.

LEAVING

◆

I passed the row of burnt-out cars, battened up shops, bare windows. I wondered whether I was in England. As nothing prepared me for such decay, I checked the Satnav on the car. Five minutes away. It was an unusual case in Hertfordshire, Home Counties personified. I was the nearest tropical disease specialist. When I pulled into the overgrown driveway, I placed my disability sticker on the dashboard.

Inside the hospice my mood darkened. Only four of the ten lightbulbs in the gloomy reception were working. My back brace set off the metal detector. The nurse at the desk slapped the alarm with a magazine.

'Doctor Rhona Binnie,' I handed her my I.D.

'In here, doctor,' she pointed at the faded yellow door to my right with her rolled-up biker monthly. 'Your first time in Letchworth?'

'Yes, your Doctor Knowles called me. Can I see him?'

'He's on his lunch break,' the nurse mimed drinking a pint of beer. 'I'd try the Pig and Snout.'

'If you don't mind, I'd like to see the patient. Jerome Folley.'

She led me into the 'isolation' room, a large windowless cupboard with a fold up bed. A fishing net hung from the ceiling. I hadn't expected the cuts were hitting this hard.

I picked up the chart. 'I see they admitted Mr Folley with stage four brain cancer with little sign of recovery. How long ago did you notice these rashes?'

'On Sunday. We thought they were bed sores but then they started on his face. Doctor Knowles was stumped. That's why he gave your department a bell. We know nothing about Mr Folley; he doesn't have a medical record. The poor soul never says much, less so now the tumour has spread.' The nurse tapped me on the arm. 'No family,' she mouthed.

'It says here his testicles have been surgically removed.'

'Weird, that is. We don't know why or where. By the looks of the stitching, bit of a botch job. Keeps mumbling he had no top knot. Beats me what he means.'

My mouth went dry. 'Top knot?' Many years had passed since I'd heard that term. The scar on my back itched. The hairs on my arm prickled. I glanced again at the bald man in the bed. Such a long time ago. It can't be? He looked different, older, wrinkled.

I recoiled from the familiar tell-tale odour of a disease from another time, another far-off place. 'Govinda.' To say the name felt like eating my vomit.

He shuddered. His eyes, heavy with morphine, stared at me. Fighting the medication, he flinched, tried to escape. His lips pursed to say something, but a spasm contorted his body. Despite the mask and gown, he recognised me, wanted to flee but couldn't move.

'It's okay. It was a long time ago. I forgive you.' I forced myself not to run away, although the lie was choking me. He was my patient, at my mercy. The branded scar in the shape of Om between my shoulder blades throbbed. His doing. This husk of a man. Old memories reborn, old wounds reopened. I enjoyed this reversal, this chance for revenge.

The nurse came running over from emptying the bedpan. 'Doctor, are you OK? You've gone bright red.'

'It's nothing. I'm fine. He reminded me of someone, that's all. I must have startled the poor wretch. He doesn't have long to go.'

The built-up rage from the two years I was caged, unable to stand, beaten, branded as cattle was overwhelming me. It felt like yesterday. Here he was, my sadistic warden, imprisoned.

'No top knot to drag you up to Heaven, have you?' I said, half to myself.

LEAVING

The man in the bed scanned me, moving his lips in a voiceless plea, his eyes darted to the drip beside him. I resisted upping the morphine. Whatever I did, he'd be dead within the day.

'Do you need me, Doctor?' the nurse unfolded her magazine. 'I've got to catch up with paperwork.'

'I'm fine. A few more tests, thanks.' I waited till she left the room and turned to my onetime torturer.

'So, Jerome Folley, or should I say "Govinda"? Let's travel in our minds towards ancient times… My name was Joy…'

Gladstone's Sorrow

Laura Ann Kenny
United Kingdom

Winner of the 2019
Student Category

GEORGE GLADSTONE CONSIDERED HIMSELF a man of good virtues and understanding of the individual desires a person might possess. The difficulty he faced in his life was the collective mind of others who didn't share in his views or, to be more specific, didn't want to entertain the views of someone like him.

George was a man of good virtues indeed, yet even now he knew that that was simply not enough to survive the unjustified hatred of others. Thinking of this just made him more regretful of his actions. You must know something about George, something that many believed cancelled out all the good and noble qualities he possessed.

George was a homosexual.

In his time the general belief was that it wasn't natural for a man to be intimate with another man, let alone have romantic feelings for each other. Oh, there's one more thing you should be aware of.

You see, George is dead.

LEAVING

He really wanted me to tell you that.

◆

It can really be quite a pain when you go to bed knowing you won't get a well-rested sleep due to sifting through the deceased memories, but one doesn't exactly have much choice in the matter when the ghost in question is rather forceful.

A frightened yet skeptical family had asked for my services on a bitterly cold November evening back in 2014 and I honestly couldn't turn down such a commission.

The moment I arrived, luggage and all, to this glorious and awe-encompassing house I immediately sensed a difference between those that resided here. The walls of the lobby were coated in a thick luxurious paper that was adorned with black swirls and gold highlights, the house had electricity but you could imagine a time in which it worked well without it given the amount of candles and oil lamps that were about the place. It was cold but personally I didn't feel like this was coming from a lack of heat in the house itself, there were lit fireplaces and heavy velvet curtains hung upon every window to keep the draft out. More so I felt that whatever spirit was linked to this house was the true cause of the morose atmosphere.

It was on my return to my room that I met the two boys, Harry and Arthur Bingham, as they played with a wooden car set on the landing of the first floor. Smartly dressed even for this time of the evening and reserved in that quintessential British way, these boys were a mix of curiosity and fear in a way I hadn't seen before.

'Hello there, you must be Harry. And you, young sir must be Arthur. It's a pleasure to meet you both,' I softly spoke to them, afraid that I might startle them further if I was too loud.

They both nodded in response. Harry, the oldest of the two, stuck his hand out firmly for me to shake whilst his brother Arthur stood silently and slightly behind him in the shadows.

'Are you Mr. Thorpe? The ghost catcher?' Harry boldly asked me. I smiled. The innocence of children always astounded me, they were never afraid of getting to the point when they were curious.

'Yes, that's my name. Though I don't catch ghosts as it were, usually they have a reason for sticking around. Tell me, have you boys seen anything unusual in your home lately? I promise I'm here to help, that's all.' I watched as they turned to each other quite comically as if to telepathically confirm whether they would tell me their secret or not.

'George.' A quiet voice spoke; young Arthur had muffled his word behind his thumb as he nervously nibbled on it. I waited a beat for him to continue, noticing that although he seemed nervous, he wasn't afraid of this "George".

'George is our friend. Mummy says to not play with him anymore, but he's nice,' he said, frowning.

'George reads us to sleep and plays games with us! Though Mother says he's not real. He is! Father doesn't allow us to talk about him anymore, but George says he doesn't like our Father much anyways and to not listen to him when he's being loud,' Harry added.

'Being loud?' I asked.

'When Daddy shouts,' Arthur mumbled my way.

Before I could ask them anymore, a yell from Mrs. Bingham downstairs had them scampering to what I imagined to be their bedroom and thus ending my impromptu interview. I was more than intrigued at the first mention of a George that only the boys could see.

It was in my room, at precisely thirty-three minutes past three in the morning that I first encountered the mysterious George.

LEAVING

◆

He was hovering. I've grown accustomed to seeing spirits since I was a child but, let me tell you, it still shocks you when they randomly appear at the foot of your bed and gaze at you all expectantly and hollow-eyed whilst you're in your underpants.

'Who are you?' I asked after scrambling to protect my modesty with the bedspread.

He didn't answer my question, but then I never really expected him to through experience. Instead he continued to appraise me coldly. I could see a wealth of emotion in those hard, blackened globes, which brought the hairs on my arms upwards out of alarm. It was clear to me in this moment that the man had died in the most tragic way.

'I'm not here to expel you from this house. I am merely here to help you, I'm on your side. So please I understand you are in pain –'

'*Pain?*' he roared.

He zipped over to me so fast my head was hurled backwards against the thick mahogany headboard, a coppery taste filled my mouth and my heart raced at the suddenness of it all.

'You know nothing of my pain, nothing of what I had to endure!' he snarled, anger completely taking over his features and almost contorting his facial structure to that of a monster.

His face, just moments before, had resembled that of a young man with pale paper-white skin and dark brown hair a floppy mess atop his head. He looked unkempt yet poised at the same time, a slight shadow of a beard cupped his cheeks and his attire was dated by the high starched collar with its tips pressed firmly into wings and his three-piece tweed suit that highlighted his narrow waist and slim figure. There was a discolouration on the right side of his shirt I noticed, as if something had overflown from his lips and fallen onto his disheveled clothes. Though now all I could see was the hatred and anger in those eyes all directed at me.

'You're right, I shouldn't have assumed anything. I'm sorry. But I meant what I said, I just want to help.' Trying my best to calm the situation I slowly scooted further back on the bed.

'How am I to be helped? I did something awful to befall this fate, and you cannot simply turn back the hands of time!'

The figure moved back, sadness lacing his words and beating down the anger to a slow hum.

'Don't bother answering, I know you can't help one such as me. I'm a vile and soulless creature, in life and in death.'

'The two young boys living here don't quite think so. You are George, aren't you?'

I decided to take a leap of faith and address him by the name Harry and Arthur had given me and watched as the confusion washed over him by mentioning the kids, melting away the negativity.

'They are just children, what do they know? Though I must admit, they have made my imprisonment here a little more bearable. They told you about me?' George asked.

'They called you their friend. They didn't have a chance to say much more, but I could tell they weren't afraid of you. Children can see through our lingering pain and simply accept us for who we are. You are kind to them; therefore, you aren't a monster,' I told him, offering the proverbial olive branch.

George became quiet for a moment. He ran his hand slowly through his messy hair, out of habit perhaps, not that it moved of course, frozen in time like the rest of him. Yet I could feel a change, not a huge one, but enough to hopefully help him move on.

He scoffed.

'Not a monster,' George almost whispered, his eyes holding back unshed-able tears. 'I doubt that very much. I think you should see what happened.' George turned to me again, except this time his face was unreadable, and his words put fear back in me.

'Prepare yourself sir.' That was all he said before he launched his ghostly self at me, and I fell into a liquid icy darkness.

◆

Swirling masses of silver fog was all I saw until I could focus on what was before me. It strained my eyes and brought that familiar burn of a headache to the forefront, I persevered willing my senses to come back to me.

When I was able to finally see things in full colour I was astounded to find I was not in the bed that just moments before had been beneath me. Something had been altered and distorted until I had been thrust into this other world. Feeling a light tingling sensation through my extremities, I glanced down and noticed my body was almost translucent, a soft veil of a glow surrounded the perimeter of my entire being and though I thought I was touching the floor I was actually in fact almost floating a few inches from it.

The décor in the room was dark and dimly lit with soft candlelight, the glow seemed to bounce off the glossed wooden furniture and was interspersed with elegant fabrics that adorned the chairs along with heavily patterned wallpaper that made the room feel smaller somewhat. A musky scent filled the air and reminded me of the comfort of old books, long nights studying and cozy cafes drinking rich coffee with my favourite novels. One thing that stood out the most was the lavish carved sign that hung above the door, centered by huge front windows, that read *Wilkin Publishing House Limited* in bold black text.

A bell brought me out of my musings, and I panicked as a noteworthy looking gentleman came into the room. Confidently striding across the parquet styled wooden floor, his steps softening when they hit the thin red patterned rug that lay across the center of the room that added warmth and colour to the space. I didn't dare move; I just waited and desperately tried to come up with a reasonable explanation in my head should he ask who the hell I was.

However, the man walked right past me and seated himself at the large desk in the back corner adorned with papers, inks, books and other writing materials that made me believe him to be the owner of the establishment I was in. I gingerly walked over to the desk and found a newspaper strewn over some of the books. Picking it up I glanced over it quickly reading the headline: OSCAR WILDE AT BOW STREET, dated Saturday April 20th 1895.

'1895!' I exclaimed, before checking if he noticed me. Not a movement from him at all, and I let out a sigh of relief at my findings.

The man at the desk looked up and focused his attention on something behind me, another set of footsteps came from that area and when I turned, I saw a very familiar face as they approached the desk.

'Ah George! Good timing, I just had lunch with Mr. Hemmings, he said to go ahead with the proposed illustrations we had made for him. Could you see to that for me?'

'I'll sort it right away Mr. Wilkin! Oh, Miss Jensen stopped by whilst you were out,' George answered Mr. Wilkin politely, but there was a hint of annoyance at the mention of the lady.

I stood there, mouth agape, at George all alive and well. There was a rosy radiance back to his face and he looked smart and refined in his clean clothes. He bent over the desk and took the papers that Mr. Wilkin was holding out for him. I watched as the exchange happened and George's fingers slowed when they brushed up against his superiors'.

LEAVING

It seemed like eternity past before both men came out of their bubble, George's flushed face and diluted pupils said more than any words could in that moment. Mr. Wilkin cleared his throat, his face a little pinker now too.

'I see. I said what I needed to say to her before, and I honestly can't see a reason why she would continue to put herself through any more embarrassment.'

Mr. Wilkin ran a hand over his thick moustache, in contemplation. George on the other hand looked visibly irritated and his lips pursed into a thin line in response.

'The woman is infatuated with you; can't you see that? It kills me that she is able to express that towards you when I am highly prohibited from doing so William,' George said with discernible distain.

'I have no feelings towards her. I know how you feel, it's not as if I don't want to fully embrace what we have between us. But look at the times, it's dangerous for us to have our guard down right now. You must be careful,' William pleaded.

George simply nodded at his lover and walked away papers in hand. It was true that during this time they were forbidden to be in love. It was a prison-able offence for a man to love another man or be caught in any act of homosexuality. The problem was that there wasn't an exact guideline on what constituted homosexuality, therefore with such a blurred line there were many cases of innocent people being persecuted for such things.

It made me think of my brother Cameron's own struggles. The sleepless nights he had before he came out to our parents, the way he made himself sick with worry over thinking how people might suddenly start treating him. Though keeping it a secret was more detrimental to his mental health, only I knew of his sexuality at the time and I lost count the amount of occasions I had rushed him to A&E after he had drunk himself into a stupor or had taken various drugs to escape the pressure.

◆

My vision distorted suddenly, and I was whisked away again in that milky mist. When the scene cleared, I was able to see George and William once more. This time they were standing with a group of other men dressed in evening attire. A rowdy debate was going on, fueled by the beer in their hand and the heated gossip about town.

'It simply isn't God's will!' a portly gentleman sneered. 'A man should not engage in a sexual act with another man, it's utterly unnatural. I can't see that this Wilde fellow will get away with his depravity!' he bellowed to the group.

My eyes focused on George and William; their eyes averted. William's knuckles were white with tension against his pewter tanker and George was clearly already drunk, his eyes bloodshot and unfocused with a swaying figure. He took markedly more gulps of his drink as the conversation deteriorated into a dissection of the nature of those that were partaking in such acts.

The night went on and further into the abyss I saw the fragile George drown. It was like a car wreck I couldn't take my eyes away from and my gut clenched as I realised where this was leading.

Darkness fell and George stumbled out, heading home with a heavy heart, sobbing and mumbling to himself about the awful things he'd just heard from those he thought were his friends. I knew then that this wasn't the first time he'd had to endure this; this secret had weighed him down and hacked away at his soul.

I cried with him only moments later when he took his own life after writing a simple note to William telling him he didn't want to bring him

LEAVING

further into a life of secrecy and lies.

One sentence stood out the most: *"We are nothing but monsters to these people, but without me I pray you have a life in the light rather than the shadows,"* which spoke volumes on how George came to this moment.

◆

I woke back in my own time and found George staring at me.

'I shouldn't have done it. I was a coward and afraid, that's why I can't leave.' George explained, head hung low.

'You are nothing like a coward George. It takes a lot of being beaten down to get to that point, trust me. Your fear drove you there, but it doesn't have to keep you here. You can move on and nothing bad will befall you. You have my word.'

'I want so badly to believe you.'

'Let go George, it's time for you to finally be with William.'

It took some time that night to convince George that he was worth 'saving' but I put everything I had into making him believe that, despite how he viewed taking his own life. By the time morning came and I said my goodbyes to the residents of the house I felt an enormous sense of relief knowing that I hadn't left him there to wallow in that darkness anymore. As the taxi drove me to the train station, I took out my mobile and dialed a number I was all too familiar with.

'Cameron, hi. I really want to talk you about something.'

The New Sieve

Colin Kerr
United Kingdom

Shortlisted for the 2019
International Writing Competition

WHEN I FIRST NOTICED THE STARS, I was confused – they weren't where I expected them to be. The more I stared at the stars, the closer they seemed. Not threatening but beckoning me; enclosing then passing into me. I would lie on the bench at the top of the local hill, the autumnal breeze passing over me, and watch them. I had always imagined them high above me, but now it was more as if sparkling netting was being lowered onto my face. The way hot plastic will mould to a shape as it cools. As I watched them, they moved, or seemed to move. Of course, it was the Earth moving but I thought about the times when people trembled at thunder and believed the stars were our canopy; the very idea of a heliocentric state of affairs being heretical; and so people would suffer for nothing more than explaining beauty. And then I started to think about how many of the stars I could see were already dead. Long exploded but their furtive messages still hurtling to wherever they were hurtling to. Delayed calls from the past. The simplicity of how a river just

LEAVING

flows; the inevitability and relentlessness, going from here to there, no reason, no excuses, always leaving.

I had started to take longer walks in the evening. I'd been walking for a regular forty minutes every night, for three years. Always the same route: along a certain street, down and across another, under the watch of the hill, then back up a wide road, lined with blossom trees, to join the street I'd started walking on. I'd been worrying about my weight and an evening walk, before we had supper, seemed a sensible idea. Sometimes she'd come with me but mostly I'd be on my own; listening to music, motivating myself about this and that and feeling my leg muscles strengthen over the months.

But now the walks were becoming longer. The blossom was long gone and at times the trees felt sinister, the way the branches were gnarled and curled. It reminded me of witches scratching at the window – when I was much younger, staying at my aunt's, I would lie awake, scared of the shadows the bare branches made on the curtains, convincing myself witches were tempting me. My walks began to last several hours. I'd come home – if it was still home – later and later. Soon it was often after midnight and sometimes, by the time I reached home, dawn would be breaking with the last shades of nautical twilight leaving.

It was about a week after she left, when I was on my evening walk, that the leaf fell. I'd stopped on one of the benches that lined the route. It was wooden, below and to the west of the hill I had taken to lying on. The hill resembled a sleeping bear – if you looked at it in a certain way. A bear with a large, round stomach, wearing boots, with a premature summit for a snout and trees for a bed. The trees skirted the base of the hill, along a sloping path, which led down to a pond. The area around the pond was a haven for bats and at twilight, back when my sight was still good, I could see black specs taunting the trees. There was a tree by the bench I was sitting on – I was taking a rest, my foot was hurting again – and I was looking up, towards the bear, when a leaf fell. I'd never seen a leaf fall with such violence. Others would drift or spin, or be caught by an updraught and loop, as if they were planes performing for a crowd, but this leaf threw itself to the ground. It seemed angry and dissatisfied.

During the day, the bench was a vantage point to the world of the suburban affluent, retired and otherwise not at work. During those first few weeks after she left, I would make sandwiches and sit on the bench. I needed structure and it gave me an excuse to be out of the flat. There were cyclists, dog walkers and, one day, a couple, pausing by the sign that marked the beginning of one of the paths that led to the hill. They were taking photos of each other, standing next to the sign. Pointing at it, pointing at themselves. I couldn't understand what was interesting about the sign, it was just a name. But I didn't know the names of the couple. They'd take photos, then come together and shake or nod their judgement. I thought about offering to take a photo of them together, but I was already losing my confidence around people; that happened so slowly I didn't really notice – or not the way you'd notice if your car had been stolen.

One of those afternoons, I saw the smallest dog I'd ever seen. It was being fed chocolate by a woman who was looking across at me with a questioning expression. She seemed to be looking for confirmation – maybe she was, but I couldn't think of what she was uncertain of – it was a dog, it was a path, it was a hill. Or perhaps it was a life defined by her dog. She was crouching, taking selfies with the dog and editing while the dog stared, perhaps wondering when the next chocolate was coming.

The afternoon of the dog, a cyclist with a large box on wheels went past. I watched it approach from a distance. There was a split in the path before the path reached me, where the path went in three directions and

LEAVING

from a distance, it wasn't entirely clear what was approaching me. Once the cyclist chose my path, I could see it was a large box. 'A dog or shopping,' I thought to myself. But no, it was a child in the box. As the cyclist went past, I caught the child's eyes. The child seemed to ask, 'Why am I in a box?' I didn't have an answer then or now.

The leaf was dark green, it didn't look as if it belonged to the tree. I felt I could hear it hit the crowd, hear the crash, hear it scream. The ground shuddered and I put my hands over my ears. I felt quite shocked, jolted back into time and space. I was there, on the bench; twenty minutes past seven in the evening, on a Sunday, with the sun drenching the bear in red, as it set beyond the houses behind me. I went over and looked at the leaf. It showed no signs of being ready to fall. Nothing indicated it had chosen or accepted its descent. It had a gloss to it, the gloss of an evergreen tree or a porcelain figurine. I began to feel scared looking at it.

That evening, mid-September, it was still light enough to climb back up the hill. It wasn't a long climb and one I had made many times. When I was younger and the hill was brown and dusty, before the trees and shrubs were planted to encourage soil retention, the climb used to be a slippery one. We – my cousins and I – would go the long way up, round by the power substation and along the gravel road. We'd carry old cardboard boxes which we had stamped on, split and flattened; talk about how fast we were going to go and the danger of sliding into the pond at the bottom of the hill; the pond was so far away and surrounded by trees, it wasn't a possibility. But at that age, when lying seems as logical as having enough blocks to reach the Moon, we would thrill ourselves with the danger. We'd go almost to the top of the hill, sit down on the cardboard, let gravity pull us and hang on as long as we could, laughing as we fell off, rolled and slid the rest of the way down.

But then it became a lush green hill with long grass near the shrubs and trees. There were no more teenagers with bicycles or older youths smoking and drinking; paths were clearly marked out for the preservation of replanted wild flowers, with evening walkers – if not their dogs – secure in order; and steps had been cut into the steepest part of the hill. When the steps started to round off, wooden slats were inserted. I would walk up the hill, balancing on the slats, pushing them into the arches of my feet, feeling the pressure. Near the top, the distance between the slats increased and I could feel the stretch in my legs as I felt for each new slat to push into.

Lying down on the bench, I'd think of the sound of waves and the noise the grass made when the wind blew. I didn't know what sort of grass it was. The greener grass on the slopes gave way to tired, yellow grass on the summit of the hill; burnt by the sun and the wind. Late summer grass. The wind made the seeds clatter and I'd think of small sprites and mischievous, mythical creatures, beating out their messages through the seeds, or hundreds of demons, rattling their tiny chains, waiting for the canopy to appear, as the light slipped.

'I'm leaving you,' she said.

With the walking and no reason to be awake at a specific time, my sleeping pattern was disrupted. Up until she left, I regularly slept at least seven hours every night, aiming for nine, without waking up. Sleep had been a lifetime of healing and solace. Back then, I was a firm believer in the adage that things seem different in the morning and, nearly always, better; with rest came perspective and a level head. I had even introduced a nine in the evening rule – no major decision to be made after nine.

But I'd also become fearful of not having those hours or still being awake after midnight. There were hours I feared in the morning and night, and I believed I had to be asleep when they came around. When I was younger, I was woken by my mother to be told of my father's

LEAVING

death and it had always stuck in my mind that that was at six thirty in the morning. There were other times I feared; for instance, four in the morning. Walking was my – at times – nonsensical approach to any of life's stresses. Perhaps it was the idea of being a moving target, constantly leaving and renewing, or there was something I read about how if a body feels it is moving, the subconscious thinks everything must be okay – I read that many years after I started walking.

We'd been together three years when I was woken at four in the morning with what felt like a spiky clove in my throat. Several hours later, it would be diagnosed as tonsillitis but at that time, rather than wake my girlfriend and ask for her thoughts, I went out for a walk. By the time I returned home, near seven, I was exhausted, feverish and she later said, green. I was sick in the hallway; she called a taxi and we went to the hospital. But walking, it solved things, mostly. Or up until she left, it solved things.

Quite apart from all that, no matter what was happening, I had lapsed into being asleep by midnight. I had become superstitious about it. No matter where we'd been out to or what argument was rumbling on, I would be asleep by midnight and there I would sleep until my alarm woke me. When we had first started as a couple, we were both at University. I lived in a noisy flat and had taken to staying with her in her halls of residence. I slept on the floor, on a rug, out of respect for her roommate – it was commonplace to have two or three living in one room in those days. One morning, the fire alarm went off and the only thing that woke me was my girlfriend shaking me.

I had expected my sleep pattern to settle down again, once I settled, but over a decade after she left, I had yet to sleep more than three or perhaps four hours, without waking up. The broken parts perhaps adding up to an average of six hours a night.

A fortnight after she left, when I had managed to establish some sort of new pattern to my bedtime, I took to waking up at three in the morning so I could sit and watch the stars from the lounge window, and watch how the light began to change as the sun began to rise; although never where I expected it. I'd not been awake at that time before, living in that flat, so the sun was at a new angle. It gave the lounge an orange glow I'd not seen before. I'd stay awake, just to experience those hours, new hours to me – I'd not been awake at five for as long as I could remember. And below on the street there would be barely a sound.

I took to cherishing the two hours between three and five. I'd stand at a window, in the dark and cold, gently shiver but not in pain. My body would be asleep or resting and although it was cold, it wasn't the cold I'd feel in the afternoon, or the sting of a January morning, dressing, readying to go out for another day. Or the cold when too much caffeine and not enough food would cause my blood sugar to sink, hormone levels to flicker and my skin to gently shimmer as it sought a balance. There would be few lights on in other buildings and I would walk around the rooms, running my hands across the cold walls, making sense of each room, the door, the carpet. I'd walk from room to room, creeping, gripping the carpet with my toes, a nocturnal hunter, catching all the droplets of time and sense, knowing that there was no more that could be done at that time. Those two hours would seem like a haven. Sometimes it was like the air itself was deep, calm water.

When she said she was leaving, it was me who left, and I began to walk. I walked for two hours to reach a friend's house, left quickly, and walked again; the friend offered little support; very few friends did. I went back towards home but then stopped, sat on the bench I would come to know over the coming days and months, and then started walking again, in a different direction. It was late in the evening when I understood that I had to keep walking, going back was not an option, and as long as I didn't go back, time was suspended.

I could retrace the route I walked that night. Across the hill, over a different hill, through an underpass, up a long street lined with hotels and guest houses, through the poorer, then richer parts of the city. Past houses with curtains tacked up, to others, where luxurious, green velvet curtains parted to reveal deep, period, mahogany walls with imposing bookcases. I walked along paths, grass and pavements, following the trails of underground cables, cracks and moulded concrete ridges; I judged and critiqued trim gardens, overgrown gardens, concrete gardens, their punctuations of trees, water features and ornaments. In the dark, I felt I had almost superhuman energy and that I could outwalk any reality, but my body began to fail.

I began to stumble. Aches that began in my knees moved down to my shins, ankles and then my feet. My right foot began to bleed; the red seeped through my sock into the canvas of my flimsy canvas shoe. It turned red and then brown, as the blood oxidised. As the hours passed, the sock, skin and canvas began to stick together. Later on, the next day, when I reached home, I had to soak my foot in the bath before I could prise the shoe and sock off. I lost two toenails; one of the nail beds never fully recovered and I started to limp. The limp stayed with me for three months and even now, when I am very tired, the limp will return. That walk finally ended in a train station – almost a full day since I had started walking.

As the autumn months gave way to another cold winter, another winter of heavy snow, which was rare by then, my weight began to drop – a combination of not sleeping much, increasing anxiety and no appetite. I lost twenty percent of my weight in three months. I had started underweight due to an overactive thyroid and by October, I looked so emaciated I removed the mirrors in the house to lessen the reminders. And when I did see myself, in the mirrors of lifts and cafes, I'd be shocked at the gaunt look in my face. New ridges and deep creases were forming in my face and my previously young and alert eyes were sagging. The genetic bags under my eyes, which up to that age I had managed to avoid, appeared – swollen and black. I developed a dent below my left cheekbone where I'd sit on the floor, rest my elbow on my knee and lean on the heel of my hand. My head twisted, staring out the window, looking at the stars, the Sun rising or the spire of the church.

When she left, I had no job, no money and no plans other than to keep going. Initially, I had the goal of making it until Christmas, convinced by Christmas, matters would be better; I'd feel safer and more secure. But beyond Christmas waited February and the likely birth of her child. My targets dropped to a month, then a week and then at its worst, about a week after she had left, to getting through the next hour. Even then, I was convinced that I would only need that approach for a short while; but many years later, I would find myself applying the same technique. There was a security that broke that day that failed to return. Or perhaps, when she left, I also began to leave, and at some point, I too, left. And if you are aren't present, then what else can you do other than drift?

My walking took on a pattern of several hours, increasingly around streets I didn't know. A human map making machine, tracking every hedge, garden and house. Tracing the land and infrastructure as I'd trace the walls and carpets with my hands and bare feet at night. I'd stand opposite the bay windows of houses and look in through the open curtains; at families and couples, project perfection onto their lives and wonder how they were there and I was where I was. I'd imagine interviewing the people in those rooms – I'd carefully note the advice they would offer me in terms of life choices. And walking home, I would work out how

LEAVING

I could apply it; how I could get myself out of the walking desolation I was straying into – I could feel it happening; each day, discernibly more desperate, more doubting, more lost.

'I'm leaving you, I'm four months pregnant.'

When I walked, I'd think and try to problem solve; I'd had a successful business career in my twenties, an executive assistant with an industry wide reputation for strategic thinking and ruthless action. I'd try and reduce my situation and what I was feeling to a puzzle that somehow had an answer; because everything had to have an answer: why the leaf fell; why the child was in a box; why that couple were taking photos; why the dog owner looked questioning; why my life was dissolving all around me. I took to carrying a notebook with me. I'd stop, lean on my knee or a wall, or sometimes on the pavement, and write something that I thought was a key, or profound, or an insight: something that would help the journey from where I was to where I was going. After several years, I had a large mound of notebooks and pieces of paper – when I found myself without a notebook, I'd write on whatever I could find: napkins, leaflets for events, receipts. I'd sit on the floor at home, surrounded by notes, cards and books – with passages highlighted, lying flat with broken spines; I'd use string and ribbons to connect ideas. I bought a flip chart and some pens, made diagrams and lists of bullet points. I'd print off motivational cartoons, sayings and pictures and pin them up around the walls.

But when the profound and insightful can fill several boxes, you know they are neither. A decade later, I burnt them all. I filmed it. It had taken a decade to realise it was going nowhere and serving no purpose other than to continually emphasise I was not okay. Or perhaps, as I later realised, I'd left too and so any search would be fruitless, until I came back.

When I returned home, when I had removed the shoe and fixed a bandage over my foot, when I had shut the door of her bedroom, when I had looked into the kitchen, looked at where she had been standing the day before, when she told me she was leaving, only then, I finally looked at what she had been doing when she told me, and I looked at the sieve, the new sieve.

When she told me, she was preparing to bake. She had been sifting flour. She stopped, put the sieve down, turned to me, wiped her hands and began speaking. On the worktop in our, now my, small kitchen, there was a bowl of flour, a jug of water with dust settling on the top, and a sieve, partially filled with flour. She had taken the time to pack and leave, but these, she left as they were. The Saturday before, on a warm day when the city centre still pulsed with school holiday tourists, we went into town on a bus, had lunch at our usual cafe, then went on the hunt for a sieve. A very specific sieve, one that would do for sifting flour. She already had a sieve but the holes were the wrong size and her previous sifting sieve had started to tear. We found a nylon one, and then we walked back, the long way. Through parks, by the pond and past the windows of the large houses, where later I would stare into. It took an hour and we talked for the whole journey; just as we had always talked. After twenty two years as a couple, we would still talk. We could talk for several hours and still not have enough time to talk about everything we were thinking, laughing about or planning to do. I remember, that day, we moved on to religion, which was never an easy topic between us. She was Catholic and I was nothing, or in denial if you were to ask her, and I reached my usual conclusion that regardless, religious or not, there was a core morality of right and wrong, a Kantian categorical imperative that guided us, and whether one religion or another wanted to appropriate it, was neither here nor there.

That Saturday evening, she had littered the floor of our lounge with papers and boxes; light blue cardboard boxes; the size a pair of boots would come in. She said she was organising all our papers – insurance, mortgage, savings, passports, you name it. She already had them organised in drawers, so I wanted to ask why but then I didn't ask why – sometimes you just know things and sometimes you know not to ask.

She left at a quarter to four, during the half time football scores on the radio. I was sitting on the kitchen bin, talking about the scores and she said, 'I'm leaving you. I'm four months pregnant, you're not the father. I'm leaving you.'

Why did she buy the sieve? In those first twenty-four hours, when I was walking, I couldn't figure it out: why buy the sieve? And why had she cooked all that food and left it in the freezer? We were a practical couple; our holidays, weekends, meals, all organised and planned ahead. We cooked batches of food, usually monthly, and froze it in meal sized portions, it saved time during the week. But we both had very different diets and ate different food, so why had she made a month's worth of food that I couldn't eat? There were thirty-two separate containers of frozen food.

An hour earlier, we had walked home, talking as always; so much to say, we'd talk over each other; about the trees and the cars; about our hopes for my new career – I was on a career break, studying full time for a degree; about how birds know to fly in formations; and the significances that couples find in minutiae. She had tried to tell me then, and earlier. We had been at the same cafe as always and she acted as if she didn't know me: it was a song playing on the radio that made me nervous. She said, 'You like that song, don't you?' in a questioning way – she'd known me over two decades. And I said something like, 'Of course I do, what a strange question.' It was asked in the way an aunt would ask her sister if a niece was routinely allowed a second portion of cake. She wanted to go for a walk at the local nature reserve, 'There's something we need to talk about,' she said, but I said, 'No.' So we went home and during the half time scores, she told me.

She wanted to talk after she told me, but I didn't and don't live in a world where two people have a rational conversation, immediately following one telling the other that they are leaving after twenty-two years of living together, that all the doubts were correct and that yes, there was going to be a family, just with a different father.

There was no talking: then or at any time since. I very carefully pushed her aside – you don't manhandle a four months pregnant woman – walked out the door and began walking. When I returned home, the next day, her room had been emptied and many belongings from the flat had also gone. I shut the door on her room and returned to the kitchen with the dusty water. After a couple of hours I went back into her room, drew the curtains, shut the door, and taped the door up; it would be a month before I could go into the room again and when I did, I took all the furniture apart, moved it out and redecorated. The more time passed, the months into years, the more I accepted that she'd left years before she physically left – I don't know that she ever arrived.

But, the new sieve? Why the new sieve? And the size twelve, polka dot, knee length skirt she left in the wardrobe? Not only why did she leave it, but why was it there? She had never worn a skirt above mid-calf length since she was fourteen. No exceptions. All her skirts were ankle length. So why did she buy it? And when? I had quite an eye for what suited her and enjoyed shopping with her, so I was usually there when she bought clothes. And if I wasn't, I would be asked for my opinion. And even then, I dealt with all the washing and had never washed the skirt, it still had labels on it. She left nothing else; just the sieve, skirt and

LEAVING

thirty-two days' worth of meals.

    I still have the sieve and the skirt. I kept the food for three years before throwing it out.

    After four months, I briefly dated a woman. She was slight with a face that was two personalities, crushed together. An alcoholic, chain smoker with a quick temper and a demanding way of speaking. On our second date, she asked, 'How much money do you earn? How much do you have saved?' I answered, 'I have no job and only debt.' The snow was icing by then, the marginal thaw each day, freezing over. The snow stayed for weeks, even down near sea level and higher up, the side roads were impassable. I'd slip on the ice, my shoes ill-fitting now I had lost weight.

    After that second and final date, I walked home, it was about three miles. I was limping and slipping after an hour of walking and near home, I fell and hit my head. I picked myself up, cleared the snow off a low boundary wall, which marked the edge of the garden of one of the larger houses, and waited for my head to clear. I looked at the stars. I was beginning to recognise constellations, be assured by their position in the sky. I saw Orion, Polaris and was thrilled to realise that I understood, that the slightly red star, close to the Moon, wasn't a star, but the planet Mars. I thought of the senseless passage of time, no reason or motive needed to leave one moment for another, and I thought of three in the morning, cold walls and my toes curling into carpet. I lifted my head and began to walk again.

Cartolandia
Enzo Kohara Franca
United Kingdom

SHORTLISTED FOR THE 2019
INTERNATIONAL WRITING COMPETITION

WE ARE BORN THE DAY WE DIE. Or if we're lucky, the day we get arrested. Us, native citizens of *Cartolandia*, the Land of Cardboard. The Land of Ghosts.

A concrete barrier divides *Avenida Vista Alegre* in two. It's our only weather-proof wall. It's our only wall made of something other than paper.

Stretching from the south-east to the south-west of rainy São Paulo, *Avenida Vista Alegre* – Happy View Avenue – could steal several hours of your day. Its traffic was a cruel mix of intense chaos with intense boredom.

As far as my brothers and I were concerned, the slower everyone moved the better. We made our living when cars were still, and drivers impatient.

Shirtless, barefoot, we'd approach our customers like thieves. If we were spotted before the right time, they'd angrily shoo us away. But if we could make it to their windscreen unseen, if we could soap it and raise our squeegees – half of the time we'd get paid to clean it, and half of the time to disappear.

Things were easier when we were younger. I'm fourteen now. My big brother Guto is fifteen. My little brother Dado twelve.

When we were all too short to reach the driver's window, our customers would always spare us a few cents, a few *centavos*. Some would give us trinkets, wish us luck. Some would even buy us warm food.

Aline was like that. Watching ten-year-old me on Guto's shoulders, holding a squeegee and a soap bar, she asked us where the closest bakery was and promised to meet us there.

She caressed our hair and bought us pastries filled with ham and cheese. She said she was studying to become a History teacher. It was while overhearing Aline talk to the baker that I learned we didn't exist.

If you're born in a real house, with real walls, you get papers. Documents that prove you're alive, that you were born on a certain date, in a certain place, and have certain rights.

Amazing things can happen if you have these papers. You can go to school. You can learn how the world works.

Happy View Avenue is our world. We're free here. Several times a week I make my way to *Villa Lobos*, a buffet restaurant in a nearby street. I stand alone outside the window. I watch TV.

Everything I know about the heavens I learned outside that restaurant. Watching a show hosted by a foreign man with a funny moustache. It's a show about the stars. It's a show about how we got here.

Mum used to love hearing me talk about the cosmos. She'd press her eyes shut, put her arms around me, and lie on the floor of our cardboard home asking for stories.

A soda can on the floor, empty but for the remains of her precious rocks, the smell of burned rubber infesting the place – I'd tell my mother about light.

I'd tell her only space itself, as it expands, can move faster than light. I'd tell her everything that exists today was once tinier than a spark. I'd tell her outside the Earth's atmosphere you'd see the sun in a black sky.

Close your eyes and look up. The sun in a black sky.

Out of us three boys, Guto is the bravest, the strongest. He promised to one day get us papers, without getting us killed or arrested.

My big brother walks with a limp. Two years ago, the bones in his right foot were crushed by a motorcycle. He was shoved in front of it – by one of my customers.

It was my fault and it wasn't.

We hadn't eaten in days. The traffic was at a standstill. I approached a car without being careful, and after pouring soapy water on its windscreen, I began working oblivious of the driver's protests.

Lowering his window, the middle-aged man took the squeegee out of my hand and started cursing me. He called me *favelado*, a boy from the favela. He called me a bum, a crack addict and a criminal.

Within seconds Guto appeared. I was twelve then. My brother thirteen.

He gripped the driver by the collar, and with madness in his eyes ordered him to give us back our property.

I saw horror in the man's face, followed by violence. The driver opened his door, throwing Guto against the side of another car. He then grabbed my brother by the ears, and shoved him just as a motorcycle was zigzagging between the lanes. The biker, a delivery guy, nearly lost his balance but did not stop, turning only to curse at Guto. My brother screamed in pain as the back wheel crushed his foot.

No one thought of helping us.

LEAVING

I know the sounds on *Avenida Vista Alegre*. I know what noises don't belong here. One of us, citizens of *Cartolandia*, screaming in pain – that's part of the soundscape.

Like old combustion engines. Like car horns blaring.

Our world is a marketplace. We're bartering beings. If we can't trade something, Guto always says, we have no use for it.

Limping, he moves from one cardboard home to another, making deals with our neighbours. He's the best negotiator in *Cartolandia*.

I trust my brothers more than anyone else, but I think Guto is wrong about the value of things.

Looking up at the skies, at the dreamy blue dawn, at the candle-lit dusk, I see Light inviting me. The starry night, infinite and imaginary, asking me to come its way. To see the Moon. The Space Station. Mars.

Am I gazing at the future or at the impossible? Or are these two the same for me?

My little brother Dado thinks we'll never leave the Land of Cardboard. Not now that mum is gone. He thinks it's his fault she's not around.

Will I ever be strong enough to tell him the truth?

Three weeks before mum disappeared, Dado and a driver became friends. *Dado*, Portuguese for dice, short for Eduardo.

He threw the dice, my little brother. He tried his luck.

Dado's friend was in his fifties. He drove down *Avenida Vista Alegre* every day. My brother called him *moço*, young man, despite his age. This made the young man giggle.

From chocolate bars to real toys, that *moço* loved to indulge my brother. Guto would confiscate these gifts, and when Mum wasn't around, he'd make deals with the baker and the grocer, and turn them into meals.

If Mum was around, she'd order Guto to trade them for cash. She needed *reais* to buy her rocks. Long ago, Mum explained to us us she had a disease of the heart, and her little off-white rocks were the cure.

They smelled like burned rubber. When I asked Mum if I could taste them, she threw me on the ground and smacked me until my nose was bleeding, my cheeks swollen. She would have gone on for hours if Guto hadn't stopped her. Crying, Mum made us swear on her life we'd never touch these rocks.

Whether this is a brain disease or a superpower I don't know, but I can use the light in my head to protect myself from pain. Being smacked, I didn't cover my face. I looked over my mother's shoulders, at the sun's rays and the blue skies. Thoughts of tomorrow protected me from today.

Tomorrow I'll become an astronaut. An explorer of space. A student of the stars.

Dado's driver friend invited him to *Parque Parana*, a famous amusement park on the other side of São Paulo. None of us had ever been there. We never went too far from *Cartolandia*. We had sworn to each other we'd never leave this place alone.

My little brother heard our voices inside his head, but failed to resist the images. The speeding roller coaster, the candy-coloured carousel. He said yes to the *moço's* invitation, and didn't tell us a thing.

Dado vanished. By the end of Day Two, we were still in denial. On Day Three we succumbed to despair.

Limping, Guto visited every resident of *Cartolandia* while I spoke to our customers. Guto was met with sympathy, I was met with suspicion, neither one of us learned anything.

On Day Four, Mum said she had to go find her son.

On Day Five our little brother returned, alone. His clothes torn. Bruises on his tummy, mouth, and neck.

They never went to *Parque Parana*. They went to an apartment in the outskirts of the city. All Dado remembered was a single bed, and a big television showing the Mirror making a speech. Denying the reality everyone could see.

Wildfire. Smoke. The vanishing green.

Twelve months earlier, tiny mirrors appeared all over the country reflecting the worst in us. The worst of our vulgarities, of our ignorance. These mirrors found each other and merged, creating a monstrous being.

According to the Book of Judges, Yair from the Tribe of Manasseh is the One Who Enlightens.

The opposite of our monstrous Mirror. Our Jair, from the Tribe of Tyrants. The One Who Conceals. The One Who Deceives.

Furious, Guto shouted at our little brother he was the dumbest, most pathetic little kid in the world, before crying and hugging him on the floor of our cardboard home.

I looked up and imagined black holes colliding billions of light-years away. I thought of home, and saw our galaxy, the Milky Way. I remembered the man on TV explaining how a day in Venus lasts longer than a year. How ironclad Venus, the symbol of love and beauty, spins backwards around the Sun.

Venus is my kind of rebel. Because a day does feel longer than a year. Because everyone – even my brothers – seem to be looking one way, while I'm looking the other.

Dado was back. Mum was still gone.

With her, the rescue procedure was different. We had been taught to wait. We had been told she'd always come back to us.

A week later, when we got word she was in the *Casarão*, I had a very bad feeling. The *Casarão* – the mansion – was a tiny abandoned apartment where people with Mum's disease came to smoke their rocks.

Frightened, my big brother and I went to get her. To hug her. To tell her Dado had come back home.

We found Mommy's lifeless body on the dirty floor of what was once a living room. Her eyes and arms wide open.

Like *Pietà*.

I wanted to use the light in my head, I wanted to find a way out of the world of pain, but the streets of São Paulo wouldn't let me focus.

Were those car horns or police whistles? Fireworks or bullets? Screams of joy or hatred?

Guto and I were stunned. We walked down *Avenida Vista Alegre*, towards *Cartolandia*. I didn't understand why government supporters were demonstrating. They had won a year ago. Why take to the streets to signal their devotion?

All I wanted was to look up. At the skies, the stars, the universe.

But smoke from the *Amazonas*, our beautiful rainforest, had enshrouded Sao Paulo.

And all I saw was him. Our tyrant. Our Mirror.

The Cruellest Leash

T.H Kunze
United Kingdom

SHORTLISTED FOR THE 2019
INTERNATIONAL WRITING COMPETITION

*T*HE COMFORTING WHIRR OF PROPULSION, *munching mile after mile, nudged this way and that by fingers too tired to let go, slave to motion, to a landscape smeared flat by nothing but gentle pressure, until outside becomes inside, the clouded mirror to a reality long gone...*

◆

ASH IS INVISIBLE

The stone's inscription pricks her floating gaze, more whisper than shout, the merest glimmer of sunlight dripping from its blackened furrows. Rachel steps up, homes in. The letters seem crudely chiselled, devoid of artistic embellishment other than the wind-streaked bloom of ages.

Large enough to flatten her car, the jagged, crystalline rock dominates the centre of this forest clearing and, unlike some of its storm-skewed coniferous guardians, exudes the unshakable confidence of enduring the worst, and then some. Even the patchy pelt of moss girdling its lower flanks and a dusting of winter-bleached pine needles fail to soften the stone's rugged resolve.

If only the words made sense. Perhaps they once did, to those who assembled here? *Clan Gathering Place*, the faded green sign had declared, with just enough time for her to slam on the brakes and crunch-slide into the narrow lay-by, gravel spraying. On a whim. For a chance to take stock, not flight. To splice her confetti of thoughts into weight-bearing strands once more. And where better to try than at a sanctuary to unity, located right beside this familiar road that once led all the way to her home? But never here, strangely enough. Not even close.

Drawn to the scent of bittersweet lushness, Rachel surrenders, squats with a sinuous bounce beside the rock to reach out and feel for its name. Soon her searching fingers are lost in the cool, sprawling islands of sphagnum, knuckle-deep in places and coaxed by nature's quirk to neatly frame the inscrutable message before her...

A tender scratch, and an adjacent clump of moss gives way, to the eager curl of her lips. Then another. She sways with excitement, toes working boot tips for balance, soil-clogged nails digging to the last letter.

THE CRUELLEST LEASH IS INVISIBLE.

◆

Yearning, flush like my open smile and worn with pride, nourished by driving rain on bare skin, written in the wistful swirls of a raspberry sky, a gift, a blessing, a coveted gem, a chink, a liability, an unwanted friend, shot dead like a lame sheep at night, a screamed sacrifice to feed to the many before the rot sets in, ever hungry, ever smiling, ever yearning for another chance to get away with it...

◆

LEAVING

'Aye, it's been there a while,' the barman mutters, turns to face the coffee machine. 'I'm pure clueless about the words, though. Sorry.'

Thistle ear stud, *OK Computer* badge, Millennium Falcon tat – he's probably around her age but has clearly skipped a few service intervals. Bending low to fit the charged brew head his glossy-backed tartan waistcoat rucks up to expose a ripple of white flesh above low-slung black denims. Rachel looks away, but too late.

'So, is it still, uh, in use?' she asks casually.

'Who kens? Bit of a stushie there, a few months back. Police called out, but... Just some local bairns, having a rammie. There you go.'

'Thanks.'

Her espresso tastes bitter. Probably made with ordinary beans. She frowns, adds a little more sugar, gaze panning as she stirs. But for an elderly couple huddled near a neglected coal fire, the pub is empty. Two framed hunting scenes on the far wall are flanked by *Brexit Means Brexit* and *Indy Ref 2* posters.

'Not the most popular beverage here.' He points at her drink by way of apology.

A forced smile. 'It's fine. I just –'

Her phone gives a low, liquid burble. It's Trish calling. Again. A sideways glance at the window confirms steady passing traffic outside.

'Sorry, I have to take this and I'm supposed to be in bed, so...' She crosses her lips at the barman, who returns a knowing grin.

'Hello... A bit better, thanks... Yeah, I must have been asleep... No, no, I keep it on all the time, but on a low ring... Yes, tomorrow, unless... Of course. Once again, please pass on my apologies to Norman... No, just my tummy, nothing to do with my 'thing'... Thanks, bye.'

Relieved, she lets her mobile slide on the counter, spins it in place.

'Your caring boss?'

'His snooping PA.' She nods him a thank-you. 'I don't usually pull sickies, but... I had to get away. And taking leave's even riskier right now.'

'Brexit blues, is it?'

Her fingers rake back windswept blond hair. 'Dig for victory, aye. We're all going the extra mile.'

'Mind you don't tunnel your way back to Europe by accident.'

A shared laugh before he heads for the coal scuttle. Rachel finally submits to yet another buzz, finds two recent messages pickled senseless in the acid cloud of her social media exhaust. Both are from Mark. The 'thing'. Some drivel about direct debit, and how he still ended up paying last month's council tax. She didn't even notice. Too busy counting coppers to stump up the monolithic mortgage all by herself. His latest text includes a bank transfer receipt as proof. What a roaster – so much for calling *her* obsessive...

'Just up for the day, like?' The barman is back, wipes his hands on a dishcloth, eyes on her.

'Looks that way, sadly. Home tonight.'

'Which is no longer around here, I'm guessing.'

She wafts him a thin smile. 'Bradford. Moved there ten years ago, soon after college.'

'And now you're ticking off Scotland's historic sites.'

'What?'

'You asked after the clan stane, so, I was like –'

'Oh, that...' She flicks her cup's handle, too hard. Forgotten coffee spills. 'No, I'm in textiles, not history. Found the gathering place by pure chance.'

'Makes perfect sense.'

'Does it?'

He nods with a steady gaze. 'My dad, he reckons that, on a moon-

LEAVING

less night, you can still see the stane, clear as daylight.'

◆

Wind through a winter's hedge, sharp, tearing, desiccating dead leaves to breaking point, a snatch, a snap, and one by one the outside leaks in, turns brown to gold, shadows to shades, a damp-grey car park into a crackling vortex, ripe with momentum, a sea of colour parted briefly by my playful footsteps, sensing and surfing the endless ocean of probability, rudderless but for the whim of a quantum breeze...

◆

If explicit mental tipping points really exist, then Rachel reached hers one hour into a heavy-hearted journey home, with the arrival of Trish's latest message. Curt platitudes followed by the bulging itinerary for an India trip to scout for alternative suppliers. Rachel's trip. Previously just one of Norman's brainfarts, an unscheduled nice-to-have. Now a fully booked seven-day route march across four Indian states, departing this Sunday lunchtime. And a vengeful wakeup call to his supply chain manager in rude absentia.

A screaming exit at the next junction. Amber-splashed doubts on a hard shoulder at nightfall. Until the satnav's omniscient arrow points her at Perth, just ten miles north.

The BusiRest hotel lives up to its name. Recently opened, its far-flung location near the provincial airport draws a ceaseless clatter of trolley-bagged budget jockeys. Mostly agricultural sales, Rachel figures from their themed ties, branded lapel pins and mud-speckled brogues.

Her corner table in the open-plan dining area beside reception feels more exposed by the minute. Not least to the three TV monitors hovering silently above tonight's captive audience, each dispensing its own flavour of a singular tonic that's impossible to ignore when trying to block out the bustling presence of new arrivals. Eyes flicking from screen to screen, she can't help feeling trapped inside a panopticon of the past: famous Victorian inventions, another tribute to the D-Day Landings, and the Great Fire of London relived through special effects. Seconds later, the slashed cloth of a lurid programme ident cleverly hints at new beginnings after a separation yet to come, before announcing the great Canadian railway journeys of an erstwhile Europhile.

'...Just one more piss-up with the estate guys, and I reckon I can kick this contract across the goal line.'

'What's the margin?'

'Storming the bridal suite, naked. Or did you mean profit margin?'

Raucous laughter from the next table, where three males now take their seats, drink in hand. Company-green polo shirts flopped over orphaned suit trousers, what they lack in dress sense pales behind the rampant incongruity of their studied predatory demeanour. The zeal for deals, epic last-minute heroics, upstaged expense fiascos and business car bragging rights – it all seems to implode in a blustery cloud of con-artistry. The same cold-blooded conviviality that Rachel detects in most guests here as they recline with intent, like sharks in a jacuzzi.

She was never one of them, was she? At least not the calculating one-upmanship type. Long hours, free air miles to Jupiter, career insomnia – yes. Goes with the managerial turf. Not that Mark ever thought so. And as a teacher and spare-time environmentalist, why would he? Civil Service complacency, annoyingly legitimised by his salary that almost matched hers to the penny. But it wasn't all about the money, she patiently explained, but about a sense of purpose, and to fulfil her educated female potential. And he had laughed. Not like the reckless outbursts splitting the air all around her tonight. But the warm, knowing laugh that needs no alibi. And it hurt all the more for it.

She had tried hard to prove him wrong: brave-faced dinners after a hard day; cheerful whistling when burning the midnight oil in her home office; the odd cancelled business trip for his benefit... Crumbs of hope, repaid in kind by Mark's decaf smile and a token interest in her latest procurement nightmare. But even as their bumpy flight path appeared to stabilise and drinks service resumed, unexpected turbulence already loomed on his radar.

Her name was Beth, or Bethan – what did she care? Art school grad, gallery assistant and general boho wastrel, much as Mark tried to tart it up otherwise at their summit talk six weeks ago. Reservist in the LGBT sorority, too, and hence unlikely to 'be the one for him in the long run.' But enough of a romantic diversion to remind him what an unbridled fulltime relationship should feel like, apparently.

Worst thing was, she hadn't seen it coming. No dodgy texts, tripping words or sheepish glances. Then again, her schedule had peaked again around that time, what with blasts of Hard Brexit strafing the headlines, Spitfire-style, and Norman's panicky field trips to China, Canada and Taiwan the inevitable result. And when it came, Mark's revelation caught her at her weakest, unintended or not, pinned to the sofa's edge that Friday night as the facts rolled in. His calm oratory form resembled a well-prepped presentation. Only, there was no beamer, no feedback session, no take-home message. But like all good presenters, he didn't outstay his welcome.

'...It wasn't my bloody fault! How can I deliver on time when our suppliers keep welshing?'

Rachel scowls at the reptilian grins from across the aisle. And her dinner still hasn't arrived. She gets up, finds the waiter idly texting behind the bar counter, and her request for room service flatly refused.

'Cancel it, then. I have to be somewhere else.'

◆

The last rancid meat stripped off the bone, divested, digested, recycled, my pale, ghostly frame now picked clean of all value but one: clarity; a flickering beacon, like feeble sparks of St Elmo's fire leaping from rib to rib, their blue flames lost on an ocean of expectation, of oneness assumed and purpose consumed. The elemental force of a single atom – unplugged and discarded for the sake of a pocket universe...

◆

The road before her coils on like old magnetic tape slipping off a giant reel. Imprinted memories stir, flashed back to life by her sweeping headlights, of fall-side picnics, churchyard kisses, of guilty fags and good intentions. She steered clear of the A9, instead wound her way up past the now skeletal Meikleour hedge, fuelled tank and tummy at Blairgowrie before crossing the swollen Ericht to follow its rugged woodland course north. A bumbling Rangie, swiftly dispatched to its obligatory horn blast, and her run is clear, with only the twinkling eyes of watchful rabbits for company.

Discounting the slew of incoming messages from Trish, of course. With their subject header 'Re: India Trip – Please Confirm...' escalating in severity and Norman now openly copied in, she stopped reading soon enough, and still hasn't replied to any of them. It's nearly eight-thirty, after all – ambitious timing, even for a testosterone junky like Trish, by now most likely wedged tight on a barstool while playing corporate battleships on her mobile. No bad blood has openly been spilled between them to date, largely on account of Trish's painfully methodical professionalism, sealed with a scaly glint from the office behind her. The dragon's doorbell, played to perfection.

Rachel smiles, at one with the belligerent song of her cornering tyres and the sharp, invigorating scent of Scots pine.

'Compassion is the female form of integrity.' Scribbled on the edge of her notepad, some months back during a return flight from hell-knows-where, ram-packed with business travellers, their stern-faced males' complacent air of ownership clumsily aped by most combat-suited women on the plane. The occasional stray glimmer of hope, quickly extinguished behind soot-black power lashes, along with care, anxiety and tenderness, to be rekindled on a shared fireside cushion at runway's end. Perhaps. If supply and demand are evenly matched, unmolested by the lucrative tendrils of emotional disruption; the insidious brain bait sprinkled by the Normans of this world into every email, team talk and appraisal form. Perhaps. Or maybe there simply is no choice anymore.

◆

Not even a pinprick, a nail jab or a love bite – just the sweet tingle of promise, and the hook is in. Tipped with desire, barbed by pleasure, looped to devotion. The close tie to a just cause, pride's anchor in an emotional storm, stabilised, anesthetised, immobilised for the next sting, and the next, until my skin crawls with their steel, my limbs become their arms, my jump their twist, until each step aches for the tremor of thousands, until one smile fills the hearts of all, until...

◆

The crimson leer from a temporary traffic light beyond the next bend draws in on her like a net. She rolls to a lone halt, mindful of lost momentum and a sinking feeling that intensifies as ticking seconds turn to minutes. And right on cue, two dazzling xenon darts round the corner, sweep in from behind, before their needle points fly up to explode in her rear-view mirror, twice. It's the Range Rover, out for a cold serving of revenge. Just as she feared.

Perhaps piqued by the long, cold stare of inevitability, her customary strategic indifference gives way to unchecked irritation, and arms flung up wide in a fit of frustration.

No response from behind. Nor up ahead, where the lights steadfastly refuse to change despite a total absence of oncoming cars.

Then a glint of red as the Rangie's driver door opens. She considers taking off, somehow resists, steeled by the crunch of a balling fist inside her chest.

'So you think you own the road, do you?' the male voice booms. West Yorkshire accent, of all places.

'Do you?' Rachel replies instinctively, glowers back at him, one finger readied to shut her cracked window.

A disgruntled shuffling of legs. He's in his late forties maybe, and tall. Angular face, its prominent features cut into high relief by the icy-blue beams behind him. Quilted green waistcoat and Harris tweed flat cap. Estate owner type.

'There's a leash of deer just beyond that hill.' His square chin wags distantly. 'Roadkill is common in these parts. Not that your satnav would know about it.'

'Much better to sell their lives to the highest bidder instead, isn't it?'

He straightens his pose. 'That's not the point! Reckless driving is. And you don't know –'

'I know these roads better than you think. And the limit's sixty. If you can't hack it then keep your grouse trawler parked in your triple garage and use the bus.'

The slap of his flat palm on her roof. 'I don't think I like your tone...'

LEAVING

He steps up close to clear the intersection as three approaching vehicles at last weave by. His head turns back and forth a few times to study her car's briefly illuminated interior. All she can do is stare out for further traffic, foot poised to punch down hard.

'So you're from Bradford?' He bends down a touch, motions at the A-Z street map on her backseat with a lopsided grin.

'Uh... I live there, yes, but –'

'Always nice to catch a taste of grit from the old homestead. I come from Halifax.'

'Well...'

Their eyes meet through the inch-wide air gap, his gaze the flinty messenger of convictions wholly impervious to hers, unyielding but for a higher code of honour, like border guards at a prisoner exchange.

A sudden flood of invigorating green trips her breath, brings the metallic sound of a finger tap from above.

'You'd best run along, little rabbit,' he sneers, licks his lower lip. 'And remember to watch out for foxes.'

She nods – not at him, but at an urgent whisper from deep inside – then drives off wordlessly. Once the spasms in her right leg subside she regains full speed control, holds it to a steady sixty where possible, checks her mirrors repeatedly. He continues to maintain the advisory distance; a casual but palpable presence. Until three miles later, when the pillared gate of a secluded driveway swallows him whole, in a moment of unspoken relief.

Her outraged thoughts quickly lose their identity, dissolve in the embrace of night's boundless sanctuary, safe in the knowledge that no amount of evidence-based reasoning can ever force the cast-iron portcullis of expectation-led men. She grins, shifts gears as the road narrows once more, skims past two picket-fenced cottages, almost a match in height to the flaking red phone box nestled ornately between them, like an abandoned shrine.

◆

Mindslip. Just a careless blink and time tears, unravels in the crack between one second and the next as reason turns to random before my weightless gaze, unchallenged. Colours fray, split to spin right through me for one graceful beat, until their tumbling fragments click and fuse into a new, flawless whole.

◆

Rachel pulls over, finds her hand hovering above the ignition button as if to cast a spell. A deep breath. Then darkness. The fading glimmer of dials, a booming slam, quickly sucked into the cloak of sudden silence that fits like a lover's embrace. She fights a shiver, pins her gaze to the sole bead of light from a distant farmhouse, until a sense of shape reawakens to paint the sweeping arc of hills against a circling, starless sky, and the inky blur of a path before her.

Firm footsteps. Slow but deliberate, as if ascending a flight of familiar stairs blindfolded. Up and over the lay-by's embankment, where the track dips, gently, ready for a crooked right turn somewhere. The whispering moan of pine trees draws nearer on a breeze, clear as pillow talk, and soon joined by the furtive symphony of nocturnal life, perfectly poised on beauty's fragile edge.

She blinks as the shimmering haze arrives from nowhere; a glistening web of joy to guide her there, safely, on soft and infinitely forgiving soil, until her outstretched fingers come home to the unshakable touch of stone.

Rootless

Hanne Larsson
United Kingdom

Shortlisted for the 2019 International Writing Competition

Mrs Yu casts one final sharp look over her grandson, ignoring her wrinkled skin peeping through the gap between her black shirt and trousers. But today they need to leave the house to soothe the spirits. She nods once; he's covered from head to toe in hat and face mask, gloves and long-sleeved clothes. Not a hint of his skin exposed.

'Are you ready?' she asks the boy and he bobs his head, any sound muffled by the balaclava and scarf.   She inhales, mumbles a prayer of protection and steps outside, feet falling into her usual speedy shuffle on the path to the cemetery. They mustn't stay out too long. Her back bends under the weight of the devotions and joss sticks in her knapsack, pushing her feet deeper into the ground each time she goes to the shrine. Someday soon she will be squashed by the ancestors that sit on her shoulders.

Her grandson has grown too heavy to carry and is pulled along at her speed. She would sink if she had to carry them both. And who will take care of them then?

Mrs Yu glances up ahead through her swimming goggles and sees only the normal burnt haze in front of her. The trucks jostle continuously past, eroding her land, and her bones will shatter if their rumbling carries on much longer.

But this way means her relatives remain peaceful. Because she stays, her grandchild is as pale as the ghosts she prays to placate. Her daughter understands this need, but her son-in-law doesn't. He wants them to move to the city – where the rain isn't death-tinted, where the windows look out over white clouds and sunshine. But Mrs Yu has heard stories of the city.

She finally slows down to let her grandson catch up. The path, flanked either side by grey grass and husks of trees, ends in woods along the base of a hill. Cut into this hill is the shrine where her family has been sleeping for centuries. A light, leafy glade for their final rest. They've farmed this land and now become this land. They worked hard for the peace that the glade provides.

Looking at the trees she wonders: if she touches them will they fold into wet ash at her feet? It's meant to be spring, but nowadays, the only way Mrs Yu knows is because she looks at her calendar. The bees used to whisper this as they flitted from blossom to blossom.

'Nearly there,' she mutters to her soft boy, who's coughing through his mask. He'll be five in a week. He's never seen a blue sky, never tasted sweet water. Ordinarily she wouldn't have brought him here, but it's time he learnt what land he comes from, despite its change. Her daughter admonishes her for being too protective. But he's the one positive light left amongst the dust.

'*Ah-ma*, stop!'

LEAVING

◆

She skids to a halt as much as her legs allow her. Ahead of them looms a machine out and over their heads – all grey angles, metal, monstrous – and thankfully silent.

Where the path once forked – left for her cousin's house, right for the shrine – there are only bite marks left in the ground to mark her memories true. Here, her cousin would meet her to visit their ghosts, pick flowers or hone their tree-climbing skills. The path is gone. The hill – her family's shrine – must surely be gone. Everything now replaced with a hole. She quietly swears as the tears fill her goggles.

◆

Her cousin tells her stories about the city: rooms so cramped and dark that they spend a fortune on lights, the food tasting of only rice paper, the air with a vinegary smell.

The clouds aren't white, her cousin confides, nor does the sun shine through, even if the rain isn't as brown there. They both try to remember the stream that used to run sparkling between their kingdoms.

But Mrs Yu can't make her son-in-law see how foolish his desire for the city is.

Her knees buckle and her trousers are now caked in the dust she's been so careful to avoid. She senses her ancestors waiting to embrace her but here is not where she joins them. Mrs Yu must do what she can to fix things.

Apologising to her father, her mother and everyone she's ever loved, she unpacks the oranges she has scrimped her money for, the dumplings her father loved so, the *char sui* pork for her mother and the rice wine. She lights the incense and places it as near to the gaping hole as she dares.

AWARD WINNING STORIES

Her grandson joins her on the ground, both pleasing and troubling her. She settles for patting him on the head. There's no response, not that she expected any. As they bow, she wishes for her family to see him as their glorious future rather than this quiet imitation of a boy.

She quickly damps down the thought of what she truly desires. Wishes are never for the dead to grant.

◆

Now they need money for food, where before they would grow their own. Her son-in-law now works in the steel-framed tower behind the farm which has turned the land from fertile to inconsolable; her daughter is in one of the factories further away.

There is nothing left here for either of them; corruption is the only thing with roots left in this canton. She scuffs the dirt with her soft-soled shoes. The ground wept and seeped with pain at the start of it all but is now as cracked as her heart. Neither of them has aged well but she at least has her memories of something greener. She doubts whether the earth can recover from the pilfering it's been subjected to.

They retrace their steps, more slowly than when they first set out. She leans into the boy for comfort but her grandson bears the weight of her without complaint. But they need to hurry. He mustn't be outside.

There are no promises left here. There's no time for any more; tonight she'll discuss leaving for the city.

Back home, they unfurl themselves from layers of clothing stained shades of ochre. Mrs Yu unpeels her grey rage and leaves it on her doorstep with her jacket; so much else has changed, she'll not stoop to bringing that across her threshold.

She sets water to boil for tea so they can rinse the sulphur out of their mouths. Her family faces the same waiting as the doomed panda, both choking on pollution as they shuffle towards extinction. She knows there are laws, knows that the officials are breaking them but this country's too vast. Greed has replaced tradition, poisoning a land that they used to make a living from.

There's much her grandson has never done. But the chief crime is that he's never tasted the family's famous pears. The trees stopped growing green fruit before he was born. By the time he could eat solid food, the pears were black and crumbling when she tried to pick them. He'll never know how their sweet juices would run down fingers, how to squeeze them to check they were ripe, how to shimmy up the trees at harvest time. He'll never learn how to pack them for market so that they don't arrive bruised and unsellable. What is she, as his grandmother, supposed to teach him now?

Mrs Yu hears the water boiling and looks for the tea leaves, then glances back at the water, sighing. It's already the colour of tea. It'll taste of tin, thanks to the factories that crowd her doorstep.

◆

Doctors came here a few months ago. The report that they sent to the government has been thumbed through until it's started to flake. Her farm is 'unfit for human habitation'. The report makes no recommendations for how she can make it fit. Instead, the doctors have recommended that the industry is regulated or stopped altogether.

Her family tried that a few months ago by chaining themselves to the gates of the biggest factory. All they have are bruises, but even this colour will fade and wash out. Her daughter will now always limp due to a security guard's kicks.

Mrs Yu knows her dead shouldn't grant her wishes, but it's the one avenue she has left. Heading to the shrine by the kitchen, guilt stretches across her brow – will they still remain peaceful after such flouting of the rules? Where have they gone now that their ground has been swallowed?

She lights a fresh joss stick and grasps it between her hands, visualising the wish she has longed to make. Her home begins to rock.

'Have the factories not got enough machines?'

But the rumbling carries on, bubbling like the water did. Pictures sway on the walls, the table shifts across the room. It pauses then starts again in earnest.

'Earthquake!'

There's no time. Grabbing her grandson's clothing off the floor, she picks him up and runs, holding a facemask over his mouth. Her crooked legs carry them out to stand amongst her orchard of soot. Their whole world shimmies out of focus – which god did her family upset for them to deserve this hell?

Her heart pounds against her ribcage, a scream lodged in her throat. It can't be allowed to escape. She's gasping for air whilst beside her, clutching her leg, her grandson is muted. Have they bundled all of his emotions into so many layers of clothing that now he'll never speak? She can't remember if she's ever heard him laugh and in this rumbling moment, she wished she could make him do so. A child's laugh is a balm like no other.

The shaking stops and, slowly, they let go of each other. There's stillness in the earth, and Mrs Yu turns her face heavenward to listen. A singular trill of a bird breaks it, her face cracking into a smile despite everything.

'There? Can you hear it?' She pulls at her grandson's arm. 'It's a bird!'

'Yes – what's a bird?' His eyes widen as it lands on a branch near his head. Perhaps there's time for a grandmother to teach her grandson all

LEAVING

of this, show him all of the memories she grew up with. What this land used to look like, how beautiful it was when the sun skimmed over the mountains in the distance. The brightness of green, of the red flags fluttering by the roadside and how people used to talk to one another and not merely hobble past. They are the only rooted family left. Everyone else is new; they don't know what they're helping to destroy.

◆

She looks to the house, sees the widened crack in it, but it doesn't matter. They've escaped and she must remember to light another candle at the shrine. Her ancestors will find her, the shrine is wherever she is. Her legs don't allow her to do a little dance, but her insides staccato-burst with joy.

She's longed for this calm for so long; but it isn't until her grandson tugs at her shirt and points behind the trees that she realises something is wrong. Too wrong. And she wonders exactly what she's asked for.

Because behind her trees, the view is clear. The monstrosity that belched and spat out sickly smoke and dripped black ooze into the streams is gone.

'Ah-ma, where is Ba-ba?' Her grandson's face is slack and Mrs Yu tries to fathom how she hadn't realised before; that her five year old bright light has realised this before she has. What the clear sky means.

'I don't know, darling. It's almost dinner time – I'm sure your father's just on his way home from work.' She adds layers of warmth to her voice; she remembers the honey her mother used to harvest from the bees. It would melt on her tongue and she hopes her voice now envelops her grandson in the same sweetness.

'Come, let's go and meet him on the road. You'll see.'

She adjusts her grandson's face mask and reaches for his hand. They walk down the road past trucks jack-knifed across their path whilst Mrs Yu prays that her grandson can't touch her fear escaping through her glove.

The Accident
C.S Lawrence
United Kingdom

Winner of the 2019
Student Category

STEVE STRUGGLED AS HE DRAGGED THE BODY from the boot of the Ford Anglia, parked outside the meat room. The car was his Dad's pride and joy, which he had passed on to Steve after he got too frail to drive anymore. It was only a few years old and he had treated it with the utmost respect. That is, until now. Now it was tainted, not with blood, but with memories, of the accident and now the disposal.

The sodium lights created an eerie orange glow, which hung in the air as a fine mist enveloped the zoo. The zoo wasn't even as old as the car; it was opened 5 years ago in 1962 by the Deputy Lord Mayor, when Steve had got the job of Head Keeper. The job came with a bungalow at the entrance to the park, an added bonus, as it was situated next door to Plymouth Argyle's Home Park. The home crowd seemed to love the fact that they had a new zoo overlooking their football pitch and Saturday mornings, when the Pilgrims were playing at home, were always the busiest. But tonight, it was just Steve and Jim.

Beads of sweat formed on Steve's forehead as the churning in his stomach increased. His eyes darted around the room, unsure of where to focus, the sound of his pulse filled his ears as his heartbeat quickened. This was the only solution he could think of. Jim was on the butcher's block, the back of his skull smashed by the road after being thrown by the impact of the car, being prepared like every other cut of meat, ready for the big cats. Inside the food store, the air was cold and crisp. The hairs in Steve's nose began to twinge. He ran to the corner and threw up in the bin, he wasn't sure he could go through with this, but he didn't see any other way. He wasn't going to prison just because the idiot who happened to step into the road was his wife's ex-fiancé. He took the old blood-stained leather apron from its hook on the back of the door and placed it over his head, the taste of bile still tainting his mouth. He switched on the radio to try to take his mind off what he was about to do.

> *This is the late evening news from the BBC. Figures announced yesterday show the new breath test as a triumph for Barbara Castle. The Transport Minister said last night 'If we can keep up the rate of reduction achieved so far; we shall reduce deaths on the road by 1200 a year.'*
>
> *In other news: Rescue boats patrolled the rain-swollen Ohio River in West Virginia today, in a search for an estimated 80 additional victims of the thunderous collapse of a steel suspension bridge carrying rush hour traffic.*
>
> *Journalists and film crews flooded into Cape Town's Groote Schuur Hospital, as news of the first human-to-human heart transplant, led by South African surgeon Christiaan*

LEAVING

> Barnard, made headlines around the world. The operation attracted unprecedented media attention for a medical undertaking, ushering in a new era of doctor and patient celebrities, post-operative press conferences and medical PR.

The blade of the cleaver smashed down into the flesh of Jim's corpse and the light from the single bulb swinging in the rafters glinted off the blade with each strike. As he dismembered the body, he kept replaying the accident over and over in his head. After a skin-full in the Millbridge, he was rushing home to check on Sandra. Their argument earlier in the evening was bound to make her head for the bottle of vodka. The figure just appeared in the road as Steve drove towards Stuart Street Bridge. But who would believe it was an accident? Just a coincidence, that it was Jim who happened to step in front of his car. Especially as he'd been wishing Jim dead that very evening. There'd been bad blood between them since Steve reported Jim for inappropriate behaviour with the stock girl at work. Jim got the sack, and Sandra left him the week before the wedding. 'Why can't he just fuck off and die somewhere?' Those were his exact words, to the pub full of zoo staff.

Sandra was curled up on the sofa when Steve got in. The vodka bottle lying empty on the floor beside her. In the kitchen, he stripped off his clothes and stuffed them into the twin-tub. After dousing them with wash-powder and a bit of bleach, he switched it on. Sandra was way too gone to notice the washing machine, but if she asked, he could say he had been sick on them. He turned on the shower and stepped into the stream of water. The cold shock made his knees buckle; there was no hot water at three in the morning and the cold December air made it even worse, but he had to get the stench off him. He took the scrubbing brush and carbolic soap and lathered his arms, the stiff bristles biting into his flesh, but the pungent aroma of the soap eliminating the sour odour of blood and guts. After what felt like an hour of scrubbing, Steve just crouched in the cold flow, staring, he could feel the anger building. What had she made him do? What had she turned him into?

◆

After the usual hectic weekend, everything seemed to be back to normal. Steve had woken early and carried on his usual routine, opening the zoo and checking on the animal enclosures, making sure no one had escaped overnight. Mondays were usually quiet, but at this time of year, the Christmas holidays, business wasn't quite so slow. Steve was walking past the reptile house, when he saw a familiar face walking up from Barn Park Road. It was Sheila Atherstone, Jim's Mum, and she was heading straight for his bungalow.

Sandra opened the front door to put out the empty milk bottles and was surprised to see Sheila on the doorstep.

'Sheila? What brings you here?'

'I just wanted…Oh I don't know. I shouldn't have bothered you.'

'Wait! It must be important for you to walk all the way up here in your state. Why didn't you get Jim to bring you?'

Sheila's face dropped as she contemplated the question, tears welling up in her eyes.

'That's just it, that's why I'm here. Jim hasn't come home. He went to the off-license on Thursday night and hasn't come back.'

'I'm sorry Sheila, but he's probably shacked up with that Tracey Hammond again!'

The bitterness rang out from Sandra's words, Tracey the stock girl had been the catalyst for the hurt that had plagued her thoughts for nearly two years now.

LEAVING

'That was a long time ago Sandra, and he regrets it every day. Anyway, she left town weeks before he came back from Edinburgh.'

'Well I haven't seen or heard from him, but I'm sure he'll turn up when he's finished doing whoever he's doing.'

Her sarcasm biting at Sheila's remorse.

'Well if he's not back by tomorrow, I'm going to the police. He'd never leave me alone like this.'

Sheila burst into tears as she set off towards home. Sandra was closing the front door when the back door opened, and the breeze snatched the doorknob from her hand slamming it shut and rattling the knocker.

'Who was that at the door?' Steve enquired.

'Oh, you made me jump! It was Sheila, Jim's Mum.'

'What did she want?' He could hear the contempt building in his voice and tried to temper it. 'Is she okay?'

'She reckons Jim's gone missing, but he's probably shagging some dolly bird he met the other night.'

'The other night?' Steve asked, feigning concern. 'What happened the other night?'

'Oh, she says he went to the offy and didn't come home.'

'Oh well, like you say, he'll turn up when he's had his fun.'

Steve grabbed his plate of sandwiches off the kitchen table and headed for the back door. 'I'll eat these in the hut, see you later,' he said and slammed the door shut behind him.

As he walked back through the enclosures, Steve realised that Sheila wasn't going to let things lie and Jim disappearing needed an explanation. He'd been missing for four days now and if the police got involved, they would definitely think it was suspicious. As he passed the gift shop on his way to the staff hut, an idea jumped to mind. If Jim had decided to go on holiday, and send his dear old mum a postcard, then that would

AWARD WINNING STORIES

account for his sudden disappearance. That would put her mind at rest. He sat in the staff hut playing the idea over in his mind. What would he need to make it work? A postcard from the gift shop would be perfect, like he'd gone on a safari, but a postmark, how would he do that? It's not like you can just pick up a postmark stamp. That's it! He'd just need a stamp, like the one they used for the guided tours, a bit of red ink and smudge it, and no one would ever notice, he thought.

After locking up for the day, Steve slipped into the gift shop to put his plan into action. He wrote a message on the card and the postmark worked out just as he'd imagined. He put the card in his jacket and went back home for his tea. Sandra was her usual apologetic self, after one of her binges. She was sorry for shouting, for swearing, for making him choose the lads over her. But was she sorry for making him mad, for making him drink too much, or for making him overly worried about her? Was she sorry that she was responsible for Jim's death? That she'd turned her husband into a killer? He knew that if she ever did find out, then she would be sorry.

Early next morning, Steve took the zoo Land Rover and parked down the street from Sheila Atherstone's house, he watched as the postman walked door to door. He skipped number 72 and crossed the road. Steve took the moment to slip the postcard through Sheila's letterbox. He made it back to the car without being noticed; it was a bit too early for the curtains to be twitching. He waited until the postie was out of sight before starting the car and making his way to work, confident that this would put Sheila's mind at rest.

It was past nine when Sheila finally woke. She put on her thick woollen dressing gown and slippers and carefully made her way down the stairs. The card on the mat looked unusual, but without her glasses she could only see a blurred animal. In the kitchen she put the card on the table and filled the kettle. Retrieving her glasses from the welsh dresser, she looked at the image on the postcard, a tiger, stalking through long grass. Turning it over she read the brief message.

> *Dear Mum, Sorry I haven't let you know where I was before now, but it's all been a bit of a blur. I bumped into an old friend after I left the off-license, he was about to go on holiday when his girlfriend dumped him. He asked me if I wanted to go with him, as it was all paid for and he wouldn't be able to get a refund. We flew out to Kenya early on Friday morning. We'll be here for at least two weeks. Sorry about Christmas!*
> *Love Jim xx*
> *ps. Sorry about the bad handwriting, these safari jeeps are really bumpy!*

Sheila made her cup of tea and sat at the table; a gentle sigh removed the tension from her shoulders and a smile lit up her face as she reread the card. Her boy was okay, although he was halfway around the world. She felt a twinge of sadness when she realised that she'd be spending yet another Christmas alone. But at least she wasn't going to have to spend it worrying about her baby. Finishing up her tea, she made her way upstairs to get dressed. I'll have to let Sandra know later, she thought, I wouldn't want her to be worrying about him, I can go on the way back from bridge club.

It was getting dark as Sheila got off the bus at Home Park. She walked up the short drive to the zoo entrance and knocked on the door of the bungalow. The porch light was dim, but it just managed to bath Sheila in its soft light. Sandra opened the door.

'He's okay Sandra,' Shelia blurted out, before any traditional niceties could be exchanged.

'That's great, Sheila,' Sandra replied. 'Did you find out where he'd got to?'

'Oh yes! He's gone to Kenya, on safari. It was a last-minute decision. He's sent me a postcard. Look!' Sheila handed Sandra the card.

Sandra took the card; she recognised the tiger on the front immediately but kept it to herself.

'That's a relief for you Sheila. I'm glad he's okay. I know we haven't seen eye to eye over the past couple of years, but I really am glad. At least he'll be warm over Christmas.'

A feeling of dread rose within Sandra and she thanked Sheila for letting her know and made her excuses to return indoors. As Sheila left, Sandra burst into tears behind the closed front door. She knew that postcard hadn't come from Kenya, she knew that that tiger was behind her house, tucked up in his bed, and she knew that postmark was a zoo stamp, however much it had been disguised. She also knew that only one person could have, would have, done this. But the why, that she couldn't figure out.

She wiped the tears from her face with her sleeve and grabbed her coat from the hall stand. As she left through the back door, she felt the chill wind biting into her still damp cheeks. The enclosures looked empty this time of year, as most of the animals preferred to be in the warmth of their beds, rather than parading around for everyone to gawp at. It felt like a ghost town with the persistent orange glow streaming through the trees. Making her way to the staff hut hidden behind the trees at the rear of the park, she noticed a light on in the tiger enclosure.

'Steve?' she shouted as she approached the gate. Juma, the tiger on the postcard that she had so easily recognised, wasn't tucked up in his bed. He was pacing up and down in his enclosure. Juma growled as she approached, baring his huge teeth, obviously agitated. He got like this when he hadn't been fed for a few days. The keepers liked to do this now and again, to keep his hunting skills in order, but this made Juma more volatile, more dangerous.

'Steve? Are you in here?' she shouted again. She unlatched the outer gate to the feeding compound and walked through, letting the gate slam shut behind her. She jumped and squealed at the noise.

'I saw Sheila leave,' said Steve as he stepped out of the dark corner behind her.

'Shit Steve, you'll frighten the life out of me doing that!'

'Gone home has she? Happy, is she? Now that Jim's okay, just off on safari.'

'So, it was you who sent Sheila that card. Why on earth would you do that? She's worried about him.'

'Well, she should be. If he hadn't come back, none of this would have happened. This wouldn't be necessary. See I knew if she brought that card to you, you'd figure it out in a heartbeat. And here we are!'

'What do you mean "Here we are!"? Here we are where?'

'Well I have to finish what I started. And it's all your fault anyway. If you hadn't been in such a pissy mood on Thursday I wouldn't have drunk so much, I wouldn't have felt the need to get back and check on you. I wouldn't have hit him with the car!'

'You hit him with the car? Jim?'

'Yes, Jim. Your precious Jim. Mummy's boy Jim. The car bit was an accident, I just didn't see him. But feeding him to the tiger, well, that was just tidying up your mess.'

'Oh god! You fed him to the tiger, to Juma. I'm going to be sick.' Sandra fell to her knees and threw-up. A stream of tears flooded from her eyes.

Steve grabbed her by the hair.

'Come on, Juma hasn't eaten since then, and it's supper time!'

He dragged her towards the gate to the tiger enclosure. Juma, still pacing, was waiting impatiently for his food.

Sandra screamed. 'Steve, you're hurting me!'

She managed to get a foothold on the slippery ground and grabbed Steve's hands on her head. She pulled herself up and launched her head up under his chin. The weight of the two bodies hitting the gate forced the latch and they fell into the grassy enclosure. Steve groaned as his chest broke her fall, winding him. She got to her feet just as Juma made his turn. She jumped through the gate, managing to pull it shut behind her, leaving Steve to his fate with Juma.

It felt like hours before the police arrived. Sandra had to go through everything she knew with three different policemen. First a constable, then two different detectives. It turns out Steve was serious about feeding Jim to the tiger after all. After they got another keeper in to make the enclosure safe; they had to dart poor Juma, the search team found a finger with a ring on it, which they asked Sheila to identify. It was the wedding band that Jim had bought for Sandra.

Left

Jennie Liebenberg
United Kingdom

It was 1952 in a Britain still rationed on some commodities, still struggling to emerge from the war years. The class of eight and nine year olds was filing out of the classroom at the end of the day. 'Filing' was, of course, a euphemism, thought their teacher, already settling at his desk, red pencil in hand, prepared to mark their compositions. The boys jostled with one another at the door, each one trying to be first through to freedom. The girls followed a little more decorously, but not entirely without their own version of pushing and shoving. He sighed and wondered for the umpteenth time why things had turned out the way they had.

His reverie was interrupted by the voice of one of the lads – Terry Magson – a skinny boy with more enthusiasm than ability.

He cleared his throat. 'What did you say, Magson?'

'I said, ain't you writing with the wrong 'and, sir?'

'What are you talking about, boy? Of course I'm not writing with the wrong hand.'

'But they calls you Lefty, sir.' The boy's eyes were fixed on him, no malice in them, only curiosity, and hadn't he always been hoping for a bit of curiosity in one of his pupils? Not a curiosity for personal details about himself, of course, but there was something so trusting and hopeful in the boy's face that feelings long sealed up inside the teacher almost started to untwist from the tight knots his experiences had tied them in. He relented.

'Yes, Magson, some people do call me Lefty, but that's got nothing to do with which hand I write with. I'm right-handed just the same as you are.'

'So… what is it to do with then, sir?'

The boy was nothing if not persistent. If only he would apply himself to his classwork with the same persistence!

'There are two reasons,' he said. 'Some people call me Lefty because my surname is Wright. That kind of thing is known as the British sense of humour. And some people call me Lefty because I served in the Royal Navy as a Lieutenant. But mark well, Magson, no one calls me Lefty to my face, because they know it would be disrespectful.'

'Coo, sir, you was in the Navy? Did you have any adventures?'

The boy was quelled with one of the teacher's sternest looks.

'Run along now, Magson – and try to be here on time tomorrow morning.'

The boy scuttled off and the teacher heard him break into a run as he headed down the corridor to the exit. He sighed and laid down the red pencil, passing his hand over his face as if this would wipe out his memories in the same way that he rubbed out his writing from the blackboard. The past was threatening to push itself into the forefront of his mind, a place he never allowed it admission; except in his sleep of course, when his defences were disarmed and dreams caused him to thrash around and deposit his eiderdown and blankets on the floor. He would wake up, heart pounding, adrenalin pumping through his body, and that familiar despair in his heart. They had nearly all been lost, including the captain. Again and again the guilt would pierce him, even though in the military hospital on Gibraltar the medics had assured him over and over that no one could have saved the men or the ship. He was wrong to lay the blame at his own door. But only a handful of the men had survived and he, Philip Wright, had been the officer in charge after the captain's demise. He couldn't shuffle the responsibility off onto anyone else no matter how many times the experts told him that the ship was doomed from the moment the bomb blast had penetrated to the engine room. The explosion had broken the ship in half.

His nightmares brought the scene back in terrible detail, the brutal speed of the destruction, the horror of the instant disintegration of men's bodies, disconnected limbs flailing, heads… He stopped himself, picked up the red pencil, determined to concentrate on something else, but of course it was no use. He would take the compositions home with him. Take some medicine. Hope for oblivion. Mark the children's work in the early morning before he came back into another day of teaching.

♦

Even five years after the end of the War this part of town was still visibly poor, pock-marked and soot-covered from the bombs aimed relentlessly at the docks in what seemed like unending night-time missions. Despite the urban nature of the area, it had the characteristics of a village. The same families had lived in these same streets for generations. It was a place where nobody stopped to consider whether they should offer a hand to a neighbour; it came as second nature to help one another.

They weren't in and out of each other's homes. The home was sacrosanct; it was for the family, not for neighbourhood gatherings. People who wanted company had the choice of two pubs, The Nelson and The

Blue Flag. Philip Wright passed both of them on the way home to his narrow terrace house, which was identical to those of his neighbours: one up and one down, kitchen built on at the back, the other amenities under a separate roof further down the mournful-looking garden. He never drank in the pubs.

At home he laid the folder of compositions on the scratched desk under the front window. They could wait till morning. Safe in his own territory he vaguely noted that the trembling had started. He was a man of massive self-control. All day teaching he somehow contained the shaking in his limbs; he was under no illusions about the gossip that could spread like a wild fire. He vaguely suspected that the gossip about him arose out of concern rather than titillation, but if he lost his pride, then he would truly have lost everything.

In the kitchen he pulled open the top cupboard. Even for a man of his height and bearing it was a stretch. Indeed he went up on tiptoe to reach inside and draw out the bottle. The trembling was much worse now. He must not drop the bottle. He went to the kitchen unit, which was neatly packed with plates and glasses behind the frosted glass doors, took out a squat, thick glass and placed it on the tiny table. Every movement was deliberately steady. He would not rush. He had more self-discipline than that, more self-respect.

It was hard, though, so hard to pour the drink, when his hands were shaking so uncontrollably. The neck of the bottle rang against the chunky glass; the fragrance of the brandy brought expectant saliva to his mouth. He sat, still determined not to rush. It wasn't that he needed the brandy, he told himself; it was just that after a day of trying to be strong, unmoved by the small frustrations of teaching and unbowed by the way the children's vivacity drained away his own energy, it was only human to want to relax. And brandy helped him to relax. It cancelled out the tensions. Enough of it would even cancel out the memories – at least for as long as he could stay awake.

He remembered how eager he had been to enlist when the War started. He had just begun teaching then and he knew he would not be called up, but he wanted to serve his country in a more active role. From boyhood he had been a keen sailor, going out with his father in the family's sailboat every weekend and every holiday. He had learned quickly, having a natural aptitude for gauging the temper of the elements and being at ease with the sea in her various moods. Before long he was winning regatta competitions, taking silver cups home, making a name for himself. There had even been whispers of his chances at a future Olympic Games. If his country wasn't going to call him up for service, then he had determined to volunteer for the Royal Navy Reserve. He had been accepted and entered as a sub-lieutenant, his ability bringing him a prompt promotion to full lieutenant on a destroyer headed for the Mediterranean. How, he berated himself now, had he not realised the vulnerability of a fighting ship in such an arena? The drone of the German bombers sounded again in his ears as the ineluctable memories began to roll out in his mind's eye like a film at the pictures. He splashed more brandy into the glass. He did not intend to allow the memories to reach the final scenes of carnage. Not tonight. Please, not tonight.

◆

He woke at around 3.00am. For a change it wasn't a dream that had woken him. His mouth was as dry as a stone in the desert; his bladder was in need of emptying. Was that what had disturbed his sleep? No. As he floundered out of the deep pit of brandy-induced oblivion he realised there were shouts outside, even screams, and lights were shining through his window, dancing, flickering lights, and what was the smell?

Full consciousness came to him in an instant, as soon as he registered the smell. Fire! Somewhere there was a fire. Oh God help me, he thought. For once the smell and the light and the shouts were not part of one of his dreams. This was real. He was out of bed the second that the realisation hit him. Out and, fortunately, fully dressed, he discovered. Ah, it had been a shameful evening, then, if he had not undressed himself before tumbling into bed. But this decadence was a blessing now.

He ran down the stairs, slipped into his shoes by the front door, and went outside. Dear God, there were two houses on fire down the road. His mind screamed 'bombs', but of course it wasn't bombs. Something else must have caused the fire. He ran down to where a huddle of neighbours stood watching and fretting. Several of the street's menfolk – those who weren't working nights at the factory – were trying without much success to douse the flames with buckets of water and inadequate hoses. In one glance Philip Wright summed up the situation: everyone was involved but no one was in charge. And one woman was screaming piteously while a group of her neighbours attempted to comfort her.

Philip strode forward, suddenly every inch the young lieutenant. He asked one question: has anyone called the fire brigade?

One of the women answered, 'Our Terry's run down to the telephone kiosk, sir.' She called him 'sir' because he was the teacher, but to Philip's ears it confirmed his leadership. He organised the women to form a chain with buckets, so there could be a constant flow of water, even though he knew what they really needed was more hose pipes, and a powerful pressure of water to run through them. It was better to have them contributing; then they wouldn't face the guilt of having stood by, helpless.

Ted Rossiter and his oldest son arrived with a rusty ladder and put it against the side of one of the burning houses. Philip Wright snapped at them, 'What's that for?'

'Kids trapped in that bedroom, sir,' replied Rossiter.

Used to running up and down companionways, Philip Wright took it on himself to climb the ladder. He knew the dangers of smoke inhalation. What if the children were already dead? Yet he could see that, miraculously, there was no smoke emerging from the partly open window. They should still be safe, but he mustn't waste time.

He pulled the window fully open and climbed in over the sill. The toddler – either amazingly or worryingly – was still asleep and being fiercely hugged by the little girl, who was scarcely school-age herself.

'Let me take the baby,' said Philip. 'I'm going to pass him out of the window so he'll be safe and then I'll take you out as well.'

'The baby's a girl!' wailed the older sister.

'I'm sorry,' said Philip, keeping a rein on his patience. 'Let me have her, please, love.'

The little girl seemed about to hesitate, but a tear-roughened voice shrieked from outside.

'Our Susan - Let Mr Wright bring our Angela out, this minute!'

Philip took the baby from her sister's protective arms and moved over to the window. Ted Rossiter was on the ladder, waiting to be handed the baby, and Philip went back for Susan. The smoke was now beginning to seep in under the bedroom door. Susan was coughing and Philip felt a catch in his own throat. He climbed out of the window and helped Susan to clamber over the sill after him, then guided her safely down the ladder, where he was received with a chorus of thanks and congratulations. The sound of the fire engine's bell stopped all that and the team of firemen deployed with speed and efficiency, telling the neighbours to retreat to the end of the street, well out of harm's way, and not to return to their homes till the fire brigade gave them the all clear.

The landlord at The Nelson, at the farthest end of the street, opened his doors so that all the residents could take shelter in the pub. His wife brought blankets for the children and, exhausted by fear and tension, the mothers tried to get their overexcited offspring to settle down and sleep. The landlord offered brandy to the men and his wife made pots of tea for the women.

Philip asked for a cup of tea. The very idea of his old crutch nauseated him now.

'Thank 'eaven you were here to take charge,' said Ted Rossiter. 'The minute you took command things got organised properly. We could all calm down and get on with the job in 'and.'

'You're a good man to have around in an emergency and that's a fact,' added one of the women.

Other people were clapping him on the back, telling him he'd been a hero, and he was deeply embarrassed. He hadn't been a hero at all. He had never been a hero. Today there had been something he could do to save lives. That was the difference.

This was common sense. In some situations there's nothing anyone can do. The trick, he realised, is to know when something can be done and to do it. This simple truth had eluded him for a decade, ever since the loss of the ship and the sustaining of his own wounds that had seen him moved to a desk job on shore, a move he had found deeply humiliating. Even so, he had insisted on completing his duty in the Navy until the proclamation of peace released all the Volunteer Reserves back to civilian life. For years psychiatrists and doctors had been telling him there was no disgrace in being a survivor, but he had never accepted it, nor ever been able to believe it. Perhaps now he could start thinking about it differently.

The clock struck six. It was still dark outside, but Philip had a pile of compositions to mark. He slipped out of the pub and walked down the street, puddled from the firemen's watery assault on the fires. The smell of smoke hung heavy in the air and the old buildings had gained a layer of fresh soot, but Philip, instead of being plunged into depression at this new manifestation of destiny's evil ways, walked with a rather longer stride than usual, his head turned up towards the pale glow in the sky that would turn, at its own appointed pace, into sunrise. And Philip conceded that it might not be as impossible as he had believed for there to be some purpose in his life. Maybe, if he could forgive himself, as his senior officers and medics had been trying to instil in him for years, he might even find some of the old aspirations huddling inside him somewhere; perhaps he did still have the heart of that eager but untried young lieutenant. In fact, he felt the softest stirring of hope that he might after all have a life left that was worth living. No matter what, from this point onward he was leaving the past behind.

The Milky Way
CHRISSIE MAROULLI
Cyprus

SHORTLISTED FOR THE 2019
INTERNATIONAL WRITING COMPETITION

HE GRABS MY ENGORGED BREASTS with lust and squeezes them together; he must have seen this in porn. Before I manage to pull away, a fountain of warm breast milk squirts in his face. He winces but I don't take offense. He rolls away from me and I realize his erection is gone.

Oh well. I might as well grab the opportunity to leave. I would probably have regretted this anyway. I click my nursing bra's cups in place and throw my sundress on. He is sitting at the edge of the futon with his head in his hands.

I look for my underwear.

Fuck. Fuck fuck fuck fuck fuck fuck fuck I can't find them.

What was I wearing?
White, cotton, high-waist panties.

LEAVING

'Have you seen my underwear?'
'What do they look like?' says he.

                Like a pair of women's panties you shithead.

'They were uhm… white, just a plain pair of panties. Can't really go home without them'.

He falls on his knees, still naked, to look under the futon. His erection is definitely gone. His manhood hangs like a gloomy little elephant.

                      Jesus, his back is so hairy.

I absolutely have to find my underwear. It's not that I care that much about the actual panties. It's not even that my husband is going to know they're missing; it's been a while since he's been interested in what kind of underwear I have on. I don't want the hairy monster to find them first because if he does find them, he will look.

                              Damn it.
        I should really start wearing black underwear.

I am not judging myself. It's not a matter of cleanliness. I wipe well and I manage to shower every single day and moms know that this is an extraordinary achievement.

It's not that hard if you think about it. I put the baby in the cot, drag it at the bathroom door and arrange a couple of shoeboxes to elevate where the head goes. I wash the dried and/or fresh vomit and/

or excrement out of my hair while peek-a-booing the screaming infant. It's quite funny, I have to shower with my glasses on too! I can't see shit without them and I cannot take my eyes off the baby, not even for one second, because – God forbid – reflux could cause the baby to choke on its own spit and die.

And who wants that, right?

Only three pushes, three lovely pushes and the little one came into our lives like a slime-covered gift sent from above, along with a complimentary horrifying case of the hemorrhoids and third degree tears, like a special offer bundle, three for one kind of thing, for mummy's exclusive personal benefit. The dad only got the cute, swaddled baby.

Defecation hurts like hell when you have hemorrhoids but I can take it. It's the leakage I can't handle. I stain all my underwear. I use over-the-counter creams but they don't help. The doctor prescribed a couple of stronger ointments but, of course, I can't use any of them because like the perfect mother that I am, I chose to breastfeed. There are active ingredients in those things that get into your milk and then the baby might get the plague.

And who wants that, right?

'Here they are,' says the hairy monster. He picks them up from the top shelf of the bookcase, raises them above his head and waives them like a white flag.

I immediately jump up to grab them. He maneuvers away from

me in an attempt to make a playful invitation for pity sex (we both pity each other at this point). In the blink of an eye, I sprint towards him, almost flying over the dusty furniture and pile of filthy clothes and leap into the air to get the panties, but he hides them behind his back and I can't reach them. I try to snatch them but he swings in alternate directions like he is holding some kind of dog treat teasing a poodle.

He is laughing. I am cursing. I jump onto his back like a monkey and dig my nails into the soft soil of his curly jungle. He does not seem bothered.

Damn it, I wish I had my pre-baby nails.

I am out of options here. I don't want to kick him in the crotch because that would make me an epic bitch, especially since he is butt naked. So I just go for what's in front of me: his right ear. I bite his right ear so fucking hard that I can feel the skin breaking and the cartilage being torn apart. My jaw locks on its prey until I start to notice his fist slowly opening and his sweaty fingers relaxing, letting go of my seemingly unimportant underwear.

He shrieks.

'You bitch did you just bite my ear off?'

He finally lets go of my white panties and I gawk at them as they gracefully fall on the ground, in a slow motion scene complete with incidental music (the soundtrack theme from Requiem for a Dream). I let him go and swiftly bend over to pick them up; I clutch them in my fist and stare at them for a moment.

AWARD WINNING STORIES

My most prized possession.

I start to go. But wait.

What the hell? There's a soft piece of something in my mouth. There is, indeed, a small piece of hairy monster ear in my mouth.

Oops.
On the bright side, the panties are safely sheltered in my handbag.

I spit out the ear puzzle piece in my stock-still palm. I rush to the kitchen sink to rinse my mouth. Of course there is no soap, only a pile of century old unwashed dishes and their unbearable stench. I shove as much running water as I can in my gaping mouth, hoping to wash off the metallic taste his blood has left on my tongue. I can hear him screaming in the next room, he must have looked at his ear in the mirror. I examine the piece of flesh in my hand; I believe I only chopped off the lobe.

Damn it. Did I take this too far?

My instinct tells me to get the hell out of there but my cloudy logic tells me I should at least stay and help.

'Get your clothes on, we are going to the ER, they'll stitch it back on.'

I open the freezer to get some ice to preserve the detached piece of flesh but there's nothing in there except a half empty pint of 'Great Value' mint chip ice cream. I throw the ear in there and close the lid.

LEAVING

'There is a medical centre two blocks away, we can walk there.'
'I'm not going anywhere with you, you crazy bitch. You ate my ear!'
'Relax, your ear is in here. I bet now you're happy I don't like to swallow huh?'

I'm making cannibalistic jokes now? Wait. This can't be right. I do not have that kind of sick humor and come to think of it, I would never bite a man's ear off!

Would I?

'I'll come with you to pay the bill. It was my fault, what happened.'

He hesitates but eventually nods with frustration. He throws on a pair of jeans and a black T-shirt from the laundry pile. He walks in front of me holding his injured ear and it suddenly hits me, I just realize how appalling his smell is. Like a moist mop you recently cleaned cat urine with.

My husband always smells nice.
Even when he sweats I love the way his armpits smell.
I love his morning breath too.

Hold it. This can't be right. This is not me, I would never, ever cheat on my husband.

Would I?
I definitely remember loving him.

'You will take care of the bill and then you'll get the fuck out of there and I never wanna see you again,' says the hairy (and reeking) monster. Well that makes two of us. I'll pay and then I'll Van Gogh.

I don't say that one out loud.

I walk behind him with the melting ice cream in my hands and I watch him limping from pain. Maybe I shouldn't have gone for the ear, it's too sensitive. Maybe I should have let him look at the soiled panties. What is the worse thing that could happen? Would it really be that damaging?

I suddenly realize that I'm going commando.
I feel exposed.

We enter the medical center and I take a seat in the waiting room. He sits as far away from me as possible and I honestly don't blame him. To him I am merely the milk squirting whore than bit his ear lobe off for no apparent reason.

A man would never understand my motives.

A male nurse approaches him; I can see them speaking indistinctly, he gestures, apparently explaining what went down and eventually points at me from across the room; the nurse turns around and looks at me with disgust. He tells the monster something, probably to wait there and then he goes to the reception, where there are two other male nurses; he whispers something and they simultaneously turn to check me out. They examine me from head to toe without any trace of discretion. They are probably saying that I'm not as fine as their girlfriends.

I hope they can't tell that I have no panties on.
I feel exposed.

    They start pointing, actually physically pointing, fully extending their arms in my direction and pinning me with their index fingers, and they start laughing, laughing deeply from their stomachs, so hard that their torsos start bending backwards and their bellies wobble like jellies, and their mouths grow so wide with pleasure that it seems like they are being pulled sideways by invisible hooks, and then I see their initially surprised eyes becoming smaller and tearing up to accompany their hysterical laughter, which is getting louder and louder, until it becomes a high pitched flat line that rings like a sonic weapon in my ears.
    Wait. This is not right. This cannot be. No decent human being would do this.

Would they?

    Oh my God.
    Am I in a dream? Could I actually be asleep, dreaming? There is no other logical explanation for what is happening. But if this is indeed a dream, how much of it is true? What will I find when I wake up? Did I have a baby or am I still pregnant or am I not even pregnant yet? Did I cheat?

I try to remember what year it is.
What month.
Nothing.

Meanwhile the nurses are still laughing; they are now on the floor, flipping their legs like beetles on their backs.

I cannot remain in this state any longer.

I try to use my thoughts to create a gun so I can shoot the nurses dead – if this is my dream then I should be able to dictate what happens next, right? I stare at my hand but nothing appears. I am only holding the melted ice cream pint with the ear.

My next strategy is to wake myself up from the inside out. I stand up with intention. I jump up and down and try to shake it off. Nothing happens. Pinching my arm does not work either. I bang my head against the wall once. Twice. Shit, now I am woozy as hell and everyone is looking at me like I am a freaking psycho. I am the ice cream psychopath.

So I scream.

I just stand there screaming as loud as a human body can scream.

I scream so loudly that the windows start to vibrate, the lights flicker and the people fall on their knees and watch me with awe (or terror).

LEAVING

I scream for soiled panties, milky bras, falling hair and brittle nails.
I scream because he once told me I am not a remarkable mother.
I scream because he once told me I don't bake as well as his ex.
I scream for all the expensive dresses that don't fit anymore.
I scream for the burned pot of spaghetti he blamed me for.
I scream for the clean clothes he never thanked me for.
I scream for backache, nausea and pregnancy brain.
I scream for the blinding sting of infected stitches.
I scream for my cracked and bleeding nipples.
I scream because I haven't slept in two years.
I scream for the money I still have to make.
I scream for the heels I still have to wear.
I scream for the swollen varicose veins.
I scream to hit humanity's eardrum.
I scream so men lend me an ear.
I scream 'cause I'm a mother.
I scream for womanhood.
I scream for parenthood.
I scream for mercy.
I just scream.
I scream.

Zilch.

I give up the screaming. I am panting. The ringing laughter of the nurses has thankfully faded but I completely lost control of myself – and the situation.

I am ready to resign and crawl into a ball when all of a sudden my nipples start to tingle like they do when I am having a let-down and the milk starts shooting itself out with such a force that it throws me back onto the wall behind me; I spread my limbs like a starfish and somehow, I become the Vitruvian Man.

My liquid gold draws a spiral galaxy, a milky way in the middle of the room and within seconds it starts to solidify from the outside in with a deafening cracking sound. In an instant, I unwillingly become a marble statue, a self-loathing Aphrodite, who cannot budge. I can only move my eyelids.

I am petrified.

Why haven't I woken up yet?

I'm starting to doubt my dream/nightmare theory.

I try to concentrate. I can definitely feel my vocal cords bleeding. I can't even swallow my own spit. I sense a gush of something coming up my throat and I open up my mouth to release it. I start throwing up.

And there it is, an extraordinary fuchsia vomit, projected like an ombre pink rainbow across the waiting room; inside of it I can see my first Barbie (the model with the removable pregnant belly and plastic infant), acrylic nails with French tips, thongs, my favorite pair of sti-

LEAVING

letto heels, more thongs, baby pink mini roses from my wedding, and glitter and unicorns, and glittery unicorns and little stars and little hearts and then I close my eyes because the pinkness makes me dizzy.

I'm not trying to leave. I decide to just stay there and wait, with my eyes closed, until the vomiting ends. Until something happens. Until someone cares to save me. I can wait.

I will wait.

I am going to wake up any minute now.

I probably will.

You know there was a time I felt whole

Tiyani Mhlarhi
South Africa

Editor's Choice

THE PARTY WAS SET TO START AT 9 PM. It's only 4 right now yet I had already checked, double checked, and quadruple checked everything on my list. Clothes, check. Shoes, check. Hair, done (in neat yet stylish way). Phone, charged. Bag, packed. Money, withdrawn. Transport, organised.

I was so nervous, I wanted to do something but there was not much to be done except chill, and I was very incapable of chilling at that moment. I have not been to a party in so long I had no idea what to expect… do they still hand out goodie bags at the end of the party?

To be totally honest, I didn't even want to go. I was invited by my best friend, Brian, who said there's this really cool girl he wants to ask out and he needs me there for confidence so, I'm doing this as a favour more than anything else. He loves the party scene; I absolutely despise it. Loud music, drunk idiots, an inhuman level of standing and dancing… nope that doesn't sound like fun. If I could pull out now and play video games all night I would.

The party was taking place at this really expensive part of the neighbourhood. From what I understood the host's parents were renowned lawyers who owned multiple mansions and plots all over the city, allowing the host to use any of the unoccupied houses at any time he wants. So, more often than not, he was using them to host these massive house parties, he is infamous for them. I cannot remember when he wasn't hosting one.

So, this was a big deal for me. I would be meeting new people, reuniting with old faces, and avoiding the rotten ones at all costs. Social encounters completely freak me out. You can never tell what someone else is thinking of you, which brings this constant pressure to say the right thing. Then there's the huge chance that you don't and you screw-up the whole encounter. At the very least if I plan everything out, I could give myself some sort of assurance. So that is how I ended up pacing back and forth in my room checking everything.

At some point around 6 I found myself standing in the middle of my room with everything I had ever owned spilled on the floor of in a huge mess. I could not for the life of me remember what I was looking for and so, as I started to pack up, I heard my doorbell go off. I had ordered my rideshare for much later so I had no clue who it could have been. I trudged out of my mess, down the stairs and to check on the door. As I reached the door, the visitor knocked on the door once, taped the glass three times, knocked again, taped again, and knocked one final time. I know who it is; that's a special knock.

'Nice,' I say as I open the door, 'Hey Brian!'

'Dean!' he says, grabbing my hand and pulling me in to hug him with his free hand. 'It's been so long!'

'We saw each other yesterday!'

'And oh, how I have counted every passing second!' he exaggerates, while trying not to laugh. He was rather comedic.

'I am sure you did. What up?' Don't get me wrong I was happy to see him and all but all the while just a little confused.

'I came to chill for a while before we head on over,' he said as I gestured him inside.

'Oh cool. Next time you should call first. I was in the middle of packing.'

'What?'

'Everything.' We laughed but he had no idea I wasn't joking, 'So, you're supplying drinks?' I asked as we walked inside. I realised I had felt the bottle through his backpack.

'What? Oh this,' he says gesturing to his bag, 'no um... actually this is for now.'

'Now?'

'Yeah we are going to have our preez here.' Preez, short for pre-drinks somehow, is a little get together among friends before a party where they start the drinking early as to avoid the outrageous prices offered at bars or clubs or even some house parties. It also helps form a circle of reliance that could be useful later during the party, helps minimize transportation costs, and helps people get warmed up for the night. How do I know this? I have heard of enough party stories to know the ins and outs like a regular. There's a certain science involved in the stupidity of it all that is very interesting; it's like watching reality tv. So, more often than I would like to admit, I find myself asking my friends to recount them.

'Preez? I didn't agree to no preez.' (Very horrible English, yes but it got my point across much better than proper English)

'Don't worry it's not like an actual preez. It's just us getting a drink before we head out.'

LEAVING

'Hmmm.'

'To be totally honest, I was just kinda worried you would be stressing out here by yourself so, I thought I should help get you warmed up and relaxed. And nothing better to calm the nerves than booze!' He seemed genuine in his remarks. I shouldn't be surprised though; he really has worried and looked out for me since the incident. It just really catches me off-guard whenever he does. He always finds a way to step up every time, even when I would expect to find the limit to his kindness. A saint in wolves clothing, I guess.

'Sure, why not.'

We took the drinks up to my room and he helped me repack my clothes while we sipped merrily on the bottle of alcohol. We talked about the do's and don'ts of parties, but I knew them all already. Then we just started messing around and joking.

I had no idea what to expect tonight, but I knew if Brian was by my side, not much could go wrong.

◆

A couple mismatched ideas later, and I can't find Brian and I'm freaking out in the middle of the dance floor.

Everything had gone well so far. Brian insisted a friend take us there, so Danny, who wasn't drunk yet, mind you, took a detour, on his way to the party, to my house. When we ultimately arrived at the house (or rather mansion) 30 minutes later, the party was in full swing. Music boomed so loud it rattled the windowpanes. There was litter and cups layered all over the front garden. All the outdoor lights were on and I am pretty sure it was viewable from space.

We parked some ways down as to avoid overcrowding the road, and I got out the car and immediately started to regret my life decisions.

'You know what guys? You go and have a fun party; I'll just hang around back here while I wait for my uber,' I said.

'Oh no ways are you going to come this far only to bail on me,' Brian said, 'Come on man, it will be fun.'

We walked up and entered the main gate, where there were a couple of people mingling in the parking space.

THUMP THUMP THUMP.

The house looked even more lively up close. The bland colours of the house were upset with the colourful frenzy that were the partygoers. Few of them had made it to the roof, where they looked down on us while chatting. 'Our first mission is to find the host,' Brian said. Makes sense, it would be rude if we didn't. I just hope he is mingling outside somewhere…

THUMP THUMP THUMP.

We walked into the main foyer, and all at once, all my senses got attacked from every angle. My ears cried to my brain about the abuse it was going through. My eyes were also trying to get my brains attention to the strobing lights but to no avail. My nose wanted to vomit, and my tongue and throat wouldn't stop whining about the hard liquor it drank earlier. My sense of touch was already numb so that was no use either. So, the only description I can offer to you is that the room seemed large.

I eventually ran into the host by the catering table, and greeted him. Brian told me to wait by the table while he sorted something out. So, I thought sure, I was starving anyway, and I didn't want to be hungover tomorrow, so I picked up some chips and started eating my way through my mini panic attack.

THUMP THUMP THUMP.

After a while I realise, Brian might have forgotten to come back. So, I decide I might as well venture in and see what this party is about.

LEAVING

Bad idea #3 (1 was coming, 2 was letting Brian leave).

I end up bumping into a few friends, who seemed surprised by my presence.

'How are you holding up?' one of them shouted as she was failing to simultaneously dance, talk and drink

'Huh?' I replied

'I said: HOW ARE YOU DOING!'

'OH, I'M GREAT, THANKS!'

'Perfect!' she mouthed 'YOU KNOW WHAT? IT'S YOUR FIRST NIGHT OUT, YOU SHOULD PLAY THE POTJIE CHALLENGE. YOU HAVE TO, ALMOST LIKE AN INITIATION!'

Bad Idea #4.

THUMP THUMP THUMP.

I was dragged over to the side to my relief, but as soon as we got to the tv room, I realised what I had signed up for. There was a medium sized, three-legged, iron pot in the middle of the room, where the coffee table should be, with a huge tube coming out from it. It was loaded with alcohol to the utmost brim. Everyone around it looked at me with such eagerness, like I was joining the most drunk cult ever. The friend that led me here proceeded to shout, 'I found a challenger!', causing the room to erupt with cheer.

The point of the game was to continuously chug on the tube for a full minute straight. If you didn't, you start again. I couldn't back out now, I thought. My whole integrity depended on this. So, I chugged for a minute and a half before someone bothered to tell me that was enough. My eyes and throat burned so intensely I thought I was dying. I tried to run to the kitchen as quick as possible, but I ran headfirst into some random guy.

THUMP THUMP THUMP.

He turned around and tried to grab me, but I ran back into the party. At this point I had lost all my bearings completely and wished Brian could reappear. Any moment now, this brute could be on me, and I'm struggling to walk straight while everyone is bumping this and that way

I eventually make it outside in the garden at the back, and I realise he isn't chasing me anymore. I don't even know if he was chasing me or it was the alcohol talking. I take out my phone and try to open the rideshare app. The phone displayed a '15% remaining' warning. How in hell? Did I not charge this thing about 2 hours ago? Then I remembered. That's exactly what I was looking for when Brian came in unannounced; my power bank.

'Yeah, he's become such a hassle nowadays,' I overhear Brian say. I realise that he too had escaped the chaos and was chilling on the balcony. He couldn't see me from up there, I was right underneath him. I gave up my rideshare mission, seeing as how I couldn't see anything on my phone anyway, and continued to listen in on the conversation.

Bad idea #5

'I mean before, he was really cool and all, but after the incident, he's become a totally different person.'

'Give him a break, he's just mourning.' I realised he was talking to a girl

'For how long? Hes been nothing but an anxious, weird, melodramatic wreck! It's extremely depressing just to be around him.'

'Then why do you?'

'Because my mom is friends with his mom that's why! She is always insisting and guilt-tripping me.'

'And why bring him here?'

'I was hoping he actually gets out of his house, out of his slump, and makes new friends, so he won't have to bother me anymore.'

LEAVING

At this point it started to rain, and I didn't want to catch a cold out here in the middle of the night. I turned back and started walking slowly towards the house when the brute surprises me from nowhere and wallops me in the socket. I woke up about 2 hours later, must have been 3AM, with spilled alcohol and vomit on my shirt. My eye stung, badly.

THUMP THUMP THUMP.

My head felt like a beehive. It didn't matter though; it was too dark to see anything anyway. The party must have died down while I was unconscious, because I couldn't hear anything. It was just dark, cold and damp. The rain had slowed to a drizzle. I pulled up next to the wall, so I could take out my phone with my free hand. My chest was wheezing as I was trying to control it with my arm wrapped against my chest. Once I eventually got my phone out, I realised it was pretty much useless. I can't call Brian. Nor Danny, had no idea if he felt the same as Brian. Can't call my parents unless I wanted to be in trouble. And can't call a rideshare, the app wouldn't let me call one at this time of night (stupid parental control). I did the only thing I knew how. I cried. Softly though, couldn't have people pitying me. My phone was on 5% (or it looked like it was, it's hard to see through tears), so I decided to use it to play the last voice note I had received from Her, from long ago. Why not? I hope it won't cut off. I could really use Her voice right about now.

◆

'So, umm... ok...

I was going to say something but then it just slipped out of my mind so... yeah

So random fact about me is that I really like the rain you know? Because after it rains it's like ummm... so there's this smell that comes out of the ground. And like it's, its fresh and its earthy. It smells like wet soil.

And like I don't know why but it's so calming and I really like the smell. It's like it warms me up on the inside and the air is cool and crisp and it's fresh, you know? And the ummm… the little…no… the sound of the water running off of the rooftops, on the sides of … and the little streams that are made on the ground. The sound of that is just really calming. *yawning/indistinguishable talk* yeah *humming*

So, I guess I'll see you tomor –'

Bitten

Adrian Mills
United Kingdom

THE HOLIDAY WAS NOT GOING WELL.
Bernard, Roderick and Harold stood staring down at Cuthbert; or at least what was left of Cuthbert. Jagged bites scarred the torso, legs torn down to the bone, the throat ripped open, mouth and eyes wide, frozen in death.

'Bloody hell,' whispered Harold.

'Well, that's ruddy inconvenient,' muttered Bernard.

'Can't say I care for this at all,' intoned Roderick.

They stood there in silence for several more minutes before calling for the help. It did not take long for the groundsman to place Cuthbert's body in some sheets and take him back to the house.

It would be a week before the river was passable again. The storm that had raged the day before had raised the river and brought down the phone line that was the only means of communication between the small island that was Grangely Manor and the mainland.

Dinner was somewhat subdued that evening, the maid noticing that the men ate hardly anything. Afterwards, none of them fancied the arranged game of poker, deeming it unseemly to play with only three. It was still early when they all retired to their beds.

That night. once again, an unseasonal storm arose during the hours of darkness, engorging the river even further.

In the morning, it was a short walk to the outer gardens north of the Manor house. Roderick and Harold stood with damp shoes in the early morning dew, contemplating the demise of Bernard. Blood soaked into the lawn, bone jutted into the damp earth, severed fingers lay scattered in the nearby rose bush.

'Well this just isn't on,' rumbled Harold.

'It's just a damn shame,' breathed Roderick.

The help was called on again, taking no time to remove the remains in another sheet that would need to be burnt afterwards.

The rest of the day held none of the thrill that it had once promised, and this was not helped by a slow, persistent drizzle. The horse riding was subdued. The archery had lost most of its appeal and the grouse hunt was decidedly empty. Dinner that evening was quiet once more and although both Roderick and Harold tried manfully to enjoy some light badinage, their hearts were not in it and it was not long before both retired to their bed.

The morning dawned bright and early, the sun strong and welcoming after the previous day's rain. An influx of insects buzzed and crawled amongst the wreckage of the topiaries in the southern grounds. Harold chewed his lip as he viewed the destruction that had been wrought upon Roderick. Body parts lay in confusion amongst the shredded shrubberies, gore and organs decorated the walkway, empty eye sockets gazed skywards.

'I think that's blown it,' stated Harold.

The groundsman arrived in short order, sheets at the ready and cleared the remains away. The rest of the day was spent in a quiet haze

LEAVING

as the sun arced overhead and time floated away on a mist of memories. Harold lazed in a long boat on the small lake to the east of the Manor. Evening came and he enjoyed a small meal on his own before once again retiring to his room.

The night passed. The sun slowly rose in the morning. The maid licked her lips and crawled back to her quarters on all fours. Fur receded from her form leaving her naked and shivering. The groundsman wandered out with fresh sheets to the Manor's main driveway. Harold's remains were burnt with the sheet.

The holiday had not gone well.

Stale Peaches
David O' Dwyer
Ireland

Shortlisted for the 2019
International Writing Competition

She wheels Paul up a ramp. She's used to checking details in advance, the access routes to buildings. 'Easy Amy,' he wheezes, as she pushes the chair through the front door, the buzzer sounding. 'Easy.'

There's nothing unusual about this door. It's heavy, stubborn, green. She continues to push.

Inside, a hallway. Weak, lemony light. Trickles of shadow, with narrow-plated windows, the types you'd see in a picture-book castle, in the highest room in a tower. Figures outside move up and down, oblivious.

In front of them a staircase, a lift with criss-cross railings. The floor is tiled black-and-white, a chessboard. Velvety fronds hang limply from a plant, the twisted bark crying out for an etching, a so-and-so was here.

The email said go right. Down a corridor. But she can't see it. But there it is, just beyond the plant. The chair squeaks on the chequered floor as she turns the wheels.

Prints of drab hunting scenes line the wall, the smell of disinfectant. There's a whiff of something else, but she can't put her finger on it. Is it that smell she got in her mother's apartment those last months? The odour from the rooms when she walked the corridors in the hospice. A fruity smell, like peaches. Stale peaches.

'Here we go,' she pushes. Apartment 23. Gold numbers. The number 3 hangs loose, a screw missing. The door is half-open.

'They give you space,' a woman who'd been through it told her, a woman on the phone. 'Take your time. Look around. Have a drink. You'll need it.'

She pushes Paul in. Her mouth is dry, her head throbbing. She hears a hum, like the sound of a fridge, only more high-pitched. It might be Paul, his chest.

'Are you okay, Paul?'

'Humph.'

A sweet smell in the air, like candy floss. A brightly-lit kitchen, silver and white. Except for a lemon-coloured box of dishwasher tablets in the corner by the sink. A coffee machine, cupboards above the sink, one door open. Inside wine glasses, stacked ashtrays, champagne flutes. Wheeling Paul in, she sees their joint reflection, grotesque and smudged, on the surface of the silver fridge door.

'*Who's a pretty boy, then? Who's a pretty boy?*' A nasal voice, muffled. Something trapped in a box. She's not sure where it comes from, whether from outside or from a room nearby. '*Who's a pretty boy then? Who's a pretty boy?*'

Amy turns around. A woman is standing in the doorway of the kitchen, a phone in her hand.

'I'm so sorry. My granddaughter put this ring-tone in my phone. I can't get rid of it...'

The woman comes forward, holds out her hand. She's tall, silver-haired, dressed in a white sweater with a pleat skirt. 'I'm the nurse,' she smiles, 'My name is Giulia.' Amy takes her hand, touches cold flesh. A lightly-tanned face. Dark blue eyes, a glint of amber. A brooch pinned to her sweater, the head of a Sphinx. Green jewel-eyes are embedded in the metal.

Amy releases her hand.

The nurse goes over to Paul, squats beside him, whispers. A patch of pink beneath her thinning hair, the glisten of a pimple on the crown. Paul lifts his tortoise head. His eyes are yellow, rheumy. Amy's own eyes water.

'Do you do this often?' Paul asks Giulia. 'Once or twice a week. That's enough.'

'We can take our time with this,' Giulia continues. 'We've all the time we need.'

Giulia wheels Paul out of the kitchen, across a hallway to another room. Amy's uncertain whether to follow or give them some time. She misses the support of the wheelchair, her anchor. She has clasped its handles - the rubber sometimes grating against her skin – and manoeuvred its brake with her foot for several weeks now.

Before the chair, Paul used sticks. A nickel-plated cane with a horse-shaped head that could double as an offensive weapon. A white ash crook with a curve that evoked shepherds. An aluminium cane you could extend, reduce or fold over. A thick, solid oak stick with a knuckled head made from a stag's antler.

He always liked his style. The leather-bound encyclopaedias, the moleskin diaries, the fountain pens. The silver hip-flask with the Tullamore Dew inscription, his Cherrywood pipe. A beautiful chess set. A shaving brush with badger-hair bristles. Club ties, silk ties, handkerchiefs with stitched initials. A gold tie-pin, a signet ring. Things he'd accumulated. Beautiful male things.

◆

In the opera he told her, the hand with the signet ring holding her wrist. Just before Act Three of *La Bohème*, before the curtain went up. Before the scene with the toll gate at the Barrière d'Enfer. Deep red curtains – words like crimson and maroon and scarlet came to her mind – quivered a bit, but would not part as the glaring lights in the auditorium hurt her eyes.

'It's not localised enough for surgery', he whispered. 'I've to start radiation therapy next week. Intensive stuff '

She released his grip and felt awkward. Her face was hot. She was afraid. Afraid of what was expected of her. Afraid of what was to come. Then it hit her. The separate lives they led. The separate people they were.

◆

Giulia is in the office talking to Paul. Amy stands outside, wants to enter. She has come this far, has taken this risk. A silver cat, with a stub of a tail, emerges from the room, humps its back. Rubbing against her leg, it purrs, an electric whine. Amy shudders, hurries into the office.

An ordinary space, a whirring fan, lots of lever-arch files on shelves around the walls. Giulia sits at a desk which slopes towards Paul. There is paper in front of him, a fountain pen. Amy sits on a small settee and waits. She sees several folded-up wheelchairs in a corner of the room. Beside them a basket, with walking sticks. Sticks and stones may break my bones. But names will never hurt me. She imagines the hands that held those sticks. Bone-white, yellow, blotchy. Mother's hands. Like latex, old and crinkled. Clotted in places with tiny brown lumps. Paul's hands.

'Would you like a drink?' Giulia glances at Amy. 'Can I get you something?' 'We'd like champagne,' Amy replies but Paul weakly raises a hand.

'No. Hot Toddy. With brandy.'

'Sure,' Giulia rises. 'I'll see what I can do.'

'I'd like a cigarette, if you have one,' Amy asks as Giulia strides across the room. 'Of course.'

The sound of her footsteps tap-tapping in the hallway, purposefully echoing in that empty space. The pottering about in the kitchen. Water gushing from a tap, glasses clinking. The hiss of a kettle, clanging objects on a metallic tray.

The silence between them.

◆

There was another conversation with Paul, a couple of weeks after the therapy had begun. She sees the orangey red box-seats, the kind you'd see in the foyer of a large building, an Art Gallery, or office block. He was standing by a window that framed a small garden at the back of the University's library. Staring into space, a Styrofoam cup in his hand, he seemed oblivious to the view of the flowering fuchsia plants, the creeper on the slate-grey wall, the cherry blossoms. As she came closer, she noticed the Styrofoam cup was crumpled in his hand; he was standing over a metal bin, undecided whether to let it drop. His other hand was pressed against the small of his back.

He turned to look at her. Dressed as impeccably as ever: navy blazer with wine-coloured hanky in the top pocket, white shirt, striped tie and grey slacks. His eyes looked dull and absent. Spittle shone on his pale pink lips.

'Won't be long now.'

'Why are you still working?'

LEAVING

'They put me in this annexe here. Away from the cut and thrust. To preserve my dignity, so to speak...'

'Come and sit down.'

On an orangey red box-seat, his hand sliding up and down his spine, she asked him. 'What the hell is going on, Paul? Why are you doing this?'

'The back pains were the worst, at first. Then I started puking.'

'And what about the chemotherapy? You mentioned the chemo. What's happening with that?'

'They advised a break first, after the radiation. There's a possibility of combination therapy, of combining the two.'

'Why not?'

'I'm tired, Amy. It's now spread from the pancreas. They're pumping me to keep me alive...'

He wouldn't look at her and she wanted him to say more. But there was only silence, exacerbated by the slow drugged movement of city centre traffic, the chugging sound of a nearby photocopier or fax machine, the persistent ringing of a telephone.

'You're not going to, Paul, are you?'

He was looking at her now, his face wider, younger, the way he once was, with blue eyes shining. Slowly, he nodded.

Giulia comes back. There's a smell of brandy and honey, steam rising from the glass. A tinkling sound as she puts the tray down.

'Let me get you a straw for this, Paul.'

Amy takes a cigarette out of the blue-and-white packet, a Peter Stuyvesant.

'Pet-er Stuy-vesant,' Paul mouths the syllables, as if trying to locate somebody in a crowded room. Amy holds the cigarette, without lighting it. Her champagne is flat but she sips it.

◆

They were sitting in their back garden, down the very end, smoking. Sitting on a slab of stone that was balanced on two rocks, in the shade of the apple trees. Flicking cigarette ash on to the ground beside the flush of red and yellow roses, looking at the flowers, the withered apples on the ground, the bark of trees. Their curling cigarette smoke twisted and merged in the air between them before trickling away. The perfume of the flowers, the cidery smell of apples, the smokiness.

'Take me with you,' Paul pleaded.

'I can't, you know that.'

'Why not?'

'They'd only get suspicious.'

'So?'

'I'm supposed to be working there for the summer. You'd be better off coming over later. For a visit.'

'Will you be alright?'

She stabbed out her cigarette on the edge of the rock. Took a deep breath. 'I suppose, but... Paul?'

'Yes?'

'Promise me you won't tell them?'

'I promise.'

◆

Giulia stirs Paul's drink, clink-clink. She raises the glass, the straw protruding, to his lips. Amy can see the skull beneath the stretch of his skin, the wisps of hair. She can't bear to look, but hears the cough raking the air, the pain she has become so used to. She has seen the bile, the phlegm swirling in silver bowls, settling into shapes: an Ireland, an Italy, a bigger

LEAVING

blob for Australia. He has come to reclaim her and this is what she has. These memories, these maps.

She lights her cigarette but can barely hold the matchstick. She lets it drop to the floor and stands up, shivering. Blowing smoke, she walks out to the hallway. She never told Paul she knew he'd broken his promise. He told her parents about the child, the little thing inside her, the vanquished hope.

Her mother's dull blue eyes fixed her, right at the end. The crinkled hand held onto her sleeve. Her lips were pale and parting. A smell of stale peaches.

In the dying light she told her. She knew about the child.

◆

A weak, yellowy light in the hallway. A low Gregorian chant comes from a room with an open door. Amy feels nauseous, but goes in anyway, her head spinning.

A bed, a bible on the locker beside it. A tray with an orange tumbler. Napkins, a heart-shaped chocolate to soften the taste of the fatal liquid. A silver bowl for vomit.

She moves to the window, tries to compose herself. Holds onto the green curtains that are tied with yellow rope. Outside, rust-coloured rooftops, spires, skyscrapers. Birds fly overhead. Their pointed wings, their forked tails, cut the air. She'll have to fold his chair. Organise his belongings. Selfishly and selflessly, he has left her nothing else to do.

She awaits a signal, a sound. The release of the brake and the turn of the wheel so she can tell him she knows.

No Answer
Eamon O'Leary
Ireland

Shortlisted for the 2019
International Writing Competition

THE BRASS BED, OVERDUE A RUB OF BRASSO, creaked with relief as Tommy swore, farted and swung two gnarled legs onto the icy linoleum. Except for rheumatic big toes which stuck out of the top, his clammy feet found comfort in a pair of originally tartan slippers. Over skid-marked Long-Johns, he wore a pair of shrunken pyjamas and an Aran sweater, minus the elbows.

Yanking back the green floral curtains, he saw only a frost-covered window both inside and out.

'I'm going to shoot that fecking dog. Yap, yap, yap since six o'clock. Non-fecking stop. I'm not taking it anymore, do ya hear me, Rose?'

No answer.

He went along the landing to the airing cupboard where, on the door, a thermometer hung from a nail. Taking a brown notebook from the pocket of his pyjamas, he noted and recorded the temperature, along with the time and date. After turning on the immersion, he went to the bathroom, took a piss, left the seat up and didn't bother flushing or washing his hands.

Back in the bedroom, he rummaged under the bed and pulled out an air rifle and a box of pellets. Dragging over an armchair only fit for the dump, he positioned it at the metal-framed window, whose hinges squealed when he opened it. Shivers reached his toes when an icy-clean breeze met the foul air. Before sitting, he went back to the airing cupboard and turned off the immersion. Then, with the ambush set, he plonked himself down on the chair, his index finger exploring high into one of his nostrils.

He entered all the details of his morning – except the subconscious nasal adventure – in his notebook.

The silver circular tin had originally held two hundred and fifty pellets. Seven, he'd used in a former unsuccessful dog-culling exercise. He sat counting as the lazy sun made an appearance and cleared most of the frost, but there was no sign of the doomed dog. With a broken spring burrowing its way up Tommy's arse and droplets from his almost pious-blue nose running to a constant flow, he suspended operations, but not before finishing the count. 'Two hundred and forty-three' was recorded in the notebook.

In the dirt-encrusted kitchen, he heated a pot of porridge that he'd left soaking overnight in milk and a spoon of honey. He stood and ate a bucket-sized portion. On the table sat a stack of books, mostly classics. A pair of ladies glasses on top of the pile. A lonely cup, saucer and spoon lay among an array of medications. Everything covered in dust.

When he'd finished his breakfast, Tommy crushed a handful of oats and stood, arm outstretched, outside the back door. After a short wait, his robin friend landed on a nearby whitethorn tree and made a few cursory security checks before coming to rest in Tommy's palm. Redbreast made short work of brunch, while Tommy gave him the latest news.

'What d'ya think? Should I shoot the dog?'

The robin took flight without answering.

'Ungrateful little bollocks.'

The details of breakfast and conversation were noted down.

In the bathroom, he shaved and washed his important bits in lukewarm water.

'Maybe it's not fair to shoot the stupid dog,' he told himself. 'Maybe it's that eejit who owns it I should be going after? Did ya see the state of him, Rose? All tight trousers and stripy shirts and what about the dog? I mean to say an alsatian or a labrador or even a fecking cocker spaniel would be a man's dog, but a bichon feckin' frise? Yeah, he's definitely a queer hawk.'

No response.

After checking the immersion was off, he left home, his departure confirmed by the clattering of the cast-iron knocker as he pulled the door shut. The dog barked, and Tommy cursed.

His two-up-two-down, the sole surviving fisherman's house, sat on top of the hill. The rest had been snapped up and razed by developers. Tommy refused all offers. Not even a house in the new complex and a barrowfull of money could shift him.

'Me father lived here, and his father before him. I've lived here all my life and I'll be buried from here,' he'd told them. He'd won. They'd redesigned the development around Tommy's place.

A narrow road corkscrewed its way from Tommy's house to the village. On one side, breaks in the stone wall gave glimpses of heather, gorse and coarse grasses, with the never-ending sea beyond. Opposite, sad, hungry-looking cattle picked at sparse grass in irregular fields.

It was a leisurely five-minute walk for most, but with thumbs

LEAVING

clenched inside white-knuckled fists it was, for Tommy, a daily nightmare fraught with danger. His route was like a jigsaw, crisscrossed with moss-filled veiny cracks. Stepping on a crack ensured imminent bad luck and disaster.

Relief came when he reached the road in the village.

McCarthy's pub, its neon sign swinging from a rusted bracket, shared a corner with Murphy's grocery. The Post Office, Curls 'n' Colours and the boarded-up Yangtze River completed the business district of the village. Opposite, facing the elements, stood a solemn, cut-stone church and a two-roomed school. All the buildings shared a sparsity of customers.

Tommy's education had ended as soon as he'd learned to read and write. He joined his father on the fourteen-footer, hunting down the herring. A tough life for little reward. He minded the few pounds he made. A match was made between himself and Rose and three kids followed. She'd sworn that 'All three of them will go to college. That'll be their passport out of here.'

A good result. Two accountants and a teacher. She'd moved well up from the back row of the church on Sundays.

Nowadays, Tommy enjoyed the half-moon foreshore, gathering driftwood, wondering what stories of storms, giant waves and foreign parts these bleached relics could tell. It mattered little after he'd dragged them up the hill. They'd all end up the same way, clobbered by his hatchet and fed to the fire. Date, time and relevant details recorded in the notebook. Other days, depending on the tides and time of year, a bucket of cockles made for a change from the staple diet of boiled spuds and streaky bacon.

Of late, usually on a Sunday, Tommy took an evening constitutional as far as the pier. Once a thriving haven for fishermen, including Tommy,

AWARD WINNING STORIES

it now hung on sadly, slowly succumbing to the endless waves. A single insipid light at the seaward end flickered as if signalling the inevitable.

Armed with a fishing rod, a torch and his thermometer, he timed the walk to coincide as best he could with the full tide. With the thermometer hooked to the rod, he lowered it into the water, retrieving it minutes later. Date, time, temperature and a comment entered the notebook.

A white bundle of fur sitting on the windowsill inside the house next door greeted Tommy on his return. It barked. A lot. Tommy shook his fist and swore.

He slammed his front door. 'I'm back.'

No reply.

Warming himself by the fire, he placed a candle on the narrow, wax-covered mantelpiece. A pile of sympathy cards and an eclectic collection of dust-coated photos cluttered the limited space: babies, children of all ages, college celebrations and weddings. In the centre, a black and white portrait of a smiling couple on their wedding day. Only memories now. The regular visits from Australia and America petered out when partners and grandchildren arrived.

'Will ye be coming home for Christmas?' A regular plea. 'Your ma will be disappointed if ye don't come.'

'Da, you know we'd love to, but with the kids, it'd cost a fortune. Why don't ye come to us?'

'Maybe next year.'

Over time, the weekly phone calls tapered off. Now they were down to just an occasional duty call. Skype and Facetime alien to Tommy.

He'd never felt the joy of a newly born grandchild wrapping its fist around his little finger. No longer babies, they were strangers to him now.

He'd given up on organised religion years earlier and preferred the direct approach. After checking the immersion was off and before climbing into bed, he'd kneel by the bedside and have a private chat with Whoever Was Up There. It always ended the same;

'Take good care of her.'

Callers to the house were rare, except for Jack McCarthy, the postman. Almost as old and wizened as Tommy, and equally cranky. They enjoyed sorting out the problems of the parish, the country and the world. Agreement on any issue was a rarity. The perfect match.

As the days shortened, December crept along and with it came the first of the Christmas post.

'I've a few for you today, Tommy. Any of the kids coming this year?'

Tommy grunted. He threw the cards into the grate unopened after Jack left.

The sun hid its face on the last Sunday before Christmas. A sky laden with snow hung heavy over the village and delivered its cargo as Tommy prepared for his evening trudge to the jetty. An effortless journey for once, a light powdery dusting covered the cracks. The full tide was in, so he took his reading.

Date, time and temperature recorded and a comment – 'Perfect.' Bitterly cold with a lazy wind that would rather go through you than round you.

About to strike out for home, he found his way blocked by a group of children singing carols, huddled together like a flock of lambs outside McCarthy's pub.

What a stupid place to bring these kids, thought Tommy. The coldest spot in the village…

Oh, should've known. 'Tis that eejit living by me that's in charge.

Not the dog-owner, but another adversary of Tommy's, the recently arrived long geek of a schoolteacher. There'd been some problem over a parking space. Tommy didn't have a car, never drove, but that wasn't the point. One child shook a collection bucket in Tommy's direction. He stopped. The teacher, expecting an outburst, held his breath and bit his lip.

Tommy rooted through the pockets of his oilskins. Yellow from top to toe, he looked like a giant canary standing under the light. A few bits of twine and an oily rag didn't augur well for the collectors with their feet, fingers and faces shivering. Pulling down a zip in the cumbersome coat, Tommy took a crumbling wallet from within the layers. With hands over his mouth, the teacher took a step back and watched Tommy empty note after note into the bucket. Fives, tens and even a twenty. The children danced and whooped, except the bucket carrier, who stood motionless, eyes fixed on the bundle of notes.

'I'm back.'

No answer. He missed the smell of Christmas baking.

Tommy went up to the bedroom. His only suit, smelling of mothballs, hung in the lopsided wardrobe among an array of dresses, some long, some shortish, all old. Winter and summer overcoats and even a full-length fur coat, complete with foxtail collar. Holding the hanger, Tommy satisfied himself that a rub of the iron would restore the charcoal grey suit to its former glory, and set about the task. He managed a crease as sharp as a razor on the trousers, the knees shiny from years of grime transferred from palms to pants. A size eighteen collar shirt, formerly white and now a delicate yellow, together with a wide maroon tie got a smoothing of the iron. He spotted what looked like a gravy stain, a relic from a wake or wedding, and doused it under the cold tap before giving it a pat of the hot iron. With a frenzied enthusiasm, a pair of mould-encrusted shoes were polished back to parade ground standard.

LEAVING

He changed into the suit and brogues and after checking the immersion was turned off, returned downstairs.

Taking the photos from the mantelpiece, he sat by the fire examining each before putting them all back except the one of the young couple. As the fire died, he blew out the candle and put the photo of the newlyweds in his breast pocket.

'Not long now, love.'

He placed the small brown notebook on the mantelpiece and tugged the front door closed after him.

The dog next door barked. Tommy gave him the thumbs-up, laughed and headed back to the pier.

Sarah

CHRISTOPHER OWEN
United Kingdom

SHORTLISTED FOR THE 2019
INTERNATIONAL WRITING COMPETITION

SARAH, COMING UP TO SIXTY-FIVE. Seated in the armchair under the window in the living room of her flat in West London, waiting for Petra to phone. She could have been a star. People had told her so. And no one could say she hadn't tried, and, looking back, it had been all right. Terrific. Then Gerry died.

It was all right with Gerry. She and Gerry had been a team. He had form. Highly regarded, almost a star. Drank of course, but who didn't in those days? In those days, people drank. Men drank. It was the thing to do. Gerry's Club – not her Gerry – the actors' club – Gerry's – Groucho's – the other one, what was its name? – the other one – closed down now. Joe Allen's, there was always Joe Allen's. Everyone used to go to Joe Allen's, it was the place to go, although sometimes, she went and she'd feel, oh God, this is so fucking awful, all those people, stars, and those hangers on – sometimes she'd feel what was the point? But Gerry and she went. Of course. No point in staying at home in the flat. The flat. It wasn't the sort of place one stayed in for long, not for too long if one could get out, Joe Allen's, the Queen's, the Lamb and Flag. Then Gerry died.

◆

She'd go and see Petra if it wasn't for that God-awful cat of hers, which Petra clearly loved a lot, a lot more than anything or anyone else. That cat with its fur all over one's trousers, all over one's skirt. Moulting, forever moulting, non-stop moulting. She's moulting, Petra said. Christ.

No one seemed to know anyone anymore, Sarah in the armchair under the window thought. No one. No one at all. And the drains. The drains were blocked. The landlord's agent – God knows who the landlord was, someone in far off places, no doubt. The landlord's agent told her she must have put something down there, fat, oil, something that's blocking the drains, as if it was her fault. She didn't use fat or oil, she told them. She phoned them, told them she went out to eat, she didn't cook in the flat. She went out. The drains were stinking the place out. Tuesday night, was it? – she'd been to that show – God, what a bore that was, that show, by the friend of Terry's – it was in verse, for God's sake. She'd got in about twelve and there it was – the drains. Lying in bed with the stinking drains all about her – getting into the bed clothes, into the wardrobe. So now she was in the armchair under the window, waiting for the landlord's agent to send the men about the drains, clean them out, unblock them. So, of course, she wasn't staying in while that was going on – she'd have to go out, even if it was to Petra and her fucking cat and its fur balls, and its hair all over her trousers. She'd go to the Queen's, but that dreadful, dreadful man Philip would be there. He was always there. Might be there. Philip, pompous, self-regarding arsehole, thought he could act, said he was writing his autobiography. Philip, always looking over his shoulder, everyone's shoulder to see if he could spot someone who'd come in who was important. God. Sarah didn't know what had happened, not exactly, couldn't remember, the two of them shouting at each other in The Queen's. It had been him saying about her not paying her way when she could get away with it, always on the cadge – the bastard, saying that. All those people, and him saying she was on the cadge as per usual. And she was shouting at him – shouting he was a total absolute failure – Philip, a nobody. She'd stormed out. She wasn't going back to the Queens, not today. So, it was Petra. She had rung her. On her mobile. Petra. Half an hour earlier. It was her voice mail. She'd tried her again, twice, always Petra's fucking voice mail. So, it was Sarah in her armchair, and the drains, now Gerry was gone.

◆

It was the ciggies that did it for Gerry. Even after he got throat cancer, he smoked, even after he'd had the operation, he'd have a ciggy. He'd always smoked, it's what one did. She had sometimes wondered, it was a nagging thought, whether it was because she didn't smoke, had never smoked, that she hadn't got the work she might have done if she had smoked. One never knew. The slightest thing could put people off. 'She doesn't smoke, you know. She's not the sort we'd want. She's not really right for the part.' No one had actually said that to her, but should they have done so, she thought that she would have said that she was not up for the part of a fucking chimney. She thought, seated in the armchair under the window, that that would have been a jolly good retort.

◆

It had been no good telling Gerry not to smoke. Gerry and ciggies were old friends. Ciggies and Guinness. Thin as a rake, all bones in the last year. People didn't recognize him. 'Oh, my God, Gerald, it's you. How are you getting along?' Bloody silly question. He was fucking dying. Before their eyes, everyone's eyes, dying. All, all bones. Refused to go into hospital at the end. Die at home, he said. Not going into the fucking hospital, he said. They'll fucking kill me in there, he said. They gave him morphine. He died of morphine, a ciggy between his teeth, half a glass of Guinness on the bedside table. Hadn't the strength to finish it.

The phone rang. It was Petra.

◆

She had started to see Dr Reynolds, she told Petra. She couldn't think why she was seeing him. She had gone to the GP with her chest, and he asked how she was getting on since Gerry, and she said sometimes she didn't know why she bothered. The GP said this and that and arranged for her to have Cognitive Behavioural Therapy. She went to a woman at St Ann's, who, God help her, asked so many questions. It was like a fucking exam, she told Petra, when she went over to see her that afternoon, with the fucking cat, its fur all over the place. She went back to the GP surgery – a different GP this time, an Indian – she never saw the same GP twice – one had to take pot luck. The Indian suggested Dr Reynolds. 'A very good man', he said.

The first time she went to see him, Dr Reynolds had asked her when her husband Gerry had died.

Two years ago, she had said.

◆

'I'm going to this psycho man,' she said to the man who'd come to clean out the drains, an African American from Brixton. He had such a nice smile. Six feet two, she told Petra on the phone. She liked him. His name was Derrick, she said.

Petra wanted her to look after her cat, she said to Derrick who was standing by the drain outside the flat.

Petra was going to stay with her son in Worcester. His wife had walked out on him and he was in a state, and would Sarah look after her cat Carlos, her fucking cat, for two weeks? Her fucking cat Carlos, its fur everywhere, all over the flat, God knows where.

She said to Dr Reynolds, how could she refuse?

So now Carlos was living with her. And she had to feed him disgusting pork and salmon in jelly. And Petra had said to her, don't forget the water. And let him out to do his business, but don't let him out at night. The bloody cat under her feet.

The flat was not big enough for them both, she told Dr Reynolds, him sitting there, the consulting room blinds half down, his trousered legs stretching out into the room, his face in shadow, so she didn't really know what he was thinking, and at some point, she wasn't quite sure he hadn't fallen asleep.

She told Derrick, when he had come back the following morning to clean out the drains, that Dr Reynolds hardly ever spoke. All she got from him was the odd word, the occasional murmur, and so she was left to do the talking, she said to him.

◆

She was in the kitchen and she had called the cat 'Gerry'. Just like that. Out it came. 'Gerry'. What was she thinking? she said to herself. She thought of telling Dr Reynolds the next time she saw him. She could have told Derrick when he came back again to try to fix the drains, but he had a workmate with him, a skinny little white man whom she didn't take to. The fucking cat had got on the kitchen surfaces by the sink and had knocked a cup onto the floor and she had yelled 'for fucks sake, will

LEAVING

you stop farting about, Gerry. Christ sake, if you can't stop your moping around, not knowing what to do with yourself, then fuck off to the pub. Moaning, complaining no work, for Christ sake.'– and, without thinking, she'd let it out at the back, and Petra had said, she was sure she had said, don't let it out after dark. And she had. She was out there in the back garden looking for it, but it had fucked off. Fuck off then, she had shouted into the night.

◆

Would it be all right if she called him James? she said to Dr Reynolds. Such a nice name. She was waiting to hear from her agent, James, darling, she said. She'd been to a casting. For a commercial. She'd been in at nine thirty and had still been there at eleven. A cattle market, James, she said. Ghastly. That's how it was now, that was what it had come to. Thousands of them waiting, she said. Dozens of them. Women of a certain age. A young man, who didn't look more than twelve years old, asked her what she had been doing, she told Dr Reynolds, and Dr Reynolds said: 'Ah'. Dr Reynolds said 'Ah', she told Petra when she phoned to find out how the cat was settling in. Oh, it was fine, Sarah said. She didn't tell her it had fucked off.

◆

Her bedroom ceiling had fallen in, she told Petra who phoned from her son's house in Worcester. She wasn't surprised, she said. She had complained more than once to the landlord's agent about the cracks. She had been in the kitchen and the ceiling in the bedroom had come crashing down. All over her bed, she said to Petra. So, now she had the builders in. Mike and a man called Beck or Bock or someone. A name she couldn't get her head around.

Before Gerry, she said to Dr Reynolds, there had been others of course. When one was young, and on tour, that was what happened, she said.

Before Gerry, there was Simon, baritone, big voice. Solid, reliable, chorus at Covent Garden, Glyndebourne, she said to Derrick who was down inside the drain, knocking out the bricks.

Before Gerry, there had been Simon, a very good baritone, but awfully dull in himself, she told Mike and Mike's mate Beck or Bock or whatever his name was, as they were pulling down the remaining plaster, and saying something unintelligible about 'drywall' and a 'botched job'.

Before Simon there was Terence. None of them were Gerry. None. He had a tongue on him, had Gerry, she said to Dr Reynolds, who sat there and hardly said a word, so it was up to her. But she felt better after she'd been to see him, walking out of his consulting room, walking to the Tube station. Although, when she thought about it, she wasn't sure she'd recognize him if she ever met him in the street.

She told Derrick outside the flat by the drains that Dr Reynolds reminded her of Gerry.

She told Dr Reynolds himself that he reminded her of Gerry. She didn't know why she had said that. He didn't remind her of Gerry. But she said it.

She was wearing Vinaigre de Toilette that afternoon which was from a nineteenth century recipe and contained an infusion of plants, woods and spices, she said to Derrick as he drank the cup of tea she had made for him. A perfume that was rather too pungent for her liking, she said.

She told Mike and his mate Beck or Bock, the Vinaigre de Toilette had been sold to her by a sales woman in Selfridges.

She guessed the sales woman's face had not been fully in evidence since the sales woman had first discovered the obliterating benefits of applying excessively generous amounts of foundation cream and blush and so forth.

She had formulated and practised this observation on her own in the kitchen over a six o'clock gin and tonic. Mostly gin, less tonic. Once perfected, she conveyed her descriptive account first to Mike, then, more importantly to her, to Derrick, and subsequently to Dr Reynolds, and was thinking of trying it out on Petra on the phone but, by the time Petra phoned again to ask about the fucking cat who, unknown to her, had of course fucked off, Sarah had become bored with the whole thing and was no longer certain it sounded all that clever. So, she didn't.

◆

She had seen a woman in a blue wool coat, she told Dr Reynolds. She had thought the coat too large for her. But anyway, there she was on the platform's edge at Baker Street. As her train had come in, the woman had thrown herself onto the tracks, which was why, James, darling, Sarah said, she was a little late that afternoon.

◆

The drains were all right now, Derrick said to Sarah. Brickwork and piping had come away, and there had been a sewage build up. But it was all done now, he said, and it was nice to have met her and thanks for the teas and all the best, and Sarah thanked him and felt she would miss him, although she didn't say so. The next day it was Mike who said his mate Beck had finished the painting of the new ceiling. It was a nice job, he hoped she'd agree, and she had agreed, and thanks for the teas and nice to have met her, and take care, Mike said, and his mate Beck, whom she now quite liked, said take care, and she waved them off in their van, as she was standing on the pavement outside the front of the house, waving.

Waving. And quietly calling goodbye.

◆

Dr Reynolds had left, she was told by reception. Why was that? she asked. No reply. Her enquiry ignored. She was to join Dr Leone Hoffman's group. She was directed to where the group was assembled. She looked in. Dr Hoffman was sitting at the front behind a desk, patients seated in rows before her. An angry young man ranting. She turned away and left the building.

◆

She was seated in the armchair under the window. She heard someone at the back door. She opened it. It was Petra's cat. He had decided to come back home, had he? Sarah said to it. Fucking about out there. God help her, he was impossible.

Petra phoned. How was the cat? she asked. Oh, Sarah said, Gerry was fine.

Running Up That Hill
Jonathan Page
United Kingdom

Shortlisted for the 2019 International Writing Competition

GERAINT REACHES THE STREAM at the top of the gulley. The sun tricks out the dark water with lines and commas. It shows him the stones glowing under the surface by his sheep shitted boots. He listens to the manic radio of the larks.

Come on. We've got to get on.

His collie Fly is barking for thrown stones from the deepest part of the stream. The dog shakes itself off and jogs towards him. A couple appear at the corner of the path, walking their mountain bikes over the yellow sponge of the moor and the dog changes course to greet them.

Geraint feels a twinge of desire, instantly supressed, when he sees the woman's oval face in the frame of her coat hood. He turns to the square faced man with her, an ageless face, her father's, her lover's, he is not sure, and says something banal about the coldest June on record. He turns his head as he speaks to take them both in. They smile uncertainly and he wonders if he seems strange to them, if he is strange, but then the woman speaks.

    Yes. It was raining. Raining over there. Better this side of mountain.

    They are tourists, Scandinavian perhaps or Dutch.

    Don't bounce up at them, Fly. Don't do that.

    The dog weaves between the bikes, threatening to trip them. He puts Fly on the lead and the cyclists walk on, smiling, nodding, to the stream. The woman pulls down her hood and her hair is a surprising grey.

    Geraint takes the right hand path for once, out over the featureless plain to the distant bluff. The cotton grass vibrates to the horizon. He leaps over the big stones the national park has laid down to mark the dried black watercourses that cut the path. There are ponies out where the moor starts to tilt again into the wet weather that is coming. The hills are dusk there, slate or a dirty green. He stands watching from the edge of summer. It is a relief to be alone again. To have escaped other people and their judgement of him. He lets Fly off again but the dog stays close to him.

    The sun rises strong out of the land and he is suddenly happy. The sun stands strong against the slate wall of the coming rain.

    He must get Jen to see this one day. Get her to climb this far.

    He wants to turn to her and say look at this, though they are both seeing it.

    He takes photos on his phone to share with his grown daughters and his step-son on Instagram.

    Geraint is an almost fit, almost happy man in the hills with his dog. A band of horses queues on the path under the rocks. The valley is faint and orderly with fields and woods. He sees the architecture of it all and is part of this order.

    How long does he have now? An hour? An hour and a half?

LEAVING

The rain arrives as pins on his bare arms. He is not prepared for the weather and feels liberated by it. The rain stains the hard ground in circles. He will give it another hour. He will get as close to the bluff as he can.

♦

Suzie drifts away from the capsule, watching the tether uncoil and grow suddenly tight. The blackness of deep space is so complete she cannot look at it.

She hates this dream and forces herself awake.

She wakes to a sunlit room. Birds chatter in the tall windows. She remembers that Ken has left her, as she always does when she wakes, though it is nearly a year ago now.. She knew he would leave one day and she thought she was ready, that she would be happier when he did, but she was lost when he went and she has stayed lost. It is not as if she really knew or loved the man. Their struggle to exist together obscured some greater question she could not answer. Her struggle to exist without him obscures the same question.

Suzie showers and is surprised as usual by the small signs of age, the grey wires in her red hair in the mirror. Some days she sees someone younger in the mirror, on other days an old woman. After coffee she gets into her hill running gear. Her smelly muddy shoes lie abandoned in the hall, her ragged red shirt and clashing yellow shirts hang stinking over the bannister.

Running is less about taking her out of herself than meeting an indifferent world head on. It is a comfort to go up into the hills and see that things continue with or without her.

No, that's wrong. That's not it. That's not why.

Running does take her out of herself. It does. She enters the world while she runs. She feels the strength in her legs and the weather on her body and is briefly part of something larger. That sounds romantic but let it stand. She must believe in something. She searches the kitchen for her car keys and fills a bottle with water.

The sun blooms where she parks the car on the common and she stretches then jogs within the wide flag of it. She runs towards the rainy hill and remembers her dream again but without fear. The pounding earth is in her muscles. The earth is taking over her body, just as she knew it would.

The first part of the run goes past a white-washed chapel. She sees what she has seen many times before as if it were the first time. She wants to turn to the invisible presence at her elbow and say look at that! Look at those tall windows! Suzie is sympathetic to the chapel and wants it to know that it is loved.

She reaches the drover's track, which climbs the sheer side of the hill in grassy zig-zags. Stones click under her trainers. Her sweat is a second skin. She feels like she is running up a tunnel or up from the bottom of a well. The fierceness of her grief is part of her joy. Grief is part of her power.

She runs she runs she runs she runs.

The valley becomes a soft picture of fields and woods. Towns and villages sit white at the joins in the patchwork. The valley and her car, a blue point on the common, are not her life any more. The sky larks are now her life. The stones under her shoes, the next patch of ground are her life.

She runs and she is here. She has reached the high country.

The moor is bleached hair rolling down into some vast obscure country beyond. The rain prickles her skin as she runs her reward of near level ground. She wanted what everyone she knew wanted long ago, a partner, children, but there is something to be said for freedom and even for loneliness. The beauty of what she sees is a cleansing weight in her.

Five horses run single file past square rocks. The lead horse is the lightest brown, almost red. Its mane is a banner in the breeze. Then she sees the man and his dog coming over the rise and he seems beautiful to her also. She judges his age as her age, though she can see only the pattern of him at this distance.

◆

Geraint sees the runner and thinks her beautiful.

He thinks this with a kind of guilty hunger. He sees at once some alternative life and sees his present life exposed, laid bare in its sadness. Fly flows down the path ahead of him, to where the path breaks at an angle over the moist black bed of a rill. The sun is a faint yellow blanket over this corner and beyond it is the black rain. The sun shows up the runner's legs, her bright red shirt and yellow shorts. Her running is a kind of dance over the uneven ground and she puts out her arms for balance.

No Fly. No jumping up.

He remembers too late to put Fly on a lead. The dog is wriggling in the runner's path and she stops to fondle his head and ears.

I'm sorry…

It's all right. Don't worry. A soppy one isn't he? Soppy as anything.

He certainly is. He loves everybody does Fly.

Where have you come up from?

From Llanandras. Well, the common above. I don't often come this way.

That's a sharp climb. I'm the other way. Do you know the chapel, on the way to Norton?

Suzie doesn't know why she's talking to this man. His hair lies in soaked black cords over the pleasant square of his face. She feels an intense joy, as if the point of the day was to stand here shivering, talking with a stranger about his dog. She senses the man's seriousness, his gentleness, that he is flawed as she is. She risks saying:

It's cleansing, you know, up here. All my problems are solved by a quick run up top.

I know. I know exactly what you mean.

And he does, she sees that. She sees the recognition in his face.

It's a different world up here, isn't it?

Yes. A world apart. A beautiful world.

They have understood each other then. They sense their likeness to each other and their differences. He risks saying:

My name is Geraint.

He puts out his hand. He never shakes anyone's hand, and who does these days, who does? Car salesmen maybe. Estate agents. Old people.

Suzie.

He takes her hand. The rain dews the fine hairs of her arm. She is very pale, freckled. He sees the fine hair on her cheek. Geraint says:

I was looking for a circular route. I thought I might go down and circle back in the valley to my bit of the common but I think I may chicken out.

Yes. I've thought about doing that too. I don't know the way back to the chapel though.

I may turn back in a spell.

Yes. Me too. I didn't even bring a coat.

Nor me.

Suzie and Geraint are both happy as they go their separate ways. They feel as if they have started something though it is already over. There is nothing to connect them and they will not meet again. Geraint puts Fly on a lead to go through the horses. The horses are a dry warm wall to either side of him and they are not afraid. He will tell Jen about the horses when he gets back and the rain running towards him over the moor, a wall you can see.

He turns and shouts at the bright figure of the woman as she is about to crest the rise.

Hey. It's stopped raining here.

Suzie turns, laughs, waves.

Lucky you. It's looking worse this way.

Afterwards the mountain is a small empty room to him, the weather a wall that preserves its near silence. He notices the pad of his feet over the still firm ground and the panting of Fly who stays closer now. The rain is indeed diminishing. The sun comes again over the moor.

◆

In the month that follows Geraint:

≈ Dreams that he meets Suzie again on the hill.

≈ Takes the dog up to the same spot where they met and is relieved to find only horses.

≈ Works on a poem to Jen for their anniversary but does not include it in the card he gives her. *(He destroys it because it contains either some obscure falsehood or some obscure truth she should not see.)*

≈ Tells Jen he loves her while waiting at the traffic lights in the rain on a Sunday afternoon after their Morrison's trip. *(She touches his hand and asks if something is up. Nothing he says. Nothing. Seeing that she sees something.)*

≈ Sees how old he looks in the mirror and takes up running. *(He runs twice, once up the steep lane behind their house and once through the wood where he usually walks Fly, then gives up on the idea.)*

≈ Dreams that Suzie is the avatar of an old girlfriend he has not thought of for years. *(He makes love to Jen that morning, with a vigour like anger, to obliterate the shame he feels.)*

≈ Tells Jen he loves her as she drops him at the bottom of the hill he wants to climb.

≈ Learns that his eldest daughter has broken up with her boyfriend. *(He briefly remembers the black hell of his divorce from her mother, his first wife. His daughter comes back to stay with them, helps them in the garden, babysits Jake, his stepson, for a night, so he can go out to the pub with Jen.)*

≈ Leaves work early to rush to the hospital. *(His Dad has had his fifth heart attack. He survives, just, but the shadow of death is now upon him. Upon them both perhaps.)*

≈ Dreams only rarely of Suzie, whose face he can no longer remember, only her bright clothes.

≈ Books a weekend away with Jen on the date he proposed to her. *(Jen tells him he shouldn't have, they are living out of their overdraft, they cannot afford it, but she is still pleased and he is pleased that she is pleased.)*

≈ Remembers he is happy as he is or mostly so.

◆

A month after meeting the man with his dog on the hill Suzie sits at a bar in a high white room. Pictures of horses decorate the walls and a mirror like a thick-rimmed porthole hangs over the vast fireplace.

Bernie the senior Partner stands over Suzie on her bar stool. His enormous head reminds her of a block of stone. She can see the hair on his chest through the buttons of his too tight shirt every time he turns to the other men for their approving laughter. The more he speaks the more the four men become one man performing to the silent audience of Suzie.

Defiance, anger.

This was what was left of her sense that the world was about to change. It has not changed. It will not change. Still she told Bernie not to be such a shit – Suzie who never says anything, who sits quietly, half-forgotten in a distant windowless corner of the office – when he made that joke about Food Banks. She argued back when he followed up, delighted by her outrage, with a joke about #metoo.

You're not one of those po-faced killjoys are you Suze? Surely not?

Now here she is, an hour into their after work drinks, watching Bernie improvise a paean to free market economics, her grief stricken arguments for a kinder world pushed aside. She wonders if he is flirting with her. If he thinks his brutal rhetoric is just the display of manly power she craves.

She feels the tug of the tether round her waist. She feels deep space at her back. Her coke splatters the bar when she dips to take the straw in her mouth. She looks back at the gorgeous mirror and sees the miniature old woman at the centre of its eye and realises the woman is her.

Excuse me. Sorry Bernie. Sorry everyone. I need the Ladies.

Don't we all Suzie. Don't we all.

She wants to say: The world is burning Bernie. Burning. But she does not say it and she never will now.

Suzie leans on the sink letting the hot water run on and on over her hands. The week after meeting Geraint she ran the same route, hoping to see him again. She ran the same route again two days later, knowing she would not. Her phone buzzes on top of the plastic soap dispenser.

Hey. I was thinking of you xx.

Ken – who says he has left the woman he left her for – has been emailing and texting this past week, almost as if he sensed her vulnerability. Changing your life is dangerous. Taking up yoga, speaking up at work, seeing more of her old friends, all of it was meant to make her stronger but to her surprise she is drifting further into the darkness.

So what then? What does she do?

Sorry Ken. Still at work. Nice to hear from you ;) x

Even though it isn't.

The corridor is a gentle yellow from the dying day. She should go back to the bar but she goes out into the car park instead. The old Suzie would return to the old pattern. She would work, quietly, inconspicuously, at her boring spreadsheets and visit her Mum every other weekend. She would do a little more gardening to compensate for her surrender. She would call Ken as the days grew shorter and he would move back in perhaps.

She closes her eyes and sees the silver tube of her ship turning above the blue earth. The tether is nearly a straight line.

Right then.

Right.

The tether is a tight-rope and the globe spins. But this is her metaphor, isn't it? She fumbles at her waist and the tether recoils, writing a lazy s-shape across the void.

Suzie is standing in a car park listening to the dark voices in the bright window. She should go back into the bar, she should smile at her boss when he asks her where's she's been, but she is not going back, not now, not ever. Suzie is cutting the tether and embracing the darkness.

◆

Over the next few weeks Suzie:

≈ Asks Ken to stop contacting her.

≈ Submits her resignation to Bernie.

LEAVING

≈ Puts her house on the market. *(She grieves for her small white house under the hill, its small tidy garden, its pond, but not as profoundly as she had thought. She has a buyer within the week.)*

≈ Plans her year-long journey across Europe. *(Suzie's Mum helps her plan her route from Scandinavia to the furthest end of the Med. She will fly out to meet her at intervals.)*

≈ Runs up top to see if she can find the man with his dog and thank him. *(She runs up three, perhaps four times, but she is really saying goodbye to the hills themselves.)*

◆

The weekend before she drives down to Dover, Suzie goes into a café on the high street. The café is crowded, her table sticky, and the coffee induces a nascent headache.

Then she sees a man with a dog at his feet a few tables away.

A handsome woman sits across from the man: the woman talks and he nods and laughs at what she says. When the woman goes to the toilet the man turns towards her. It is the man from the hill. She smiles gravely at him and the man, whose name she no longer remembers, smiles frowningly back and turns away. Suzie turns back to her book but when she looks up again she sees that the back of the stranger's neck has turned terracotta.

Chrysalis
Dylan K Page
United Kingdom

'WHAT WE DOING ABOUT THAT PUFF FOR?' Martin Hines shouted from the back of the class, earning a snigger from his mates. Everything he said was in the tone of a street corner yob starting a fight. For a moment, Mrs. Wright was merely impressed that he'd even heard of Oscar Wilde.

'What, we reading gay porn?' chimed in Martin's spiritual twin, Raafi Assad.

'Ew!' – Martin.

'We're studying *The Picture of Dorian Gray*,' she said, wondering whether her subconscious had done this to her on purpose. 'It's about...'

'I don't wanna read about men touching each other,' interrupted Martin.

'You're soooo secretly gay,' said Alice Coombs in her own trademark stupid-is-cool drawl despite the insight of her comment.

'I'm fucking not!' – Martin.

'Why you so fucking defensive then?' Alice smacked over her gum.

'Language!' Mrs. Wright snapped.

'That's well gross,' Raafi said, oblivious to her authority.

LEAVING

She looked around the room, gaze pausing on camper-than-camp Jason Smith, pointedly gaming on a mobile, his stylish personal tweaks rebelling against the drab school uniform; Adaku Okereke, who brought two dads to parents' evenings, pen poised, hanging on the Head's every word.

'Read the first chapter and answer the questions on the handout,' Mrs. Wright ordered, then sat at Mr. Daniels' desk and tutted at the mess of papers, stationery and lost property half-burying the keyboard. She gathered and tapped the sheets into uniformity, brushed a dusty whiff of pencil shavings into the waiting wastepaper basket.

In the shadowy vignette around her consideration of where to place a stray, striped school tie, some of the teens had started to read the photocopied excerpt of *Dorian Gray*, turning the pages at the corner-staples she'd punched in over early morning coffee. One or two, including Adaku of course, even jotted down answers to the questions on the handout.

Others, most, had sensed the edge of desperation in her command to work. The lack of conviction was the smell of blood from an open wound: the sharks closed in, pulling out their mobile phones, opening internet browsers, chatting, giggling, spinning around on their wheeled chairs.

She'd been a teacher for two decades and knew their many excuses, evolved merely with the technology: *I'm just making notes in an app, I can work better with a video in the background, We're talking / messaging about the book, honest,* and, of course, *Soz, Miss!* as they continued without pause. She had delivered training on behaviour management and knew she must make the boundaries clear, instruct the pupils to recap the classroom rules, reward the hardworking with compliments and attention, lean over and casually exit browsers without too much fuss. She must…

She must...

She must challenge their bigotry. She must tell them that a non-heterosexual author doesn't mean porn. She must show them that it's okay to be gay or bi. That even their boring old Head Teacher was... was...

She stared into the dead computer screen and the pupils faded away, a periphery of chaos. She could just about make out her face in the reflection, two shadowy pits for eyes, contemplating coming out to a class full of shocked, gaping faces, who'd then pass on their dropped jaws to parents, staff, governors, friends, family, who'd think, like Raafi, 'gross', spread their misguided gossip: 'She used to be married but now she's a lesbian.' They'd wonder if she was a corrupting influence, the respect they'd had dissolving as they assumed a new, libidinous 'lifestyle' – suddenly she'd be 'Rug-muncher Wright', though she was never 'Cock-sucker Wright' before, but always just Mrs. Wright, Head Teacher.

As for Roza, the PE teacher, her memory of every prior moment of closeness would tarnish in the shedding of light. She'd be repelled by the one-sidedness of her platonic affection. She'd fail to hide her distaste behind a veneer of politeness, an awkward formality replacing their easy companionship.

The room's banter volume was rising. Emboldened, someone was watching a YouTube video without headphones. Miraculously, Raafi had actually started to flick through *Dorian Gray*, but Martin soon put a stop to this betrayal of their mutual determination to fail. They cackled over something on Martin's phone, asserting the education system's lack of power over them through their boisterous, loud-mouthed commentary.

No. Coming out to this class would be ripping out her heart and expecting a frenzy of ravenous sharks to perform lifesaving surgery.

And yet...

And yet, Mrs. Wright stood up, palms on desk. 'Everyone face the front!' Her conviction kept the sharks at bay. They quieted down, videos and chatter muting, and turned towards her.

She faced them. She could feel the revelation swelling inside her, willing her torso to sit up and force her face through the heavy dirt. The rigor mortis fought back, holding her in place like it always had. She was rigid in her grave as ever, the soil piling into her throat, choking her into silence.

Her arm twitched. If she could just reach up, she could drag herself out of this darkness. Yes – she would talk to them about homophobia, biphobia, stereotypes. She would use herself as a role model, making Martin and Raafi think twice about their misconceptions; lending validation to Jason, who was still bashing at his phone, avoiding everyone's eyes; strength to Adaku, waiting for the next words to defend her parents' love; back-up to Alice, still chewing, the only one who had attempted to speak up.

She would tell them bigotry was wrong and that she, their Head Teacher, was bi. Therefore, it was okay; it was normal.

Yes, she could do this…

'Shut up and get on with your work!' she snapped.

They returned to their distractions and chatter like they'd never even paused. Mrs. Wright sank back into her chair and sighed.

Cowboys Boots are Waterproof

Andrew Peters
Egypt

Editor's Choice

WE HAD AN UNCLE FROM AMERICA come stay with us awhile. A surprise visit. We came back from a walk one Sunday afternoon and he was sitting on the backdoor step, and we thought at first he was a tramp, he was so sunburnt and trampily zoned-out. So we stopped a little way off and watched him shiver in the long fetch of winter wind.

'Hello?' my mother said. And he snapped up sharply from the step, and picked up his old leather suitcase and swung it by his side.

'I got a taxi,' he said. 'The driver didn't know if anybody lived way up here.'

'Oh my goodness your colour,' my mother said, 'I didn't recognise you. Oh my *goodness!*'

'Don't cry,' he said, 'I can't look so bad as that.'

He lived so far away that he ate his breakfast while we locked the front door at night. They never saw the same stars or sun, brother and sister. He was six-three in his socks, six-five in his boots. Uncle Donald. And was getting old, the face burned-out, with chorizo scalding on the uplifted parts, the heavy-crimped ears, the delicate nose tip he shared with my mother. But still there was a shining wing of black hair hooding his face, so that in time we recognised him from the old photographs my mother kept in the dining room cupboard.

She cried on and off for hours, she was so happy. And was embarrassed about her hair, and the old tracksuit she was wearing under her winter coat.

'But why wouldn't you tell us you were coming?' She smoothed her hair and my father handed her a roll of kitchen paper for her eyes and nose. And in in the kitchen she took her brother's hand and bumped his arm with her shoulder, a movement fetched from childhood, and said to us, 'Here is your Uncle Donald. He's going to stay with us a while.'

This was the year our house in town was being fixed up and we moved onto the high moor, that part of the hills where the fields run into purple heather, and where there were no road signs, or public amenities, or other people – only the endless helter-skelter of the clouds.

We were supposed to like it. The air was clean and healthful and when you stepped out of the house there were vast spaces to choose from, the slow echoless extension of rising ground was at our bidding. From the valley road a single gravelled track rose over the flat nose of our hill, and we floated at the end of it, in our old stone house, and felt ourselves to be the only significant things up there.

But winter was coming, and we found that, after all, we weren't so sure about the place, and its new-planet atmosphere. And were stunned in its wide spaces, we children, and frozen through, and somehow pressed by the darkness which crimped both the ends of the day.

'Why have you come here?' my sister said. She had been listening carefully, her mittens dangling from her coat sleeves.

'He has come to see *us*, of course,' said my mother, wiping her eyes.

'There are dead sheep outside,' my sister said.

'I thought I saw a couple from the car,' said my uncle. 'But then I figure that dead sheep is better than dead people.'

He had way of saying things that pulled a little wagon of quiet behind them. And he served them to you flat, with no tugging for an answer in his look, which was a sort of brown molasses steadiness under the heavy lids. He went to America young. He came back with a cowboy accent and some funny clothes.

'I guess you guys are too old for presents,' he said into our silence. He hadn't brought us any. The cording of his suitcase was split, blossoming rubber. It was an old case, humped and bossed with straps and buckles. In the winter damp it was somehow dusty and worn dry – just as he was, the elbows of his suede jacket smooth polished and the pocket tassels disordered twigs. He wore cowboy boots, also, but swapped them for a pair of my father's wellingtons when he saw what the white mud of that place did to their leather.

He slept a lot the first days. We kept our voices low. We didn't run. My mother explained the new rules to us. When he came downstairs before dinner she tried things on him. Herbal teas. Citrus infusions. Hot chocolate. He slumped on the couch and the miles twitched in his legs as he received my mother's attentions. Their faces were the same, we saw, only his was drawn more loosely, deeply clawed around the mouth and eyes, as if he had been exposed to bigger and more terrible things. And while my mother approached him bright and pointed with glasses, flasks, tumblers, full of brittle cheer, he was all broad endurance and slow traversing looks, doggish, guilty.

She put liquids in his hand and he cupped them with his whittled fingers and thanked her and shut his eyes to sip. Intense, religious sipping. Beyond the outer limits of the fact nothing to see or do, he drowned his nose in the cup and we could run about then, bang up and down the stairs and loudly harvest what had been lying sullen all the day long.

And my parents stopped taking wine with dinner. And cleared the dining room and pantry of beer and spirits. My father loaded the booze into the car and drove it clinking into town to give it to the workmen fixing the house. They rubbed the dust off the bottle necks and joked, Christmas has come early. And asked no questions. The house would be ready by spring, perhaps, they said.

'Why have you come here?' my sister said.

'Why not? Isn't it a nice place?'

'The foxes chase the lambs in the night. When they tear them you see their brains coming out of their stomachs.'

'Foxes gotta eat, I guess.'

'I want to live in our old house.'

'Your mom says you'll be going back after Christmas, when it's all fixed up.'

'There was nothing wrong with it.'

'There must have been something wrong with it. And when you go back it will be better.'

'It's cold up here.'

'Now you're preaching, sister, now you're preaching.'

He didn't contradict as much as make slow twists of our dismay and fear and homesickness. And did not try to make us any more unlost or lather us in hope. As if the contract by which adults bear away from the real and the sore and the wicked was unknown to him.

'There are sheep bones by the fence,' my sister said.

'I saw 'em. It's like they're grinning at you, isn't it? Big white grins.'

'I don't like to walk there.'

'They look as though they're going to jump right up at you. Or they look like big white combs, the ribs. A little like combs, they look like. Combing all the green grass in the fields. Dontcha think?'

'Why do the foxes kill them?'

'That's just the cycle of life, darlin'. The big cycle.' His tobacco-stained finger made a circle. 'And I expect many of them were just very old folks, in sheep years, and kind of had it coming.'

The foxes went after the sheep. And there were sinkholes on the moor, very deep, and holding the heartless light of still water. Under the mirrored cloud the fathoms self-devouring and soupy with weed. The tendrils coiled and clutched, pulled the clumsy sheep to the bottom. There they lay on the bleached uproar of bones. And became bones. And there was cold cutting everywhere, the wind-slicing wire, the ditch shrubs thrashing in the clean blocks of the wind.

'Didn't you like it in America?'

He didn't seem to mind my sister's questions. She ran into the room with them and soaked up the answers wide-eyed and ran out again.

'I liked it a lot,' he said.

'So why did you come back?'

'I dunno. I guess I was just sick and tired of being sick and tired.'

He clutched a pack of Rich Tea to his chest. He didn't use the plate my mother left on the arm of the couch, the crumbs gathered in the valleys of his paisley shirt. And I thought it must be a terrible thing to leave the plains of cactus and the spiky dust-coloured mountains and the beating of danger in the hard earth, for this. To live on our cold moor, with its wind and white clay mud.

The Crews came up in their Land Rover one day. Mrs. Crew brought some things from the village fete. A plant with sick tongues for leaves, red and green, which my father did not like. And a banana cake for Uncle Donald. A welcome present. She had heard at the church. Something about America? Mrs. Crew asked questions and Uncle Donald looked flat out dead leaning against the breakfast table, and Mrs. Crew threw glances at my mother and got fat in the cheeks as if something was tickling her teeth.

'You'll find it very quiet here after Las Vegas,' said Mrs. Crew. 'The town is quiet enough, but there is nothing at all to do in the villages. All the young people have gone away, you see. They run after the bright lights.' She flashed jazz hands and rolled her eyes, and we got the squall of her sugary perfume. 'Our daughter lives in London. Will you be visiting London on your holiday, Donald? Is it a holiday you are having?'

Uncle Donald knuckled the table, leaning.

'We're all go-ing on a sum-mer holiday,' sang my father, leaving the room.

Mrs. Crew wanted to hear all about America, its many dangers and interests. She had owlish glasses with heavy lenses which blew out her eyes, and these she turned on Uncle Donald whenever he spoke.

But Uncle Donald didn't say much. The adults talked standing up and after a while it got to an embarrassing kind of quiet and my father came in again to walk up and down the kitchen as if he had forgotten something. And when Mrs. Crew said she had to leave my mother got busy with the banana cake and said everybody should try a little, but Mrs. Crew really had to go, ta-ra all, and so we waved the Crews down the drive and down the track which led to the valley.

'Sorry,' said my mother when we were back in the kitchen.

'Oh my ears, my legs,' said Uncle Donald.

'If I'd offered her a seat she would have stayed for hours.'

My mother got a message to the church. No visitors, for a little while.

And so the house got quieter and the days shorter and the moor pushed the square fields of the valley further under the drowning winter sun. It was a heavy stone house with thick walls and a castle depth to the windows, and downpressing ceilings that put Uncle Donald into a bony hunch, made him awkward in doorways, ducking from the lintel, clambering from the frame.

But he wanted to like it there, and wanted us to like it with him. The way a drinker doesn't want to drink alone. And whenever he could he reached for my mother's lightness, the more certain smile he almost shared with her.

'You know, I think I can see the sea from this window.'

'We used to live by the sea,' my sister said.

'Yes, there it is, just on the horizon. I guess the town is just below that ridge.'

'My school is a long way away now. Ten whole miles.'

'In fact, I think I see the top of a steeple. You'll be going back there after Christmas, to the town.'

'Will you come with us?'

'Oh, I don't know about that. I don't know at all.'

By then he was done with sleeping, and was mostly resting on the living room couch. My father called it the Couch of Donald.

DO NOT UNDER ANY CIRCUMSTANCES PRESUME TO SIT ON THE COUCH OF DONALD. ONLY DONALD IS PERMITTED TO DONALD ALL DAY ON THE… HA HA HA HA.

Uncle Donald never laughed. He did not like it when people shouted. His eyes closed over when noise hit him, his chin tucked birdlike and a queasy ripple washed his mouth and he sat very still, like he was waiting for a great pain to hit.

LEAVING

He needed to sit and be quiet to get better. Let Uncle Donald have a rest. Turn the TV down. Don't run up the stairs, kids.

We put on our winter coats and went out into the garden to look for the whisper of sea that marked the place where we had come from.

And he ate biscuits and sipped tea and stared through the deep windows at the cruising winter clouds, the slow squadrons, the long grey-painted passages. Or was washed over with television warble. His eyes on the screen but not dancing along, finding other ranges, rubbed numb by what they had seen, the wild hollering, gunshot, all the scrabbling endeavour and galloping bloodspills. The lines of his face were my mother's, but pulled to the ground, pegged taut. And messy under the eyes, melted and stitched. And her floating smile out of his reach, no matter how he tried.

We told him about the American sinkhole. On the moor he wanted so much to like. How in the war it swallowed a tank. How there was a camp in the valley and the tanks came out of it to drive across the heather. On the woollen back of the moor they charged and practised killing. Perhaps they didn't know what a sinkhole was. Mistook it for a puddle. Or maybe they were too busy in the fire and noise to notice the failing ground ahead. And so a tank drove into the American sinkhole, which was what we called it, and went straight to the bottom, settled on the nail-bed of bones. There was no time to save the crew. Death must have come quick, dark and cold. And there was a war on, anyway, so the place was all around bricked in by death, which lived in the sky even, spilled out from the clouds. But all that was a very long time ago.

'Those poor boys,' said Uncle Donald, when we told him. He turned to the window and raised his chin and closed his eyes and nodded, and my mother, coming in and understanding, said, 'Don't tell Uncle Donald such sad stories.'

'Uncle Sad,' my sister said. Not unkindly, transmitting plainly, and the wide eyes recording.

My mother took her from the room. At the threshold she shouted, 'Dinner time, dinner time nearly,' the voice poured from a height, cleansing, undoing. But too late.

And then she was tender with him at the table, her older brother. Filling his glass and patting the back of his hand. He ate in a buzzard hunch. When he spoke the sound was as serious as canyon boulders, slow-rolling, and my mother stared glassily, encouraging, and her fingers chasing the skin on the back of his hand as she nodded at the words laid down like stepping stones.

We asked him about the weather in America. Which was hot, where he was. And sometimes cold nights. But pretty much T-Shirt weather all year round. And the roads were longer and generally more straight. You could drive for days. And the supermarkets bigger, with more things to eat.

My mother filled his water glass. And he sipped two-handed, the blind ends of his fingers touching. And his eyes flickered shut and there was a stillness in the room as after a gunfight, the air plucked to trembling absence, something giant rolled away and forgotten already, and lower down, very deep, the crushed rustle of our thoughts.

It rained for days. A misty vaporous wet from no place or level in particular, the sky a heavy even shade. And then it stopped, and there was a crumble of slow clouds and wells of silver winter light dropping to the valley floor.

'You should get some fresh air,' my mother said to Uncle Donald.

'Oh yeah?'

'Yes. Look where we are. The nature.'

'Yep. There's enough of it.'

'Bring the kids for a walk. They're dying to go for a walk and I can't take them.'

'Is that so?'

'Take them.' She ran out to the hall and came back with one of my father's long coats. She made Uncle Donald stand as she hooked him into it, tapping his arms up, bidding, willing. The coat was small on him, but it fastened. She was delighted the buttons closed. For all the days the rain had fallen she had looked for bright things to settle on, glints or flashes, fissures in the slabbed hours she could lead my uncle's treacle gaze to. And he hadn't moved or spoken much the while.

We walked down the track which fell from the moor. And to the brook to the west which bottomed a fold of the hills. And to the east, where the forest climbed from a ravine and raised its hackles over a ridge. Then sometimes to the moor behind the house, and the white staining paths and wind-sprung heather and the mats of dead bracken, flat drowned, releasing dark odours.

'You're looking better,' my mother said to him. He sat in the current of the television, low in the couch, sipping a Lucozade. And in the long reach of his sigh there were the horizon fragments, spinning golden, the platelets of baked earth and strange blooms of desert spoor. He ran a casino in Vegas, and later in Reno, Nevada. Was married once, not so unhappily at first. He might have had a kid or two were it not for the. And he did okay for a while, all the same. And. Well, here we are. He wore cowboy boots with his suits and sometimes a Stetson as he stalked the gaming tables. He wore a brass badge the size of a belt buckle with his name engraved on it. Running a casino wasn't easy. It was a tough life that knocked you up the ribs, was bone-threatening, and worse.

My father said he must have been a galloping gallant in his Ten-Gallon.

Uncle Donald looked from the windows to impossible distances. When his eyes came back there was still something of sky in them. He gave you those cottony looks and at once you saw all the parched spaces he had looked upon, heard their enfilade echo.

'When is Uncle Sad going home?' sang my sister.

My mother slapped the back of her hand. 'Please don't call him that again.'

On our walks we didn't stop to look at anything. We went in Indian file, my sister at the back. Uncle Donald walked hunched, his tall weight thrown forward. The same as the tight-rope walker we saw that summer. One step doubtful of the other, and forbidden volumes either side.

'You'll stay for Christmas,' said my mother.

'It'll be cold up here.'

'It will snow. It'll be beautiful. You must stay.'

'I guess I could.'

'Of course you will. And we'll have Christmas pudding and all the things you miss.'

'I was never a fan of the pudding.'

'Bread sauce, crackers, sprouts. It's been so long, Donald.'

He couldn't ride a horse and he never shot an Indian. He drove a brown Datsun Maxima, which he thought must still be in the airport carpark, if nobody had towed it. He did okay with money and owned his apartment, not so big, but near a manmade lake that attracted wild birds, ducks and such, and made the place less of a desert. He could sell the apartment pretty easy, if he had to. What with the ducks. Working casinos wasn't so bad, but when people smiled at you over the tables they meant something other than friendliness. It was a tough life that made you do things. Things maybe you shouldn't do or didn't want to do or might run into something hard doing. And so you hurt yourself on the cruel edges of it. It may or may not be why he was sad sometimes. Probably not. He liked my sister, really, although she said such things. She was just a snotty little kid, that was all. And a scalping, a proper scalping done with a hunting knife or maybe a tomahawk, and leaving your head looking like a raspberry popsicle, would indeed be a terrible thing.

He rumbled from the couch, and lowered his heavy-lidded looks on us. The gold of his eyes buried deep and lighting unseen things, and he didn't mind our questions, he said, as long as we asked them politely, which was all he had ever wanted from anyone.

Then the real winter rolled in and it was snow and ice and a skimming sea wind that threw smooth drifts against the house. My mother called the school to tell them we wouldn't make it. For a day or two or maybe a week, the sky looked so curdled, thick-skinned.

'Donald, why don't you take the kids to play out there?' she said.

◆

There was a red plastic sledge in the pantry, which somebody before us had filled with vegetables. We rolled the old potatoes onto the floor and took it outside. Dragged it in circles as Uncle Donald wobbled into his boots.

He didn't want to go down the track. If we went down it we would only have to come up it again. It was such a long way. So we went out onto the snow-sheeted moor and the speckling heads of the heather pushing frozen through. And walked until the house was small. Until the house was gone and there was only the pearl string of our footprints and the snatches of wind-jumped horizon folded white around us. Uncle Donald heavy shouldered in my father's down coat, we stumbled in his track and felt the chill bottoming our lungs.

We were a long way from home when he stopped and raised his

hand, scout-style.

The sinkhole was iced over, the misty edges snow-webbed.

'I think it's the one the tank went into,' I said.

We approached the edge. Uncle Donald with his careful walk, high-stepping. And stood around it. The milky cataract of the frozen hole staring. And the many darknesses at its centre revealing gross depth.

'How do you know?' asked Uncle Donald.

But I just knew, as we all did, that it was the very hole. The way events of dread magnificence sing down the years. You carry their hum unaware, find yourself matching the tune under your breath, and are sure of something suddenly, with surprising hold on a thing rising from the deep, wriggling, thrashing.

There were fingers of wind at our necks, our cuffs, and the carried spits of snow stinging our faces.

'That's good ice,' said Uncle Donald. He placed a foot on it. Gave it his weight.

My sister ran around the hole, tralalalalala. At the other side she did a star jump. 'Uncle, uncle, uncle,' she shouted.

Uncle Donald took a creaking step. There was movement, bubbles scuttling under the lid, but the ice held. He took a few steady paces, arms outstretched.

'Can I get on?' I said.

He gave me his bottomless stare and nodded. And of course it is that look I remember most, which had no entries or borders, would have done for anywhere or anything, and might have been given to a desert sunset as much as a frozen kid dropping the rope of a sledge.

I stepped after him. On the far side my sister jumped, 'S'easy peasy.'

We stood in the middle, and for a moment there was a narrow balance, crisp, sugarspun, and the teetering rush of possibilities above and below.

And then the tight cracking. There were shooting forces, brittle and terrible. And only at the last moment did he sharpen, and look down at me to say quietly, 'Best get off.'

I ran for the edge, and turned. 'Uncle Donald,' I shouted.

It was quick, like a trapdoor, when it happened. He broke straight through. The sinkhole took him to his waist and the weed held him there, his arms thrown across the ice.

And I saw that if he raised his arms above his head he would go straight down. Countless darkening fathoms. To the forest of bones, to the poor boys in the tank. And so I watched his fingers in their spider hunch, frozen without purchase, as I ran to the sledge and pushed it out to him.

'Grab the sledge, Uncle Donald.'

Maybe he didn't see the thing sitting dumb behind him. But within reach, certainly.

'Go and get Dad,' I shouted. My sister had stopped jumping. She plugged her mouth with her hand, dumb with catastrophe.

'She'll get lost. You both go.' The cold snatching his voice, winding it thickly. His shrunken head nestled in the rise of my father's down jacket. 'Goddamit,' he said, shooting breath, 'you both go along now.'

And the sensation of running along a familiar track, the moor opening either side and that old tune coming into the head, and a certainty of destination felt deep in the gut, so that I said almost slyly, 'I think I'll leave her here, Uncle Donald.'

'Take her!'

'I'll go, and leave her here.'

I placed her in his view. She sat cross-legged and watched him as I ran off. He must have put that drifting look on her, it must have caught.

And I hope she sang to him, or something. Or was polite, at least. It was impossible to tell when my father roped him and dragged him out, and he slid sideways across the ice with his loose, cloud-staring face.

'Why oh why oh why oh why?' my father said. Busy and embarrassed, and twitching with a buried anger. Picking the weed from Uncle Donald' trousers.

But Uncle Donald was too cold to speak. He stood bowed and dripping as my father slapped the weed from his legs. And shaking, wild and feverish, and the castanet of his teeth making my sister laugh, not unkindly.

We rushed him to the house. I offered him my shoulder, and when his hand came down I saw the purple moons of his white fingers and felt his heavy grip jerking steeply, the way an old person troubles a stick.

And that night he got drunk. He must have had a bottle in his suitcase. At first he kept it hidden, but when he got loud at dinner, in a red sweat and banging the table, my mother cried a bit and said he might as well bring the bloody bottle downstairs. Wild Turkey. He placed it in the centre of the table.

They sat up late, and we kids were sent to bed. And heard for the first time the boom of Uncle Donald' laughter. And their loud talk. And other noises. Steps on the stair, whispers, scraping, suppressed fetching and carrying. And the snow feathering the window, so that when the music started and I switched on the bedside light I was shocked by the way it climbed flat against the glass.

I found them all in the living room. My sister asleep on the Couch of Donald and the adults standing in the centre of the room, wearing Christmas hats. There was silver tinsel stuck around the windows, furring the mantelpiece. And streams of concertina paper sagging from the corners. The angel with the toilet roll dress that my sister made the year before was propped on the coffee table, and the cardboard box marked 'Xmas Decs' lay on its side in front of the television, spilling its rainbow guts.

And there was that snowglobe giddiness, the sickly kiddy anger and fear at the shaken world. That comes when the fundamentals are upended, when an adult cries or drunkenly grins or music is played on the trackless ground between day and night.

'We're just about to pull some crackers,' my mother said. She threw me one. Her mascara ran black on her cheeks. 'Come over here and pull a cracker.'

Uncle Donald was laughing and kind of dancing. Jigging up and down to the sound coming from the dining room, where my father's turntable was kept.

'Hep, hep, hep,' he shouted, clicking his fingers squirming in his socks. 'Cracker time.'

I was angry at the tilting world. When I approached them their faces were lowered to me, worried looking, and I was suddenly in their vapours and tired heat, and was surprised by the stubble of Uncle Donald' cheek. He gave me a loose hug, his whiskey held level.

'Uncle Donald is going back to America tomorrow,' my mother said, 'so we are having Christmas tonight.'

'We'll be snowed in tomorrow,' my father shouted, like it was the hundredth time he had shouted it. 'Nobody is going anywhere.'

'I'll be gone in the morning,' boomed Uncle Donald. And I saw the adjusted face, properly tuned now, as he took the end of my cracker and showed a level of white teeth, a good American grin.

He let me win. It was clear by the way he shuffled his thumb away from the crimp. The cracker burst open and the contents spilled onto the carpet. My mother, laughing, disastrous around the eyes, got down on her knees to unfold the paper crown and place it on my head.

'Merry Christmas,' shouted Uncle Donald, raising his glass again. And he led a conga later, as I joined my sister to sleep on the couch, my singing parents towed behind him and dappling the carpet's pile with their conga shuffle. And they sang along with Bing Crosby to Old Lang Syne, and woke us up to join hands, and Uncle Donald hugged and kissed us all again and told us how he would go away for ever.

And when he left us the next morning he tried not to show how happy he was, in deference to my mother's tears, and said that of course he would come back to visit us some day. He would go and he would return, this was the way things went, always, and his finger came up to make a circle in front of his nose. And my sister was worried he would drown in the snow, or wet his feet, it was a two mile walk along the buried track to the valley road, but he said he would go very carefully and he would follow the fence posts all the way to the bottom and not wander into the wide spaces either side, the dangerous drifting planes, and didn't she know that cowboy boots, well, *his* cowboy boots, are waterproof?

More Ways To Leave Your Lover

Don Rhodes
United Kingdom

Shortlisted for the 2019 International Writing Competition

I. Poison in the Ear

Spring 1993, Berlin
'Fraulein Heidinger. Rosa. Join us. Don't sit alone.'
　'No thanks, Frau Herbertz. I must be back at my desk soon.'
　I turn back to my soup.
　I can't stand office gossip. *Harmless gossip*, they call it. Gossip wasn't harmless in our dearly-departed German Democratic Republic. Someone was always listening, someone always twisted what was said. And some poor sod always suffered in the end.
　I lunch alone by choice. I'm not short of offers from the office casanovas. I'm still only thirty-one after all. OK. I'm slightly faded since my trouble. But I catch the men stealing a look on the long corridors of the head office. I smile a little smile. Maybe it's the athletic figure that Thomas loved so much.

'We'll produce wonderful athletes, you and I,' he'd said, as we lay together on the lake-shore. 'Olympic champions for the glorious GDR!'

But we haven't and we won't now. No Olympic champions; no GDR. No Thomas.

The men of Allianz Insurance think a little secretary from the East will be grateful for attention from an important manager. But I'm not grateful, nor *just* a secretary. I have a university degree in history. And I have my own personal history. But neither of these has any value in new Germany. The two Germanies didn't unite. The West took over. Everything from the East is now sneered at and cast aside. That's how I feel.

I've ended up typing letters for men with half my intelligence. I correct their crap German surreptitiously so as not to embarrass them. *Surreptitiously*... not a word many of them can spell.

'Fraulein Heidinger. What a surprise! May I join you?'

It's a man I haven't seen for years, Herr Richter, our neighbourhood Stasi snitch. Not someone I'd have chosen to see again, ever.

Before I can reply, he plonks down his tray and sits rather too close beside me.

'How good to see a friend from the...' He leans closer and drops his voice, '...*good* old days.' He looks around furtively.

His breath smells of schnapps. I shuffle away.

'You don't have to whisper. Nobody's listening in any more, Herr Richter. What are you doing here, anyway? I thought you were a printer.'

'I'm Schmidt now. Lots of Schmidts in the Berlin telephone directory. Good camouflage.' He sighs: 'Some people can't forgive and forget.'

He forks mashed potato into his mouth and swallows it quickly so he can continue talking.

'No call for old-fashioned printing any more. I sell insurance now.

Can't say I like it but I do OK. People seem to trust me.' He sounds surprised. 'Everybody's so scared of life in the West, especially people from the East. They'll buy insurance for anything. Might rain tomorrow? Policy for that. Wife might run away with the butcher? Sign here. They're shit-scared of ending up on the streets... Excuse my language, Fraulein Heidinger.'

More potato.

'That's why I'm here today. Being trained in payment protection insurance. Beautiful product! First, we loan them money to buy something expensive. We make money on the loan. Then we ask, casually, like a friend: *What happens if you're ill or lose your job and can't pay it back? Disaster's what happens! The Mercedes goes back. You lose the flat. Out on the street. A mean street in the West!*'

He leans in. I catch the reek of schnapps again.

'The trainer says to let them stew a bit. Then ask: *What about this new policy? It will pay off the debt if any of those awful things happen?* They sign up in no time.'

He looks around him, then drops his voice again:

'We had one insurance policy to cover all those risks in the old days, Fraulein Heidinger. It was called: the State!'

He taps the side of his nose and then pushes his empty plate away.

Perhaps he realises that I've said little so far. He looks at me with phony concern and says:

'Sorry to hear about your little brush with the law...'

He's not sorry at all I think. He was probably involved in my arrest.

'It was hardly a *little brush with the law*. Two years in jail for trying to join my boyfriend in the West. More than a bit of bad luck.'

His lips twitch. The twitch turns into a smug smile:

'Oh. Luck had no role, Fraulein Heidinger. It wasn't ever left to luck with the Stasi.'

I am livid. 'Was it you? Did you inform on me to the Stasi? You were their man, right?'

'It wasn't me, I assure you. I got in trouble for being as surprised as everyone else.' He pauses. 'I think you'd have to look closer to home for your informer. Much closer, I'd say.'

I look him straight in his shifty eyes: 'What do you know, you little creep?'

'No need to be rude, Fraulein Heidinger. I'm just sharing my experience with an old friend. Do with it what you will.'

He stands up, loads his dirty crockery onto his tray and leaves.

I look nervously around. Frau Herbertz and her gang have detected juicy gossip. Their flat faces, like the TV antennae on an apartment block, are all tuned in my direction.

My own face is flushed, my stare fixed. I look exactly what I am. Someone who has just had a very dark thought. My father? Karl and Brigitte, my prospective in-laws? Thomas, my lover? Who had betrayed me?

◆

Weeks have passed since my chat with Richter. I'm having another sleepless night trying to work out who the informant was. *Closer to home*, he'd said. The words taunt me. The most likely suspects form and fade in my mind. My teeth grind. I turn angrily in my twisted sheets and lie face down, clutching the pillow.

Finally, I can stand it no longer. I decide I must to apply to read the file the Stasi kept on me. I can live with any outcome. It can't be worse than not knowing.

LEAVING

II. First Love

1966, East Berlin

It was hard not to notice one particular boy at the school where I was enrolling on my first day. I turned up clutching my mother Renate's hand and keeping as close to her as I could.

My mother pulled me back as we started to cross the road towards the school entrance. A lone car was approaching slowly. As it passed, a boy's head stretched up from the passenger seat and swivelled to get a good look at me as we waited on the pavement. The head was topped with a mop of black curls. A tongue pushed was out and was wriggled about. The eyes in the head crossed momentarily. I started to laugh but my mother tutted her disapproval, jerked my arm and I quickly stopped.

'Rosa! Try not to play with that boy. And don't sit at his table if you can choose.'

The head, tongue, curls and eyes belonged to a boy I would come to know as Thomas Feld. Thomas and I ended up on the same table after all, at the front, under the teacher's nose. This met both our needs; mine because I could listen intently and his so that his behaviour could be closely monitored.

◆

Some years later, I was made Brigade Leader in the school Young Pioneers. I had to record the achievements and behaviour of other YPs in school and report it to our leaders. One year, I was told to check whether the pupils in my brigade were ready for the May Day celebrations. Of course, our bunting at home had been in place a while. I established that every other family had also got their decorations on display, except, to my horror, Thomas'.

AWARD WINNING STORIES

Thomas himself didn't seem concerned at all: 'Oh, we've got plenty of time,' he explained. 'Dad didn't bother at all last year. Richter, the Stasi man, came to see him. He blustered in as if he owned the place. Dad told him he'd been too busy looking after his sick father, Helmut Feld. Dad just dropped it in casually.'

The *Helmut Feld?* Richter had asked. *With the Patriotic Order of Merit? For opposing the Nazis? That Helmut Feld?* Thomas mimicked Richter really well. 'A bit of bunting didn't seem to matter after that,' he added.

I hated reporting on Thomas, but he didn't care. Thomas's family operated to different rules. It went against everything I'd learned. But he had become more important to me than any of that. By now we were inseparable, at school, Young Pioneers, weekends.

1978, East Berlin
It really caused a stir at home. Thomas' parents invited me to spend Republic Day at their dacha on a lake outside Berlin. My parents argued endlessly about it. My father was dead against the trip:

'She should be here, celebrating with her family, not off in a secret hidey-hole with people we hardly know…'

'We know he's a Spanish lecturer. He's organised youth trips to Cuba. He was even on the Committee for the World Festival of Youth last year. He must be sound.'

'I don't trust them. I've heard he might be under surveillance.'

'Like half the GDR,' she replied. 'Maybe even you!'

'And his mother's some sort of artist! How did they get a dacha anyway?'

'Actually,' I piped up. 'It belongs to Thomas' grandfather, not them. Thomas' grandfather has the Patriotic Order of Merit. For his opposition to the Nazis. He had to flee to France before the war. He's invited back each year to celebrate French resistance to the Nazi occupation. Thomas went with him this year.'

My father thought I was fibbing.

'Thomas brought the medal to Young Pioneers and gave a speech about it.'

The Felds were a family esteemed by the State. My father was defeated. I could go.

◆

The Felds' dacha was set back from the lake amongst birch trees. A bark path led down to a wooden jetty.

The first thing Brigitte did was to turn around a framed photo of Erich Honecker that hung over the fireplace so that our General Secretary ended up facing the wall. On the side newly facing us was a poem of some sort, painted in a beautiful illuminated script. I was shocked about General Secretary Honecker's treatment but concealed it.

After our evening meal, Karl and Brigitte wrapped up warm and sat on the veranda, smoking and drinking. Thomas and I stayed in the main room in the glow from the fire.

Thomas took some records out from a hiding-place behind a bookcase. Inside every LP cover by an East German group, there was a second LP by a western band. I was shocked yet again. Thomas finally pulled out *Let it Be*.

At least I'd heard of it. Stuff like that wasn't really banned any more except in our flat. Father kept bans going for years after everyone else. It was embarrassing. Banned or not, it was still difficult to get hold of those things.

Thomas played the title track.

I expected the Stasi to come crashing through the door at any moment but all I heard above the music was tipsy laughter from the veranda.

When the title track ended, Thomas flipped the LP over and played *The Long and Winding Road*. I gradually relaxed. I was lying on the floor with my head on a big cushion. Thomas came and lay down at ninety degrees to me, his head on my stomach. We both closed our eyes and listened to the haunting song. I ran my fingers gently through his soft black curls.

I knew then I'd never be able to report him to the Party again.

♦

I awoke first next morning. I read the poem above the fireplace. It was called '*On Children*' by someone I'd never heard of. It ended:

You may house their Bodies but not their Souls
For their Souls dwell in the House of Tomorrow,
Which You cannot visit, not even in your Dreams.

I couldn't make head nor tail of it. This family scared and excited me in equal measure. I asked Thomas about the poem when we took a walk along the lake.

'Oh, that guff. She found it in an old book when she was expecting me. She painted it on a piece of cloth and Dad framed it.'

'But what's it about?'

'It means we kids are not owned by our parents or anybody else really. We've got to find our own way in life. That's what they believe. Pie in the sky stuff. They think they're hippies. They're embarrassing!'

'That's why they called me Thomas,' he went on. 'You know, the sceptic in the bible. They want me to be my own person, not swallowing all the crap thrown at us.'

This was so different from my own naming after the communist martyr, Rosa Luxembourg.

'Is the poem an approved text?' I asked.

'Hell no! That's why Dad made the frame reversible... for any snitches like Richter calling unexpectedly. Dad thought it was safer down here at the Dacha, out of the way.'

'Yes, of course,' I said, as if we did such things at home all the time.

III. First Leaving

January 1984, East Berlin

Thomas had talked more about leaving for the West recently. He first thought of escape when he returned from his last trip to France with his grandfather. Life had turned from colour to black and white the moment he crossed the border between West and East Germany.

He raised leaving the GDR again. We were sitting by the lake, one of the few places we could talk without being overheard. We'd gone over the same old ground...him talking about the future we could share, the opportunity, the travel, the freedom; me talking about justice, equality, my family, the GDR's *better* way.

He said his parents supported him leaving. They'd raised him to be free.

'No more answering to little shits like Richter.'

I stared down the lakeside.

'And the constant surveillance, having to be careful, even in our own

AWARD WINNING STORIES

apartment. Walls have ears, as do corridors, light-fittings, radios. Most household implements. The GDR is all ears. I can't breathe.'

'Ultimately, Rosa, it's not enough, the double life. I want to be properly free.'

He was holding something back. I was scared again. When he finally came out with it, my hands went to block my ears but I still heard him:

'I'll go without you if I have to.'

He didn't look at me but carried on speaking: 'If you love me, you'll come with me. You won't keep me in this half-life. The West has found a better way than ours. I'm going to be part of it. It's what I was made for. You can come across later if you change your mind.'

'But I don't think *I'm* made for it, Thomas. I'm not sure I'd cope...'

He wasn't listening. The West was what he wanted above all else. Even above me, it seemed.

I was upset for weeks. Eventually, my feelings settled enough to realize what I had to do. I would have struggled to live without my family and the GDR. But I was absolutely sure that I couldn't live without Thomas.

When I told him, he seemed pleased. Thomas insisted he alone would deal with all the escape arrangements. The less I knew, the better. He was protecting me. I went along with it because I'd given myself up to him. We were now bound together by an escape plan.

August 1984, Ostbahnhof, East Berlin

'My name is Helga Bartmann.'

I repeated it silently again and again.

'I am twenty-three years old and a West Berliner. I am a German Studies undergraduate at Bonn University...'

I was on Platform One of Berlin Ostbahnhof, East Berlin. I was waiting for the 11am express to the Baltic coast, where I'd transfer to a ferry to Denmark.

Repeat!

'... my name is Helga Bartmann. I am twenty-three years old and a West Berliner. I am a German Studies undergraduate at Bonn University...'

I must have looked nervous. That was OK. I was a supposedly a West German in transit through a hostile country after all.

In reality, I knew this station very well. It was only half a kilometer from my home. Former home, I should say.

What was really making me nervous, terrified even, was the fact that of course I wasn't Helga Bartmann at all. She was probably hundreds of kilometers away in Bonn, totally unaware of me.

I knew all about *her*. We shared eye-colour, height and age. I'd got her passport containing my photograph in her shoulder bag, hanging from my shoulder, which was in her coat. Yes, I knew a lot about Helga. My real name, of course, was Rosa Heidinger. I was East German, at heart still a proud citizen of the GDR. I was fleeing to my lover, Thomas Feld, who had made that self-same journey to the West ten days earlier.

I had with me a suitcase containing clothes and personal items for my trip, all sourced in the West. I had nothing at all of my past life. No family photos, no certificates, no old teddy bears. The hardest thing of all to accept was that my family and the record of my whole life would be left behind a wall that was getting more impenetrable by the day. I was like a snake, shedding my skin. The old skin had quite suited me. But it was too late now. There was no turning back.

My heart pounded away. My head was full of Helga Bartmann, but my blood coursed with Rosa Heidinger's fear. I paced up and down to dissipate the tension but I kept an eye on the snack-bar exit. If it was safe to board the train, Mischa, the escape organizer, would come out of the snack bar holding a green book in his left hand ten minutes before departure. If he was holding a red book, we had to abort the escape. In that case, I would exit the station calmly and go to the public baths on Gartenstrasse, where someone would be waiting with a change of clothes and further instructions.

As the platform clock flicked towards 10:49, I looked again at the snack-bar door, willing Mischa to emerge with the green book.

The clock flicked to 10:50, decision time. I picked up my case.

Before I could move, I was expertly clasped at both elbows from behind. I looked round in turn at the men holding me. Neither of them held a book. They were totally non-descript. They could only be the Stasi.

'This way Fraulein Heidinger. No trip abroad for you today.'

My suit-case was eased from my hand. I was swept away towards the exit, my face turned down and flushing with shame.

December 1984, East Berlin

Justice was swift in the GDR. No one I knew attended my trial. I was sent to Hohenschönhausen prison for two years. The prison wasn't too far from home but I had no visit from my family. They wanted nothing more to do with me.

I convinced myself that it had been Stasi efficiency that led to my arrest, that I wasn't betrayed. Betrayal by someone close to me was unthinkable.

IV. Fresh Hope

November 1989, Berlin

Three years after my release from prison, the Wall fell live on TV. Alone in my small apartment, I watched aghast as it all unfolded. I'd already lost Thomas, my family, my career. Now my country was crumbling before my eyes.

I half expected the throng on our side to be forced back from the Wall and ordered home. I wanted that to happen because I couldn't comprehend what this chaos meant for me and my country.

Eventually, a faint smile shaped itself on my lips. I started scanning the thousands of grainy faces on the western side of the wall. I thought I saw Thomas ten times at least. Perhaps I could now join him in the West. If he was there still. If I could find him. If he wanted me to. So many 'ifs' I couldn't keep them all in my head. In the following weeks, I expected him to contact me.

A growing industry developed serving two-way information and link-ups between East and West. I also found stuff out about Thomas' new life from former school and university colleagues who'd picked up snippets about him. Thomas was in Düsseldorf. He'd done well. He was Sales and Marketing Manager for an American company. He had a riverside flat on the tenth floor of a swish Düsseldorf apartment block. He wasn't married.

The months passed quickly after the Wall fell. I could well understand why Thomas hadn't contacted me immediately after his escape. That would have been dangerous, especially for me. But why hadn't he found a way to do so now there was little to stop him? Possible answers to that question were torture. The pain of the torture lessened with time but time also took away the hope. There was no word from the West.

AWARD WINNING STORIES

V. Truth Will Out

Summer 1993

The Commission for Stasi Records, Berlin (Former Stasi HQ)
Once I have my appointment with the Commission, I busy myself with a plan for each possible betrayer. I am driven by Richter's phrase *closer to home*. As the plans develop, calm gradually replaces the anguish.

If my father was the informant, his ideological belief would have overridden any feelings for me. We Germans have a way of committing absolutely to ideas. We have form for it. We lack the capacity for scepticism. Sometimes it makes us dreamers, artists, great thinkers, heroes. Sometimes it just makes us wicked, capable of turning neighbours into sub-humans. I had cast-iron belief myself once. Life has beaten it out of me.

If it was my father, I can do nothing about it now. He died suddenly in 1990, hollowed out first by my actions and then crushed by the destruction of all he held dear when the Wall fell. It was as though the crowds were hacking away at him with their picks and hammers the night the Wall fell. At least if my father was the betrayer, I'll be the wronged one now, not him. Quits.

If Karl and Brigitte betrayed me it was not from loyalty to a state they despised. I knew they thought that their darling Thomas could have done better than an electrician's daughter from a poor part of Berlin. We had snobs even in our worker and peasant state. They thought I'd hold their precious son back in his life in the West.

They are big cheeses now in united Germany. Karl is a Professor of Spanish at the Humboldt University. Brigitte has a PR consultancy. He has a side-line as the go-to man for the German media on survival under

LEAVING

communism. He's never off TV. It's part of the wave of nostalgia for life in the GDR. He wasn't so fond of it while it was all happening.

But they'll be finished if it was them and I expose how mired they were in all that Stasi slime.

As for Thomas, could he really have betrayed me after all we'd been through? Perhaps he thought I wouldn't adapt to the West or would hold him back. Maybe he regretted ever persuading me to try to leave. He may have met someone else in the drama of the escape. I convince myself it can't have been him for no other reason than that it would be too much to bear. But German as I am, I still plan diligently for the unthinkable.

So, what's the plan if it's Thomas? Well, if it were him, it would prove he was capable of absolutely anything. And so, now, am I.

◆

I'm at the Commission a good half hour before my appointed time. I am security-checked and shown to a large room. There are already a dozen or so people there, working away at files on plastic-topped tables set far enough apart that no one can read about the lives of others. It's calm and orderly. They could be reading the train time-tables.

I wait for the official to bring me my files. It's four years on from the fall of the Wall but I feel I've stepped through a hole in it back into the drab of the GDR years. The room is bare. No curtains, no carpet, dull green walls, tubes of fluorescent light, one of them flickering. Not much has changed... dingy buildings, surly officials, submissive citizens.

The woman brings me two files.

'Please let a member of staff know if you need to leave your table for any reason. Don't remove documents from the files. Just ask if you need explanation of any unfamiliar terms. We are not allowed to interpret content but can clarify facts.'

'Thank you. Thank you very much.'

My fists clench in frustration at me again being so supine. It's my own life I'm getting back. They aren't *giving* me anything. Why so grateful? Years of obedience-training I suppose.

She turns to go, pauses and adds:

'You need to know. Regrettably, it's been necessary to install CCTV in this room to prevent theft from the files.' She points to a small camera in the far corner of the room.

I laugh out loud. 'I wouldn't have expected anything else!'

Not a muscle moves in her flabby grey face.

I continue digging my hole:

'It's a nice touch. Maintaining the traditions of the good-old-GDR, I mean. All that surveillance equipment left in the basement. Shame to waste it.'

People at the other tables are now glowering at this interruption.

'Sorry… It's not funny really,' I tell the official.

'No,' she says. 'It's not a laughing matter.'

She turns and leaves, her flat-heeled shoes slapping down on the tiled floor.

◆

I feel light-headed. The going is slow at first. The first few pages contain trivia, stuff I'd forgotten myself. Attendance at Young Pioneer events. Conduct in school. I scan-read it.

I smile when I discover they knew about what they call *sexual congress* on the lakeside when Thomas, described as *an unknown youth*, and I were there alone.

I blush. I put my arm around the file as nonchalantly as I can, like a teenager guarding her diary. I look around sheepishly but no one has lifted their head from their desks.

Then more trivia. I scan-read again.

Towards the end of File 1, I sit bolt upright and grab my pen. My pulse quickens. I am now at the key entry:

> *04/08/1984 7:00 am*
>
> Phone-call to Stasi Officer K-HK 11 from Informant: *Berlin-7349*
>
> Summary: *An escape attempt will be made tomorrow by a female, Rosa Heidinger, travelling as a West German student. The traitor Heidinger will board the 11:00 o'clock train to Warnemünde intending flight to Denmark. No other details are known.*

I call for advice. A different official, a Westerner this time, attends.

'How I can find the name of Informant: *Berlin-7349?*'

She says they thought that would be what I'd want. Even now, total strangers are one move ahead of me in my own life! She explains that *they*, whoever *they* are, need time to ensure there's no reason to withhold the information.

'And what reason might that be?'

They must exclude any threat or violence, or vulnerability on the part of the informant apparently.

'What about the violence done to me? My vulnerability?'

She looks at the floor, pretending to brush away a scuff on the tiles with the toe of her shoe. Her neck is colouring.

'We can't do much about that now, I'm afraid. I'm sorry if you've found something to upset you. Access to the name is almost always granted. I can arrange counselling if that would help.'

'No. Just the name.'

AWARD WINNING STORIES

VI. Second Leaving

November 1993
The Feld's Dacha outside Berlin
At last I know. It's all in place. The control I feel is calming after all the guessing.

I go in mid-week. Most of the properties are locked up for the winter. I park by the Feld's dacha. It's been smartened up. It's bright and modern against the drenched autumn trees and the brooding sky. The cold lake stretches away into mist. I stroll around the lakeside for a while but no one else is there.

It's time. I go to the boot of the car. I put on my walking boots. I fill a rucksack and all my pockets to the brim with pebbles bought at a builder's merchants on the way down. I heave the rucksack onto my back. I lumber to the driver's door, put the key back in the ignition and close the door gently.

I walk clumsily down the path from dacha to lakeside, the rucksack pulling my shoulders backwards, my legs quickly draining from the extra weight they're carrying.

I trudge past the place Thomas and I used to make love, shielded from prying eyes we always thought.

I reach the side of the lake. I walk in. The cold seeps into my boots, numbs my calves and soon reaches my waist. I stop momentarily. I want to fix my eyes on something specific, not the nothingness of the merged mist and water but there's only grey. I drag myself forward anyway, drawing each foot in turn out of the shale on the lake bottom.

I reach the point where the lake floor drops away steeply. I turn carefully, struggling to maintain my balance, and face the near bank.

LEAVING

I stand stock-still for a few moments, looking back towards the place where I spent all that time with Thomas. I summon up his face one last time. It's not the face I saw yesterday, glassy-eyed on the carpet of his Düsseldorf penthouse, with blood oozing from the hole in his temple. No. Not that face. The memory I conjure up is of him lying with his head on my stomach, dozing off in the warmth of the dacha, listening to the Beatles. I see myself drawing my fingers gently through his soft curls. It's the nicest memory I have. I hold it and allow myself to fall backwards into the water, slowly at first, then sharply, as the weight of the rucksack pulls my head down to the bottom of the black lake.

Freeing Yasmin
WENDY RILEY
Australia

SHORTLISTED FOR THE 2019
INTERNATIONAL WRITING COMPETITION

ONCE THERE WAS A GANNET LIVING PROUD, strong and free in the Pacific Ocean. He haunted the empty sky, diving deep below the velvety surface of the sea for his dinner.

One day, Nigel discovered an island where all the other gannets were made of stone. Nigel is a funny name for a gannet. It's the name the scientists gave him as part of their experiment – to create a colony of gannets where before there were none.

But then Nigel lost it. Like us, he had been alone too long. He fell in love with his concrete friends and ignored the real gannets when they came to call. Nigel courted them. He nuzzled them. He gave them his tastiest fish, which rotted on the ground. Nigel didn't mind though. It was his destiny to serve them; to be hopelessly, desperately unloved in return.

I discovered Nigel on the scratchy computer in the school room. He posed in a picture with his statues. If ever I'd been lucky enough to meet

LEAVING

him, I would have given him this message: *Come live with us in Crazy Town and we'll all go mad together.* After all, most of us turned to stone long ago. And most of us will never leave.

◆

My name is Yasmin and I am 12. I live in a Pacific island prison with my mother, father, the ghost of my brother Behrouz and a whole bunch of other people who sought freedom only to find despair. We came when I was seven and when my parents still believed in the Australian dream.

Kol Khara! is all I can say to that one. I am young but never stupid. A dream is a lie if it cannot come true.

We survived the treacherous alleys of Jakarta, then the violence of the ocean, only to end up here. The Australians calls it offshore processing. We call it Crazy Town, because it is a town filled with crazy people. The crazy people are us. We are eaten from the outside by mosquitos the size of helicopters and from the inside by the poison of our lost dreams.

The captives of Crazy Town come from the hard places in this world. Kurdistan, Iraq, Iran, Syria, Afghanistan, Somalia, Sri Lanka. Because we come from war, we continue to fight each other. Or maybe we fight because we are bunched together like animals in a cage, forced to beg for bread, aspirin, paper and pen. In the beginning we were comrades, brothers in arms, but love fades quickly like the violets of summer. It is hard to love when you are suffocated by the sounds, smells and bodies of too many people just like you. Then cold and darkness set in. We are cold in our hearts, while the tropical sun scorches our eyes and skin. We are dark in the shadow places, which kill us from deep within.

We want to love, but loving has left us.

The Australian Government sends its little people to tell us the bad news: that we are nothing, and to nothing we must return.

There is another island just like ours, where the mosquitos are even bigger. The men in Crazy Town 2 now believe the future does not exist. Many have been told no country on earth will take them. So, they wrote to the Australian Prime Minister and asked him to arrange a mass suicide based on one of the following methods.
1. Carry us out to sea on a navy ship and drop us in the ocean.
2. Set up a gas chamber anywhere you like.
3. Instruct the guards to give us lethal injections.

All three will be better than living like this, they say, as leftovers in a sated world.

◆

My father's name is Darius. He was a jolly man until he came to Crazy Town. I remember a rubbery face with eyes that shone with mischief. Even on the boat, which nearly took us down, he told me dad jokes as the wood splintered and the sea spat in our faces. The wind howled and the waves crashed, yet still he smiled, still he laughed. His mouth stretched wider than any mouth should. It became almost a scream. He is physically smaller now; his body has shrunk with his spirit. He spends time in the prayer tent but finds nothing to pray for. Besides ball games – he was never a sporty man – and the occasional outing or computer session, he has little to do each day except think about the failings that brought us here. Life for my father is a series of odd little circles. They take him in pointless loops from the minute he opens his eyes in the morning to the blessed time he can lose his consciousness in the night.

Father is cynical now, grown dark with resentment.

'The Australian government thinks we are rapists and murderers, terrorists in the making,' he told me. 'They will never embrace scum like us.'

LEAVING

When rumours started to circulate – 'New Zealand will take us', 'The US Government is sending ships!' – my father scoffed and called all politicians, everywhere, *sons of dogs.*

No ships come to our island, no planes touch down to take us to a new home. Meanwhile, father still makes his funny face at me, with the googly eyes and the flapping mouth. And I still laugh, despite the fact it is no longer funny. It is no longer funny because it is no longer pretend. The clown has lost his mischief, he curses in Farsi, he has found despair. No child should *ever* have to sit and watch this wretched circus of real life.

I saw Rakine wrecking the Comms room again, smashing chair legs against the wall and this time painting words in blood across the dingy paintwork: Let Us Go. He had a familiar look on his face when they marched him out of the building in a neck-hold. It was a face coming apart at the seams. I don't know who we are underneath as we lose our surfaces... leaving dark thoughts blowing around in the wind, always finding new places to grow.

My name is Yasmin, and I don't think we are what they say we are. But I'm not quite sure either.

◆

While we wait to start new lives, children must be taught. It's all part of the big pretend.

I work in a corner with Amira and Dada, trying to be good at all things, in all ways. The heat is wicked, creeping down our throats until we choke. A fan whirrs on and on, shifting blocks of hot air from one side of the room to the other. We work in small groups, which ebb and flow. Our teachers change, but recently it has been Helen from the Salvation Army. You can tell she thinks we need to be saved from ourselves.

Our selves being rapists, murderers and terrorists in the making.

Yet Helen tries. She thinks we're cute but annoying too, because can't we see she is trying to look after our future?

'What is future?' Dada asks, his mouth tilting up at the corners.

'Is it good? And can I go there?'

'Future is full of piss and shit,' says 10-year-old Amira. That's what her dad Farouk thinks. Amira was five when the family came here, fleeing the Afghani war. Farouk's darkness is gaping open now; he has been in Crazy Town too long. Helen looks shocked.

'Those words won't help you in your new life, Amira,' she says.

'My new life is now,' Amira replies. 'This is now. Now is here. Here is piss and shit.'

Helen's face crunches into a frown.

'It upsets me to hear you use those words,' she says, looking prim.

Amira is suddenly in a rage; her anger is black and cold like slabs of stone.

'It upsets me to breathe,' she hisses. The air presses in. She looks like the old man Pez who rattles around the camp, fed up with his body and his ridiculous life in Crazy Town. But she is a little girl, with black curls and wide eyes, which are now filled with old-man hate. She is young become old, gentle become savage. She is the self they made her.

◆

I'm glad we have our dog. He's not really 'our' dog, but we look after him as much as he looks after us. So special is Birdie, he has even wormed his way into the hearts of the guards. His body is grey and thin, his tail just a wisp of feathery muscle. Yet his eyes are deep pools of devotion. They reflect his vivid soul.

I'm not sure why the dog is called Birdie. I think because the only

LEAVING

survivors of Crazy Town are the ones who can fly away. So, Birdie is a symbol of hope. Yet he will never have wings. He will die here in this swampy madness, just like us.

The locals throw stones at Birdie; they say he is the devil's dog. We are the devils who own him. We are less than dogs anyway; to them we are the rotting humans the whole world has decided to put in the bin. I expect the people who live on this island are annoyed we have been put in *their* bin.

Crazy Town is a human garbage can. It is filled with corpses that are still alive. We are dead men walking, that's what Omar says. He is so full of wisdom and hate. One day we will all just walk into the ocean and be swallowed by the blue, frothy waves. The water will accept us even if it cannot love us. For love can never be given to wretches like us.

◆

In the school room, Helen lets us use the computer. If the internet is up, we can find a favourite thing to look at. Dada chooses soccer. Amira chooses horse riding or hospitals depending on her mood. Once she asked for a coffin and Helen scolded her. As if little girls should never look at death, even when it is all around them.

I choose birds, which is how I met Nigel and Trevor. Nigel you know about. Trevor is a mallard who made a mysterious journey across the ocean. Helen thought Trevor was a cute duck with a funny story, so that was all okay. She was less pleased with Nigel trying to mate concrete gannets instead of live ones. But Helen missed the point. Out in the wild Pacific he was one tiny bird, alone. Surrounded by his statues, 'no mates Nigel' found himself again. He felt love when before there was none. You stop being fussy when reality shows you how small you are. Most of us just wriggle around until we fit.

We try to be good for Helen's sake. She pretends that Crazy Town is normal and we all have to play our part. So, we learn our English words, and what food we should eat to be well, and where Crazy Town is on the map of the world – a dot among dots in the dizzy blue of a sea which sloshes halfway around the battered globe in our classroom – and how children usually play in parks with their friends, wear clean bright clothes, go to birthday parties and study to be a doctor, a banker, a teacher or a vet.

Amira spits when Helen shows her pictures of children in Australia. Patting a koala. Surfing at the beach. I will spit too if you tell me one more time that everything is possible. That God is good. Amira has already moved beyond God. Her God has deserted her. Her God is the devil. *So, don't mention God to Amira.* She just knows he doesn't care.

◆

Trevor was good for me. He helped fill empty days. He gave me someone to feel sorry for other than myself. I thought about him a lot.

Most mallards know their migration lines and follow them. Not Trevor the duck. Maybe he was daffy, maybe he just got lost, but he flew all the way to the Pacific island of Niue, where no mallard had been before. He became a celebrity. Trevor made his home in a puddle and the locals made sure it was always full of water. He had his own Facebook page where he talked to all the people who loved him and cared about his future. The papers said he was the loneliest duck in the world, but he had more friends than we do. Even the Governor of New Zealand wanted to bring Trevor to his shores so he could be with his own kind. Trevor said no, I think.

Take us instead. We will come, we will be good, we will say the words you want us to say, learn the facts that will make us good citizens,

LEAVING

grow the beliefs acceptable to your people.

Take us now. We are dying, mad, washed so far out in our own heads that we cannot find shore again. We are decaying in a world beyond our own, without the people who know and love us. We are unseen, unloved, unlovable, forgotten before we are even remembered. Aching to leave, we are birds without wings.

◆

The Australians wage war on our parents. The Government says they put our lives in danger on rickety boats in high seas. Then, in Crazy Town, the mothers and fathers abandon their children by crying all day, refusing to wash, staying in bed and cutting their wrists. Don't they care about their little ones?

I will tell you this. They suffer too much. My mother Azedah looks at the walls of her prison without seeing. She mourns the loss of her beautiful baby boy on a deadly voyage over the sea. She writes letters in her own blood to a Government who never reads them. My father moans and grinds his teeth at night, fighting imaginary demons in dreams he cannot remember. He makes long lists of countries in his head, trying to find the country who will take us. Every day, my brother Behrouz haunts our steamy cell with echoes of life that can no longer be. He is the grieving we no longer name and the memories we no longer share.

My parents have fallen and cannot get up again. They are tortured. They are mortal. They are not how you want them to be, I know. Fallen people never are.

My father chose to leave on the boat because, as Iranian Kurds, our old life in Ilam Province left us on the bottom of the pile. It was scary and it was dangerous. Farouk says the Kurds are like the Jews – despised on all sides. It doesn't matter what the problem is, it is always our fault.

Father knew there were no guarantees, but he couldn't put up with the persecution forever at our back. He is a driven man. That's why we ended up here. Nothing can save us from own choices. Nothing can prevent us from being human.

The Government wants us to go back where we came from. That's why they keep us trapped in the machinery. Officials tell us to apply for refugee status, make us wait so, so long for a reply, then generally turn it down. If they make life really horrible, we will probably go home. That's what they think. That is the end game.

My family is lucky. I think. Refugee status makes us ready for the call. Yet there is no open door, we are still 'illegal arrivals' who jumped the queue ahead of well-behaved refugees. We should have used the proper channels, gone to our embassies like good little Kurds and Afghanis. But how? Could we even find one? And would we get blown up or shot if we tried to go in? If we make it to Indonesia, we are illegal once more. We must live in the shadows, then catch an unsafe boat to an unknown destination. It is a cycle with no beginning and no end. We are really just people in pain with no place to go. That is why we trash our flesh and sew our lips together to shut out the world. No more food, no more troubles. No more pain.

Mother tells me to stay away from Farouk who has his own Afghani axes to grind. Three, in fact. He insists we are screwed three times over.

1. Our home Governments make us live in mess, war and fear.

2. The people smugglers take big money for leaky boats which spew us into the ocean.

3. The Australian Government says *Screw You Refugees! Eat Shit on an Island and Die!*

I try to avoid him, but he knows I am a good listener. I soak up this poison like water in a sponge. I am always seeking a way out, so I must

LEAVING

stay open, keep looking, be ready.

◆

No-one leaves Crazy Town. If you go, you go out in a box. When you are nearly dead, a judge in Australia tells the Government it is very naughty, and you must come to an Australian hospital to get better. The island hospital is small and tinny. It cannot do important things. Even if you go to Australia, you come straight back again. Australian Border Force makes big trouble for little people like us who say they want to stay.

Every week more of us try to end our crazy lives. My friend Poya poured petrol over himself in the dusty yard. A Tamil boy tried to eat a razor blade; it must have tasted better than false promises. Young girls cut their veins with the sharpest stones they can find. We are self-destructing. Omar says boat people will soon be extinct like the dinosaurs and the dodo. I expect he knows. He lost his whole family in Iraq when Daesh burned his house down.

Yet boat babies are still born in the island hospital. They meet this world in chains. If you are born in darkness, how will you ever know what to do with the light? And how will the light know what to do with you?

Nida was a thin new-born who barely cried. As a toddler, she guarded her few toys – a doll made of out of lollipop sticks, a dented spinning top and a Barbie with one leg. In her third year, she started to eat things – anything she could find. She would stuff them into her mouth and bite down hard, so no-one could take them away again. Barbie ended up legless. Nida pooed out the lolly sticks. Her baby teeth broke on the spinning top's hard metal.

But then Nida turned four. She began to realise she couldn't break her chains. She watched her family bumble about – mother Lilla lost in tranquillisers, father Ahoora vengeful and furious, kicking his way around the camp, every day picking a new fight. Nida was a nothing person, a number, an unlawful arrival, a boat person, an intruder, a queue-jumper, a taker-up of other people's space.

Nida didn't like that. She took it badly. She started sticking her fork into other people. Nobody dared give her a knife. She'd jab it in as you walked by or leap out from around a corner. When she did it to a visiting Australian official, all hell broke loose. Mutterings were made about 'poor quality arrivals' and 'unfit material'. Lilla and Ahoora begged her to stop, telling her she was threatening their chance of a normal life in the promised land. But Nida didn't stop. Perhaps she knew it was too late anyway. This land had already broken its promises. Didn't we know that dirty boat people weren't allowed?

So, Nida decided to eat dirt. While the other kids played in the sand pit or made mud pies in puddles, Nida scooped up spoonfuls of soil. She was often ill, lying for days in the dark, sweaty nurses' room with its faded curtains. Sometimes she smiled as if she had great secrets to protect. Other times she turned her face to the wall.

Nida got more violent too. Every day I tried to talk to her, to break the strange witch's spell. She ignored me or launched at my face, screeching. *You must come back*, I begged, *you will go mad and die*. But her eyes didn't see me. They saw something else, the thing you only see when you cross to the other side.

Nida spent more and more time locked up to keep others safe. I pestered Helen, telling her to show Nida photos of birds and bright colours and sunny houses to make her want to live again. Helen would always shake her head. She looked shocked and far-away.

'You don't understand, Yasmin,' she said one day. 'Nida needs professional help.'

LEAVING

'So, get it then.' My voice was loud and rude. It didn't sound like mine.

'We've called the doctor,' Helen replied.

That's the mind doctor. It usually went like this. The doctor comes. *It's all wrong*, the doctor says. *Take this patient to Australia*, the doctor says. *This patient might die.*

This patient is illegal, Australia replies. *They made their own choices*, Australia replies. *We decide who comes to this country and the manner in which they come.*

'Just bury us now and it's done,' I said. My voice was hard and flat, as flat and hard as the pain which turned Nida's face to the wall.

The doctor came and went. Nida began to draw all over herself in biro and felt tip pens. Maybe she'd seen the tatts some of the men got from a tattooist in the village – 'Son of Crazy Town', 'One Day Freedom' and 'Crazy Town Kills'. Nida decided to cut out her own pictures with any pointy thing she could find. She knew there wasn't much time. Nida was already in God's waiting room.

From then, whenever we saw her, Nida was covered in blood. Born in darkness, she wanted the light so much she killed it.

One day, I pulled Birdie by his rag-tag collar and led him to the window of Nida's room. Peering in, I could see her propped on her pillows, staring ahead. Knocking hard on the window, I hauled Birdie up in my arms and waved his front legs in a hopeful kind of way. Birdie gave a happy yip. I smeared the dirt off the window with my arm and knocked again, louder. I thought the glass might break. Nida's eyes looked at us but they didn't see. My stomach twisted in a tight and tiny knot. Nida was death before death came to call. Kissing Birdie, I set him free to wander off through the debris of coconut palms and banana leaves.

Australia is a shifting dream, lost in the darkness, like me. Only the bright eyes of Birdie light my way.

Our broken places cannot be mended. Sometimes I remember our journey on a rocky boat, I feel the roaring wind and waves attacking us. As we lie in our narrow bunks, listening to the ocean throw its energy around, I am there again. The sea pulls at my baby brother, greedy for his youth. Behrouz spins overboard only meters from the shore. There we find him, washed up on the sand like a chunk of chubby driftwood. My mother screams when she sees his body, an empty cherub shell with the murmur of the ocean in its ears. She doesn't stop screaming for a long time. She screams all the way from Cocos to Christmas Island on the navy ship, then all the way to Crazy Town on a plane like a sardine can. She is still screaming inside, where no-one else can hear.

Behrouz got so far, so close, so *almost there*. And then he just disappeared.

His body lies between us still. None of us get past him. We feel his baby weight, hear his squeaky voice call to us at night. I tell him he must leave us alone, he has no business here, stepping on living dreams. But I don't think he hears from his berth in the island cemetery. If he does, he is angry and tearful, determined not to set us free. Perhaps Behrouz doesn't even know he is dead. Sometimes I think we are all dead, in Crazy Town, and no-one has told us yet. Behrouz was just a baby and he doesn't know how to leave us. He cannot swim away all alone in the sea; it is up to us to let him go.

◆

I remember only patches and spots of my life in Iran. Bodies bumping in the souk, sunlight playing on fountains, dust motes spinning in the rooms of our home. The few photos we have of Life Before Now are rotted by sea water. I can still make out my father's parents – Daryan and Gizem – on the big family photo which crossed the world in our backpack. But my mother's parents, Peros and Lilan, have been eaten by the ocean. They are now just bodies without heads. Mother is angry because I can no longer remember their faces. Crazy Town is also eating my memories. It's hard to link the bits into a whole. When I do, the whole is a burden I cannot bear, the pain of it spears my heart. Little bits, little pieces, I can push into places which torture me less. Otherwise I will end up like Nida, like Amira, a banshee wailing at the Pacific moon; a bitter old woman before I am even adolescent; an exhausted, wrung-out person that life has disposed of.

My name is Yasmin. *I am still a child*: that is my weakness and my strength. I will bleed from childhood into adolescence, here in Crazy Town, like a stain spreading slowly, slowly into clean spaces. My guilt and my failure follow me always.

I wish Nigel would pick me up in his beak and carry me far away, until we are just a dot against the sun. I would be happy among concrete gannets. I'm sure they have just as much to say as anyone else. Yet Nigel is dead now, he died among friends, so his feathers and bones will be part of the island his stone companions rest on. I could join them all, laying down my head with those who are gone and those who remain.

Nigel arrived at his Mana Island home the same year we arrived on Crazy Town. Out of 80 concrete gannets, he chose his love. Then he built her a nest, groomed her, courted her and had endless chats. Five years later three real gannets arrived, just as the New Zealand scientists had hoped. Nigel ignored them. He died soon after, surrounded by statues. But he had played his part. The real gannets wouldn't have set up home there if not for him.

The Australian Government says it has stopped the boats, so it is happy. Yet good souls continue to die in vain. Those who remain survive like Nigel, pinning their hopes on dreams which can never come true.

We are a colony of zombies and clowns. No-one knows who are the living, who are the dead.

Tomorrow I will go down to the shore. I will burrow my way through the jungle roots, leaving only footprints in the sand. I would like to shout out to Birdie, but he cannot follow me. Too many lost souls need him. Reaching the ragged water line, I will remember Behrouz and our battered boat.

No boat is needed now.

Goodbyes are too hard. I will take the plunge fast and easy. With pockets full of Pacific stones, I may flail around a bit, but nothing more. My spirit alone is heavy enough to take me down.

I will think of Nigel as I go, surrounded by my own stones. On an island inhabited by ghosts.

The Levensons
Tara Roeder
United States

2ND PLACE IN THE 2019 INTERNATIONAL
WRITING COMPETITION

THE FIRST TIME LOU HEARD THE NAME Grete Nilsson Levenson she was focused on prying tiny mussels out of their shells in a sliver of a restaurant on Île Saint-Louis. Marcello Marciano, her companion du jour, was notable for two things: 1.) He'd sculpted his way through several decades on three continents, never once becoming irrelevant. 2.) When it came to dining out he had an unerring nose for the microscopic and blissful.

At the time Lou had yet to master the art of the interview.

'Blaston Glaze wrote about the specter of Giacometti haunting your latest exhibit,' she remembers beginning solemnly, grasping a tiny silver refillable pencil.

'Your pupils,' Marcello Marciano stopped her, 'melt into your irises in a delightful way. And because of that I promise to answer all of your questions about specters and exhibits after we eat. Allow me to recommend the Cevit de Cerf?'

'Not a deer,' she said sharply. Being in France, she might go as far as an occasional scallop, a Dover sole on Easter Sunday, but nothing further.

Marcello Marciano was an acquiescent dinner companion. He ordered blanquette de crevettes and launched into the type of understated gossip that was his trademark.

He stopped abruptly in the middle of an intriguing story about a Persian poet Lou knew only by sight.

'I didn't know she was back in Paris,' he said suddenly, his voice trailing off in the way Lou would later learn to recognize meant that he was remembering something.

'Who?' she asked, craning her neck despite being at an age when one prefers to appear aloof.

'Grete Nilsson Levenson,' Marcello said, his voice oddly prayer-like. Lou caught a glimpse of the back of a gold shingled head.

'Who?' she repeated, trying not to sound as interested as she felt.

Marcello Marciano looked at her as if seeing her for the first time, possibly intrigued by being in the presence of someone so unworldly. 'The explorer,' he said.

'Explorer?' she repeated, surprised. Vague illustrations from 1980s middle school history textbooks floated through her mind, none of which corresponded to the tall blonde figure about whom Marcello Marciano spoke so reverently.

'Her work in the Arctic is legendary,' he said, lighting a cigarette, 'And her photographs are unparalleled. True art. They've been in museums.'

Lou might later, of course, read all of her interviews, every published field note, and some of the unpublished ones.

Lou liked the Paris of Marcello Marciano. The pair spent the rest of the evening drinking whiskey in Marais cafés where he seemed to know everyone, or everyone seemed to know him, or both. He took her home that night to a small and sparsely furnished apartment on the Rue St. Denis. Marcello Marciano was an interesting lover, detached yet tender. That was the first, and last, time they slept together. In the morning she wore one of his sweaters and he took her to a café for breakfast.

It was an image Uri Levenson would recall often, the sight of young Lou ravenously tearing a croissant to pieces in smudged eyeliner and Marcello Marciano's maroon pullover.

'Who is our new friend?' he asked, sliding into an empty chair at an adjacent table. (Uri Levenson's voice has alternately been described as cinnamon cake, or buche de noel. There's no point in describing the somewhat rotund figure, the slight bald spot, the beard.) Uri Levenson's eyes crinkled disarmingly at the corners; they x-rayed you kindly. Uri Levenson's hands were sturdy and expressive.

'This is Lou,' said Marcello Marciano, 'and Lou, this is Uri Levenson –'

'The collector,' Uri said, as Marcello finished, 'Grete Nilsson's husband.'

There was a momentary pause.

'Lou is writing for an American art magazine,' Marcello said, almost unwillingly.

'I don't know many writers,' said Uri.

His eyes dwelled appreciatively on her, and Marcello abruptly asked about Grete.

'I hear the Norwegian exhibit was a huge success,' he said.

'Absolutely,' Uri said, smiling. 'You know Grete. Every photograph a masterpiece. You'd think Norwegians would be bored as hell of snow, but even they were dazzled. The Arctic fox stills sold for an amount it would be uncouth to mention.'

Lou's image of Grete Nilsson Levenson, heretofore based solely on the back of Grete's head and the awe of Marcello Marciano, expanded.

Marcello lit a cigarette. Uri waved the smoke away with his hand absent-mindedly.

'I hope to see more of you, Lou,' he said warmly.

'Likewise,' she said.

'You shouldn't see him again,' Marcello Marciano said abruptly after Uri Levenson had left. Misattributing his warning to jealousy, Lou discarded it. She looked forward to meeting an actual explorer, and she didn't have many friends in Paris. When she came down with the flu the following week, she only had two visitors – her landlady, and Marcello Marciano, who came to call with onion soup and a Grete Nilsson Levenson catalogue.

Lou was awed by Grete's work. (Despite making a living out of the written word, she still lacks the language capable of describing the stark sublimity of the images of Grete Nilsson Levenson.)

Uri Levenson came to visit Lou while she was recuperating. He brought macarons.

'I'm going to take you to the country,' he said decisively, cupping her chin with his hand as he examined her face carefully. 'You need fresh air.'

Looking back, Lou doesn't remember if she was vaguely annoyed or oddly touched at such familiar solicitude. Perhaps both. She does remember that the first time she felt the unusual combination of comfort and excitement Uri Levenson would never fail to arouse in her was in his car that day, speeding from Paris to Chenonceaux with their overnight bags tossed in the back seat.

She'd never seen the châteaux of the Loire before. Their solemn decadence delighted her. Uri Levenson seemed to know the history of every pane of glass and staircase, every titillating story of Renaissance perversity. That night they stopped at a small roadside inn with a squinting, anxious proprietress who seemed eminently relieved when Uri requested two rooms.

The following afternoon, tipsy from the expensive wine they'd spent hours tasting in damp cellars, Lou told Uri she wanted to explore the forest. On the list of things she no longer remembers is whose hand brushed whose first, but she doubts she'll ever forget the mossy carpet of leaves or the urgency with which she and Uri Levenson fell to it. That night over dinner, bruised and contented, she listened to Uri talk about his childhood in London, his trips around the world, his extensive collections. He tactfully avoided mention of Grete Nilsson, and, for a while at least, Grete retreated into the background of Lou's mind. At the time, Uri seemed like the fascinating one.

Marcello Marciano had left Lou several annoyed messages over the weekend. He'd assumed, correctly, that she was with Uri Levenson.

Once in a while she dreams that things ended there, that summer, eating ripe peaches in bed with Uri Levenson in the afternoons, drinking whiskey with Marcello Marciano and his friends at night. She eventually returned to New York satisfied with the memories she'd accumulated. There was a tasteful book about the Val de Loire inscribed by Uri Levenson at the bottom of her suitcase.

◆

But it didn't end there. Two years later, he randomly knocked on her apartment door.

'It's been a long time,' he said.

His appearance, unexpected as it was, somehow also had an air of inevitability. Or so Lou felt.

'Where can we get a drink?' he asked.

And that's how it started again, on the Lower East Side of Manhattan.

One whiskey in she asked after Marcello Marciano.

Two whiskeys in she asked about Uri's latest acquisitions.

Three whiskeys in she boldly inquired into Grete Nilsson Levenson's latest show in D.C.

'Her photographs are pure oxygen,' Lou said, attempting to display a casual worldliness she didn't yet feel.

'Would you like to see the tundra?' he asked.

Lou suddenly felt annoyed at the very idea of endless glistening. Of pure white melt, desperate carnivores, the cold edges of a precarious planet.

'Would you like to screw in the bathroom of a dive bar?' she responded.

Maybe they could have floated off into a world of icicles and white wolves that night. Or else tacitly decided to leave the memory of their one summer together pristine and singular, enclosed in amber. But Uri Levenson was something of a sensualist, and Lou thought she was too. The experience of ramming her against the stall of a Lower East Side men's room was an interesting acquisition for Uri, Lou could tell. When she woke the next morning she found herself vaguely surprised in capable arms, her clothes on the floor beside her bed, his folded neatly on her armchair.

Two weeks later Uri told Lou that Grete would be visiting her sister in Sweden for a month. Søster tid she thinks he called it. He invited Lou to accompany him to Montreal.

'Costa Rica,' she said firmly.

He had them on the next flight.

Their first night there she idly wondered what Marcello Marciano would think if he knew she was sleeping in a rainforest tree house with Uri Levenson.

'This was a magnificent idea,' Uri said, smiling contentedly as they slid into sleep, 'You'll have to choose all of our destinations.'

His casual use of the first person plural possessive both pleased and vaguely troubled Lou. The next morning she awoke to a curious spider monkey on the tiny verandah. Uri seemed touched by her joyful disbelief, and, remembering Grete Nilsson Levenson's photographs of polar bears, she felt momentarily abashed. But back then it seemed there was little lasting room for an impulse as banal as embarrassment.

Lou ended up returning to Paris shortly after that trip. She told her publisher that she was a more disciplined writer there, though she'd already acknowledged to herself that the reckless pursuit of Uri Levenson simply brought her an unparalleled sense of pleasure. Eight months after Costa Rica, Grete Nilsson Levenson intrepidly trekked to the Antarctic for a 12 month project, and Uri and Lou rented a cottage in Normandy.

The happiest year of Lou's life so far was the one in which she lived with Uri Levenson. They knew no one, and no one knew them. Every morning Uri went to the local bakery to buy warm croissants; the discreet baker assumed they were on honeymoon. Lou worked on a biography of Melanie Klein; Uri caught up on the classics. They rode bicycles, made vichyssoise, and occasionally travelled south to plunge themselves into the sea at Juan-les-Pins.

To Lou's increasing annoyance, she found herself beginning to feel quite possessive of the body that slept next to hers. One afternoon she caught a glimpse of her suntanned face looking at Uri Levenson in the mirror of the local brasserie. In it she recognized the expression of Marcello Marciano whenever he spoke about Grete Nilsson Levenson. She had a sudden recollection of his warning years earlier, and felt a fleeting stab of unease.

'What are you thinking about?' Uri asked, his eyes (as they often did) crinkling warmly.

'You,' she replied, flippantly and honestly.

When the year was up they returned to Paris. Uri seemed sad but fundamentally unchanged; for him, the loss of daily intimacy with Lou was no doubt mitigated by the reclamation of his illustrious wife. Lou herself had nothing to reclaim, and resentfully started seeing a waiter she picked up at a bar unfrequented by Marcello Marciano or either of the Levensons. But the first time Uri called to ask her to lunch she mentally ended that budding relationship immediately. If Uri Levenson wanted to ask her something, she wanted to answer.

'It's about Grete,' he began haltingly.

She looked at him without speaking, wondering how someone so worldly could so suddenly remind her of a prom date from Long Island.

'I want you,' he said, 'to write the story of her life.'

Whatever she'd expected, it wasn't that. A surreal calm descended on her. She imagined a golden peach, dripping with juice, floating in the air between them.

Either misreading her silence, or reading her silence correctly, he continued.

'You're a hell of a writer, and it's a hell of a life.'

In a play, Lou supposes, the moment that followed might have been called a pregnant pause. The imaginary peach was spinning slowly around.

'She doesn't know about us...' Uri trailed off.

The peach was gone, replaced by a globule of beautiful words tangled together, breathing Arctic air, covered in tiny stones and iridescent shells. A litany of glistening strangeness. Taiga. Caribou. Cottongrass.

LEAVING

'Will I write,' Lou asked, over-pronouncing her words, 'about your marriage?'

She could tell by the almost imperceptible indentation of his nostril that he was troubled, inexplicably frustrated by this reminder that there was something about which they might not be on the same page.

'Oh, I think it can just be about the adventures,' he said lightly, his voice strange in its echo of her feigned brightness.

'Marriage is an adventure,' she replied, unwillingly.

(Here she remembered being pinned to the ground in the forest of Chenonceau, her back pressed hard against the damp ground, his teeth sinking into her neck so deep they left a mark.)

Uri Levenson's eyes were opaque. His lips twisted in a grimace of pain and surprise.

He doesn't know what to do with this, Lou realized. She felt tired.

The topic never came up again. The Levensons remained in Paris for many months, and Uri and Lou kept a standing appointment for Monday evenings, Wednesday afternoons, and any weekends that Grete Nilsson Levenson decided to travel. The following spring Uri and Grete went south. Lou received tender postcards from Greece. Her latest project was about lesser-known Roman goddesses; her apartment was silent with the exception of the occasional visit from Marcello Marciano. One day he arrived to find her packing a suitcase.

'I'm going to Rome,' she said. 'To research Cloacina the sewer goddess.'

'That's interesting,' he said, 'Because the Levensons are in Italy as well.'

Her wince was barely perceptible, but Marcello Marciano caught it. The brief look of savage amusement that flitted across his face made her own turn red.

-446-

'You don't like thinking about them like that. But that's who they are. An institution. The Levensons,' he said.

'I know who they are,' Lou snapped.

Grete Nilsson Levenson was delivering a series of lectures on Arctic flora in Florence. As Marcello had insinuated, Lou never didn't know her whereabouts. Uri had arranged to meet Lou for a weekend in Venice. She'd become so accustomed to the vague and perpetual stomach ache his absence caused her that she was surprised to discover what it was like to feel well again. She and Uri locked themselves inside an apartment for three days, getting out of bed only to cook and shower. On the last night, Uri haltingly told her he was going to accompany his wife on her upcoming expedition to North America. The trip would last eleven months.

She vomited on the train ride back to Rome. She still credits Marcello Marciano for the almost maternal concern he exhibited on her return to Paris a few days later. She found him in her apartment flipping a chive omelet, a pack of Gauloises and bottle of scotch on the table. He said nothing. Later that month, he ripped a first edition of Death In Venice into pieces with his teeth and hid the scraps in a sculpture he would never finish. Rumor has it that Uri Levenson purchased the piece in its unfinished state after seeing a photo of it. He cabled the money from northern Alaska.

Those days Lou's gut was a perpetual furnace. Her mind too. Momentarily unable to write, she took a page out of Marcello Marciano's book and shredded the Nilsson Levenson catalogue from the Norwegian Exhibit. She used the strips to make her own rough, imperfect paper, which she plastered with images of the spider monkeys and honeycreepers who inhabit the dense jungle canopies of Costa Rica. Marcello Marciano was oddly enamored of the piece, and had it installed in a small gallery in the Rue de Thorigny, where it was purchased by an anonymous patron shortly after the Levensons returned to Paris.

    Uri showed up at Lou's door with hothouse orchids and a tiny opal the day after his arrival. She waited until after they'd been to bed to tell him that she'd decided to go back to New York permanently. She'd wanted to enjoy the spasm of pain that momentarily marred his normally placid face, but found she couldn't, and was numb on the plane ride back.

◆

Another two years would go by before Lou saw Uri again. Despite every fierce promise she'd made to herself upon her return to New York, when Uri Levenson randomly asked her to meet him in Florida for a week, she said yes. Feeling master of herself, she believed she was finally capable of accepting that the Levensons would always be, as Marcello Marciano proclaimed, The Levensons. That she could capture the detached sensualism of that first summer and appreciate the legacy of Grete Nilsson Levenson in a mature, disinterested way even as she slept with Grete's husband. But obviously, one night, her hands tied to a motel headboard in St. Petersburg, she realized that none of that was true. Remembering how cautious he had always been in Paris that she should never leave a mark, she dispassionately bit Uri Levenson's neck as hard as she could, thus ignominiously ending the affair that had begun in Chenonceaux almost a decade earlier.

◆

When Lou finally did meet Grete Nilsson Levenson, Marcello Marciano was there. Uri Levenson was not. It had been five years since Lou and Uri's final meeting in Florida, and she'd heard the Levensons had more or less settled down in Oslo.

    She could pretty much say 'The Levensons' without gasping for air at that point. She was back in Paris to meet with a publisher interested in translating her biography of Catherine de Medici, and she was excited to attend the latest exhibit of Marcello Marciano, who was also back in Paris after a three year residence in Brazil. He had recently begun working in bone.

'You look wonderful,' Marcello said, scrutinizing her face with satisfaction.

'I've missed you,' she said. She hadn't realized how much.

They seemed to sense the gently hovering presence behind them at the same moment. Marcello turned first, and Lou watched him melt into an embrace with the striking explorer who had so often consumed the thoughts of her younger self. When they detached, Marcello grabbed Lou's and Grete's right hands, gripping them tightly.

'This is Lou Conway,' he said quietly, 'And this is Grete Nilsson Levenson.'

'I'm a great admirer of your work,' Lou said.

Grete Nilsson Levenson's eyes, Lou remembers, flashed like sapphires.

'And I of yours,' Grete replied, her accent soft and rich. 'The biographies of course, but also, I believe I have a collage of yours hanging in my apartment,' she continued, 'A junglescape. The warmth is comforting for someone whose life is so often spent buried in snow!'

Lou found herself incapable of responding.

'Lou and I were planning to get dinner if you'd like to join us,' Marcello said quickly.

Grete Nilsson Levenson hesitated.

'Please do,' Lou urged. (She thinks she meant it. She wanted to mean it.)

'Do you enjoy sea urchin?' she asked, 'I know a place where it is simply luscious.'

'I no longer eat animals,' Lou said, almost apologetically. 'Even the bloodless.'

Grete Nilsson Levenson nodded absent-mindedly. Her left thumb and forefinger were slowly twisting the solid silver band on her right ring finger around in tiny circles. Like ripples in a tide pool.

They let Marcello Marciano pick the restaurant.

No Two Ways

L.F Roth
Sweden

Shortlisted for the 2019 International Writing Competition

SOMETHING IS WRONG. Warren looks at the key, tries it a second time. Nope. It doesn't fit. She must have changed the lock. Just like that. No word of warning.

He rings the bell. No footsteps. Not a sound.

He scrolls down his list of contacts to call her. Does so. No reply.

Irresolute, he hesitates. Then, having put two and two together, he shouts: 'Michelle was a mistake. You're the one I love. Always was.' That is a lie, of course. A man needs different fare occasionally.

Still no response.

He bangs on the door and finishes with a hard kick.

While he hops around on one foot, the neighbour across the landing sticks her head out. A right nosy parker, that one.

'Oh, it's you,' she mutters. She is about to make some kind of comment, but he frowns and she is gone. The lock clicks shut.

He raises his fist for a renewed attempt, but stops in mid-air, having caught sight of a suitcase and a holdall, leaning against the banister. On inspection, he sees that the tags bear his name; the address has been crossed out. Stella can be subtle when she sets her mind to it. What better mode to signal that this is no longer his home? He unzips them. The case holds socks, underwear, a few shirts, tossed in any odd how. His. In the holdall are files and backup disks. Will she have erased them? Does she know how to? He gives the door a final kick, using his heel – never too old to learn, he would have boasted, had there been an audience – and carries the luggage down to his car, where he tosses it in the boot, beside the spare tire. Spare tire, spare shirts, none of which counts among his favourites. This in itself may have rankled her – the fact that what he's been wearing around the house are clothes he doesn't value. He ponders the matter briefly before he slams the boot shut and eases himself into the driver's seat. Thrown out by two women on the same day, wife and mistress. Well, locked out, in one instance, but the distinction is minimal. Not his dream scenario. He could have kept things going for a good deal longer, but, as some would hold, there are two sides to every relationship. Each to his own.

He stares into the rearview mirror.

Where to?

Friday night and nowhere to go.

It is at this point it strikes him that they must have been in collusion, Stella and Michelle. This is a joint effort.

He sighs.

There is no trusting women, is there?

Well, given the set-up, some might put the blame on him for what has transpired. But that would only show that they haven't got the whole picture. He had done what he felt was required. 'I'm in a relationship that isn't much of one,' he had told Michelle, not on their first date, to be sure

– that would have brought everything to an immediate end – but after they had gone through the early experimental stages and she expected him to stay the night.

'What's the hurry?' she would say, echoing some women from the past, her fingers tiptoeing across his chest as he reached for his wristwatch. 'The night's still young.'

And he had blamed work: an early start the next day; a huge backlog that had to be dealt with. Casual excuses that didn't call for much deliberation and were easy to accept. But by and by he had sensed how her frustration grew. It's generally the same: becoming involved with a woman turns into a chore. You can't leap in and out of bed at your convenience. If you're not there, your absence has to be accounted for. In a way, having an affair is like having a job, at least part-time. If you fancy a break, you have to call in sick or else you are in trouble.

So the day had come when he had to make Michelle aware of how things stood. Well, within reason: he'd never considered her a permanent presence in his life. He enjoyed her. She differed in a number of respects from Stella. In truth, it was their differences he appreciated most of all. But who wants to be apprised of that? Who wants to be considered a third wheel? 'I'm in a relationship that isn't much of one' was the phrase he had found handy in the past and used on Michelle.

But though his remark was meant to sound offhand, she froze.

'What's wrong with it?' she'd asked. 'I'm here for you and have been from the start. Tell me.' Her voice rose on the last two words.

He hushed her, putting his hand over her mouth the moment he realized her mistake – or his, for that matter. 'I wasn't referring to us, honey,' he assured her. 'You're doing fine. I meant my wife. Our relationship.'

He'd expected her to echo the word 'wife', but what followed was silence, the kind that raises walls. There were jagged bits of broken glass along the top. She shut herself off. She closed the door on him.

'She needs me,' he had pleaded.

But that proved a bad tactic.

'And I don't?' Her tone was bitter.

Careful, he'd told himself.

'Not in the same way.'

He had regarded the ceiling. If her neighbours had their bedroom above hers, were they listening? What would they hear? A bed that no longer squeaked? One that might never squeak again?

'We go back years,' he'd explained. 'Without me, she'd be nothing. She'd kill herself. I can't let that happen.'

He'd paused, wondering if he should suggest that Michelle put herself in Stella's shoes, but instead, when there was no response, he brought out the ace he had learnt to keep up his sleeve, metaphorically – in Michelle's company, needless to say, he rarely wore clothes, other than arriving and departing.

'Unlike her, you give me strength,' he had declared.

He had smiled to reassure her, but to no avail. The wall she had put up didn't crumble.

Still, he hadn't been unduly worried. Time had always been on his side and he trusted it would remain so. Only once, barely out of his teens, had he resorted to that clichéd gesture, a bunch of roses, and with disastrous consequences: judged by Sally – was that her name? – to be an admission of guilt, she'd used them to prick him every time he tapped on her door, till he insisted that she throw them out.

With Michelle, he'd let two weeks go by, before he attempted to pick up where they had left off. 'Honestly, she means nothing to me,' he had repeated and soon they had been back on their previous footing. On an improved footing, actually. For as he had hoped, his having introduced

Stella to Michelle, in a manner of speaking, brought nothing but advantages. No longer did he have to watch his tongue in case of an inadvertent slip. 'She's got a cold,' he could inform Michelle whenever he felt that Stella had begun to eye him askance, which might indicate that she was on to something. 'An ordinary cold, but she tends to overreact. You know how it is. She will want me around for the next few days.' Allergies and migraine, he knew, along with PMS and similar complaints that he preferred to give a miss, could serve the same purpose, clearing the road for a night out – with Stella, that is – to blot out whatever suspicion she might harbour. Michelle, he didn't take anywhere. Being with her in her flat constituted their nights out. Well, his, at least.

Hazel, had been her name, not Sally. Or was it Marion?

There had been a number of occasions, it goes without saying, when he had contemplated pushing things, opening up to Stella as well, to a degree. It might simplify matters. They could set up a weekly schedule, the three of them. Share and share alike. He could knock on Stella's and Michelle's door every second night. Or alternate weeks. That was how many divorced couples arranged matters for their offspring, handing them over on Fridays, say. Why shouldn't lovers? But he had been stumped for an opening. He would have to approach the topic in a roundabout fashion or else run the risk of giving it all away prematurely, which could result in catastrophe. The trick would be to get Stella to implicate herself. But how?

'You ever been attracted to anyone else?' he could ask.

But no. She would be on her guard. 'Else than who?' she would respond, leaving him no other option than a strident 'Yours truly, naturally' – which, given where it was meant to lead, would ring false. How exchange confidences without committing oneself?

Women, he is fully aware, have a way of parrying your every move instinctively.

Anyway, the more he'd thought about it, the less inclined he'd been to let someone come between him and Stella. He'd hate it. He wanted her to himself.

Therefore, with Stella, he'd had to go on resorting to subterfuge. Doing overtime topped the list. Taking a customer out for a meal came second. Attending a two- or three-day conference out of town was a feasible alternative, but must be used sparingly. Provided he didn't lay it on too thick, Stella would swallow whatever he told her. He'd let her know that in his line of business, there was no sitting on your haunches. You had to stay ahead of the competition. Work had to be your top priority.

And it had run pretty smoothly, on the whole, until today.

The music, when he stepped into Michelle's hall, having spent two nights with Stella, indicated that all was not well – a classical piece that put him in mind of some funereal passages of German origin, played by a churlish teacher at school. This was a far cry from Norah Jones, Michelle's favourite.

'It's me,' he had been about to shout, but didn't.

Not that it would have made the slightest difference.

Michelle, he learned, and this came without warning, before he'd even stepped out of his shoes; Michelle didn't want him any more. She wanted something different. He no longer moved her. He wasn't it.

He wasn't it.

That hurt.

She'd waved no list of grievances. She issued no ultimatum. There was no 'me or her'. He just wasn't right for her. Sorry it had taken so long to find out.

And how long could it have taken her to inform Stella? A few hours? One day? There she had most definitely gone behind his back.

Women.

Oh, well. There's nothing he can do about it.

With a shrug he starts the engine, asking himself again, Where to? But how much choice does he have? He heads towards town. Once there, he can call on a colleague, for a night's kip, or book a room at a hotel.

As it happens, he does neither. Near the centre, the sign for The Greyhound catches his eye – one of few pubs where the clientele doesn't simply call in for a drink but does so in order to meet like-minded – or unlike-minded – people. He brakes and turns into a side street. This was where he had met Michelle. Having spotted her early on, along with the two women with whom she shared a table, he had placed himself strategically by the counter in case she came up for a refill.

'Nice outfit,' had been his opener. 'Not everyone could wear it, but it suits you. The cut. The colour.'

She had thanked him and given him the once-over.

He'd passed.

And they had gone on to dip their toes in the water to make certain that the temperature suited them both, neither too hot, nor too cold – which had thus remained the case, except for some brief interludes, until today. Or so he had thought.

He is in luck. Less than a block away, he finds a vacant space for the car. Having retraced his steps, he pushes at the door to the pub a little hesitantly, not entirely sure what to anticipate. She won't be there now, will she? No. There is no more than a scattering of people – the after-work crowd must have headed for home, while those who are going to take over won't show up till later. The only one he recognizes is the barman.

'Quiet tonight,' he says. He orders a lager and takes a seat at the bar, where he will be less conspicuously alone – after all, the barman is there, too. Sipping at his beer, he tries to recall the Michelle he had met ten months ago, not the one who had cold-shouldered him today. Her eyes, in spite of the soft light, had had a sparkle in them. Her lips had been full of promise. The quick movement of her head as she kept an eye on what was going on, without losing sight of you for a moment, had been reassuring.

He stops himself. In the mirror behind the bar, between the bottles, the door has swung open; two women are making their way in. One of them heads for a table, but the other beckons her on. He observes their clothes, the style, the length, how the colours of each match what the other is wearing, and rehearses his standard opener. Here is beauty. Here is poise. Having turned around slowly, he raises his eyes. Then, abruptly, he pulls back. He frowns.

'Is this a trap?'

He hopes they didn't catch the quaver in his voice.

If they did, they don't let on. They looked in on the off chance, they inform him.

'We thought a confrontation, if there is to be one, had better occur in public,' is the excuse they offer.

The barman serves them their drinks and makes himself scarce.

Stella raises her glass. 'Cheers,' she mumbles.

Warren nods.

'So you've met,' he notes.

The phrase hangs in the air. There is no background noise. No music. The silence grows.

'Michelle contacted me,' Stella replies, finally.

And at that point the dam bursts as she gives vent to her pent-up anger with him, but, parallel to that, they both take turns describing, however incompletely, how they have discovered, over the last few weeks, after Michelle's first phone call, the close affinity that exists between them.

'It goes beyond you,' says Stella. 'In fact, to put it bluntly, it excludes you. We were meant for each other. I've never felt so close to anyone. I'm leaving you – well, I already did. I want a divorce. I'll get in touch with a lawyer who can help with the formalities. It's a good thing there are no children.'

'Wait.' Warren puts up a hand. This is going too fast. 'What about…?'

But they are on their feet. 'The flat,' he'd meant to say. But the lease is in her name. What is his he can pick up at some point in the future. He watches them walk towards the exit. Stella puts an arm around Michelle to escort her through the door. They smile at each other. The door falls shut.

Stella. Michelle. Until late afternoon, he'd had two women. Or thought he had. Now he has none.

He stares in front of him.

They hadn't even finished off their drinks.

The barman returns and Warren pushes his glass towards him.

'Same again.' He nods absentmindedly.

Not taking much in, his eyes wander among the whiskies, vodkas and their reflections in the mirror, lose their way temporarily between more unfamiliar brands of cognac and liqueur, there to cater to anyone's taste, only to fasten, as before, on a figure that approaches the bar, a woman in her thirties. She is blonde. She is chic. He turns around.

'Nice outfit,' he comments. She has stopped only a few feet away. He draws a deep breath. 'It held me captivated from the moment I caught sight of you. It wouldn't suit everyone, but it looks great on you. The colours. The cut.'

'Thank you.' She glances at him and rewards him with a smile.

He smiles back. 'Can I buy you a drink?'

LEAVING

She inclines her head.

So many, he thinks. Hazel, or was it Elaine? Others, leading all the way up to Michelle. So different and yet so similar.

'What will it be?'

And her choice, once she has made up her mind, had also been Michelle's. It had been Stella's. There are so many things that never change. Indeed, there are.

'I'm Warren,' he says. 'And you?'

Elaine, he thinks. Or Hazel. Whatever. Really, it doesn't matter in the least.

Miriam.

How To Become Crimson
Richard Salsbury
United Kingdom

Shortlisted for the 2019 International Writing Competition

Duncan travels home in a state of joy. He knows how this will play out: Melinda will be annoyed that he's late again, but once she sees his color her mood will change.

There is always a moment of weightlessness as the lift begins its descent from the office, but this time it seems to last all 37 floors and into the basement. The doors open onto the MRT station and the train arrives for him as if summoned. The ride is smoother than usual – gliding, effortless.

Of course, there is the walk from the station to the lobby of Zero Plaza, the only part of his journey home that is not air-conditioned. Two years in Singapore and he still hasn't got used to it – the baking acres of concrete; the green, jungle heat trapped between the skyscrapers. Tonight it must be pushing 30°C, and by the time he's approaching the doors his short-sleeved shirt is drenched with sweat. He will shower before they eat.

LEAVING

There is a cluster of greens hanging round the entrance again, five or six of them. One looks up as he passes – the look of someone who has been caught at something, white eyes flashing from a bottle-green face. Duncan hurries past.

'Hello, Mr Duncan,' chirps the duty manager from behind his desk. Why doesn't he move the greens on? Duncan will have to speak to him about it, but not now. He won't allow a little thing like this to chip away at his elation. He nods in acknowledgment and takes the lift up to the fourth floor.

Melinda is on her feet as soon as he opens the door. 'Where have you been? Do you know what the time is? Why haven't you been answering your phone?'

She often does this: questions in batches of three. Best to avoid the one about the phone – he had switched it off to concentrate on work – and answer one of the others.

'I had to stay late. But …' He steps further into the light and draws her into a half-embrace. She resists, not yet willing to surrender her annoyance, and he ends up holding her elbow with one hand, their forearms parallel. He looks down, drawing her eyes so she will see the difference. Before she responds, he notices someone else in the apartment behind her – Bhaskar.

Duncan blinks. 'It's not tonight, is it?'

'Of course it is,' she says. 'That's why I was trying to phone you.'

'God, I'm sorry… both of you. It was… I was really onto something.' He turns to Bhaskar. 'You know what it's like.' But does he? His colleague has never seen this kind of success.

Duncan offers his hand – a formality to dismiss the awkwardness. 'How's it going?'

'Oh, you know…' Bhaskar shakes vigorously. Good for him; cheerful, no matter what.

Bhaskar says what Melinda must surely have noticed by now. 'You're looking redder.'

'Yeah. This week has just been… amazing.'

He is too polite to make any mention of Bhaskar's color, which these days is more yellow than orange.

'Get a color strip,' he says to Melinda. 'Go on, humor me.' He turns to Bhaskar, 'I hope you don't mind if we…'

'No. Go ahead.'

Melinda returns with a strip and places it next to Duncan's arm. He's well into the tangerine.

'You still should have phoned me,' she says.

'I should,' he concedes. Then, after a suitable pause, 'I don't want to get your hopes up, but this could just be the beginning.'

And he sees her irritation melt into a kind of hope, just as he foresaw.

'Enough to get Autumn into the American school?' she says.

'Not yet, but… fingers crossed.'

She is too mild, too easygoing, to hold a grudge for long. He loves her for it. The extra time at work, the late nights, the missed social engagements – she knows they'll be worth it. Duncan hugs his wife, giving her a little of his red. She will get more tonight, much more.

'Is she in bed?' he says.

'Yes. We tucked her in half an hour ago.'

'I won't disturb her, then.'

'Autumn seems to have grown each time I see her,' Bhaskar says. 'Last time it was fairy princesses, now it's Lego. We built a house together.' He indicates a haphazard, multicolored structure with a tower at one corner.

LEAVING

'Well,' Duncan pushes out a laugh, 'anything that keeps her away from the green kids.'

Melinda and Bhaskar exchange a glance. Yes: they must be hungry.

Duncan claps his hands. 'I'll just jump in the shower and then we can eat. Is the food okay or have I ruined it with my tardiness?'

'I've done Laksa,' Melinda says. 'It'll reheat.'

◆

On Monday, at 9:00am sharp, Duncan connects his console to the Immanoke and puts into action the plan that cost him so much of last night's sleep. He keeps an eye on the colors of other locations, especially S, JP and DB, but most of his work is closer to home. Too many color managers react to what is going on elsewhere rather than actively encouraging red more locally.

He swipes the colors from sector to sector, dials them up and down with a virtuoso precision. If he had devoted this much effort to his childhood piano lessons back in Woking he would be playing the concert halls of Europe by now. But this is his instrument: more difficult, more unforgiving, and finally – after so much rehearsal – more satisfying.

He has the courage to allow sectors to swoop alarmingly into the green because he knows that in an hour's time, with some more creative shuffling, he can push them back at least to a comforting amber. Many of his colleagues would balk at the risks, but he makes it work. He is breaking new ground, a Haydn, a Stravinsky.

He creates empty, jungle-green silos and through careful manipulation hoards enough red to color their cells, then he drains them, uses their contents elsewhere, closes them down. All the while, more and more of the cells entrusted to him by the company blush crimson, scarlet, ruby.

AWARD WINNING STORIES

They are like the cells of his own blood. An affinity has developed between them, an intimacy, almost as if he can push them redward by force of will alone. He is alert for signs of overconfidence, of a slip back into mediocrity. At a recent meeting the company psychologist warned that prolonged connection to an Immanoke console might cause Color Misperception Syndrome, a condition characterized by confusion, poor judgment and misplaced optimism. Duncan suspects the psychologist of making things up to justify his salary. But just in case, he puts things to the test in the simplest way he can conceive – by placing a color strip against the screen. There: an undeniable crimson. CMS. What a joke.

He skips lunch and carries on into the afternoon. There is nothing easy about the work. It still demands his full attention.

At two o'clock, Bhaskar makes an unexpected appearance at his console.

'Hi, Bhaskar. What brings you up to the 37th?'

'Listen, I wanted to thank you for dinner last Friday. It's always so good to see Melinda and Autumn. And that Laksa! You're a lucky man.'

'You're... welcome.' Duncan frowns.

'So,' Bhaskar says, 'how are things?'

It's an odd question, given how much he has told Bhaskar about his recent success. 'Well, things are ...' Duncan finds it difficult to express just how well it's going, so he simply gestures at his console.

It takes only a few seconds for Bhaskar's jaw to go slack. 'Wow.' He might not be a top flight color manager, but he can read a console. 'You have... this is... wow.'

'Tell me about it.'

'Isn't this a bit more, uh... stressful than usual?'

'What, this? It's wonderful. Why wouldn't it be?'

What is Bhaskar doing here? He has risked some embarrassment

LEAVING

coming up to the 37th – to be so glaringly yellow among all these oranges. For a few moments, there is only the sound of other color managers swiping and tapping and dialing.

'You're putting in a hell of a lot of hours,' Bhaskar says.

Yes, and look at the results.

Bhaskar chews on air for a few seconds. His head dips. 'Are you sure you're not working *too* hard?'

'Huh! You sound like Melinda.'

'Well, she has a point.'

'Look, this is *for* my family – better schooling for Autumn, a bigger apartment. When the wave comes, you ride it.'

Bhaskar's eyes stray back to the console. He looks like a man who hasn't eaten for a week. It's undeniable: if Bhaskar were in the same situation, he would act no differently.

Duncan says, 'Look, I really have to get back to...'

'Sure.' Bhaskar heads for the door. Before he disappears, he says, 'Hey, when you're rich and famous remember your mates on the 32nd.'

Now why did he have to say that? Duncan sighs and turns back to the console.

There is another interruption about half an hour later. Duncan can sense someone standing behind him, and is ready to tell them he's too busy. Then he sees who it is. He stands.

'Sir.'

'Please, call me Hong.'

Hong stands with his arms clasped behind his back, broad-shouldered and so resplendently scarlet that Duncan thinks he can feel the heat of his skin even from a meter away.

'Duncan, if I gave you ten times as many cells to manage, do you think you could turn them red for us?'

AWARD WINNING STORIES

'I, uh... yes, of course. Yes, sir, I could.'

'In that case, I would like you to pack your things and come up to the 46th floor.'

The *46th*? Holy shit.

'That would be wonderful, but...' Duncan glances at his bare arm.

'I would not worry about that. Continue like this and by the time you collect your color on Friday, you will fit in perfectly.'

'You want me to... you mean now?'

Hong beams paternally. 'Yes, I mean now.'

With hands that don't quite seem his own, Duncan gathers up his coffee cup, his Landmarks of London calendar, his photo of Melinda and Autumn.

◆

Their new penthouse apartment is a wonder. So it should be. Duncan's color had taken a worrying dip at the estate agent's, but once he was colored the following Friday he was back up to a glowing cinnamon. Melinda had been surprised with his sudden decision to move them to a better apartment, but he had done everything possible to smooth the way. A removal firm had transferred all of their possessions, and he had given her a generous budget for new furnishings. It was never, he explained to her, a bad idea to have capital in property.

The panoramic windows make the interior seem brighter, the city outside bigger. Standing in the living area on the east side, he is rewarded with an uninterrupted view over the Downtown Core. A direct link to the air-conditioned MRT station in the basement means that during his commute he no longer has to face the sweltering heat, or the congregations of greens.

There will, however, be one green with a much closer role in their lives. He introduces her to the family on Saturday afternoon. She stands modestly before them, hands clasped, wearing spotless white.

'This is Hijau,' he says. 'She's going to be our housemaid.'

Autumn is wide-eyed. Duncan can see how this might be confusing for her.

'Hijau has been carefully vetted by the agency. She has an excellent record.' He turns to her. 'You know your duties, Hijau.'

'Yes, Mr Duncan. Keep the apartment neat and clean. Help with domestic chores. No touching the family.'

'Very good. I think we're going to get on fine. You'll get Sundays off and you can catch up with anything that needs doing on Monday.'

Hijau's nod is almost a bow. She has a neutral expression and a pleasant half-smile. Of course she does.

It's not just Autumn; it will be strange for him too. But it's their numbers that have always worried him; the prospect of being overpowered and dragged off, to be immobilized in a basement somewhere with a dozen clammy hands pressed to his flesh, slowly leaching his color away. Hijau is petite and polite. She is no threat at all.

Still, there is a sense on her first day that each of them is performing for her. Ridiculous, really. He looks forward to the time – Hong has assured him it will come soon – when she is invisible, appearing only when summoned.

After lunch, Autumn shows him her Lego house, now extended and embellished, but clearly based on the one she made in their previous apartment. There are little figures too: a Dad with a briefcase, walking in through the front door; Autumn herself, sitting at the top of the tower, reading a book; and in the lounge …

'Who's this?' Duncan asks, indicating a yellow figure sitting opposite Mum.

'Bhaskar, of course,' she says.

'That's nice.'

'I'll need a green one too.'

'What?'

'A green one. For Hijau.'

'Yes. Yes that's a good idea. I'll buy you one.'

He looks up to see Hijau's reaction. Perhaps she is flattered to be accepted so readily into their family. But no. Nothing about her expression has changed.

◆

Rare fillet steak with a redcurrant sauce, grilled vine tomatoes and sweet potato, accompanied by a particularly fine Cabernet Sauvignon. It's a big change from their last meal together. It's also a sham. The slip has begun, inexplicable and frictionless. Duncan can think of little but tomorrow's session at the console, attempting to dig in his heels and prevent further loss of red.

Bhaskar shifts in his chair as Hijau serves him his vegetables. Her polite stoicism has come to obsess Duncan. No matter what task he sets for her, she seems content with it. Cook the meal, clean the toilet – it's all the same to her. Behind the mildness of that gaze there must be thoughts of her own, secret and safely stashed away. Does she harbor a fierce jealousy of his wife, a series of fantasies in which she usurps Melinda? It must be what all greens want. Is it only the agency rules – and the prospect of never being able to find work again – that keep her in check?

He imagines her naked and astride him, her professional mask cast aside, while he, a slave to his own pleasure, feels the red leaching from him.

'So, throw me a bone, will you?' Bhaskar says, out of nowhere.

'What?'

'What's your secret?'

'You mean at work?'

'Mmm.'

Why are they eating with Bhaskar again? An act of charity?

He tries to make light of it. 'Well, that's my little secret, isn't it?' If everyone has an advantage, no-one has an advantage.

Something in the Immanoke has changed, possibly something in the L or DB locations, something he has taken his eye off. Or was there only a limited window where his techniques were effective, a window never to be repeated? If Bhaskar got his hands on Duncan's methods, could he make them work? A week ago he would have laughed at the idea.

He must redouble his efforts.

'This is very nice,' Bhaskar says. 'So, is this is the sort of thing you eat with Hong and the boys?'

There's nothing snide in his tone, but the words speak for themselves. It's jealousy, pure and simple. Or maybe it's something worse. Maybe Bhaskar can already see the failure written on him. Maybe this is his way of gloating, now that he can sense the end of Duncan's brief surge of red.

Duncan tells Hijau to open a second bottle. Even if the company is second-rate, at least the wine is good. A couple more glasses embolden him for what he must say to his wife.

'I need to do some work at the weekends.'

Melinda is swallowing a mouthful of steak, and coughs before she can get it down.

'What? Are you serious? For how long?' she says.

'It depends.'

'And how do you think your daughter is going to feel about this?'

'The whole point of this is to get her into the American school. No mucking around with half-measures. We put her straight in at the top.'

'But what's the point of a good education if her father is never around?'

'Never? I'm here now. Our daughter is ten feet away.'

'Yes, and she's asleep. She hasn't seen you all day.'

'These hours are temporary.'

'They've been temporary for months.'

She has never understood the intricacies of his work, the sheer amount of time it takes to get things right.

'Look, this week has been...' He won't confess failure in front of Bhaskar. 'To maintain the red I have to put in some extra hours.'

'Why?'

'Melinda, this might be the only opportunity we ever have to –'

'Why can't we just go back to how it was?'

'What? And throw away everything I've worked so hard for? I've got ambitions for this family. I'm not one of those people content to just –' He casts a glance at Bhaskar, and manages to stop himself from finishing the sentence.

But why? Why should he stop? The wine pulses in his veins and he experiences a moment of horrible clarity. Of course, it's so obvious. And now he knows, he is capable of finishing any sentence.

'Oh, I see what's happening between you two.' He turns to his wife. 'You prefer yellows, don't you?'

Bhaskar starts to speak but he's drowned out by the scrape of Melinda's chair as she stands and says, 'You apologize to our guest, right now.'

'Our "guest" is here because he thinks he stands to gain from it. I don't think it matters to him what he gets, as long as it's something.'

LEAVING

Bhaskar's jaw is clenched shut. Duncan wants him to explode, for the whole jealous tirade to spill over, but Bhaskar stays rigid and contained as he gets to his feet. 'I think I should be leaving.'

'No,' Melinda says. 'You have no reason to.'

Bhaskar shakes his head. 'It can do no good, me being here.' He heads for the exit.

Melinda waits for the sound of the apartment door to shut before turning a furious gaze on Duncan. 'How can you say those words to –'

'Are you sleeping with him?'

'No, I am not!' She shakes the words off, like a dog shaking off water. 'He's a *friend*, Duncan. Are you too busy at work to remember what one of those is?'

No, he's a parasite – a covetous, maneuvering parasite. Why can't she see this? He tosses his napkin onto the table. Enough of this. He needs to be alone. On his way out of the apartment he sees that Hijau has been watching everything from the corner of the room.

'What are you looking at?' he says.

She casts her eyes downwards but shows no sign of fear or contrition, no sign of anything. Just that infuriating half-smile.

He slams the door.

◆

Duncan stumbles into the apartment at seven o'clock, blinking and deflated. Tomorrow he will launch another assault on the Immanoke. Tomorrow he will feel more positive, more energized.

The note is taped to the fridge:

Autumn and I have gone to stay with a friend. Now you can spend as much time as you like with your precious work.

This isn't real, of course. She has already forgiven him. He has already witnessed the tilt of her head, the sigh of resignation, the little smile of acceptance. But, no: these are episodes from the past, so numerous he has mistaken them for the present.

He reels into the kitchen area. With a hot jet of anger he stamps open the pedal bin and throws in the bunch of roses. He unholsters his mobile and phones Bhaskar.

'What?' comes the blunt voice from the other end.

'I want to speak to her.'

A pause. 'Melinda? She's not here.'

'Bullshit.'

'Come round then, if you must. She's not here. Everything you think –'

Duncan stabs at the phone, ending the call. He must do something, urgently, but what? What?

'Hello, Mr Duncan.'

So, there is at least one person still here.

'Where did they go?'

'I was not told.'

She probably helped them pack.

Hijau says, 'I have finished my duties for the week, Mr Duncan. Is there anything else you would like me to do?'

Yes. Wind back time. Change Melinda's mind. Make the red just a little easier to get hold of.

'No, Hijau. You can go home.'

'Thank you, Mr Duncan.'

But once she has gone he will be truly alone. Even her paltry company is something. He could command her to stay, but that would imply he needs something from her.

When did she become so powerful?

She gathers up her things, and as she leaves he decides to follow her. He takes the other lift, guessing, correctly, that she will take the MRT. She spends a few minutes in the ladies' toilet, emerging in a frayed, grubby tunic, her work clothes stowed away in her shoulder bag.

She takes the Downtown Line to the Botanic Gardens, then switches to the Circle Line. Duncan follows at a discreet distance, traveling in the next carriage, making sure there are always other people between them.

At Marymount they emerge into the wet, throbbing heat of evening. She walks west, towards the reservoir and the jungle. There are fewer people now and he has to keep his distance, hoping that the dying light will be enough to conceal him. The tarmac becomes a dirt track and leviathan plants close in from both sides. He has never been in the rainforest before. Insects shriek at him, a cacophony of miniature saws and drills and car alarms.

Hijau takes a tributary off the main path and her journey ends at a jumble of planks, car tires and sheets of corrugated iron, jigsawed between the trees. It had never occurred to him that she might live in one of the jungle shanties. There must be a hundred greens crammed in here.

Two children, leaf-colored and spattered with mud, abandon the hammock they are weaving from vines and throw themselves at her. She lifts one of them high above her head while the other attaches himself to her leg. A man steps forward and folds them all up in his arms. It's a tottering, precarious arrangement, and for a moment Duncan thinks they might fall. But no, the hug ends, the child is returned to the ground.

He gets closer; he has to see. Yes, the mask has gone. As Hijau speaks to them – an unhindered babble he can't make sense of at this distance –

she has become another person entirely, someone he has not met before.

Why is he here? Confusion, poor judgment, misplaced optimism – he has all the symptoms of CMS, and yet… he is red, and they are green. Even in this light it is obvious. He is seeing clearly.

It must be his color that gives him away. Hijau spots him and her expression resumes its practiced neutral once again. She communicates something to the others, he doesn't know how, and one by one they slink back into the jungle, green against green, vanishing.

He wants to speak to her. He wants to ask her – what? What, exactly? He must try to articulate what he feels, what he needs. Duncan opens his mouth and takes a step forward.

Hijau moves sideways, into a pocket of space he cannot see, and she too is gone.

Tall Tails

Peter True
United Kingdom

Frank knew Tom would be dining with the devil tonight, but they played *Stairway to Heaven* at his funeral nevertheless.

It had all started three months ago.

The bar was your usual border-world fare: weather-beaten on the outside, people-beaten on the inside. Nothing relieved the tension and frustrations of a marooned colony of grade-three workers better than getting tanked up in a dank room that smelled worse than your own bunk room. Rusting, damp and angry it may have been, but the border-world bar was the sanctuary tired men and women sought after a hard shift breaking rocks and digging holes.

Frank and Tom had worked together as part of the same drilling team since they were assigned to this golfball of a planet two years ago. Golfball was as good a description as any; it was small and covered in craters. So long as you pictured a golfball that had spent ten decades festering in the stinkiest of weed-choked, mud-bottomed, gator-shit-filled water traps on Earth, golfball was just what it resembled.

They weren't best buds. Nether were they staunch enemies. When their paths crossed, they tolerated each other. It wasn't through any personal grievance or history; it sometimes just helped to have that one guy on the crew who just happened to rub you up the wrong way. And if that other person felt the same way about you too... well that was just economical, wasn't it?

The beer they served at the bar was yellow and it had bubbles in it. As for taste? Who gave a shit? The fact is, it had alcohol in it and as long as it had that, the taste could go to hell; as could the colour and the bubbles for that matter.

After a few jars you pretty much had four options: you fight; you tell godawful jokes; you find someone willing to fuck you; or you tell tall tales.

Tom was a fan of telling tall tales. The truth of the tales took a low priority after the violence and the bare-breasted women. Tom could tell a tale so tall you'd get the bends if you followed it too closely.

Frank was more into his fighting. But nine previous warnings and an at-present broken hand meant that his favourite pass-time was off the cards. So, it was begrudgingly that he sat at the only free space left in the bar and settled down to hear one of Tom's comic-book 'true' stories.

'I'm telling ya,' Tom was saying, 'this elephant of a one-armed man was coming at me with his laser pistol pointed straight between my eyes!'

The others at the table had heard this one a hundred times; enough to know that there were at least a hundred different versions. They weren't really paying that much attention and they were willing to let the odd discrepancy and impossibility slip by. However, Frank was new to all this. More so, Frank was in a bad mood because he'd rather be fighting than listening to Tom spouting his mouth off.

'So the beam shot out,' Tom continued, 'bounced off the glass of my goggles, hit the door of the whore-house cubical and burnt his other arm clean off!'

LEAVING

The regulars at the table took the conclusion of the story as an opportunity to get more beers or take a piss. Which left only Frank sitting at the table with Tom.

Tom nodded and gave a wink, as if to proclaim the excellence of his story and acknowledge the forthcoming plaudits.

Frank stared at him.

'You talking outta your ass,' Frank said from between clenched teeth.

That's where it all started to properly get started. Tom called Frank out and Frank eagerly excepted. Only it was pointed out that it wasn't a fair fight, what with Frank's busted hand. This lead to the suggestion Tom should tie an arm behind his back. Which lead to Tom proclaiming he wasn't gonna be no one-armed monkey. To which someone remarked that he'd be just like the one-armed elephant from the story. And well, that was that. Seems as the fight had been called because Frank had accused Tom of making it up and a fight was not forthcoming, Tom decided to hit back by proving his story true.

It was decided that this spectacle had better not take place right away. Pure blind luck had caused the events told of in the tale and no man on this rock had enough luck in their possession to not be on this rock in the first place. So, it would be skill that would have to take luck's place. As such, Tom was given two weeks to practice.

He took the practicing pretty seriously. He even took on a coach, of sorts, in the form of Dead Shot Harry – squirrel hunting champion of Alabama 2067.

When it came to the day of reckoning, Frank had to admit to being impressed by the effort that had gone in. The scene had been recreated down to the finest detail, with the positioning of the thick metal door of crucial importance. A dummy had been employed to take the place of

Tom, complete with the same model of goggles and sat in the same position – doubled up with pants around the ankles.

Confident in his newly honed skills, Tom took aim. Now at this point it must be clarified that, of course, safety precautions had been made. This was a mining colony after all and they lived with danger every day and knew the importance of taking the necessary safety precautions. That they only counted on the demonstration being a success, and so only protected Tom's arm, is succinct testament to the poor survival rates of such mining colonies.

The demonstration was not a success. Either Tom's aim was off or the story had indeed been false and Tom truly had been talking outta his ass. Whatever the reason, the laser beam reflected straight back at Tom, rather than to the door.

His head popped like a boil on a grave-digger's ass.

Still, Frank's hand had mended by the time of the funeral. So afterwards he was looking forward to a good fight. And it was decided amongst the rest of the crew that it was probably safer for everyone that they just let him get on with it.

Bloodletting
Kyle Waters
United States

Shortlisted for the 2019 International Writing Competition

'You can change your life like you can change the blood in your veins boy.' Anton's father shouted in the kitchen down the hall as he threw something.

A 9-year-old Anton sat at his desk and stared down at an open book as he started to cry. He tried to focus enough to read the words, as his father's drunken raging tirade continued.

'The blood of a slave!' he sang out to an impromptu repurposed song tune. 'Your father's a drunk and your mother was a whore.'

Anton cringed at the sound of his father stumbling around the kitchen, knocking down anything in his way. His roughly hobbled together desk supported a small stack of borrowed books.

'Your father, the drunk cripple.' He held the tone as he opened the door to Anton's room. He slurred heavily as he leaned against the door, towering over Anton. 'What are you reading, boy?'

'Nothing,' Anton quietly said, sniffling.

'What was that?' his father asked as he wobbled back and forth, eyes glazed over.

'Nothing' Anton said louder, wiping a tear away from his cheek, refusing to look away from his book.

'You answer me boy!' his disheveled father shouted, drooping against the door frame. 'Are you crying? I didn't cry when your mother left. She left -' he stumbled over his words and paused to collect himself. 'She left 'cause, she knew who we were.'

Anton clenched his teeth at the sound of the word 'mother'. He quietly sat there, trembling as he stared at the book. He knew turning and engaging with his father would escalate just as it always had before.

'Slaves. Both of us,' Anton's father said as he pathetically threw his bottle down. The bottle clanged and rolled across the floor, hitting a small bed of rags lying on the floor.

'You're wasting your time with that book, trust you me, boy. Learn you whatever you want but that blood. My blood,' he angrily snarled, pointing to his chest. 'It's the blood of slaves. You'll always be under the heel of better men. Smarter men. Or worse men, just better off. You'll never be anything. And you'll never change that.' His father spat on the ground and waved to dismiss his son, not being able to get a rise out of him. He turned and continued to coarsely sing an old sailing song as he limped down the hall.

Anton looked at the words on the top of the page. He ran his finger along each letter as he sounded out each word. 'Lo-lo-cus of con-trol, locus of control' He read aloud, nodding his head. Anton was not a fast reader. Most of his education had been a charity from others. This year was the first year he was allowed to sit in the back of the classroom, with the agreement he help the teacher clean chalkboards and other menial tasks.

LEAVING

Anton squinted harder at the book. He looked up to his window to see the sun had already set, taking with it Anton's reading light. Even if he wasn't done for the evening, that would have to be a stopping point. Discouraged, he crossed arms and rested his head, as he stared out at the waterways below his third-floor apartment that was filled with other degenerates and poor of a similar caliber. Through his cold frosted window, he could see the eerily black water that ran along the canal, snaking its way through the city. Behind the canal, the dock's wooden cranes, frayed ropes, and rundown buildings incongruously jutted into the overcast grey sky. Anton much preferred the sun to the overcast but lately, he had learned to love the somber sky. It was easier to think under, somehow colder and less intrusive to him. A rock for him to hide under.

He watched until he could see the faint shimmer of the moon through the cloud cover. Most of Anton's time not reading was spent just watching the canal. The slow pace of the gently moving steam ships that puffed along calmed him most days. If nothing else, it was at least something to watch, as he spent most of his time alone in his room. He wondered if the moon would shine bright enough to light his book, but it was cold and late, and he had to be up early for his chores at the schoolhouse if he wanted to be able to sit in on the class. Anton sighed and closed his book, patting it on the cover to reassure the book that he had not fully given up on him. His father had really bothered him that evening. Worse than most nights. He curled up on his scavenged bed and pulled an old shabby blanket over him.

Anton rolled back and forth as he tried to sleep in the cold that seemed to seep in through every rip and tear in his poorly stitched blanket. The more he tried to keep still, the colder his extremities got. His father's song bounced around Anton's mind as he huddled for warmth. As he held his arm, he felt the vein that pulsated beneath his goose bump covered skin. Lying there for what seemed an eternity, he decided that if he wasn't going to sleep, he might as well be productive and read.

He looked for a candle that he had hidden from his father under a loose floor board. It was Anton's hiding place for his most prized possessions: a mostly unused candle, a locket, a sewing needle, and couple of coins. Anton slowly opened the door as he looked down the hallway at the warm soft glow of the embers in the woodstove still smoldering in the kitchen. He had not heard from his father in some time. Rubbing his arms for warmth, Anton tried to quiet the chattering of his teeth. The worn, wooden floor boards creaked under his bare feet as he gently made his way down the hall, running his fingers along the wall to try to feel his way through the dark.

Reaching the kitchen, Anton opened the small hatch in the front of the stove to the cindering remains of a fire and lit his candle. The hot metal stove radiated as Anton held his hands over the top of it. He thought about how nice it would be to sleep curled up in the corner next to it, but his room was the only safe place in the apartment to sleep, if you could even call it safe. The kitchen was bare. A table and a chair a neighbor had thrown away. A counter made from scraps, just as Anton's desk was. A wood stove that the previous occupants had left, not wanting to carry the hulking mass of pot metal down the stairs.

Turning to go back to his room, Anton was startled to see his father, now illuminated by the candle, sprawled on the floor next to the kitchen table and an overturned chair. He looked down at his father passed out in a puddle of liquor, bile, and small bits of bread. Anton suddenly froze as the giant sleeping beast inhaled abruptly. Anton held his breath as he refused to make the smallest of sounds. His father's back slowly drifted down as he exhaled. Anton's eyes darted back and forth, and he plotted an escape route back to his room. He slowly backed away from his fa-

LEAVING

ther and back down the hall as the candle light flickered over his father's body, until it was out of sight.

Slipping through the doorway, Anton wished he hadn't warmed himself, as his room now felt twice as cold. He smiled at the successful mission he had embarked on and closed the door behind him. He scooped up his tattered blanket and wrapped himself in it as he sat on his wobbly, uneven chair, and folded his legs underneath him. He leaned up on his desk over his book, clutching the candle closely. Between the cold and the sudden burst of fear, he was energized to get back to reading. Under the dim candlelight, he slowly got back to using his free hand to run across the words.

Anton struggled his way through the sentences then paused to digest what the words truly meant. He continued on, pausing to take in the words after sounding them all out. Back and forth until he slowly got into a rhythm. Anton loved books. The ideas that felt like forbidden knowledge to him. Things that had been just out of reach for his entire life until just a few months ago. He worked hard to convince people to lend him books, bartering his labor in exchange for the privilege to borrow a book to read. Anton always gave them his word on when he would return the book, and Anton always kept his word. He borrowed from his neighbors and people he met. Most people just lent him whatever book they had lying around, and most of the loaned books were far out of his skill level. Out of his level or not, he was determined to extract whatever they held.

Anton sat back as he tried to piece together the last sentence with the others he chewed off into a comprehensible, cohesive paragraph.

'The locus of control. The degree to which people believe that they have control over the outcome of events in their lives, as opposed to external forces beyond their control. It is far better to believe yourself a hard worker, than naturally gifted. Motivation blossoms from the events you have the ability to affect change in. Strive to see all events, situations, or challenges within your grasp. Shift the burden of responsibility to your shoulders rather than the cruel fates.'

He sat in his chair and thought about what the words meant. Anton quickly sat up as an idea struck him. Going back to his loose floor board, he dug around to find his mother's sewing needle that was hidden down there. 'Strive to see all events, situations, or challenges within your grasp.' He said as he looked down. He held out his finger and pricked it with the needle, squeezing the wound to draw a single drop of blood. Anton tasted the drop, as he made a note that this is what the blood of a slave tastes like, as he looked around his room. Anton promised himself that he would bleed the slave out of him. Drop by drop. Every day.

'I am not smart. I am a hard worker. I am not lucky. I am a hard worker.' He recited to himself as he squeezed both of his fists in the air, clutching his new life philosophy.

Anton worked and read until the sun started to come up. Extinguishing his candle, he set it back in its hiding place. He looked at the sewing needle, and thought about putting it in the hiding place, before threading it through his shirt to keep it with him. Anton picked up his slate and chalk. He was especially proud of finding his slab of slate. Not many people throw away a perfectly good school slate when they are done with it. He snuck past his still asleep father and set off to the school house.

He walked through the city on his usual route, looking at all the familiar sights, sounds, and smells, just happy to breathe the air outside of the apartment, that smelled as bad as the canal tasted. People gave him odd looks or ignored him as he walked down the foggy cobblestone streets, avoiding small pebbles to keep them out of the large hole in the bottom of his shoe. He got to the school house and began his chores. He picked up the rags from the front of the room, under the chalkboard, and took them outside to shake them out. He went about happily cleaning as he looked at the school desks and imagined himself in one, one day, just as the other students began to file in.

Anton quickly took a seat at the back of the room on a bench. The other students quieted down as the teacher came in to begin the morning routine of looking over the students' work from the past assignment. Sitting quietly at the back of the room, Anton watched the teacher float from student to student. Happy to be there, he sat more upright than the rest of the class, despite how tired he was, with a cheerful smile. The teacher walked around the room correcting students, as Anton carefully listened, before the teacher returned to the main chalkboard and taught the day's lesson.

When lunch break came, Anton decided to put his new philosophy to work. Instead of playing like he normally would, he would take the time to work on the assignment, even if it wasn't meant for him. He sat at lunch, looking down at his chalk and slate trying to piece together what the questions were from memory. As he scribbled away on the fringes of the school yard, a group of boys approached, and stood over him.

'What are you doing? Just go and play. Why do you even take lunch? You never have one,' one of the boys said.

'You're just going to end up a drunk cripple, like your father,' another said.

'Speaking of fathers, my father put a coin in your father's cup yesterday,' the boy said, cruelly sneering. 'So, I thought I'd do the same.' The boy threw the remnant scraps of his lunch, which hit Anton in the face, then fell to the ground.

Anton sat his slate next to him and looked down at the food with an immense shame. Not for his father, but because of just how hungry he truly was. The other boys stared intently with bated breath at the sight of Anton reaching down and picking it off the ground. Anton closed his eyes and took a bite out of a half-eaten sandwich, as a tear ran down his cheek. The boys laughed, throwing up their arms in amazement at the deranged behavior of the poor, drunk cripple's son. As they ran off to tell the rest of the children what happened, Anton sat there humiliated, slowly finishing the rest of the scraps, and held back the rest of his tears.

'I am not smart. I am a hard worker. I am not lucky. I am a hard worker.' Anton recited it over and over again in his head. He took out the needle he had pinned to his shirt and pricked his finger, tasting the blood with the food. 'This is what the blood of a slave tastes like,' he said to himself as he looked around. He finished the food and got back to trying to figure out what the assignment was. He worked until lunch was over and waited for the rest of the kids to take their place before he finally did.

Anton sat lower, coming back from lunch, as the other children occasionally looked back at him and sneered. He listened to every murmur and word from the teacher but kept his eye contact with his slate as he tried to take notes. After the class was dismissed for the day, Anton approached the teacher, at his desk, slate in hand. Even while sitting, his stern, wiry teacher still lorded over him.

'What is this?' The teacher said, taken off guard as Anton handed him the slate. 'Oh, no Anton, you don't have to do the assignments.'

'It would really help me if I could,' Anton said.

Annoyed, the teacher looked down his nose at Anton and took the slate from him. 'No. Wrong. No.' he said as he marked the slate with chalk. He handed the slate back to Anton. 'I doubt it could possibly help you that much. Just focus on your chores, Anton,' the teacher said, turning back to his desk.

'With all due respect sir, do you mind if I continue to do them?' Anton asked.

'Fine, but maybe next time put in effort?' The teacher said.

'Yes sir,' Anton said, as he excitedly nodded. He took his slate and looked over the confusing marks.

Anton dreaded returning home, but had nowhere else to be; however, when he opened the door to the kitchen, he found the apartment was empty. It wasn't uncommon as his father was probably out begging for money or in a pub, if he had actually received any charity. Anton looked around the empty kitchen, at the vomit that was still on the floor. He got a pail full of water from the canal and a rag and cleaned up the mess. He used the quiet of his father's absence to study the marks his teacher gave him. He sat at his desk frustrated he could not comprehend what he was supposed to do. He looked at the stack of books and thought about giving up and reading for fun.

'I am not smart. I am a hard worker. I am not lucky. I am a hard worker,' Anton said, as he stared at the slate.

Two years passed.

Anton had gone from trying to keep up, to thriving in school. He took pride in the chores that allowed him to be there. The children largely ignored him, as the teacher did not want any of them disrupting his source of labor. Every night, he sat in his room and studied, then pricked his finger, tasting the blood, before reading until bed.

One day, Anton walked along the city street on his way home from school until he came up to a crowd outside of his building. His father was always making a drunken spectacle of himself on the street. Crowds weren't unusual. However, this was not the usual crowd of rowdy by-passers gathered around his father to mock him, but rather a somber crowd quietly whispering. Anton pushed his way to the front and saw his father slumped over against a wall, vomit on his shirt and around his blue lips.

Anton's lip trembled and he slowly backed out of the crowd and ran up the stairs to the apartment, clutching his slate close to his chest. He opened the door and looked down at the chalk dust on his shirt to see he had erased all of his notes from that day. He threw down his slate on the kitchen table in anger. The slate landed on its corner and shattered in half. Anton dropped to the floor devastated in a ball and rocked back, hands grabbing his hair, spitting while talking to himself. 'No. No. No.' He sobbed as he rocked alone in the world.

As an orphan, he would have to quit school, most likely ending up in an orphanage or other home for wayward children. Anton bit his lip as the slow creep of fate took control out of his hands and placed him back into cast lots. His mind panicked as he ran through scenarios to take back control. Maybe he could get adopted. Maybe he could live at the school.

Anton pulled at his hair as he wrestled to bring his adrift life back to the shore. He took out the needle and pricked his finger. 'This is what the blood of a slave tastes like,' he angrily grumbled as he put the drop of blood to his lip. There was a knock at the door. Anton opened it and looked up at the apartment's landlord.

'I saw your father, Anton. I am going to sell his body to cover some of the unpaid rent,' the portly landlord said, looking into the room to see what else of any value was in there. 'You need to leave,' he said, looking down at him.

'Please let me cover the debt. I will get a job. I will pay you. I know my father owed you money, and I will pay you all of it and take up the rent if you just let me stay here,' Anton pleaded with him. 'I don't care about my father's body. Just. Please -' he begged as he frantically thought how to put the situation into something he could change.

'The books!' Anton exclaimed as his eyes lit up. 'I have never kept a book from you longer than I said I would! Not a day late sir! Ask any of the people I have borrowed from. Let me get you the money.'

'Do you have a job?' The landlord said as he stroked his beard and appraised the offer, still looking around the room.

'I don't sir. But I can get one,' Anton said.

The landlord nodded quietly. 'I might know of a job for you, but I warn you,' the landlord bent down to Anton's eye level. 'It ain't easy work.'

'I'm a hard worker.' Anton said with a look of determination.

The landlord gave a toothy smile as he took Anton by the hand and led him down the street and to a factory. The landlord had not exaggerated; the job worked Anton down to the bone.

'I am not smart. I am a hard worker. I am not lucky. I am a hard worker,' Anton recited to himself the entire shift. Arriving back at the apartment, he lit a fire in the stove and curled up in a ball next to the fire. Now free to sleep next to the warmth, Anton hadn't been that happy for a long time. He smiled and looked at his room from down the hallway. It was small, but it felt like progress.

It took Anton years to repay the debt, but he kept his word, and after all those years of reading, Anton knew what he wanted to be. He skipped meals and looked for loose change until he saved up enough to buy a typewriter, now in his late 20's. He didn't have much money, but he had found a rhythm to his life. Every day, he worked his shift at the factory, before heading home, pricking his finger to see if he still had the blood of a slave, and writing.

In his stories, he traveled the world and helped children across the seas, in his imagination. He was a friend to all the people who were just as lonely as he was. He did all the things he wanted to do. He told all the stories he had wished someone had told him. When he didn't have enough money for paper or ink, he sat and thought about his stories, watching the canal. Anton finally found himself on the other side of the books he had cherished.

Anton also found himself struggling with the arduous task of writing. Reading was easy, but finding his own voice was difficult. He kept telling himself that if he could just write another page, if he could just finish another chapter, if he could just cross the finish line, it would all be worth it. Slowly, as he began to slow down under the immense weight of the task he faced, the negative thoughts seeped into his mind.

'Who would want to read your stories?' his father's voice taunted him as Anton read over what he had written that evening. 'It was so much better in your head,' the voice taunted. 'That isn't how you saw it.'

'I am not smart. I am a hard worker. I am not lucky. I am a hard worker,' he said, pressing his hands into his head.

Anton worked for months until he finished his book. He felt like a man who crawled along his stomach up a mountain, but he had done it. He had to bribe several people to publish and print his book, but it was published. He even had gotten a local book critic to write a review of it in the newspaper. He raced to the newspaper stands every day after his shift to see if the review was out. Finally, the day came as he excitedly bought the paper and set off back to his apartment. The entire trip home, he refused to look down at his hand, just in case he might see a single word and spoil something. His smile beamed as he briskly walked along the streets, apologizing to people he accidentally bumped into as he day dreamed what the review held. Arriving home, he sat down in front of the typewriter, and lit a lamp to read the review. He looked through the paper to find the title to his story.

'The plot makes no sense,' he read out to himself. The smile washed from Anton's face. He neatly folded the paper and gently set it down.

LEAVING

He took out his needle and pricked his finger. 'This is what the blood of a slave tastes like,' he said to himself as he looked at the newspaper. Callouses had started to develop from him pricking his finger so much. Something on the keys of the typewriter caught Anton's eye, as he leaned forward to inspect them. He wiped one of the keys with his finger and noticed the flecks of dried blood from all those previous evenings. Anton smiled as he stood up and tossed the newspaper into the slot of the wood fire stove. He sighed as he sat back down and stared at the typewriter.

'I am not smart. I am a hard worker. I am not lucky. I am a hard worker,' he said as he racked the next piece of paper and began his next story.

Each new story faced the same struggle. Upon the publication, critics would laugh at him. They talked down about how some borderline illiterate nobody kept paying his way into publication. But Anton refused to stop. If they despised his story, Anton would learn from his mistakes and write another one. He was so close. In his mind, he etched every single word the critics said about his work, hoping to learn as much as he could. He was so close he could taste it as he furiously wrote every evening. The crushingly tedious work was always offset by the enormous high and hope that came from finishing something, only to be let down by the cycle he found himself stuck in.

Anton wrote a story, and the critics mocked him. Anton wrote another story, and the critics hated it. Anton wrote another story, and the critics lambasted his grammar. Anton wrote another story, and the critics jeered at his prose. Anton wrote another story, until one day, the critics genuinely enjoyed it. Anton wrote another story, and the critics recommended it. Anton wrote another story, until someone loved his work. Anton wrote, until his fans cherished his words. And Anton wrote, until his fans wrote him back. It had taken Anton a lifetime, but he had finally done it.

After the countless years of battle, an old, withered, grey-haired Anton, now in his 80's sat in a beautiful robe, in a nice house, far out of the city he grew up in. He began his morning by looking down at a pile of letters that his wife had placed on his desk for him. He grinned from ear to ear, thinking about how long it would have taken him to read the letters when he first started to read, or how such a sight was only a fantasy all those years ago. He ran his hand along the sleeve of his robe to feel the softness of it as he thought of his tattered blanket.

He opened a letter, with his calloused finger, and read the writer's praise and questions. Leaning back in his comfortable chair, he took a moment to think about how to answer the writer's questions. His hand trembled from age as he took out a needle from his ornate lavish wooden desk drawer. He pricked his finger and tasted the small drop of blood.

'I don't think I have a drop of slave left in me.' Anton smiled at the sweet taste, while looking around, thinking that this is what the blood of a human being tastes like. Taking out a piece of paper, Anton began the first of many response letters.

> Dear David,
>
> Thank you for writing. Your letter means the world to me. Although I don't have a one-step solution to improving, rather, I would tell you just tid-bits of knowledge. Bricks in the foundation of my mind I have collected over the years that have helped me when I felt hopeless or when I felt like giving up; just as everyone does. You're not alone. Improving is day by day, Word by word, drop by drop, until your blood is replaced by the blood of a human being.
>
> You must become an expert at leaving. Leave the past be-

LEAVING

hind until you look in the mirror and don't recognize the person staring back. Leave your feelings at the door when learning from harsh criticism. Leave the preconceived notions about yourself in the past. Leave the things you don't like about yourself behind as you move forward.

Don't rely on being smart or lucky, instead, be a hard worker. You must write until your words become books, until your books become better. Love yourself and put out those horrid voices you hear in the back of your mind. Learn that it is okay to fail, because you will. Don't give up.

And most of all, always remember that nothing is truly out of your control.

Sincerely yours,

Anton.

'Write about this man who, drop by drop, squeezes the slave's blood out of himself until he wakes one day to find the blood of a real human being – not a slave's – coursing through his veins.' - Anton Chekov

Max Mustermann

Lara Weddige
Germany

Editor's Choice

H E JUST KNEW IT; FOR SURE HE WOULD get in trouble now. On the platform, the hand on the clock ticked forward one notch to 18:07. He had been dreaming and lost his train ticket. Again.

Max turned in a circle on the spot and scanned the floor. No sign of the thin beige strip of paper. *Dang it.* He wondered if he could hide in the bathroom this time or if he should try his luck with the conductor, explain that he had bought a ticket, truly, but had lost it, and could not afford another. He scoffed. *As if they would believe me.*

He wanted to sit in a seat and take the train. He had workbooks full of exercises in want of answers, but it was hard to concentrate, sitting on a toilet in a rickety train, with people intermittently knocking, pounding, yanking on the door. *At least I was on time leaving class and will get the train today.*

He checked his pants pockets, front and back, in his jacket pockets, all three outside and the one on the inside for the satiny lining as well, even though he never put anything there. He glanced up at the clock again. The hands didn't seem to be moving. Only 18:10. He had some time.

There were only three people on this end of the platform with him. He crouched and upended his pack on the stained concrete floor. When his bag was empty he started fishing through his things, refolding a page here, untangling headphones, clamping a pen on a notebook, placing item after item back in his bag, until there was nothing left on the pavement but the confirmation his ticket was gone, nothing but the knowledge he would now have to choose between hiding in the toilet or trying his luck against incurring a fine. He had been here eight months already but converting from the Euro still gave him trouble. Not that it mattered, having no money was the same in every currency.

18:15. Another 15 minutes still. Where the roof above the platform ended, the rain was gaining strength, and probably would for another hour, before the storm abated and the latent heat of the evening simmered on.

'Unfortunately, and contrary to what you may be told by politicians, up there, far away from everything, from the reality on the ground, the net effect of this migration we are experiencing, these waves and masses of migrants, these hordes of immigrants, has *not* been positive. I repeat: Has. Not. Been. Positive. And let me be clear, I am, totally, a humanitarian. But these swarms, these droves...'

Max sighed at the screen. The talking faces changed, but the words out of their mouths, the glint in their eyes, were the same. Everything was terrible, everyone was about to die, everywhere was about to be a disaster zone after the next attack. And it was always their fault. His fault.

Up and down the platform the face was repeated on each of the concrete columns supporting the roof. He watched some of the other passengers glance at him with feigned disinterest, their eyes dodging his. Some time ago he would have averted his eyes, cast down his gaze to not call attention to himself, but when the talking screens were spewing such nonsense, he had to hold something against that. He straightened his back, pushed together his shoulder blades, and held his head proud.

Today's news bulletin featured the usual, more of the same, today's particular complaint being that all illegal immigrants were selling drugs and left their trash strewn about.

Max had to smirk despite himself. *If I told any of my old friends I was being called a criminal, a thief, a dealer they would laugh.* But there was no one left to laugh with him, not anyone he had known before getting to here anyways.

18:19 and the news bulletin was still on about the crisis. Sometimes the segments felt unbearably long. As the unrelenting seconds ticked on, more and more people flicked their eyes over towards him. Try as he might, he was not about to be black. Twice now, old ladies had patted him on the head and told him to spend more time outside in the sun doing God's honest work, and he would become nice and dark like them. He had not, though redness eventually took the place of paste.

At least he wasn't having his hair *pulled*. It only had to happen twice until Charlotte had wanted to cover up. Max was referred to as an unbeliever, but he wasn't being spat on or treated rudely because he was 'uncovered'. He could never pass as local anyway, and he hoped never to reach the level of self-denial necessary to convince himself of this. He would always look different. He knew.

18:20. The news had shifted away from the refugee situation – finally. But only so much. Now they were interviewing people on the street.

'They are harassing us,' a tall man said, diagonally facing the camera. 'We must fear them. It is for our own protection!'

LEAVING

The montage cut away from his face to show a younger woman with strong eyeliner. 'All the locals, they know this can't go well. They don't speak our language, and their English is so accented it is hard for us to understand! They sound like they have trouble breathing.'

He heard worse all the time. At least sometimes the put downs had some originality to them. Except of course he was about to confirm one of their stereotypes in the train. Max shivered. He hated this.

18:26. As if he would ever want to live here; for once everyone was agreed. He didn't want to be here, and they didn't want him here. But, what options did he have? He willed his pounding heart to calm, counting slowly. He was going to hide in the toilet on the train. He didn't want to be caught without a ticket, not today.

◆

Max sat on the floor of the room he was sharing, staring ahead at the wall. Behind him the door opened.

'What?' he snapped. *Now is not the time.*

'What?' an unfamiliar voice responded, surprised. Max turned around, somewhat taken aback. He had been expecting the director of the home.

'Hi, hello.' *Fuck, that first impression was bad. He had told himself he was over this. Model behaviour, model citizen, role model, I promised myself.* He unfolded his legs and pushed himself up. 'I'm Max,' he offered, adding: 'Mustermann,' and extending his hand.

'Emmanuel,' the other replied. 'The director sent me to talk to you. He felt you were in need of some guidance.' Emmanuel grinned at him.

Max glanced at him, slight skepticism not entirely hideable from his eyes. 'Ok...' he began slowly. 'So does that mean I am in trouble again? Will I be able to stay here?'

Emmanuel smiled again. 'Yes, and yes. I think you should be a bit more considerate of the rules, but yes.'

'I had a ticket, I just lost it!' Max disagreed immediately. 'It-won't-happen-again-I-know-what-I- did-was-wrong-I'm-sorry,' he added. *Cool it.*

'I believe you,' the words spoken a touch slowly, 'but not everyone does.' His eyes were not unkind, and now that Max had a closer look, they seemed to be close in age.

'Makes sense, of course, that you wouldn't believe me. Seeing as how according to everyone here I'm an 'unbeliever', don't support the 'same values' as you, am dangerous because 'what if our children see his behaviour and turn away from their believing ways?' and the worst thing for anyone of you would be to be like me. Does that about sum it up?' He gave a sideways glance to Emmanuel. *Why am I unloading on this guy? He doesn't deserve this and I sure as shit am not helping my cause. God-damn.* He sighed and hung his head lightly.

Emmanuel had a shrewd look on his face. 'And I'm sure you want to build churches and impose biblical law. Did you know people here say your countries were sinful, which is why they have been punished by God, so now they look like the 'third world' you accused us of wanting to escape?' Max stared blankly at him. Emmanuel started to laugh and slapped him genially on the back. His sunburn ached only slightly.

'Right, right,' he laughed. *Fucking lucky break.* Max looked straight at Emmanuel for the first time and found him staring straight back. 'I don't want to convert anyone or be converted, I just want to blend in, to be like everyone else here.'

Emmanuel had to laugh again. 'You mean black?' Max grinned. *If only he knew how many times I've had this thought since arriving.*

'I can lie out in the sun as long as I want, maybe one day I will stop burning and will get a tan. But all my best efforts, and I still won't be black. I've thought about dying my hair and brown contacts, but all of that only takes me so far.' He shrugged.

'There will always be idiots out there,' Emmanuel offered. Max nodded. 'It's about proving them wrong. It's about showing them we are all only human.'

'I want to do that,' Max said.

'Of course you do, I get that. Who doesn't?'

'Right…' Max stared off into the distance, thinking about home, what was left of it. 'We used to think you guys didn't.' Max looked at Emmanuel for a second, then hushed his eyes away in shame. 'I mean – I don't mean you, I mean – you probably never wanted to leave here. I mean, when people used to want to come, to Europe, to come there, we didn't want to take them.' He pressed the tips of his shoes together, moved them apart, stepped his heels together, back apart. 'I'm sorry,' he said in a small voice. Emmanuel laughed again.

'As if that was you. Do you make the rules?' Max looked up at him. 'No, of course you don't. The same way I don't make the rules here. Maybe both of our countries would be better off if we ran them. But do we? No.'

'No, we don't.'

'Right. I didn't get a say, really, nor did you. Maybe that is part of the reason there is a problem. And now you are here, and now I am here. Do you want to play some basketball now and next time you will pay more attention and not lose your ticket?'

◆

'So let's say you move to China.' Max threw a pass to Emmanuel, who chucked the ball up towards the basket.

'Yeah?'

'Do you learn Chinese?'

'It's a hard language. It's so different from English and what I speak.'

'Right, but do you learn Chinese?'

'Depends.' Emmanuel bounced the ball without thought.

'On what?'

'On how long I will stay.'

'Right.' Max held out his hands for a pass. 'If you plan to stay, it makes sense to learn. If not, why bother?'

'Is that why you have made no efforts?' Emmanuel gave him a hard look.

'What?'

'Why you've made no efforts. To integrate more here.'

'*What?*' This time with incredulity. *Is this guy for real right now?*

'You don't know anyone from here, you don't know much about our culture, you don't know our history...do you want me to go on?'

'What? Are you serious right now? I've been trying to understand the basics and you want me to sit with a history book?' Max looked at Emmanuel with wild eyes. 'For real? And anyway, I know you, I know others. But mostly, I know the people here, in this home. You. know. that.' He paused, his flare up of anger momentarily dissipating. 'And plus, I don't want to stay.' He shot the ball and airballed. 'Fuck.' Emmanuel scoffed and grabbed the ball.

'So you want to leave, huh? Is that how it is?' Emmanuel stepped back for an arching shot.

'Of course, I'm not from here, I don't belong here. I would love to go back home. There just is not a whole lot of Europe to go back to.' Max ran towards the basket. 'I'm not wanted here – I'm not stupid, I can tell. If I could go back I would. If there was somewhere to go back to I would.

I guess I just don't know where else to go.'

'I'm sure there's something. Go rebuild.' Emmanuel scowled at Max with poorly hidden indignation.

'Like you wouldn't want to go back?'

'Of course! This is my home; this is where I belong!'

'Exactly.' Max sighed. 'If you thought you were going to go back, going to not stay, how much would you integrate?' He raised his eyebrows at Emmanuel as he angrily drove towards the basket. 'Plus, you guys won't let me integrate, this shit goes both ways.'

'What?' Now it was Emmanuel's turn to look incredulous. 'We have accepted you, have taken so many of you *poor Europeans*. Other countries want nothing to do with you, they have no white people, so you would be treated badly, and don't want that either. And now you tell me we don't want you to integrate?'

'As if everyone here was agreed you should take refugees.' Max sighed. He had talked about this back at home, when others had come, and it was somewhere to live and build a future.

'But we did. What do you want?'

'No – no, no you didn't.' Max shot the ball. 'Someone in your government took pity on us. Said we deserved to go somewhere. So now we are here. We both know –' he drew a deep breath to calm himself, 'we both know there are many people here who would have nothing rather than for us to leave.' He steadied his breath some more before continuing 'And for us to integrate, well, you need to spend time with me so I can learn from you. And no one but you is doing that. So how am I supposed to learn? How is Charlotte going to learn? What about my parents?'

Emmanuel retrieved the ball, dribbled it slowly. 'Your parents, well, I don't know. And they are older too – it is harder. You, all of you, can try harder to learn the language. Charlotte will be fine, she has lots of friends.' He set his feet to take his shot.

'Yea, it's easier for us I guess.' Max panted, after running after the ball. 'Thanks, by the way,' he added meekly after another shot bounced off the rim.

'Sure,' Emmanuel said. 'You know my parents are against me helping out, right?'

◆

Charlotte came in, removed her shoes, and flung her shawl on the cot. 'I understand,' she vented at Max, who followed her, stepping on the back of his shoes to fling them off his feet. 'Your feet stink,' she added, making a face and plopping down.

'You stink.'

'Wow. Original.'

'Ugh, fuck off.' Max was in no mood. 'You almost got us in real trouble this time! You need to learn to shut your mouth sometimes.'

'Anyway...' Charlotte started again; she was not done with their conversation from before. Max fixed her with an unwavering stare.

'Really? You want to keep going with this?'

'Yes, yes I do, of course! Don't you? This is mental!' Charlotte finger-combed her hair and glared back.

'How many times, Charlotte? How many times?'

'I can't not speak my mind! If that offends you, fine! Be *so* offended. *So fucking* offended. But argue with me! Have a better argument! If you don't – well, that's your problem.' *She wants to provoke me. The problem is she's right.* But that didn't matter here.

'We've been over this. You can't go around being rude to people.' Max sat on the floor and dumped out his bag, a lump of sweaty clothes, his phone, some notebooks.

'They deserve it,' she huffed. 'And actually, I'm not being rude, I'm being honest,' she corrected. Charlotte crossed her legs and started braiding her hair.

'Charlotte...' *We've talked about this so many times.* 'I'm scared you're going to get hurt one of these days.' He sighed. 'Call it what you want to call it, but you need to be a little more considerate of people.'

'Political correctness.' She scoffed. 'We've had this so many times, it's useless. Anger gets pent up, like here–' she pointed emphatically at herself, 'and the same goes for everyone else too. They should speak their mind, however rude they are to me, get it all out. Better out than in, right?' She raised her eyebrows at him, ready for his retort. 'If they keep their bigotry bottled up, their racism against us isn't going to go away, it's going to be hidden.'

'Well... I know what you mean,' He rubbed his eyes with his fists and blew air out his nostrils. 'You've always been like this, I know, but not everyone knows. And any stranger you meet in the street is not immediately going to know where you're coming from, you know?' Unimpressed, Charlotte kept staring at him. 'Political correctness ...it's hard ...you need it in measures, but censorship–'

'Censorship is bullshit!' Charlotte interrupted. 'I should be able to say what I want, when I want. This is ludicrous.'

'You need to be *respectful*,' Max pleaded.

'Yes, respectful.' Charlotte's face indicated she agreed not in the slightest. 'If someone wants to tell me I am a drain on their stupid country, they should be able to. Say it to my face. Come at me, I can take it. You want to tell me your country is spending too much on new arrivals? Cool, tell me, no need to say anything else, say what you think. But own it. Have facts to back you up. No need to lie.'

'It's about more than that...' Max sighed. *This is pointless. We're go-*

ing around in circles. *And anyway, there are no answers.*

'You can't hide from ideas you don't like,' Charlotte said flatly. She had finished one braid and was moving on to the second. 'If people can't say what they want openly, that doesn't mean they won't think it. They'll whisper it when they think people agree. And pester me when they think they can get away with it. I'd rather have unpleasant ideas thrown at my face than someone pull my hair or spit at me. But. That's. Just. Me.' She yanked her hair hard and made a face.

Oh Charlotte.

'And you know,' she began again, 'what about the people like expats, who have been here their whole life, but are now being lumped in with us? They aren't new arrivals, but are being treated same as us.'

'I don't know.' He shook his head. *No one will wear you down in an argument like Charlotte.* 'Your braids look nice.' She made a face at him.

◆

'So what do you think we should do?'

'When? You mean now?' Emmanuel asked, barely looking up from his workbook.

'No, in general.' Max had stopped focusing on his maths and was demolishing the eraser end of his pencil.

'Burn all passports.' Emmanuel replied offhandedly, still focused on his assignment.

'The eruption helped us out a bit there.' Max hated thinking about all the people who had been unable to leave in time. All those whom he had left behind, who they had left behind.

'But there are still so many people who have them.' Emmanuel kept writing in his notebook.

'And still so many people without them.'

'True.' He scribbled out a number.

'We would also need to get all the information stored about people's nationalities deleted from servers.' Max went on. *Is daydreaming out loud like this even allowed?*

'And coordinate it so it's all at the same time.' Emmanuel sat up and turned to face Max.

'I think we should go all out – we don't target one country; we threaten the *idea* of the country. Get enough people on board so we destroy every border checkpoint. All at the same time.'

'You're angry today.' Emmanuel shook his head at Max with an amused look.

'No, not today. Every day. At everything. At the fact we can't go where we want. I thought this was all one planet. Who thought they had the authority to draw a line in the sand and say 'ok, so over there is something else, and over here is mine now, stay out'?'

'Someone who thought they had a mandate from God.' Emmanuel's amusement had faded to a bemused concern. 'Have you learned nothing in your history classes?'

'No, we did. I understand the people created chaos, I get all that. I'm confused why and how we have let this continue. Shouldn't we be past this by now?'

'Sure, but we always want more – more for us, less for them. Because we are scared 'they' might be screwing us over, taking more than us, getting more than us.'

'Sure.' Sometimes the things they talked about scared him, most of the time they made him angry. Max turned for a moment back to his workbook, trying to figure out where he had left off.

'So – as I was saying...' Emmanuel paused for a moment, trying to recall. 'People want to protect what is theirs, it's the same everywhere.'

He looked off to the side for a split second. 'Of course. And you used to wonder why things didn't work here, that's why, plain and simple.'

There was a long pause after this.

'People – everyone – voting along tribal lines. We are not past this!' *Same shit, different toilet. The problems are all variations on a theme.*

'Can we just burn our passports, please?'

◆

'I see the question being whether or not you, or the leaders of your nation, place any value on the humans who are non-citizens when this incurs some disadvantages for the humans who are citizens of your nation. However you answer *that* question to me is the hallmark of what makes you as a person – how you see life that does not pertain to your tribe, of your blood, yet lives, breathes, sees, smells, touches, feels, dreams the same as you. Could these others be different in their customs, yet similar in our shared humanity? Is that so hard to imagine?' His face was flushed red and his voice rising with every word. 'How – how can it be so hard to imagine? How do you not think of this?' His mouth was still moving but he was producing no sound. The frustration was at a boiling point, too heated for words.

He turned and walked towards his bedroom, the door closed behind him. After some minutes he emerged in the living room of the family house for the last time. 'I'm going to go for a while now. Max is coming, too. I don't know if I can come back.'

'Where are you going? When will you come back?' his mother demanded. Her hands were on her hips, concern written on her face.

'Somewhere we think we can be more at peace.'

'But where? And why are you going with Max of all people?' she implored.

'Exactly. Because why not? Because why do you think we all have to be so different?!'

'But why, Emmanuel?' she plead. 'And you know better than to use such language under this roof.' She stood up and took a step towards him. 'Stay here. Why do you want to go? You have nothing there, anywhere else.' There were tears in her eyes, but her expression was one of fury.

'I need to go.' He readjusted the strap of his bag on his shoulder, edging the pack between himself and his mother.

'Don't do this,' Esther whispered. Emmanuel looked at the floor, then at his father staring hard, from his chair by the wall. He passed one last look over his son and his wife in the living room, scraped his chair along the floor as he pushed off, got up, and left. They could hear a ferocious kick take down the bedroom door.

Esther burst out in tears, reached over his pack, and pressed him in a tight embrace. He didn't know what to make of her expression when she released him. As he was walking towards the door, he could hear Esther repeating the word 'why' between heaves of sobbing.

◆

Max had packed the few things he held dear in minutes and sat on the edge of his bed contemplating his bag with his head in his hands. Emmanuel was rifling through some stray papers in a vague effort at helping.

'What will we tell Charlotte?' Max asked, breaking the silence.

'That we left for greener pastures and for peace. For somewhere we can both be foreigners, where everyone is foreign, where we can share in the peace.'

'I don't want to concede. To admit– to say we gave up.' He didn't know what came now.

'Well...' Emmanuel began, stockingly, 'sometimes, when a situation becomes this toxic, maybe, this is the way forward. It may look like we gave up, that we can't stand it here anymore... but, this is true.' He looked up, but Max did not respond, so he went on. 'We are going somewhere else to build a better future, so people have somewhere to go.'

'There has to be somewhere we can go...' Max sat up straight. 'I remember... on the way here, there were people going part of the way with us, talking about some place in Portugal, saying it was good there, that there were some towns and people there, ruins, but still.' He paused, excited by his memory. 'I don't think anyone believed him, or cared about what he was saying, since he wasn't coming here like everyone else. But he was talking about finding somewhere to stay there. Let's go there!'

'It's as good a plan as just about anything else we are going to come up with,' Emmanuel shrugged. The gravity of the situation, of the unknown they were about to travel into, was only starting to hit him; his departure from his family had yet to sink in properly in any way. 'Ready when you are.'

As the two stepped outside, the sun smiled on them. A light breeze ruffled Max's hair. The air smelled fresh and new. They walked slowly, foot in front of foot, left right left right. They slowly floated upwards, serenely, gently, flowing against gravity into untold heights.

Blessed Trinity
Gordon Wilson
United Kingdom

Shortlisted for the 2019
International Writing Competition

DAN LIMPS UP THE NOW PAVED access to the sea-wall, pausing awhile to scan the estate that covers the former marshland he raced across with Tom and Sue, through childhood and youth.

The air is still but silent. Gone is the song of skylark and croaking frogs. Gone the smell of the cows and the shaded bands of grass and scrub. Just the familiar hint of muffled waves beyond the wall. Gone too, the flocks of plovers, their white underwings flapping mysterious semaphore. But there she is, Susan, unfailingly; strolling across the sand, passing through the flock of feeding dunlins, as on every day that they have met across the year since Tom left.

What noise they had made, that wild trio. Adventure, excitement and mischief marking the years of their growth from the first days that they met; fugitives all from the domestic realm, creating their own joyous chaos on this coastal fringe that seemed their private haunt.

Dan and Tom were first. Neighbours for as long as they remembered. From push- chairs to bikes, to belly-boards and surfboards. Through school and scouts they had been inseparable. The dynamic duo they had been called. Dan, sharper, more thoughtful, but only just. Tom, the doer, decision-maker; though only by a whisker.

Tom, the stronger, the playground protector on rare occasions; the quicker to temper or to challenge injustice.

◆

Sue had discovered them one day when they were all twelve.

Tom had seen her first, cycling on the sea-wall and they wondered at her thick blonde hair. Dan recalls that as the first and lasting memory of their meeting. Sarah corrects him. It was bobbed at the time, she says, that she'd grown it longer later.

They were diving from a slip-way at high tide and Tom had called her down to judge their diving, to settle an argument about finesse in flight and entry. She'd said it didn't matter as she was so much better; and she'd put aside her bike, thrown off her jeans and tee-shirt, tossed a shoe to each of them to hold, then leapt like a salmon, hovered and plunged, barely disturbing the back of the wave. They loved her from the start; and three became one.

◆

Dan and Sue meet once each year at this same place and time but never in between. They always speak about the same things, their tales never varying as they walk the wild stretch of beach, beside the green silk-lined breakwaters remembering yesterdays; watching the tide withdraw and the sun come down. He recalls days like their trespass in the boarding school pool, about how cold it was and she remembers the quality of light, reflections in the water and the type of gulls that joined their pic-

LEAVING

nic. But they always skirt around the subject of Tom. Dan doesn't dare go further and Sue has never tried. And they never talk about that last day. Dan knows it has to be different this time.

◆

She always looks and moves in the same way, it seems to him, as he reflects on his now uneven walk and tighter chest. Her voice seems deeper, more resonance in the huskiness he's always loved.

'It's all changed over there,' says Dan, pointing inland. 'Not here.'

'The sand is higher up the slipways than before and a lot of rocks are covered over.' 'I see it as it was,' Sue says, 'nothing changes for me.'

'But the breeze and the wind are the same. I went to buy a kite that last time,' Dan says, his pulse racing now.

'And there wasn't a breath of wind that day,' she says. And Dan remembers.

It had been after midnight that the phone rang. 'Dan... Dan... It's me, Tom... Dan... I...'

'Calm down, Tom. Take your time. What's up? What's this all about?' It's Sue, Dan. She doesn't want me...someone else... wouldn't say...' 'Tom what are you trying to...'

'Dan, I am so sorry. Can't explain...' Tom's words had drowned in sobs before he hung up.

They would never speak again.

◆

They had all spent the morning talking, laughing, swimming, sun-worshipping. Tom had been at his athletic best; doing hand springs off the groyne, making Sue laugh with playful innuendoes, paying her compliments via questions to Dan about how lucky they were, how jealous the world must be of their good fortune in having her as their special friend.

He'd teased her once or twice about her tan, wondering about its range, tweaking her white bikini pants, laughing as she gently pushed his hands away. Dan had never felt more like a fifth wheel than then and, after the night before, the situation was becoming unbearable.

'Let's swim,' Sue said, rising from her lotus position, pulling her sun-bleached hair back into a thick ponytail.

'Great idea,' Tom grinned, flicking a fist of damp sand at Dan. 'Let's go before the tide turns.'

Dan was slower to rise. He couldn't take this now.

'Not this time, I think I'll stretch my legs. See you folks later.' He needed distance for a while. Time to think.

Dan remembers the way he returned from his walk; in his hands, the kite he thought they might fly, thinking about him and Sue making love the night before. He had been tormented by what it meant for friendship and the future of this trinity, blessed with beauty, joy and love. The scene had been empty, silent, in a way he could not remember it ever being. He'd never seen Tom again; and hopes of loving Sue had gone forever. And he sees in his mind a letter from Amsterdam:

> *Dear Dan,*
>
> *Please forgive me for everything. For betraying your friendship. For disappearing with no explanation. For the pain and confusion that mad, wild telephone call must have caused you when I lost it and did not know what to say.*
>
> *Forgive me for making it impossible for us to ever meet again.*
>
> *Forgive me for not being man enough to accept Sue's rejection. For not walking away. For not talking first to you, you who*

have always known what to do, what to say, when I messed up. Forgive me for what I said and did to our best friend. For what I can never undo. For what Sue will never be able to forgive me for.

I am in a railway station and my train leaves in the next hour. Thank you for being the best friend a man could ever have had. Tom.

◆

'Sue, I've come to see this might be the last time I can come here.'

'I'll miss these meetings, Dan.'

'Thing is, I might not be around here next year.' 'I sensed something like that.'

'It's been a long time.'

'It has.'

'I need to ask for something.'

'Then ask.'

'Forgive me.'

'For what, Dan?'

'For being the cause of what Tom did to you. For betraying him and causing the madness that came over him. I never knew he had such jealousy in him.'

'He'd nothing to be jealous about, Dan.'

'But you were his. He told me. I've always thought that you told him about us.' 'I did tell him, Dan. On that day you chose to take a walk.'

'So then...'

'He and I were never lovers, Dan. I owed him nothing. Never offered anything. He became very amorous in the water, so I told him about us. That seemed only fair. We needed him to know. There was only ever you, Dan.'

'So...'

'So there is nothing I have to forgive you for.' 'But Tom. What he did...to you...'

'I don't think that was really about me, Dan.'

Dan wonders at the meaning of this as he watches her step away for the last time, striding seaward, as if in slow motion, fading into the place where sand meets tide and sky and forms the portal of time.

Tenacity Penguin
Matt Wixey
United Kingdom

1st place in the 2019 International Writing Competition

STATIC.

Foxtrot Two, Tenacity Base. Are you receiving?

Foxtrot Two, Foxtrot Two, Tenacity Base. Is anyone there?

Static.

Foxtrot Two, you don't have to speak. If you can't speak, key the radio, or tap it, or something.

Static.

Or cough, or sneeze, or anything. I don't care what it is, but give me something.

Please.

I just want to know if someone's there.

Static.

OK. OK. Maybe you can't move, maybe there's no-one, but I'm saying this anyway, and if there is someone there, you're going to hear it. Because you lied to me. It shouldn't bother me, not now, but it does.

Because you promised me penguins.

'What about Cyprus?' I said to one of you at the recruitment office.

'Forget about Cyprus,' you said. 'It's overrated. It's hot, and it's crowded, and we've got all the signals people we need out there. *You're going to the North Pole. Tenacity Base. You're going to monitor satellite feeds and make snowmen and have your piss freeze into an icicle.*'

I said: 'I'll get to see penguins at the North Pole, won't I? I've always wanted to.'

'Oh yeah, yeah, of course there'll be penguins,' you said. 'Penguins as far as the eye can see. The place is practically infested with them. You'll be sick of penguins by the time your team's relieved. You won't want to see another penguin for as long as you live.'

'OK, I've made up my mind,' I said. 'I'll go to Tenacity.'

'We're at war,' you said. 'You'll go where you're told.'

'As long as there's penguins,' I said, 'I don't care where I go.'

It's been eight months, Foxtrot Two. Not one bloody penguin.

And now you're dead, and I'm not.

◆

George told me why, right before he left. And then he disappeared into the big white and black, so I think he's dead, too.

George. Oh, George. I wonder if you lied to him too. I wonder what you promised him. George with his books and his guitar and his Coco Pops. He hoarded them like dragon treasure. That fucking monkey grinning on the box.

'Let me have a bowl,' I used to say to George. 'One tiny bowl. You won't even notice it's gone.'

All I wanted, Foxtrot Two, was a taste, to feel that sugary, chocolaty, chemical-laden payload hitting my veins, after all those months of

LEAVING

tinned food and packets of powder.

But more than anything, I wanted to see if Coco Pops tasted the way I remember. I used to have them before school. And after school, and most weekends. It was the milk I used to love, when the Coco Pops had turned it all sticky sweet brown. I'd let the cereal soak, bleaching out its colour, and then I'd throw it away, leaving only the milk, and then I'd tip the bowl up and drink it all down in one blissful, shameful gulp.

I told George all of this. He asked me why I hadn't just bought chocolate milk.

'It's a false economy, George, and you know it,' I said. 'Let me have the milk. Forget the cereal. Just that sweet, sweet, chocolate milk.'

I begged him. I pleaded with him. Let me suckle at your chocolaty teat, George.

Let me be your little Coco Pops piglet.

'So you'll give me the milk?' I said.

George said no.

I only wanted to remember that things were the same. George told me once about this French guy who wrote a really long book because he ate a cake or something that reminded him of being a kid. I didn't know if it would be the same with Coco Pops. I didn't want to write a book. I just wanted to drink some chocolaty milk, have a wank and go to sleep.

But I wondered if the taste would bring everything back, like that French guy and his cake.

I said all this to George and he still said no, he only had one box and there wasn't enough to share. This was three months in, when we'd run out of things to say. I wasn't about to stop asking, so after four months in, he started locking the Coco Pops away. He wore the key around his neck on a cord, so I couldn't get it.

I used to close my eyes and see myself strangling him with that cord. Eating Coco Pops off his lifeless body. Still in a bowl, of course. I'm not an animal.

But now George is probably dead anyway, and the world has ended and they're definitely not making Coco Pops anymore, never ever again.

So fuck it. Fuck it, Foxtrot Two. I'm having George's Coco Pops and I'm going to taste that chocolaty milk.

♦

The satellite dish had been broken for weeks. We were used to stuff breaking, and not getting any response from the radio. We'd come to expect it. It's the North Pole. Nothing works here. It's the middle of a frozen ocean.

We thought the dish was broken because of the storm and it was, sort of. We just didn't know where the storm had come from.

When the relief hadn't arrived and we were still there, three weeks after we should have gone home, we started to worry. We thought you'd been attacked, Foxtrot Two. We started monitoring the radio all day and all night. Most of the time, it didn't work, and when it did, all we could hear was a Japanese man and usually he was crying and he kept saying something like *sausages, sausages.*

He couldn't hear us.

I asked George what he was saying and he thought it probably wasn't *sausages, sausages* because the Japanese word for *sausages* was probably very different to our word for *sausages*. But neither of us spoke any Japanese and the radio was barely working. I don't even know if it's working now. You tell me. Can you hear me?

Static.

We never heard anyone else, and after a while even the Japanese man was gone and we never heard him again.

We waited and waited and argued about Coco Pops, and George

LEAVING

read books and one day I went outside by myself into the white and black and I looked at the dish and opened the panel.

The receiver had been working all along, getting the transmissions from the satellite, but the output feeds had frayed. I resoldered the connections and there it was. Three weeks of satellite footage, waiting for us to play it back.

So I played it back. I watched it, I sped it up to save time, and oh, if you're listening, Foxtrot Two, you should have seen it. It was beautiful. Stunning. Like watching the stars go out.

There were these flares, all over the world, huge blossoming summer blooms, tulips opening on a stop motion time-lapse and then dying. Collapsing, like broken hearts. One at first and then another and then more and more. Fireworks in November. Bang. Bang. Bang.

Until it all covered the world like a film of flame and then, right before the end, the entire earth, all of it, shrank, like it was breathing out for the last time.

I wonder if there were sirens, evacuations, helicopters on embassy roofs. Or if there was no time. If that was it, that brief, sharp beat. That one last breath.

And then everything was dark. All except one tiny glimmer, one pathetic spark, sitting so quietly right at the very top of the world, and that was us. That was me and George.

It was gone.

You launched. I couldn't tell from the playback who'd started it, but you launched, everyone launched, and everything's gone.

Yeah, the war had been going on for a while, and a few times over the years it had got really bad and really close. A few times we'd put the gun to our heads and stared at ourselves in the mirror to see how long we could stand it. But to shrug and say 'fuck it' and pull the trigger – we never thought it would actually happen. We never thought you'd actually go ahead and do it. You said you wouldn't, Foxtrot Two. You said it would never come to that.

All I wanted was penguins.

◆

I sat there for a long time by myself and then I told George.

I asked him: 'What does it mean for the penguins, George? Do you think some of them made it, and they're still out there somewhere?'

He looked at me like I was crazy, and he said: 'Are they fuck.'

And he must have seen something in my face because that was when he told me.

'They lied to you,' he said, 'right from the start. There aren't any penguins at the North Pole. Never have been, never will be. They're at the South Pole. About as far away from us as you can possibly get.'

And I asked if he thought the penguins at the South Pole had survived and he said something about big military installations, much bigger than Tenacity, that were probably tactical targets for the missiles and so no, no they hadn't.

The penguins were gone.

I think I lost it there for a bit. I don't remember a lot.

But I remember George was crying and he got a bag and started throwing clothes and food into it, and he said he was leaving, he was going, to find his family.

'You didn't see it, George,' I said. 'You didn't see the footage. I did. They're dead, George. Everyone's dead. The whole world lit up. You won't find anything. There's no transport. There's nobody on the radio. George. What are you doing, come back, George. Watch it with me, George. Watch it with me. I'm watching it again. I'm putting it on a loop.'

He didn't say anything.

'George,' I said, when he was loading the sled. 'George, why don't we talk about it in the morning?'

And he looked at me, and his face was strange and empty and he said: 'It's the North Pole. It won't be morning for three months.'

He had a point. And then he shouted: 'I am just going outside!' and he was sort of laughing and screaming and then he left. He was in the white and black.

I watched him until he disappeared, which wasn't long because the lights from the base only reach so far. He didn't even ask if I wanted to come with him. I didn't, I think, but it would have been nice if he'd offered.

And he forgot his precious Coco Pops. I wonder if he remembered them, before he died out there. I wonder if his last thought was: *that was the last box of Coco Pops in the universe, in all of existence, and I've left it back at the fucking base.*

I hope so. I hope it was. Because he did and now it's mine.

◆

There's an encyclopaedia here. I don't know whose it was. Maybe it belonged to someone from the team before me and George. I'm going to start reading it. I can do anything I want. There might be some language books too, in the basement. I can learn French, like that guy with the cake. Not that there's much of a France anymore. But if I'm the only tiny spark left, why shouldn't I burn as bright as I can? I can be the last French speaker in the world.

I can't go out into the white and black like George did. I can't.

I have to talk to you.

I flicked through the encyclopaedia. I looked up the North Pole.

Virtually no life, the book said. No penguins, like George said. Not even polar bears this far north. Birds, sometimes, but flying ones, and some Russians found some crustaceans once, and that's about the lot.

That's what I have. Flying birds and shellfish. I don't even like shellfish.

And definitely, absolutely, no penguins.

I don't know why it had to be penguins. I liked the way they looked. They seemed friendly. Nice. I watched this David Attenborough thing when I was a kid, and he said they didn't even mind people, they weren't scared of them, they'd walk right up to them to say hi. I've always wanted to see if that's true.

I saw some in a zoo once but it wasn't the same. They looked hot and lazy, and didn't seem like they wanted to say hi. I wonder if they were sad about the fake plastic ice grey with dirt and the dead fish they got fed, like I was.

George used to say penguins were pointless and twats. Sometimes he would make fun of me, and other times he would look almost scared of me, or not scared but surprised. But most of the time, he was kind.

I think that's why it took the end of the world for him to tell me about the penguins. Eight months of me going on and on about them, I think pretty much every day, and he didn't say a word. Not until right at the very end. He told me how it was, when it mattered.

Not like you. You fucking cunts.

And I have to give it to him; he was brave, leaving like that. I wonder if I'd be brave like George, if I had a family. I'd like to think so. I'd like to think I'd be like the name of this base. That I'd have tenacity.

I've always liked that word. I loved it the first time I heard it. Tenacity.

Maybe there are some people left, somewhere, and maybe they'll

LEAVING

make it and rebuild everything. And one day a hundred years from now maybe there'll be kids in schools learning all about me and George and the war and the base, and maybe we'll be legends.

Maybe they'll say: 'Tenacity Base' to each other excitedly as they memorise it for their exams. 'It was called Tenacity Base. Tenacity. Tenacity.' And maybe they will know that words like that meant something. Maybe they will understand that words like that were important to us.

There are different kinds of bravery, aren't there? I don't think I'd get a medal for this; staying put. If you're there, Foxtrot Two, if you're listening, I don't think you'd get one either. But I don't think medals matter so much now.

◆

I found some language books. Dictionaries and guides. I hadn't seen it before, didn't think we'd have it, but there was even a Japanese one.

So I read it, and first of all, fuck you George, because the Japanese word for *sausages* is *soseji*, and that sounds a lot like *sausages* to me.

I've been trying to find other Japanese words that sound a bit like *sausages*. I want to know what the Japanese man was trying to tell us.

The best I've come up with is *son'nani shi*.

If that's it, if that's what the man was saying, I think I know why he was crying. I think I know what he'd seen.

◆

A few days ago I went outside and looked up and there were stars everywhere in the black. The whole sky burned with them, tiny craters of white phosphorus, little fizzing bits of debris left over from prehistoric violence. They looked ancient and bitter and they weren't anything I could ever hope to understand.

And then high across the sky there was a flash of light, blinking, soaring. I waved at it, and I shouted, because I thought it was a plane, or a helicopter or a drone.

For a few seconds, I thought it might be George. Maybe he wasn't dead, he'd made it and he'd found someone and come back for me. That wouldn't have been so bad. I wouldn't have his Coco Pops anymore, wouldn't be able to drink that chocolaty milk like I'm about to, but I think I would have been fine with that.

Or I thought it might have been the relief we'd been waiting for, the team that should have shown up all that time ago and who were probably boiled into nothingness somewhere a thousand miles from here.

But it wasn't. It was a satellite. I don't know whose. Ours, theirs. It blinked a few more times and then it was gone. It might have been the one that took the footage I'd seen. I don't know.

It'll be up there for hundreds of years, probably. Wheeling around the world in its silence.

◆

I've given up on the language books and gone back to the encyclopaedia. I looked up penguins.

The encyclopaedia says that, in winter, penguins huddle together on the ice. It's to keep themselves warm, so they don't die in the cold. They generate so much heat that they have to keep moving, otherwise the ice would melt under their feet and they'd all plunge into the sea. That's how they survive.

The ones on the edge don't.

If you can hear me, tell me you're there.

I don't care who you are. Even if you're not Foxtrot Two, I don't care. Maybe it's better if you're not Foxtrot Two. We can talk anyway.

LEAVING

You might be the Japanese man. It would be nice to speak to you again. I'm sorry. I'd like to learn Japanese. You can teach me, if you want.

Speak to me. Tell me you're alive.

Don't let me be alone.

Static.

Well. That's OK. I'll keep talking, and you tune in when you can. I'll be here.

Foxtrot Two, if it's you, I'm not even angry at you anymore. I understand. You needed people here. I get it. It didn't do anybody any good and I know you lied about a lot of things, but I do get it, and it's OK. It doesn't matter. I forgive you, Foxtrot Two.

I'm here. I am alive, and I'm not leaving.

I'll keep talking for as long as I can.

I don't know how much food is left. I haven't looked, to be honest with you. I'm not sure I want to. George and I were running pretty low, but it's only me now, so it should last longer.

Thank you, George.

I'll wait until I've finished everything in the cupboards and then I'll check the stores.

It'll be fine, everything will be fine.

I hope you've got enough to eat, wherever you are.

I hope you're OK.

Static.

If you were here, Foxtrot Two, I'd share these Coco Pops with you. I can imagine the look on George's face if he heard that. He'd be seething. But I don't care. You can have some, when we meet. There's a whole box here so I'll save some for you and we can eat Coco Pops together.

But this bowl is the first bowl, and so it's for me to have alone.

I can't wait to remember.

Static.

Oh, fuck.

Foxtrot Two, Tenacity Base. Anyone, Tenacity Base. Have you got any milk?

Static.

HH | HAMMOND HOUSE

Hammond House is a social enterprise membership organisation founded by students at the *University Centre Grimsby* and run by volunteers. We aim to encourage and support creative talent in art and literature, providing opportunities for members to showcase their work and develop a succesful career.

Our current activities include publishing, literary competitions, filmmaking, TV productions, writing workshops, festival and community engagement programmes.

Members benefit from reduced competition fees, and opportunities to showcase their work or get involved in our wide range of creative activities.

We are planning to offer a range of publishing options to new writers, and expand our programme to engage with isolated people in both rural and urban communities through art and literature.

www.hammondhousepublishing.com

University Centre Grimsby

2019 International Literary Prize

The fourth year of this prestigious literary prize saw a record number of entries spread across five continents.

1st Place	Tenacity Penguin	Matt Wixey
2nd Place	The Levensons	Tara Roeder
3rd Place	Locked In	Peter Hankins

Twenty-nine entries were shortlisted, and two were added as Judges Choices.

This years' judges were:
Peter True, Anjali Wierny, Hugh Riches, Alex Thompson, Adrian Mills, Sarah Hunter-Carson and Steve Jackson.

Additional judging was done by:
Lynette Cresswell, Jackie Collins and Jennie Liebenberg.

Awarded by the *University Centre Grimsby*

www.hammondhousepublishing.com

HAMMOND HOUSE PUBLISHING

2020 International Literary Prize

Awarded by the University Centre Grimsby, winners receive a cash prize, and worldwide publication of their work in an anthology, together with twenty-four shortlisted entries.

1st Prize	£500
2nd Prize	£100
3rd Prize	£50

Worldwide publication for the shortlisted stories

Theme: SURVIVAL
Short Story: 2000 - 5000 words
Entries open from 5th February 2020
Submission deadline: 30th September 2020

OTHER 2020 COMPETITIONS:
International Poetry Prize
International Screenplay Prize

www.hammondhousepublishing.com

HH | HAMMOND HOUSE PRODUCTIONS

Hammond House Productions is a Grimsby-based media company that tells compelling stories through corporate videos, documentaries, promotional videos and TV programmes.

We help forward thinking organisations respond to the challenges and opportunities provided by search engines, social media, local and regional television channels, and digital communications.

As part of the Hammond House group we support and encourage the development of creative talent.

www.hammondhouseproductions.com

BillboardTV

Billboard is a monthly programme produced by members of the Hammond House group, covering theatre, music, art and literature in East Yorkshire and Lincolnshire, going behind the scenes of your favourite shows, reviewing the latest film releases, books and art exhibitions. interviewing local celebrities and showcasing local musicians.

Billboard provides a great opportunity to showcase member's skills and pursue the Hammond House mission to encourage local talent and engage with the local people.

www.billboardtv.uk

LINCOLNSHIRE WRITERS

Funded by the National Lottery Community Fund, the Lincolnshire Writers project aims to establish and support new writing groups in the county, bringing together both experienced and new writers to share their love of writing

The support, provided by Hammond House, includes help with venue costs, creative writing workshops by qualified professionals and publication of the work produced by members.

If you are interested in leading or joining a group, you can find out more information and details of current groups at:

www.lincolnshirewriters.com

COMMUNITY FUND

LITERARY LONELY

HAMMOND HOUSE

University Centre Grimsby

The University Centre Grimsby, as part of the Grimsby Institute, is built on high expectations, a focus on learning, commitment to achievement and an engaged, practical education for all students.

A wide range of degree level courses are available including BA (hons) Creative and Professional Writing.

www.grimsby.ac.uk

CPSIA information can be obtained
at www.ICGtesting.com
Printed in the USA
BVHW030558040220
571296BV00018B/19